Praise for Dan Jenkins's Hilarious

YOU GOTTA
PLAY HURT

"Marvelous characters, witty dialogue . . . and a hip, flip, profane prose style. . . . Dan Jenkins may be the funniest man in America. . . ."

—*Florida Times-Union*

"A laugh a page . . . Jenkins is back at the top of his game, one that's dazzling enough to rank him among the top U.S. humorists."

—*Arizona Daily Star*

"Crackles with one liners . . . Jenkins is in his usual raunchy and wry form."

—*San Antonio Express-News*

"Shines with its own cynical brilliance."

—*USA Today*

"This is funny stuff, page after page. PG-rated funny, XXX-rated funny. Gut-busting funny."

—*The Washington Times*

Books by Dan Jenkins

Novels

You Gotta Play Hurt*
Fast Copy
Life Its Ownself
Baja Oklahoma*
Limo (with Bud Shrake)
Dead Solid Perfect
Semi-Tough

Nonfiction

You Call It Sports But I Say
   It's a Jungle Out There
Football (with Walter Iooss, Jr.)
Saturday's America
The Dogged Victims of Inexorable Fate
The Best 18 Golf Holes in America

*Published by POCKET BOOKS

DAN JENKINS

YOU GOTTA PLAY HURT

POCKET STAR BOOKS

New York   London   Toronto   Sydney   Tokyo   Singapore

This book is a work of fiction. Names, characters, places and incidents are either products of the author's imagination or are used fictitiously. Any resemblance to actual events or locales or persons, living or dead, is entirely coincidental.

 A Pocket Star Book published by
POCKET BOOKS, a division of Simon & Schuster Inc.
1230 Avenue of the Americas, New York, NY 10020

ISBN: 0-671-78461-7

First Pocket Books printing January 1993

10 9 8 7 6 5 4 3 2 1

POCKET STAR BOOKS and colophon are registered trademarks of Simon & Schuster Inc.

Cover art by Jeffrey Lynch

Printed in the U.S.A.

*To the memory of Andre Laguerre,
last of a breed—a writer's
Managing Editor.*

PART ONE

NOBODY SAID IT WAS GONNA BE EASY

1

HERE'S HOW I WANT THE PHONY LITTLE CONNIVING, NO-talent, preppiewad asshole of an editor to die: I lace his decaf with Seconal and strap him down in such a way that his head is fastened to my desk and I thump him at cheery intervals with the carriage on my Olympia standard. I'm a stubborn guy who still works on a geezer-codger manual anyhow, so I write a paragraph I admire, the kind he likes to dick around with, especially if it's my lead, then I sling the carriage at him, and *whack*—he gets it in the temple, sometimes the ear. Yeah, it would be slow, but death by typewriter is what the fuckhead deserves.

I was daydreaming. I was sitting alone at a table under an umbrella on the veranda of the Regina, occasionally glancing up at the jaunty white duncecap of the Jungfrau, bonus Alp.

I had my Scotch and water, my Winstons, my pot of coffee on the side, my *Herald Trib*. Nice day. Sunny. Windbreaker weather. If you want the truth, I was doing three of my favorite things: smoking, drinking, not giving a shit.

Switzerland was where I was in that week that was the beginning of the rest of my life. I was there to watch a pack of ski tramps slide down a mountain so I could glorify them in the magazine that sent me over there to write a story about them, a story I would file to New York so an editor with no ear and no taste could take out a carving knife and flail at it like one of those chefs in a Japanese restaurant.

This was late February. I had already been sitting around for two weeks in the French Alps and Italian Alps. I was making my way, ski race by ski race, to the Winter Olympics in Austria. Always a thrill, the Winter Olympics. You get to watch waiters and babysitters figure skate, Americans fall down in the snow, and inhale the quaint odors of sweating Scandinavians who grow icicles in their noses and wear oversized flyswatters on their feet. Cross-country skiing's not a sport, it's how a fucking Swede goes to the 7-Eleven.

The managing editor or one of his lukewarm drones likes to cut that line. I put it in, the clean version, and they take it out, like they take out everything else they don't get.

Magazine journalism practices tyranny from the bottom. Editors become editors in the first place because they can't write. Then they jack around with stories that are written by the people who *can* write in order to justify their squalid existence.

It's an eternal truth in magazine journalism that an editor exists in large part to kick a writer where and when it hurts the worst. In all my years, I had known very few editors who could take a so-so story and improve it with their pencil, but they were absolute masters at fucking up good ones.

That was my view, anyhow. Some people said it was too harsh, but I'd never known a writer who disagreed with it.

It was a curious thing, I was thinking to myself at the Regina. I used to go to sleep dreaming about pussy. Now I went to sleep dreaming about killing people.

The Regina Hotel was an old haunt, a Victorian wedge of gingerbread from which you could look down on the village of Wengen. No cars in Wengen, and no way to get there except by a bunch of trains that stopped in Spiez four or five times. This had once given Wengen a certain charm, but now it was over-hoteled and sprawling with shops that sold nothing for everybody. The tourists were multiplying like fruitflies, hopping off green-and-yellow cograils every twenty minutes to swap ski pins and observe the engaging Swiss art of wood-stacking.

Nobody can stack firewood like the Swiss. Designer firewood. They study chocolate in grade school, Rolex in high school, numbered accounts in college, and get their MBAs in wood-stacking. Well, why not? The Swiss haven't had anything else to do for seven hundred years.

Every time I arrive in the country, I'm reminded of the old joke about God creating Switzerland. God asked the Swiss people what they wanted in the way of a country. They said they wanted huge Alps, deafening streams, and beautiful pastures where their riotous cows could ring their disco bells through the night. God provided all this in three days. The first Swiss innkeeper was so pleased, he asked if there was something he could do for God in return. God said yes, as a matter of fact. He was a little thirsty. He would like a glass of milk. "Fine," said the innkeeper. "That will be ten francs."

You can't get a laugh with that joke in Switzerland for the same reason that nobody has ever been able to name a Swiss comedian. Mention to people that you're going to Switzerland and first they smile and say, "Oh, it's lovely," then they change expressions and say, "Of course, there *are* the Swiss."

Funny thing is, I kind of like Switzerland. It's clean, it's civilized, it's quiet, it's almost as picturesque as a weather map in *USA Today*. The phones work, the trains run on time, they keep the roads clear. Everybody seems to have a job. On the wall of no john are you likely to read, "Call Bruce at the Cafe du Cerf for a real good time." It seems to me that the only way you can get mugged is when you pay the bill for the raclette.

Of course, I could never live there. No college football.

Whenever I went to Wengen, for the past twelve or fifteen years, I had stayed at the Regina. It was too expensive for all the ski teams and European journalists, and it wasn't modern enough for American tourists; hence, there was a good chance that no American bore would find me on the veranda or at the lobby bar, and say, "Who do you think will take it, Jim Tom?"

Amazing how people always think a sportswriter is supposed to know who's going to win something. I'll cover a football game, golf tournament, tennis match, World Series, whatever, and invariably somebody will come up to me and say, "Who's going to take it, Jim Tom?"

I usually predicted a human being would take it, or a team of human beings, unless I was at the Kentucky Derby, in which case I would predict an animal would take it.

So there I was that day on the veranda of the Regina, thinking I was safe, when I got trapped. This guy intruded on my table like he figured I must be tired of reading the *Herald Trib*. He might have guessed I was a fellow American from my brown penny loafers, beige corduroys, white golf shirt, and navy-blue windbreaker, but in fact, he knew I was Jim Tom Pinch from the picture that ran with my column in the magazine, the picture of a man in tinted glasses with gray streaks in his hair, a thin mouth, a rusty complexion, and the expression on his face of someone who might be suffering from a stomach disorder.

"Hi, there," the guy said in a big voice. "You're Jim Tom Pinch!"

"Guilty," I said, looking up over the top of my glasses.

The guy was a vision in stars and bars. Bright blue stretch pants with a white racing stripe down the side. Red sweater with white stars all over it. White turtleneck and blue ski cap with white stars on it. He was dressed for burial at sea.

"I'm Clipper Langdon," he said. "Good friend of Bryce."

Bryce Wilcox, head drone, my managing editor.

"Really?" I said, absently.

"The Brycer's my neighbor up in Westchester. We've been known to bat it around Winged Foot together."

"Good golf course," I said, "considering it's not Pine Valley."

Only a slight insult.

My eyes returned to the *International Herald Tribune*, to a book review about a savagely incoherent Ecuadorian novelist who was in line for the Nobel Prize in literature.

"So . . . who do you think will take it?" he asked.

"Take what?"

"The DH."

"The DH?"

"The downer."

"The *downer*?"

I looked up at him again and briefly studied the round, eager, amiable face of everything wrong with living in Westchester County.

The Lauberhorn race was why I was there. It was the toughest downhill, or DH, in Alpine ski racing. The Masters, the Wimbledon, of the circuit. Its name was taken from an Alp near Wengen that had an animal-shaped rock on top of it, looking as if nature had been helped along by a sculptor in search of a logo.

I had covered the Lauberhorn many times in the past, even in those years when there was no Winter Olympics coming up. Covering the Lauberhorn and the Hahnenkahm in Kitzbuhel, the other big ski race in Europe, was a way to get out of the office and away from ice hockey and pro basketball in the winter, and Europe wasn't all that bad a thing to do between football seasons and other sports that made sense. Golf, tennis, college basketball.

I predicted a ski racer would win the Lauberhorn. I said it with a straight face.

"A ski racer?" Clipper Langdon squinted. "Heh, heh."

"On the other hand," I said, "if it's a pole-vaulter, I'll have a hell of a story for the Brycer."

"You guys," he said, shaking his head, smiling.

"You aren't staying here, are you?" I inquired with a certain amount of fear.

"Oh, no. We're down the hill at the Palace in Gstaad. Mucho train rides. Just came up for a slope check."

The "we" to whom he referred were the "mega-clients"—his term—on the ABC-TV junket. They were on their way to the Winter Olympics. It was a way for the network to entertain advertisers and hopefully create more business.

"I know the Palace," I said.

Which was true. I knew the Palace in Gstaad from a summer three years ago when I had skillfully stretched an assignment on glider-soaring and hot-air ballooning in the Saane Valley into six weeks with the ulterior motive of working on a novel.

I spent those six weeks cradled in unheralded Alps at the Hotel Valrose in Rougemont, only five miles from Gstaad. I had stopped at the Valrose to ask directions to Gstaad but had stayed for dinner and discovered the best fresh trout, omelettes, and entrecotes in the civilized world and decided to make it my headquarters.

The glider-balloon story required only a week of my time. I hired a long-haired college kid named Horace, who was traveling around Europe by bike, to go up in those silly things for me and tell me what it was like. Horace said the glider was like being on "good weed," and in his considered opinion, the hot-air balloon farted more than a high school football coach.

For the next five weeks I stayed in a room at the Valrose that overlooked the train station, ate luxuriously, and wrote 140 pages of *The Past*, which might have been the dumbest novel ever perpetrated on the American reading public if it had been finished and had found its way into print. But the bulk of it blew off my lunch table on the sun deck of the Videmanette one day. I like to think the worst chapters settled into the cow-watering pond below the sun deck, and the best chapters, if there were any, had been taken by the wind and were now frozen in the Jungfrau glacier.

The Past was a futile effort to change my life and career, but the only thing the tiring experience did was convince me that for better or worse I belonged in the dodge of sportswriting, where at least I knew my way around. There's no need to outline the plot of *The Past* for you. I will only say that after 140 grueling pages, the narrator was still knocking up cheerleaders and playing high school football in Texas.

Not that I hadn't been "published." I had once been the mechanic, the as-told-to person, on a book by an NFL running back named Puckett. The book had been a success if you only counted the money it made and not what the critics said, but I hadn't made nearly as much money out of it as the running back did.

There had been other opportunities to write books like that, books for famous coaches and famous athletes, but I never intended to do it again. Famous coaches and famous athletes have very little to say about anything. You have to make it up. They can't even remember anything accurately. My immortal, Billy Clyde Puckett, would say, "That was the Sunday I de-lipped three niggers and stuck two sixes in the Dallas end zone," and he would be off by two years and four niggers. You have to invent almost everything, try to put it in their words, then argue with them about the facts and the tone. Aside from politicians and movie stars, it's my opinion that famous coaches and athletes might be the most unaware and worst informed people in society about anything other than what *they* do, which is not to say I don't like a good many of them and enjoy their company. I just don't want to write any more books for them. It's carpentry, not writing.

Anyhow, I knew the Palace Hotel in Gstaad. I had once enjoyed four cappuccinos there at ten dollars a cup.

Clipper Langdon looked as if he might be dangerously close to pulling up a chair to my table, so I said, "Listen, I'm kind of hung over, but tell me something—do I still have that sign on my back that says, 'Please Talk to Me'?"

"Hey, that's funny," he said. " 'Please Talk to Me.' Heh, heh. I can use that at F and W. Didn't mean to intrude, Pincher. I can see you're sitting here working on the old *lines*. Writer at work, as they say."

I was reminded that it's impossible to insult ad salesmen or ad agency people. If they were insultable, America would never know there were differences in toothpastes and insurance companies.

Clipper backed away with all good cheer, saying, "Glad we met. I might be coming on board, by the way."

"On board what?" I said, looking up again from the newspaper.

"The big bird. Bryce is lighting the runway for me. The publisher's job is opening up, and my feet are rather stuck in concrete at Floyd and Warren. Incidentally, that's graveyard about the pub job, but I guess it doesn't hurt to mention it to a crew member."

"Our publisher is leaving?" I would have used our publisher's name if I'd known it.

"They're taking him upstairs to the war room. I've never been around print much, but everything's commerce, isn't it?"

I made a noncommittal noise as I turned a page of the paper.

The fact is, it didn't matter to me if Clipper Langdon became publisher of the magazine. A magazine publisher was in charge of the ad salesmen only. This was something the average person didn't understand. Publisher to the average person sounded like the man who was most responsible for all the stories and pictures, and most publishers didn't go out of their way to discourage this thinking.

But all publishers were the same guy, as I had observed them—glad-handing nincompoops—although they did serve one useful purpose. They were boisterously artful in soothing and stroking advertisers who might get angry over a certain story because the clueless jerks had missed the point of the story in the first place.

As Clipper reached the corner of the Regina, he called back to me. "Guess you'll be talking to the flight deck, Pincher. Tell the Brycer you saw the Clipper."

The Pincher made a mental note of it as he dropped his head and reached for a cigarette.

2

THE SKI RACERS FROM ALL THE DIFFERENT NATIONS WERE lodged in a group of smaller, less expensive hotels in Wengen, and I thought this made good sense for the brainless to be concentrated in one area. I once stayed in that type of hotel when I was a younger man and didn't know any better and occasionally found myself traveling with the U.S. ski team in order to report firsthand on its calamities. Four to a bath down the hall, set menu, bread-throwing at dinner, and radios and boom boxes blasting out European rock music, which is what happens when a jackhammer runs into a tuneless songwriter.

In those carefree days, ski racers were interesting to observe at times, and they often added to the frivolity of the circuit by shoving Volkswagens into hotel lobbies for the sheer French fun of it, by playing "drop trou" on the practice slopes, by eating wineglasses—yes, grinding up the glass in their teeth and chasing it down with beer—and by interrupting dinner when one of them would take a mouthful of lighter fluid, strike a match, and blow a terrifying flame across the dining room.

10

Ski racers were no smarter nowadays, but with the big money to be made, they were calmer, more serious, and more tedious, as were most athletes in most sports.

Luckily, I didn't have to try to talk to many ski racers anymore. Christine did that for me.

Christine Thorne was the magazine's researcher on winter sports, track and field, and other funny sports, most of which you only thought about in an Olympic year. She spoke very good French and German, a dab of Italian, a dab of Spanish. She was in her mid-thirties and had been with *SM* since it started, coming over from *Newsweek* where she had gone to work after graduating from one of those eastern colleges where they stamp out magazine researchers. Christine was a good friend and running mate of Nell Woodruff, another researcher who had been with *SM* since its inception and was roughly the same age as Christine. Nell, a long-legged blonde whose good looks were often obscured by her unattended hair and careless use of eye liner, was an even better friend of mine. My best friend, you might say. The three of us were close, part of a gang in the office that included a couple of other writers.

Christine was on this trip and headed for the Winter Olympics to get me quotes from all the winter sports athletes, not only the ski racers but the precious young men and dreaded teenage witches who figure skated. At the moment, Christine was off getting me quotes from Pepi Henkel, the arrogant Austrian Nazi, and Emile Louvois, the arrogant French nobleman, both of whom were trying to become the new king of the slopes now that Jean Aubert, the arrogant Swiss, had been killed, along with three Japanese tourists, in the collision of a glider and a hot-air balloon over Chateau-d'Oex.

Christine would bring me back the quotes and I would slip on my surgical gloves, do the piece on my Olivetti portable, the geezer-codger machine I used on the road, and beat everybody to the nearest bar.

I had always written fast. It was partly due to my newspaper training back on the *Fort Worth Light & Shopper*, and partly because I had discovered a long time ago that my first impressions were generally the most accurate. I had also learned that if I took too much time on the piece, I would screw it up to where nobody might comprehend it but a savagely incoherent Ecuadorian novelist.

I seldom needed to worry about Christine coming back from an interview with something usable. She had big tits and was quite pretty—coal-black hair, wide green eyes, a perpetual look of wonderment on her rosy face, and, so far as I knew, she had never met a cock she didn't like to suck, except for mine.

I don't know that it's a universally held belief among women that all men think with their dicks. I only know that a few magazine researchers of my acquaintance seemed to be convinced that this was the quickest way into a jock's mind.

Nell Woodruff once took delight in confessing to me how she had been able to obtain a crucial bit of information from a Cincinnati Red when she was helping me cover a World Series.

After a particular game, Nell, without any great difficulty, had lured the Cincinnati Red, a particularly attractive fellow, into bed, and in the middle of doing him what must have been an immensely satisfying favor, she had asked him why he had been thrown out at the plate on a suicide squeeze.

As I said, Nell was a close friend and she couldn't resist sharing the humor of the situation with me as she imparted the crucial bit of information.

In its completeness, what the Cincinnati Red had said was something on the order of:

"Oh, God . . . oh, shit . . . they stole our sign, and . . . oh, Christ . . . the third baseman . . . oh, Jesus . . . was yelling squeeze before . . . oh, yes! . . . before the pitch."

It was a comfort to me in Switzerland knowing that Christine Thorne was as much of a dedicated journalist as Nell Woodruff.

3

THE LAUBERHORN DOWNHILL WOULD BE RUN THE NEXT DAY, not that I would see any more of it from somewhere up near a turn or at the finish line than I could from the veranda of the Regina. You can't see a ski race unless you're watching it on TV. At the finish line, I had long since learned that all you can do is stand around, sip coffee, smoke, and listen to a PA announcer shout things like, "Achtung! Seeban und drysig, sepps und trysig!" Which means hold the gravy on the sauerbraten.

Then here will come a tuck of lycra in a helmet and goggles, taking air, slats chattering, a couple of golf clubs under his arms, and maybe if you're lucky, he'll fall and plow into a little restraining fence and suffer brain damage. Two minutes later, here will come another one.

A downhill race is over in about thirty minutes. The first fifteen racers who push out of the starting gate are ceremonially seeded on past performance. They deserve to benefit from the smoothest trail, according to ski racing rules. The other seventy madcaps who follow don't matter unless one of them falls and has a good quote later, like, "I vas swooshing down the mountain and my mind vas all confusion."

Thousands of recreational skiers will line the mile-and-a-half or two-mile course of a major downhill. They make strange, muffled, European sounds as the racers fly past them, but they can't see any more of the competition than the crowd at the finish line. They just like to be up there with their knapsacks of apples and cheese, yodeling. The average yodel means: "My dick is freezing."

I found out the hard way that you can't see a ski race. It was in another life on another magazine but in the same village of Wengen and at the same race, the Lauberhorn. It must have been twenty years ago, now that I think back on it.

Since I was at my first ski race, I had stupidly asked a French writer from *L'Equipe* where I should go to watch it. Up at the start, he said, to get the full flavor, the drama, the tension. He persuaded me to rent a pair of skis and board a cograil with him and a group of other European writers and photographers. The cograil would take us up the mountain to a spot near the start.

I explained to the Frenchman that I was only a beginner on the slopes, I couldn't handle anything difficult, but he assured me that I could stem or sideslip my way down—it wasn't all that steep where we were going.

So the cograil churned up the mountain and wove its way through the Alps, and like a Mongoloid, I sat there gazing idly out of the train windows, taking in the picturesque scenery. I watched the finish line go past. The cograil finally stopped at what was supposed to be a train station but more closely resembled a bench with a roof on it. Everybody jumped up and got off the cograil, so I followed. Two minutes later, the Europeans had all stepped into their bindings and were gone. There they went, wedeling down the mountain, the tail-wagging swine, fast becoming specks in the distance.

The day was cold. The sky was gray as a Nazi uniform. The wind sounded like Agatha Christie sent it. And I was now alone on this Alp. I could look *down* to see the start of the ski race, about a mile down.

My first thought: take one step and you fall to Interlaken. My second thought: I don't have enough cigarettes to wait for the spring melt. I was forced to try to ski.

But when I attempted to put the boot on my right foot into a binding, the left ski vanished. It was last seen sliding down a wall of ice toward the sun deck of a restaurant in Kleine Scheidegg, a village where you're supposed to go to eat marrowbone soup and watch French climbers falling off the north wall of the Eiger.

Fuck it, I'll walk, I said to nobody. I left the other ski and the poles in the shed in case a one-legged skier came along. I took about five steps down the mountain before I fell. Suddenly, I was spread-eagled against the mountain, clutching at roots and stumps, inadvertently making snowballs, causing such noises as a ski jacket does when it mashes against a sheet of crushed ice.

I slid on my stomach until I was hung on a ledge, clinging to a root. Here, I was reaching for a Winston and my Dunhill when a ski patrol person came out of nowhere.

He did a hockey stop, spraying me with fluff, and said something in fluent Himmler.

"Fool American," I said, forcing a grin.

He helped me to my feet, or boots, and with gestures and more Himmler, I understood that he wanted me to stand on the backs of his skis and hold on around his waist so I could ride with him to the bottom of the mountain.

Unless you've ever tried to stand up on two blocks of ice going forty miles an hour, you may not know how difficult it is. We skied about ten yards before my boots slipped off his skis. The crash took us end-over-end for another twenty yards down the slope.

Digging out of the snow, the ski patrol person said, "Ve try again."

"No!" I said, sternly, digging myself out of the snow.

"*Ja*, ve try."

"Fuckin' der tryin'," I said.

"*Ja*, ve must try. You havin' no skis or der ski pole-ins." Words to that effect.

I said, "Das iss goot. I valk."

"*Nicht* valkin'," he said.

"*Ja*, I valk," I said. "I go valkin' down. Donka bitter, bitter donka."

I groped around and lit a cigarette and smiled reassuringly.

"*Nicht rauchen*," he said, gesturing naughtily at my Winston.

"Calmin' der nerves," I said. "You go. I valk. Valkin' und *rauchen*. Goot."

He schussed away.

I was scared shitten but I valked.

Rather I slid on my butt, I slid on my side, I was frequently spread-eagled again, clawing, scratching at roots. Now and then, I paused to *rauch*. It took about an hour to get down.

I reached the finish area in time to see the last few racers of the day glide under the Ovalmaltine banner.

The winner had long since been determined, held his press

conference, and was back in his hotel being nibbled on by a cluster of Heidis.

I limped over to the press tent to beg for coffee. Several people, it seemed, had been watching me negotiate the mountain off to the side of the racecourse.

I recognized one of the faces. The man was, that winter, the assistant manager of the U.S. ski team, but he was someone I had known better as the sports information director, the SID, of a university in the Big Eight.

"Jim Tom!" he said, laughing. "Goddamn!"

"Ski racing is my life," I said, wearily.

Still laughing, he said, "I knew it had to be somebody from *Sports Illustrated*, but I didn't expect it to be *you*."

In those days, I was writing for *SI* instead of *SM*, *The Sports Magazine*, America's only other four-color national sports weekly. *SM* was an experiment that had worked, much to *SI*'s annoyance, and we were fierce competitors now. At least we thought so.

On the veranda of the Regina, I was thinking about that first experience in the Alps when Christine Thorne joined me.

"Bryce wants you to call him," she said, taking a chair at the table in her snug jeans, white cableknit sweater, and white headband. A fellow of looser morals might have noted that the bulky sweater obscured her tits.

"Why do I have to call Bryce?"

"He wants to put Emile Louvois on the cover, even if he doesn't win tomorrow. He likes the idea of a cover that says 'Vive la France.' "

"Why, because it's never been used?"

"He wants to talk to you about the story. He wants you to hammer the angle that Louvois is the best ski racer in the world."

"Even if he loses?"

"Yes. To support the cover."

"That's stupid."

"I know. I tried to tell him Pepi Henkel has won more races this winter. I said Pepi would probably win tomorrow. I said he would probably win the Olympic downhill. I do think Pepi is better than Louvois right now, but Bryce said he read in *The*

New York Times that Louvois is the best ski racer in the world."

"There's nobody here from *The Times*," I said. "*The Times* hasn't had anybody on the circuit all season."

"They sent a stringer here. I met him in the press center."

"Does he have a pointed head?"

"He's nice. He lives in Brussels. He normally covers NATO and the World Bank."

"That's fucking great," I said, rising from the table.

On the way to my room to call New York, I didn't cuss *The New York Times*. The only two newspapers I read regularly or trusted in general were *The Times* and the *Washington Post*. But I couldn't help thinking about the absurd influence *The Times* had on my profession. Researchers at *SM* and *SI*, or *Time* and *Newsweek*, for that matter, relied on *The Times* for accuracy in checking facts. I was sure that if there had never been a *New York Times*, there would never have been a *Time* magazine. What made this funny was that *The Times* could be as wrong as the *Fort Worth Light & Shopper* on occasion, but nevertheless, it had become common practice among the Bryce Wilcoxes of the magazine world to trust the accuracy and postures of *The Times* over their own writers and reporters in the field.

It was safe. A Bryce Wilcox would never have to defend a writer's stance on something controversial or provocative to upper management if he hung in there with the opinions and reporting in *The Times*. To a questioning superior, he could always say, "Well, it was in *The Times*," and thus, he would be blameless for whatever inaccuracy might have appeared in *SM*. This came under the heading of "plausible deniability," a thing that CEOs in America had raised to an art form.

Bryce Wilcox was a nice-looking, dark-haired, well-dressed man in his late thirties, ever mindful of his image, who was on the move, keeping a sharp eye on any opportunity that might elevate him within the company. He had taken the precaution to marry the perfect wife, Monica. Bryce's wife couldn't tell you where the Persian Gulf was but she could find Bloomingdale's blindfolded.

Staying blameless for anything that might go wrong on the magazine, Bryce thought, was the surest way to get himself promoted to the 33rd floor, the corporate floor, from where, someday, he envisioned that he would have more time for golf as he presided congenially over the supply of paperclips in the building and would live happily ever after in his bloating stock portfolio.

In my experience, it had been a rare managing editor who cared as much about the magazine he ran as he did about his profit sharing in Fund A and Fund B.

4

IT WAS 8 A.M. IN MANHATTAN BUT I KNEW BRYCE WILCOX would already be in the office. He liked to arrive two hours ahead of the staff, proof to the corporate floor, he imagined, that he labored more diligently over the content and appearance of the magazine than anyone else. Not many of us on the staff were fooled. We were aware that all he ever did in those two hours was calculate the end-of-the-year bonus he would receive for staying under budget and hiring minorities.

Bryce only thought about minorities when it was quota time. In the past few months, he had stocked the copy room and picture department with a Pakistani, a hyphenated Hispanic—a double coup—and an Oriental who barely spoke English, and had hired as a researcher a black girl who had graduated from medical school at Johns Hopkins and had been interning at New York Hospital.

Charlotte Murray, the black girl, had aspired to be a doctor all her life. She had no interest in journalism whatsoever, or any knowledge of it, but Bryce had offered her a starting salary of $70,000 a year, which she could only have refused if she had wanted to run the risk of having her housekeeper mother and janitor father back in Detroit have her committed to a mental institution behind a tall wire fence. Charlotte's salary was well over three times as much as a starting researcher at *SM* had ever been paid, and the only reason Bryce had gone after Charlotte was because our CEO, an oily dwarf named

Fenton Boles, had casually mentioned to Bryce that it would be nice to see another black on the staff in some capacity or another.

Bryce had met Charlotte in the emergency room at New York Hospital. He had taken himself to the hospital one morning to be treated for a minor knife wound in his rib cage after having been mugged by the Puerto Rican who was substituting for his regular limo driver. A limo to transport Bryce back and forth from Westchester to Rockefeller Center was one of his perks as managing editor, as was his membership in Winged Foot, and the six-TV-screen "media room" he'd had built onto his narrow, two-story, wood-frame house on Old Shipwreck Cove in Larchmont. Elsewhere in the house, Monica had worked hard to make every room resemble a page out of *Better Homes*. When Monica led you on a tour of the house, she would stop and pose in each room, then continue on.

Not everyone knew about Charlotte's whopping salary. It would cause a revolt. You needed to be a friend of the gossipy Eileen Fincher, Bryce's secretary, a slender brunette in her forties, or Nell Woodruff, or Christine Thorne, or a pal of mine among the senior writers, Ralph Webber, who had been servicing Eileen, among others, for a number of years, and whose nickname was Wooden Dick.

Ralph was known as a quiet writer. He enjoyed doing those long, studious, mostly unread features on such enthralling subjects as sneaker manufacturing, flags, raccoons, sports diets, and the construction of soccer balls. Still boyishly handsome for a man of fifty-one—curly hair, quick grin, holdover Georgia accent—Ralph was usually findable around the office either prowling the halls between paragraphs or peeking into doorways or drawing the newest female staffer into an extended, confessional conversation. Almost everyone on the staff knew Ralph had a wooden dick. He had spent more three-hour lunch breaks and closing nights in midtown Manhattan hotel rooms with adventurous female co-workers than anybody in the history of magazine journalism. He commuted by bus and train from a town in New Jersey nobody had ever heard of, and he was, of course, a happily married man, the father of five.

I hadn't betrayed Ralph's confidence and let it slip to any

outsider about Charlotte Murray's salary, nor had Nell or Christine. We all liked Charlotte. She was cute and feisty and would do well on the magazine despite her lack of knowledge about sports. Common sense would see her through once she got it in her head that there were four quarters in a football game, five players on a basketball team, eighteen holes on a golf course, and other such mysterious things.

Charlotte endeared herself to me one day when she said she wanted to learn about golf. I asked her why.

"So I can be a credit to my race," she said.

Bryce accepted my collect call in New York, and said, "Hey, big guy. How's it going over there in Switzer-rama?"

"Oh, we're fondue-ing along," I said, but before I could get to the point, he said, "You missed a whale of a sales conference in Ponte Vedra. I played the Big Track. Shot thirty-nine on the front, forty-one on the back. Two three-putts. Played from the blues."

I said, "Bryce, listen, I can't . . ."

But he said, "I hit sixteen in two with a driver and three-wood. Is that any good? Played Marsh Swamp the first day. Good members' course. Lot of bulkheads."

I said, "Bryce, about the Frenchman. I think . . ."

But he said, "Four of us went down in the Gulfstream. Wheels up at Butler at nine in the morning. We were on the tee at twelve-thirty. Not bad, huh?"

I said, "Bryce, I hear you want a cover on the Frenchman, but if he loses tomorrow, we'll look silly."

"The Frenchman's sexy, big guy. He'll sell."

"You must have a picture you like."

"Heck of a picture. He looks like a movie star. He's wearing a red sweater."

The old survey thing again. Red outsold any other color on the newsstands, or so Bryce had been led to believe by a group of marketing ferns.

I said, "Just for the sake of discussion, what if he finishes tenth?"

"You'll make it work," he said, blithely.

"What if he breaks his leg?"

"Might be better. The best ski racer in the world breaks his leg. We were there."

"He's not the best ski racer in the world, Bryce."

"Best average."

"Best average of what?"

"Best average of finishes. It was in *The Times*."

"He hasn't won a race."

"He's been second three times, third twice."

"Pepi Henkel's been *first* three times."

"Henkel falls down a lot."

"Right, he's reckless. He either wins or falls. Which makes him more interesting—and three wins makes him better than Louvois."

"Hey, big guy. You're forgetting something."

"Like what?"

"The Frenchman is the best ski racer in the world if *we* say so."

The arrogance of national magazines had always amused and amazed me. It was as if slick paper and four-color art made something a fact. I had been victimized by this arrogance many times, and as recently as a year ago. I had written a long feature on Notre Dame football after the Fighting Irish had won their twenty-ninth straight game, a win streak that covered three seasons. The piece hadn't come close to suggesting that Notre Dame was unbeatable; in fact, it hinted strongly that the streak was in jeopardy, seeing as how a very good Southern Cal team was the next opponent and an even better Miami team was waiting down the road. But with a Notre Dame running back on the cover and in blazing type almost as large as the *SM* logo, Bryce wrote a cover billing that said: WHY NOTRE DAME IS UNBEATABLE.

The issue hit the newsstands and reached subscribers two days before the Trojans whipped the Irish 34 to 7. I was still living down the humiliation, not with my chums in the trade but with letter-writing readers who insanely think that the by-line person also writes the headlines and cover billings.

Now, I said, "Louvois is not the best goddamn ski racer in the world in any story I intend to file from here, Bryce."

Silence.

"Are you there?" I said.

"Yo. Have you still got that old Armour putter in your bag?"

"Have I *what*?"

"The last time we whipped it around West up at Winged Foot, you had an old Armour putter in your bag. Want to sell it? This Ping is killing me."

"Bryce, I didn't bring my clubs to Switzerland. I know it sounds crazy, but I rarely travel with my golf clubs in the winter. Can we get this settled?"

I thought I heard another voice on the line.

"Who's in your office?" I asked.

"I've got CNN on," he said. "The market's on a roll in Japan."

"That's a relief," I said.

"Damn!"

"What now?"

"Gold dropped seventeen dollars."

"Bryce, I'll compromise with you. I'll do a feature on Louvois. You hold it till he wins something. If he wins tomorrow, fine. If he doesn't, I write the game story on the winner and you go with a basketball cover."

"No way, Jose."

Bryce had a knack for original phrases like that. He often inserted them into my stories, and everyone else's. You could get them taken out if you were in the office at closing time, but on the road, death. He was also fond of hard as a rock, fast as the wind, and the ever-popular cold as ice.

He said, "Wayne Mohler just did an NBA piece, and I don't want to put back-to-back niggers on the cover."

That word came easy for him around me, a native Texan, and other southerners in the office. Bryce thought it made him sound macho, one of the gang. He had never understood that I only used the word humorously, as a lot of blacks themselves did, including Charlotte Murray, but Bryce, after all, was originally from somewhere up around Boston, and one of the best-kept secrets in America is that Boston is a more racist city than Birmingham, Alabama.

What I didn't say on the phone was that I was going to write the story on whoever won the race, and if it didn't happen to be the movie-star Frenchman in the red sweater, then one of Bryce's lukewarm drones would have to toil through the night rewriting it, or "saving" it, to borrow from the language of the drones.

Our conversation ended when I did say, "You're missing a big opportunity, Bryce. If the Austrian wins, you could have a better cover billing than 'Vive la France.' You could say, 'Look Out, Jews, Here They Come Again.' "

5

THE MORNING OF THE LAUBERHORN DOWNHILL, CHRISTINE and I went for a stroll through the village before we wandered down to the finish line, which was below the train station near the old church. We walked past bakeries, ski shops, gift shops, other hotels, and a *pension* where I glanced up to see an elderly ex-Gestapo agent sunning himself on a balcony while Magda Goebbels read a newspaper.

It was when we stopped for coffee at a sidewalk cafe that Christine said, "I don't know why you complain so much, Jim Tom. You have the best job in the business."

She was probably right, and I suppose before I go on any farther, I ought to explain some things about myself and how I got where I was.

The job was one I had designed for myself when Ed Maxwell started up *The Sports Magazine* eight years ago as a direct competitor of *Sports Illustrated*. Ed was my old boss, a man who had been managing editor of *SI* for fifteen years. Ed had hired me off the *Fort Worth Light & Shopper* after I had freelanced five pieces to *SI*. He had brought me up to New York, to what most people in my profession would romantically refer to as the big league. This was an opportunity of a lifetime, of course, and I had leaped at it and felt confident that I could handle any assignment. I had learned how to work hard and write fast on the newspaper. I had studied all of my heroes in sportswriting, the men who had taken the profession to another level. Ask me to name my all-time starting eleven and I would give you John Lardner, Red Smith, Jim Murray, Damon Runyon, W. O. McGeehan, Henry McLemore, Blackie Sherrod, Furman Bisher, Grantland Rice, Doc Greene, Bob Considine.

I wrote for fifteen happy years under Ed Maxwell at *Sports Illustrated*. Ed was a managing editor who cared about writers and their words. He admired all kinds of writing: risky, flippant, provocative, opinioned, analytical. Ed deserved most of the credit for making *SI* a success. He showed confidence in the people he hired and stood behind them. He was an aloof man, a pudgy fellow who drank his lunches but could hold his whiskey and often said that more good story ideas came out of a bar than a story conference. Back then, he once told me the three greatest things I would ever hear from a boss. One, I couldn't receive too much hate mail to suit him. Two, I couldn't spend too much money on the road. Three, if any editor jacked around with my copy, he would have him killed or fired, my choice.

Ed was too good to be true, of course, and those glory days came to an end when Ed was forced into retirement at the age of sixty-five, although he was a young sixty-five and could still outthink and outperform most men half his age. He didn't take kindly to being pushed aside and immediately began trying to start up his own magazine. It took him two years, and in the meantime, I got along okay with Ed's successor at *SI*, Clinton Dowdy, even though Clint's idea of what *SI* should be evolved around the dictum that, essentially, writers should write more and spend less.

Ed eventually found a man named Les Padgett at a cocktail party. Les Padgett was willing to bankroll *SM*. Les was the chairman of the board of The Padgett Group, or TPG, a conglomerate that was making a fortune in toilet paper, pet food, diapers, other grocery products, cable TV, and was already in publishing. TPG was the parent company of five other magazines: *World Events, Celebrity Parade, Vibrant, Southern Mansions*, and *Essence*. Les was a man in his forties whose daddy had invented nondairy creamer, and he primarily occupied his time getting married and divorced to socialites and movie stars, but he gave Ed the millions needed to start up *SM*, saying he would just as soon do this with some of his money as give it to the "Federal gubmint."

I was the first writer Ed money-whipped away from *SI*. Other so-called names followed, like Wayne Mohler from the *San Francisco Chronicle* and Ralph Webber from the *Atlanta Constitution*. I like to think it was the writing that made us an instant success, but more likely there had simply been a market for *SM*. Today *SM*'s circulation was 2.4 million. We were still a million behind *SI*, but there was little doubt in my mind that the gap would be narrower if Ed Maxwell were still alive. He died of a sudden heart attack four years ago. I was out in LA on a story when I heard the news. After shedding a few tears, I did the only thing I thought would please Ed. I picked up a dinner check at the Beverly Hills Hotel for fifteen hundred dollars.

Unfortunately for the staff, the one thing Ed hadn't done was put his successor in place. Bryce Wilcox came to us out of nowhere. Bryce was chosen by Fenton Boles, the oily dwarf who had murdered his way up to CEO of The Padgett Group. Bryce's single qualification was that he was the assistant managing editor of *Celebrity Parade*, the man responsible for putting some of the movie stars on the cover that Les Padgett married. As I look back on it, I think Bryce must have got the job because he was a golf nut and convinced Fenton Boles that a sports magazine should have a sporting fellow as m.e.

Bryce would have his brain locks, but I didn't regard him as quite as big a sap as did some others on the staff. I had been getting along with him for four years. He understood that my by-line was of a certain value. Therefore, I was doing the same job for Bryce that I had done for Ed Maxwell. I was writing a thousand-word column every week on the back page, subject of my choice. I would occasionally write a lead if there was no game-story writer on the scene, which was the case in Switzerland at the Lauberhorn. For these chores, I was now earning a hundred and fifty thousand a year.

Which was all the more reason why Christine didn't like to hear me complain. She knew how much money I made, thanks to Ralph Webber, the old salary detective in the office.

"Complaining is part of the deal," I said to Christine at the sidewalk cafe in Wengen. "If you don't complain a lot, people get the idea you don't do anything but have fun—go to sports events with parking passes and working-press credentials that put you on the inside of everything and give you the best seat in the house. People don't think about the writing part. I live with idiots who come up to me, and say, 'Are those your words in the magazine? I mean, do you just write them or what?' "

I told Christine the story again, maybe for the fifth time, about the guy who sat next to me on a flight to Houston one day. He kept looking at me as if he recognized my column picture. Finally, he summoned up the courage to nudge me, and say, "Listen, I really like your sentence putting-togetherness, paragraph-wise."

Such things, I said, were responsible for my premature gray hair, my height shrinking to six feet, and the fixed sardonic expression on my face that made it seem like I was about to complain about something, even when I wasn't.

I said my salary might sound like a lot of money to a researcher, but it wasn't much money if you were feebleminded enough for your primary residence to be in New York City, where it was a known fact that the federal, city, and state taxes eat like a Labrador retriever. It wasn't a lot of money if your job had cost you three wives, two of whom you had been in love with and one of whom you had liked tremendously. It wasn't a lot of money if you had been separated from your only son most of his life and he was now in his eighth year of college. And it wasn't a lot of money if you were now fifty-four years old and in a death struggle with the exact opposite of a stiff dick and a limber back.

I asked Christine to consider the arithmetic. After federal, state, and city taxes, I brought home only $75,000 a year. The mortgage payment on my two-bedroom co-op at 72nd and Third Avenue was $30,000 a year. The maintenance on my co-op was $12,000 a year. The monthly bills in New York, whether I was in town or not, added up to another $12,000. The annual tuition for James Junior, who was now at the University of Georgia after pursuing a phantom degree at TCU, Oklahoma, and Auburn, was $10,000 a year. I loved that kid,

I said, and some of my fondest memories were those rare times when I had been able to take him on trips with me and introduce him to a Roger Staubach or an O. J. Simpson or a Jack Nicklaus, and I still laughed about the time when he was twelve and said his favorite soup came out of the vending machine in the Minneapolis airport and his favorite salad dressing was what they served on Delta Airlines, but nevertheless these days his gasoline, beer, golf balls, guns, drugs, and ammo were costing me $5,000 a year. His mother and my first ex-wife, Earlene, was getting $400 a month, or roughly $5,000 a year for dental bills, auto repairs, and hush money. On the plus side, my other ex-wives, Janice and Priscilla, didn't need any money. They were both married to rich guys now. This left $1,000 to dole out regularly to my co-op building staff—the doormen, hallmen, and handymen—a bribe to keep the doormen, hallmen, and handymen from burglarizing my apartment when I was on the road, which was constantly.

Take away my expense account, I said to Christine, and I might as well be one of the homeless, sleeping in the tunnels under Grand Central Station.

Christine had no sympathy, as I might have suspected, for in order to survive in Manhattan, she was sharing a third-floor walkup in the Village with two other researchers, Joel from *World Events* and Rachel from *Celebrity Parade*.

"You poor thing," she said, snottily, and we went to cover the ski race.

6

THE FIRST RACER ON THE COURSE WAS PEPI HENKEL, THE arrogant Austrian. The big electronic scoreboard near the finish line flashed his interval at 1.03.98. The point nine-eight might be vital because ski races are usually, if not frivolously, decided by fractions of a second. I was often entertained at my typewriter when I would think to myself that I was making a hero out of a guy who had skied two miles down a mountain and had defeated his nearest competitor by two one-hundredths of a second. It wasn't as though he had broken six tackles and dashed for a touchdown in the Rose Bowl, or birdied the last three holes to win the Masters, or hit a game-winning World Series home run in the ninth inning off a left-hander throwing gas. The skier hadn't even raced the guy side-by-side. All he had done was avoid falling down better than the other racers, but I would have to appear authoritative and say it was perfectly obvious that the winner had been quicker at the top, faster on the steep, smoother on the flat, and more fearless when he negotiated Das Nose of Der Rabbit, the most dangerous turn on the course. It was silly. But so was putting funny things on your feet and wanting to plunge down a mountain at eighty miles an hour.

The Austrian, low in his gleaming yellow racing suit and helmet, suddenly came into view, soaring off a ledge. He landed easily, went into a fetal position, and schussed under the finish banner.

Austrian flags waved in the crowd, and a chorus of a thousand Himmlers, going ohhh-ahhh, accompanied him to a scratchy stop. He was clocked in 2.05.28. When the next eight racers were slower, Pepi Henkel began to pose for the dozens of photographers surrounding him, one of whom was our man, Shag Monti.

Pepi made sure all of his logos were on display, especially the logo on his skis, which he removed and held in a vertical position near his photo-op heart.

Christine advised me that Pepi Henkel was earning more than two hundred and fifty thousand a year for using that particular make of skis—Panzer-Messerschmitts, or something like that—and another two hundred and fifty thousand for using specific brands of boots, bindings, poles, goggles, and sun creams.

Not bad, I thought, for a young Austrian with the brain of a rooster and the personality of a rock formation who would never know how to do anything in life but ski and fuck himself into comas. But I didn't envy him all the unhappy, middle-aged American wives he would have to be fucking ten years from now when he was running the ski school in Vail. That would be tougher duty than sportswriting, surely.

Just then, Pepi stopped grinning and stared up at the electronic scoreboard. Emile Louvois was on the course and the Frenchman's interval was faster than anyone by a full second.

Louvois lost part of his lead on a mogul or a turn somewhere—how was anyone at the finish to know? But in his French blue racing suit and matching helmet, he tucked his way into our sight and came under the finish banner in 2.05.20, or eight one-hundredths of a second faster than Pepi Henkel.

The Frenchman saw his name flicker to the top of the scoreboard and raised his arms in victory. French flags emerged in the crowd and people shouted things that sounded to me like, "Cafe-croissant chateau!"

The Austrian scowled, as the photographers fled from him.

I scowled, too, but for another reason.

"That French prick just made a genius out of Bryce," I said to Christine. "Bryce can't wait to tell everybody on thirty-three how he closed the cover early and saved forty thousand dollars, he was so sure Louvois would win the race. He'll be a hero at the weekly managing editors' luncheon, pointing out how much smarter he is than the writer and researcher he sent over here."

"Louvois was fantastic," Christine gulped. "Did you see how he took the last bump? He was very low. He won it at the bottom."

"He did?"

"Oh, yes."

"Remind me of that when I'm typing."

With nothing better to do at the moment, I went with Christine to stand in the midst of the other writers and photographers—shooters, they like to call themselves—who were encircling Louvois.

Shag Monti, our ace shooter, was in the throng, busily sputtering Nikon motor. Other cameras hung around his grimy relic of a safari jacket. Shag was a Renaissance man, a fading memory of the sixties. Ex-dope dealer, ex-carpenter, ex-tennis pro, ex-waiter, ex-guitarist. His hair was still long and matted, his body lean, his chin bearded. He took pride in his nickname of Earth Dude.

I tried not to hang out much with shooters. They couldn't talk about anything but lighting and lenses. They made their own travel arrangements, stayed in their own hotels, mingled with their own kind.

"Earth Dude," I said, acknowledging Shag.

"Hey, man," he said. "What it is?"

"Raclette and fondue."

"I'm blimped out, man. Fondue fever."

I asked if he had been assigned to Innsbruck.

"I'm there," he said, "but it's gonna be a long three weeks if I don't score some discipline."

Dope, he meant.

For a moment, I listened to the Frenchman's babble.

"Yes, it was in my mind to do well," Louvois was saying. "Yes, the winning is better than the losing. Yes, I must give credit to my skis. Yes, the skiing is very good in my village. Yes, my father owns the *pension* where we live. Yes, I knew what I had to do, but, as you can see, I have done it, no?"

It was Christine who picked up on the frantic achtungs being shouted over the PA. She nudged me, then Shag, and called our attention to the electronic scoreboard.

A racer from the third seed, starting thirty-sixth, was on the course and his interval was a full two seconds faster than Louvois.

"Who is he?" I asked Christine.

She looked at the start list.

"Drin Hoxha," she said.

"*Drin Hoxha*?" I responded. "That's not a name, it's a dance."

"I've never heard of him," Christine confessed.

Shag Monti said, "I better get a position in case the dude stands up."

He shuffled away.

Delving into the press kit, Christine broke into a slight grin. "He's an Albanian."

"You're shitting me?"

I don't mind admitting that the prospect of an Albanian

winning that race made my heart swell. Albania didn't have any athletes. Albania didn't have any *people*. Well, it had one person. Peter Lorre in *Casablanca*.

We heard roars from up on the hill, out of our sight, which indicated the Albanian was still on his skis.

"This is great," Christine said, actually excited.

Now here came Drin Hoxha in his black-and-white racing suit and red helmet. He took a little too much air off the last bump and came down unsteadily, up on one ski, but he regained his balance and went into his tuck.

Our eyes darted from racer to clock, from clock to racer.

"Christ," I said. "He can fall and still win."

"Go, Drin!" Christine yelled.

I looked at her. "No cheering in the press box, please."

Drin Hoxha then glided under the finish banner and our eyes shot to the electronic scoreboard. The Albanian not only won, he beat Emile Louvois by three seconds. In Alpine ski racing, that was a drowning.

"You've got some work to do," I said to Christine, calmly. "We don't know anything about this guy."

"Not the kind of work you think."

"What do you mean?" I said, innocently.

Coldly, she said, "I am *not* fucking an Albanian, Jim Tom."

7

PERSONALLY, I THOUGHT DRIN HOXHA EVEN LOOKED A LITtle like Peter Lorre in *Casablanca*. He was a stubby fellow with a shiny face and distrustful eyes. I therefore concluded that the Lauberhorn had been won by a Monsieur Hugarte, who had shot two German couriers at the starting gate, robbed them of the letters of transit, and sped down the mountain to have a glass of wine in Rick's Cafe Americain. Only this time he didn't get arrested and dragged away by Claude Rains' henchmen. He got rich from endorsements, bought the joint, scooped

Ingrid Bergman, and became the most famous Albanian since Zog. When last seen, he was strolling toward the Winter Olympics with Emile Louvois, saying, "I know your name's not Louie, but this looks like the beginning of a beautiful friendship."

A lot of that, I fear, was in the story I wrote on the geezer-codger Olivetti in my room at the Regina that afternoon, a story Christine checked and faxed to New York for me.

I fully understood that when the story was received in New York, the deadening process would begin. It would first be handled by one of Bryce Wilcox's glorified clerks, or senior editors, who were known to most of us as Drones One Through Ten. The story would then be passed along to an assistant managing editor named Lindsey Caperton, then to another assistant m.e. named Doug McNiff, and then it might be given a final trampling by Bryce himself, but only if Bryce had nothing better to do. In the end, the story might read as if it had been written from a pharaoh's crypt.

Drones One Through Ten never stopped the rhythm of a piece completely. Drone One was usually too preoccupied with *The Times* crossword. Drone Two would be drunk from a four-hour lunch and slumped at his desk, pissing in his pants and muttering to himself, "Windy boy, windy boy." Drone Three would be locked in his office, screwing a tall weepy woman from the copy room. Drone Four would be working on his seventh unpublished novel. Drone Five would be swimming laps at the West Side Y. Drone Six would be playing bridge in the art department. Drone Seven would be interviewing for a job at *People*. Drone Eight would be helping organize a labor union. Drone Nine would be searching for a slow-closing feature he had lost behind a filing cabinet. Drone Ten would be in Bryce's office, trying to explain why he had forgotten to assign a photographer to shoot a Duke-Georgetown basketball game.

Whichever drone would "catch" my story—dronetalk—would only do the following: read it haphazardly, scratch out the most entertaining sentence in the lead, change every other comma to a period, kill the third paragraph, insert the word "happily" somewhere, replace the most crucial paragraph with something off the AP wire, kill the kicker line, and be rid of it.

The story would now find its way, either by taking flight from an outbox to an inbox or by flashing from one word-processing screen to another, to Lindsey Caperton's office.

Lindsey was a devious, cherub-faced, lifelong SAE from the University of Virginia, now in his middle thirties, who had never written an interesting sentence in his life, particularly when he had covered pro football for a time, so Bryce had naturally promoted him to assistant m.e.

Lindsey was now in charge of putting a parenthesis in every paragraph he touched and pretending that he never liked anything in the magazine, story or photo, unless Bryce liked it, in which case Lindsey liked it enormously. In a story conference, you could always count on Lindsey to say one of two things: "You're exactly right, Bryce," or "I couldn't agree more, Bryce." Lindsey liked to tell staff members that his door was always open if anyone had a personal problem, but every staff member knew to be cautious about Lindsey and his door—it could be slammed on your neck.

Now the story, chock full of Lindsey's parenthetical facts and observations, would reach the office of Doug McNiff, who for some wildly arcane reason was known as a "good word man."

Doug's great sorrow in life was that he hadn't gone to an Ivy League school. He tried to compensate for this by affecting a British accent, which wasn't easy for a man who came from Oklahoma City. The accent would come out of a void and disappear just as mysteriously. Doug also figured it enhanced his image never to remove the coat of his suit or loosen his tie as he sat in his office editing copy. He would sit erect at his desk, clearing his throat or humming old Broadway melodies, while he made theatrical slash marks with his blue pencil on the pages before him.

Equally infuriating was that Doug and Lindsey never dealt honestly with a writer. They would never say, "I don't think this works," or "This doesn't seem clear to me." What they would say was, "Bryce feels rather strongly that we owe the reader some clarity here," or "Bryce rather imagines we can do without this paragraph."

It was always on Bryce, the superior. But Bryce would seldom have seen the story at that point, so there would be no use going to Bryce to get something changed back the way you wanted it, if not the way it might be more accurate or make better sense. The only thing to do, if you were lucky enough to be around the office before the issue closed, was sneak into the copy room and work with the tall, weepy woman, Miriam Bowen, and get it fixed. For once the magazine was on the newsstands or in the hands of the subscribers, Bryce and Lindsey and Doug never looked at anything but the pictures.

When writers gathered for drinks at Fu's Like Us, a hideous Chinese restaurant but friendly neighborhood tavern on the ground floor of our building in Rockefeller Center, the conversation nearly always got around to the baroque things that Doug or Lindsey had done, at one time or another, to somebody's story. Their worst atrocities occurred when Bryce would glance at the rough file, fail to grasp the humor or subtlety in it, and instruct Doug or Lindsey to "liven it up." If you were filing from out of town, as I was from Switzerland, the finished product could look as if Yorkshire terriers had been chewing on it.

An office joke turned up on the bulletin board in the main hall one day two years ago. Examples of Lindsey Caperton's editing talent. Wayne Mohler and I were both accused of the joke. We collaborated, was what happened. What stayed on the bulletin board until Lindsey yanked it down was:

BY CHARLES DICKENS

It was the best of times—and, ironically—the worst of times.

BY HERMAN MELVILLE

Beats me why but somebody hung this moniker of Ishmael on me, but it stuck. You can call me that.

BY ERNEST HEMINGWAY

He was an old man (58 last October) who fished alone in a skiff (a small light sailing ship or rowboat) in the Gulf

Stream (part of the Atlantic Ocean) and he had gone eighty-four days (a new NCAA record) without taking a fish (*SM*, July 18, 1951).

In Fu's Like Us, I would argue that Doug McNiff could be more dangerous than Lindsey Caperton at times. Doug was always poised with "faster than a speeding bullet," ready with his references to Frank Merriwell and Hairbreath Harry, and it scarcely need be said that he was a staunch advocate of the exclamation point.

Still burned into my soul was a job Doug had done on me when I covered a Super Bowl in Miami, one of those Super Bowls where Joe Montana won another one for the 49ers. Over the years, I felt I had said just about everything there was to say about Joe Montana, as had every other writer in Western culture, so I led with:

"Joe Montana, comma."

Bryce didn't get it and told Doug to "fix" it.

What appeared in the magazine, with MY by-line on it, was:

"Whoo-boy! Joe Montana did it again!"

When I returned to the office a few days later, I marched into Doug's office, but not to call him a mangy motherfucker and a menace to journalism, as Wayne Mohler would have. I simply slumped against the door facing and asked Doug in a calm, pathetic voice how many more whoo-boys I might expect to find in my stuff in this calendar year.

Doug had smiled graciously, and said, "I rather liked your lead, Jim Tom, but Bryce felt it was a bit oblique. Did the best I could at a late hour. Nice piece, by the way."

The poor bastard. We writers were already having our revenge on him. He lived in the far reaches of some gloomy county above Westchester in a town that didn't even have a deli. He faced a two-and-a-half-hour commute to the city, one way. He was married to a loon named Claire who wore culottes and thought of herself as a ceramicist. Doug's runaway daughter was thought to be on crack and laid up in Harlem, and his dropout teenage son, highly skilled in drive-by shootings, was last reported to have been sighted in the vicinity of Jacksonville, Florida.

In fairness, I guess I should say that these journalistic horrors I mention only happened to me when I wrote in the lead area, up front in the magazine. Nobody tampered much with my weekly column on the back page. Bryce assumed that my column was only read by a handful of cynics anyhow, but more important, it sold a full-page facing ad on the inside back cover, to J & B Scotch whisky one week and to Winston cigarettes the next. In Bryce's mind, I wrote money, not a column.

It was Lindsey Caperton who called the Regina and told Christine that Bryce was "very disappointed" with my story. It seemed there had been far too much about the Albanian, who won the race, and far too little about the Frenchman, who was on the cover. Lindsey was running it through his word processor to do what he could to "save" it.

As Christine reported to me later in the Regina bar, Lindsey had been greatly troubled by one particular reference I had made in the piece. She was laughing so hard she could barely repeat the question Lindsey had asked her, which was:

"Who is Claude Rains?"

8

I SAW NO REASON WHY CHRISTINE AND I SHOULDN'T SPEND A couple of days in Geneva on the expense account. We needed the rest before we moved on to Innsbruck to get all tense and keyed-up over the Winter Olympics. Geneva is one of the great eating cities. I rank it up there with Buenos Aires, Brussels, Rome, Paris, Fort Worth, and Austin in this respect, although the Texas towns only come into it for barbecue and Tex-Mex, which was what I dreamed about that winter when I wasn't dreaming about killing people.

In Geneva, the management of Le Hotel Richmond was acquainted with me from previous visits; thus I was able to get us each a room with a balcony and a view of the lake for only four hundred and fifty dollars a night. The hotel was conveniently situated, near the only place I wanted to dine, but for Christine's enjoyment, it was also near all of the elegant shops where you can watch Arabs buy emerald elephant's eyes for no more than eighty-nine thousand dollars and change. Over the years, I had seen West Germans buy diamond-studded cake pans in Geneva, Japanese buy diamond-studded golf clubs in Geneva, and I had seen my first pair of diamond-studded Guccis on a North Vietnamese diplomat in Geneva.

I made Christine eat three meals at Cafe de Paris. I had been going to Cafe de Paris for many winters. Nothing fancy about the place. It was more the equivalent of a Swiss diner. You only needed to say one thing to the slow-moving waiter: "Bring it on, *s'il vous plait*."

What would be brought on was the only dish the restaurant served, a Cafe de Paris steak, which came out lean and sizzling on a platter with French fries and a green salad. The steak would swim around in a delicate brownish-gold sauce. The true gourmet would slosh the French fries and salad around in the same sauce. All this, along with three Scotches, came close to being my favorite meal, European category.

After dinner the second night, we hit a nightclub in Geneva's Old Town. The first highlight of the show was hearing a male vocalist sing, "My kind of town, Geneva is," then "I left my heart on Zurich's Bahnhofstrasse." The second highlight was the headliner, a stripper named Heike. She was made up to resemble, I think, Marilyn Monroe, for the benefit of the Japanese businessmen in the audience.

Heike's act started slowly but she finished in a blaze of glory. Her main prop on stage was a Honda motorcycle. The engine miraculously cranked up on its own each time Heike went down on the gas cap or dry-fucked the rear fender.

Eventually, we returned to the Richmond and made the hotel bartender wealthy. We both got a little drunk, I'm afraid, or why else would I have pulled my chair closer to Christine's, slipped my arm around her, and said, "I love you, my treasure. I want to marry you"?

Christine didn't remove my arm, but she said, "You don't love me and I'm not going to marry you."

"Why not?" I said. "I'm available and you're a borderline spinster."

"I can't think of anything worse than being married to you, Jim Tom."

With that, she threw down another vodka.

"Because I'm too old?"

She took a drag off my cigarette, although she didn't smoke, and said, "You're not old. You don't look old, so stop acting like you're old."

I took that as a definite indicator and gently turned her head toward me and gave her my best Cary Grant kiss.

I thought she was enjoying it until she suddenly burst out laughing, practically spitting on my face.

"What the fuck are you doing?" I said, romantically.

"I'm sorry," she said. She was still laughing.

"What's so funny?"

"The idea of us going to bed together—after all this time."

"I didn't say anything about going to bed with you. I said I wanted to marry you."

"Jim Tom, you know we can't go to bed together. It would ruin our friendship . . . our working relationship."

"You're right," I said. "The next thing I know, you'd be bringing me coffee in the office—a dead giveaway to everybody that we're fucking."

"I *have* thought of going to bed with you."

"I've thought about going to bed with you."

"Not that much."

"Me neither."

"I used to think you didn't like me."

"With those tits?"

"You don't like many people, Jim Tom."

"I like everybody. I just don't like to talk to most of them. There are over two hundred million people in America who don't subscribe to newspapers, don't subscribe to magazines, don't buy books. What am I supposed to talk to them about? I like to talk to people who can fix things. I'm in total awe of anybody who can repair something. I would much rather talk to a garage mechanic than a CEO."

"Of course, you hang out with a lot of garage mechanics."

"More than insurance salesmen."

"You hate foreigners."

"I do *not* hate foreigners. I respect foreigners, most of them. They don't tear down their ruins to build condos. You *do* have to keep one thing in mind about foreigners. They like soccer."

Christine said, "If you want to get married again, you ought to marry Nell."

"Nell comes from too good a family for me. Her father belongs to five country clubs. Her mother is on three museum boards."

"Nell's in love with you. She's been in love with you ever since you told her she had dirty hair."

"Nell loves me as a friend, the same way I love her. It's different with you."

"Ha!"

I motioned to the bartender for backups.

"I want to ask you something in all seriousness, Christine." She looked at me.

"I don't want you to be offended," I said.

"You've offended me so many times, I'm used to it. What?"

"Since you won't marry me and since we shouldn't go to bed together because it would spoil our friendship . . . our working relationship . . . does that mean a blowjob is out of the question tonight?"

"You really are an ass," she said, giggling.

"I guess that answers the question."

Christine was just drunk enough by this time that I got her to talking about all of the men on the masthead she had nailed, and I have to confess that even I was stunned to learn that in addition to three young male researchers, and Ronnie Zander, the art director, and practically every senior writer but myself, she had also fucked Drones One Through Seven.

But Christine maintained certain standards. She had never fucked the loathsome Lindsey Caperton and certainly not Bryce Wilcox.

"Or Doug McNiff," I said.

"Once."

"*What*?" I hadn't expected to hear that.

"It was a long time ago," she said, apologetically.

"Why?"

"I felt sorry for him."

"How did it even come up?"

She said Doug had taken her out to dinner one night after work. He had missed his last train. He had said he would go to a hotel, but it had been snowing and they had been near her apartment and her roommates hadn't been home. They had drunk some wine and wound up fooling around on the couch. Doug had cried as he talked about his wretched homelife with Claire, the loon.

"He cried so you fucked him?"

"It wasn't like that."

"Maybe I can cry."

"You're incapable of crying, Jim Tom—unless a paragraph gets rewritten. Your feelings are all in your typewriter. You are quite obviously a man who doesn't care if he gets laid. You've done all that."

"What about Auld Lang Syne?"

"I'll let you in on a secret. Women like to screw men who care, or know how to act like they care."

"I used to care," I said. "Life took it out of me. I *am* hoping for one last hard-on before doomsday. We're nearing the end, you know? You could be part of a pretty special occasion tonight."

Christine detected a glint.

"See there," she said. "You're laughing. You're not only a smartass, you're a hopeless cynic. That's why you should marry Nell. She's as cynical as you are."

I was lighting a Winston as I said, "Why do I think Doug has a big dick?"

"He does."

"It can't be bigger than Ralph's."

"Ralph doesn't have a big dick."

Another jolt. "Wooden Dick doesn't have a big dick?"

"Ralph has a beautiful dick."

"It's not too big?"

"No."

"Not too small?"

"No."

"Not crooked?"

"No."

"Always hard?"

"*Always.*"

"Lucky old Ralph," I sighed.

We drank a while longer and discussed other dicks. When we went upstairs to our rooms, which were next door to each other, I put my hands at Christine's waist and drew her to me.

I looked deeply into her eyes and said, "*Il pleure dans mon coeur, comme il pleut sur la ville.*"

She laughed as she translated it. "It rains in my heart as it rains in the city?"

"Yes," I said. "That phrase has served me well with many women."

"The mentally deficient, you mean?" She kissed me on the forehead and went into her room and double-locked the door.

9

NELL WOODRUFF WAS ON THE PHONE FROM NEW YORK THE next morning, waking me up to ask if I was interested in having a meaningless relationship. Actually, she was eager to tell me she had made the traveling squad for Innsbruck.

"That's great," I said, reaching for the Winston that would get my heart started. "Who else is on the team?"

It wouldn't compare with the fourteen people *Sports Illustrated* would have on hand, but Bryce was sending two other writers to do the game stories, another photographer to have Nikon wars with Shag Monti for the covers, a drone to "coordinate," and herself. Counting Christine and me, *SM* would have to squeak by with a humbling staff of eight.

"You may have to do a sidebar or two if things present themselves," Nell said, "but otherwise, you'll just bat out the old columns. Wayne Mohler will do the lead-lead and Ralph Webber's coming to do the second lead."

"Don't kid me," I said. "Ralph's only coming to help out with the fucking. Who's our drone?"

"Dalton. Bryce is rewarding him for the fine job he's done lately."

"He wrote a headline that rhymed?"

"Two."

Dalton Buckley was Drone One, master of *The Times* crossword. His headlines and cover billings had been thrilling *SM* readers for years. THE PACK IS BACK was Dalton's. KNICKS HAVE THE KNACK was Dalton's. MIAMI THRICE was Dalton's. RAIDERS OF THE LOST SPARK was Dalton's. 'BAMA AND TONGS was Dalton's.

"Bryce may come for a few days," Nell said. "He's never been to an Olympics. He says he has a good friend over there. Clipper somebody."

"I met Clipper. He's out of Muffy by Skippy. He may be our next publisher. Who's our publisher now? Brad Terry?"

"I think it's Jimbo something. I'll have to look at the masthead. How are you?"

"Same old hungover."

"That was a good piece on the Albanian. I read the rough. Too bad they ruined it."

"Don't tell me what they did."

"I wouldn't dare," she laughed. "How's Christine holding up?"

"She beat her personal best in vodka last night."

"That's one of the dangers of traveling with *you*."

"Did you know she's fucked Drones One Through Seven?"

"I'd say it's closer to One Through Nine."

"That lying bitch," I said, and we both laughed.

When she was scrubbed up, Annella Jean Woodruff—"Call me Annella and you're a dead person"—could pass for the nearest thing to a homewrecker in our office. Her long legs belonged on a swimsuit model. Her crinkly hair was golden when clean. Her cheekbones were to be envied by most women. She had a lush mouth and gray-blue eyes that darted with playfulness, suggesting she might be willing to try anything that revolved around whiskey, drugs, and infidelity. There was a time when she had, and it may have been responsible for her divorce from an editor at *Business Week*, although Nell insisted that Edward suffered from an arrogance of unknown origin and could ad lib with more authority than anyone she had ever known. I had first met her and become friends with her when she was a secretary at *Sports Illustrated*. She was the high-born daughter of a San Francisco lawyer and she had met her ex-husband when they were at Stanford together. After graduation, they had come to New York to carve out careers in journalism. Edward had hooked on with *Business Week* right away, but the best Nell could do was the secretarial job at *SI*. They divorced after two years and one abortion, and by that time Nell had become a researcher at *New York*. I talked her into moving over to *SM* when I went there, when the magazine started up.

Nell was the best researcher on the staff—even Christine admitted it. Nell could save you from most any error made in haste, in any sport. She didn't possess the kind of confidence or ego it took to become a writer, but she deserved to be jumped up to the status of senior editor, for she recognized good writing. Bryce had promised her the promotion, just as he had promised Christine the job of research boss, but he was taking his time getting around to both things. As an editor, Nell would be a standout among the drones, somebody with an ear, taste, and a soft pencil. But it was distressing her at the moment to think she might have to fuck Bryce to make the promotion happen before she was too old to care about sex anymore. She was now thirty-seven, which wasn't old in my judgment, but Nell said it was old if you counted all the time she had spent on her knees with a dick in her hand.

What seemed remarkable to me at present was that Nell and I had somehow managed to avoid getting involved romantically, or even enjoying a sport-fuck occasionally, even though we were both single, and when you considered how often we had been drunk and lonely on the road together, especially when she was younger and kept everything in her purse that anyone might care to sniff, inhale, or smoke, along with a jumbo vibrator. But the truth was, we had never hugged or kissed in any way other than as the best of friends.

"What's Innsbruck like?" she was now asking. "It sounds charming."

"It's about as charming as Dayton," I said. "It's not a quaint little village in the Tyrol, it's a fucking city. Every Olympic event will be an hour away in godawful traffic with Nazis barking at you. I wouldn't expect a lot of sleigh rides."

"Maybe I'll just go to Ohio and watch it on TV."

"That's what I'd suggest if I didn't need a drinking buddy who can keep up with me. Get your ass over here."

"See you in Dayton," she said.

THE SPORTS SM MAGAZINE

Mr. Rollie Ambrose
Editor, Nonfiction
Fust & Winslett Publishers
New York, N.Y.

Dear Rollie Ambrose:

I know my agent thought she was doing the right thing when she sent you the first nine chapters of my book. She wanted you to see that I *have* started on it. But I told her at the time that I thought it was a big mistake, and now I have the proof, which is the manuscript you have returned.

How many different kinds of birds shit on it, or was it just your own red-cockaded woodpecker?

I seem to recall it was *your* idea for me to write a book about a year in the life of a sportswriter, namely me.

I also seem to recall you saying at a lunch that the book should be written in my voice.

So what are all of these margin notes and suggestions and deletions and language corrections all about? You haven't even met some of the main people yet.

If you wanted William Faulkner to write this book, why didn't you go dig his ass up?

My agent says I have to show you Part One when it's finished in order to get some more money.

I will send you Part One, of course, because I can use the money, but do me a favor. Try not to get too much birdshit on it. That's if you want me to finish the son of a bitch.

I might add that it's a little demoralizing at the moment to think I'm writing a sports books for an editor who believes I've got Joe Montana's name wrong.

Trust me on this. It's not Joe Dakota.

Onward,

Jim Tom Pinch

Jim Tom Pinch

10

CHRISTINE ARGUED THAT IT WAS FOOLISH FOR US TO DRIVE TO Innsbruck when we could fly or take a train, so I had to straighten her out on some things. First, I said, you never fly around Europe in the winter because most pilots of most European airlines like to take off and land in blizzards and, whenever possible, bump into an Alp. A train ride of such distance was safe but inconvenient. We would have to change trains constantly, in Bern, Lausanne, other cities, and all of the smoking cars might be full, and you couldn't get in the toilets because burned-out dopeheads always locked themselves in there to avoid buying tickets.

"I'm the writer and you're the researcher," I said. "I'm pulling rank. Go rent the Opel while I finish breakfast."

"You're punishing me for not going to bed with you."

"You did in my mind."

Christine drove all the way to Innsbruck while I read, dozed, snacked, and listened to country tapes on my Aiwa. We spent a night in Munich, so Christine could visit Dachau the next day. We checked into a modern hotel on the outskirts of the city—we might as well have been in Dallas—and ate ham sandwiches and potato soup at the lobby bar and watched transient businessmen open their briefcases and try to swindle each other out of yen, marks, and francs.

The next morning, Christine insisted on her side trip to the suburb of Dachau. I had been to Dachau and one or two other Nazi theme parks in earlier years. I now felt the same way about concentration camps as I did about cathedrals, castles, madonnas—if you've seen one, etc. So I sat in the car and reread Raymond Chandler while Christine took the tour.

Before we left, she made me take a picture of her with her no-fault camera as she stood in front of the huge jagged black sculpture, an appropriate symbol of the Holocaust. The sculpture rises over a sign that says, "*Nie Wieder*—Never Again."

Christine was painfully moved by Dachau, as I had once been. You come out of those places, your mind reeking with horrors, and you want to throw a sidebody block on the first German or Austrian you see.

We talked about it on the drive to Innsbruck.

Christine was roughly the same age as Nell Woodruff, somewhere in her middle thirties, so what she knew of World War II had come from her parents, from reading, from documentaries on public television. But I was old enough to remember it as a kid. I guess I was five or six the first time I saw Hitler in a newsreel. You're not supposed to know much when you're five or six, but I could recall thinking, "What, that's *him*? That's the guy my folks are talking about? The little creep in the scary armband with the funny mustache? The guy who's yelling like Rev. T. Hugh Arbuckle? Where did he get all those tanks, and why are all those people sticking their arms in the air and looking like they'll do anything the little dope says?"

I was eight or nine when I watched my dad and uncles and cousins put on khaki and sailor suits and go off to fight the Germans and Japs, and I was ten when some of them didn't come back, like two uncles and a cousin. I didn't mind telling Christine that it was a festive day around my folks' home in Fort Worth when we heard that America had dropped The Big Stereo on Hiroshima, and, as my dad said, college football could get back to normal.

"That's awful," Christine said.

"Oh, yeah? I'm just sorry they didn't take out Berlin."

"You don't mean that."

"I don't, huh? Listen, Christine. All these pricks we're going to run into in Innsbruck? Same people. Fifty years ago, they would have been graduating with honors from the Hitler Youth. The handsome guy who'll stop you from going into the Olympic Village because your press badge is pinned on at a slight angle? Storm trooper. The humorless asshole who'll take pleasure in shoving me away from the door to the ice stadium? SS. There's a Gestapo guy waiting in the press center to tell me I've got the wrong credential for a Coca Cola."

"We're going to Austria, not Germany."

"The Austrians were the real Nazis."

"I've never heard that before."

"I just told you."

Christine said, "You get inconvenienced everywhere you go, Jim Tom. The slightest thing pisses you off. You say it yourself. It's big moments in small minds. The Germans and Austrians didn't invent it."

"They polished it. Here's what I say we do. We turn Dachau into a disco. It becomes the 'in' place. All the new generation Nazis want to go there. They have a great time dancing to their thump-thump music and inhaling the cocaine we provide. It seeps down out of the vents in the ceiling. But it's not cocaine. It's Zyklon B. They die screaming."

"This generation's not responsible for all that."

"I know," I said, "but don't give the motherfuckers guns or armbands—they'll be in France tomorrow."

11

OUR HOTEL WAS ON A MAJOR BOULEVARD, THE MARIA THEResienstrasse, and was aptly named the Emperor Maximilian Marriott. It was across the boulevard from a McDonald's, the Sheraton Tyrol, the Alpin K-mart, and a towering billboard advertising Kentucky Fried Chicken. Innsbruck wasn't

Salzburg, I quickly remembered. The only Mozart who ever lived in Innsbruck was Helga Mozart, who worked behind the counter at Avis.

Although the Winter Olympics had yet to begin, the city was already smog-bound, traffic-clogged, and spilling over with visitors of every size, shape, color, and dialect. Two attractive Austrian girls in front of our hotel were wearing familiar ski jackets, offering evidence that the only invaders who might outnumber the tourists and athletes would be those from ABC-TV. In a week's time, courtesy of network technicians, every pretty girl in town would be wearing a ski jacket with the ABC logo on it and a *Wide World of Sports* pin.

I kept my mouth shut during the predictable argument about our reservations at the registration desk. Christine handled it in German. I was well aware that Austrians took a dim view of being called Nazi assholes.

After we settled in and unpacked and bumped our heads six times on the slanting eaves of our cozy rooms, the first order of business was to pick up our credentials at the press center.

The press center was a cavernous prefab warehouse that had been thrown up in a city park. It was easy enough to get past the security guard on the front door. All you had to do was show him your passport, driver's license, two major credit cards, birth certificate, admittance card, preregistration form, and return-home plane ticket.

The press reception desk was fifty yards long and manned by two dozen ex-bureaucrats of the Third Reich. We stood in line for an hour behind Finns, Japs, Frenchmen, Italians, Swedes, what have you, and were finally greeted by a stone-faced man in his fifties who asked to see our passport, driver's license, two major credit cards, birth certificate, admittance card, pre-registration form, and return-home plane ticket.

I let Christine handle this, too. She filled out four forms for me. The ex-bureaucrat of the Third Reich stamped them all with authority. We were then presented with a badge, an ID card on a chain that would hang around the neck, a media armband, a plastic card, a pin to be worn visibly at all times, and a book of tickets to be used for boarding press buses that would take you to any of the upcoming events.

I crammed all the stuff into the pockets of my lightweight khaki sailing jacket from Abercrombie, an alternative to my arsenal of windbreakers, and wandered into the working press area to see what kind of typing space I would have.

As yet, there was nobody around from the States that I recognized, only a few chirping members of the European press.

My space was between a brooding Spaniard and a cute girl who was idly clacking away on her Tandy laptop. She was in her late twenties, I guessed, and unquestionably American. Her jeans were patched and faded, she wore sneakers, and the sleeves were cut off at the elbows on her light-blue sweatshirt that bore the emblem of the North Carolina Tar Heels.

I plunked down in my chair and sorted through all the crap in my pockets. I draped the ID card around my neck and fumbled around with the badge that was supposed to be affixed to my body.

"Hi," the girl said, cheerfully. "Oh, my God, you're Jim Tom Pinch!"

"Guilty," I muttered.

"You're what I want to be when I grow up."

"What's that, pissed off?"

The girl was startled, but then broke into a laugh and went back to her Tandy laptop.

I saw Christine on the other side of the room and went over to see if she could make my badge work.

Christine was chatting with a heavyset man with two chins who wore a fur cap. I was introduced to Boris Svetlov and informed that he was an expert on figure skating, which meant that he knew about the Lutz, the Axel, and the toe loop.

Boris spoke decent English and was asking Christine if she had brought along anything to trade for his excellent caviar. A Walkman, perhaps? Some jeans?

As Christine pinned the badge on me, I said to Boris, "Tell me about Tatyana."

That was Tatyana Romanova, the Russian hope in figure skating, a sixteen-year-old porcelain beauty—I had seen pictures—who was said to be the next dreamgirl on ice.

"You are the writer?" Boris said.

"I'm it."

"But what does Christine do?"

"She does all the work."

Christine said, "That's not true. Jim Tom is a wonderful writer. All I do is check the facts."

Boris said, "This is interesting. It is also curious."

"Do you know motor sports?" I said.

"But of course."

"Christine is the pit crew, I'm the driver."

"Ah-HA," he laughed. "Now I understand. It is still curious."

Boris reached into the pocket of his Chevrolet-blue suit. "You will have a Russian cigarette?"

"Thanks," I said, producing my Winstons. "I have my own."

"Good, I will have one of yours."

He took three.

"Here," I said, handing him the pack. "I have more."

"Yes?"

"By all means," I smiled, and reached into another pocket and opened a new pack. I had brought twelve cartons along. You can buy European Winstons, but to me they tasted like medicine. I lit Boris' cigarette with my stainless steel Dunhill. He lit my cigarette with his gold-plated Dunhill.

"You have a Dunhill," I said.

"Ah, yes. It belonged to a man I know on the *Daily Telegraph*. He likes caviar. We traded."

"We are all friends," I said. "British, Americans, Russians."

"Yes, it is so."

"One of these days we will bomb all the ragheads together—take back the oil we found for them. There will be no more trouble in the world. Ragheads today, toast tomorrow."

Boris looked at Christine. "A raghead is what?"

"He means Arabs," she said.

"Oh-HO," Boris said with a big grin. "You are an interesting man, Tom Jim. We must drink to all this later."

Christine said, "Boris was telling me that Tatyana Romanova is going to win the gold, no question about it."

"I don't think so," I said.

"Oh, but you have not seen her," Boris said. "This girl is fantastic."

I said, "She can't win the gold. It's already been won. The winner is sitting over there."

I gestured toward the girl in the North Carolina sweatshirt.

"He means what?" Boris asked Christine.

"He's talking about Jeannie Slay."

"Who?" I said.

"Jeannie Slay . . . *Los Angeles Times*."

"You speak of the skinny girl?" said Boris, looking at Jeannie Slay.

"That's the one," I said.

Christine said, "Naturally, you don't know her, Jim Tom. You seldom read anybody but yourself. She's good. She wrote features for the *Miami Herald*. Now she's a sports columnist for the *LA Times*."

"How do you know her?" I asked.

"I've read her. I've met her."

"How come I haven't seen her around?"

"I don't know. She wrote a lot of offbeat stuff in Miami. She hasn't been a columnist that long."

Boris said, "We still speak of the skinny girl?"

"Yes," I said. "She's from Miami and Los Angeles."

"Miami is a place of gangsters, is it not?"

"That's part of its charm."

"I would not wish to see Miami, but Los Angeles is another matter. I would like to see all the movie stars."

"You mostly see them in traffic," I said. "I like Miami. The gangsters only kill each other, and there are hardly any Arabs around."

"We must have many drinks and discuss the world," Boris said.

"We'll do that," I said. "With whiskey, we will eliminate many Arabs."

"Ragheads!" Boris shouted, chuckling, pointing his finger in the air.

I excused myself from Christine and Boris and walked back to my workspace. That skinny girl, I decided, shouldn't have dinner alone tonight.

12

IF SPORTSWRITERS HAVE ANYTHING IN COMMON, SINCE WE basically fall into six different groups—dreadful hero-worshippers, sickening alibi artists, scandalous persecutors, gullible saps, distrusting infidels, and terminal cynics—it is the state of sheer ecstasy into which we can all lapse upon hearing our work quoted to us. Jeannie Slay could quote me at length, even from some of the old *SI* stuff. Subsequently, over the next few days and nights, she became what I said was my new best friend and what Christine said was an embarrassing obsession, if not someone who, owing to her looks, talent and youth, was going to send Nell Woodruff into a smoldering rage.

When I returned to my workplace that first day in the press center, I said to Jeannie, "What are you working on, the big hard-cover breakthrough?"

"Scene-setter," she said.

"You're not on deadline, are you?"

"What's a deadline? We're twelve hours ahead of LA."

"I'll set the scene for you. God invented misery and the Winter Olympics on the same day."

She twisted her laptop toward me so I could read what she had written. A writer never does this unless the writer has a great deal of confidence or an inflated idea of his or her importance. I leaned over and squinted at the screen.

"By Jeannie Slay.

"INNSBRUCK, AUSTRIA—In the land of those wacky, nutty folks who gave you *Mein Kampf* and once turned Europe into a garage sale, the Winter Olympics will begin Monday when an exquisitely blond and strong-willed German lad soars off the 90-meter jump and, with any luck at all, lands in Poland, where he expects to be joined by ten armored divisions."

Hiding a smile, I said, "You might get by with that if you put a disclaimer in the next paragraph."

"I'm not going to file it. I'm just fooling around."

"Go with it."

"Really?"

"Sure. All you have to do in the second graf is say, oops, sorry, gang, only kidding, the Austrians are swell people. They're going to host a very hospitable Olympics."

"Then I can go back to lampshades?"

"Maybe not that far."

"I'm Jeannie Slay," she said, extending a hand.

"I know who you are."

"You do?" She looked surprised, pleased.

"Yeah, you're that smartass bitch who writes a column for the LA Times."

"Does that mean we can't have dinner tonight?"

I studied her for a moment. "Are you married?"

"Of course."

"We can have dinner then. What does your husband do in this life?"

"He's an editor on the national desk."

"That means you can't be happily married. You're always on the road. He's always rewriting the Washington bureau chief."

"We are happily married, thank you. Craig's a great person. Are you married?"

"No, not presently, but I'm a grizzled veteran at it."

"How many times have you been married?"

"Three."

She grinned. "Only three, huh?"

"Yeah, but I was actually in love with two of them and I liked the other one."

"What happened with all of them?"

"I got canceled due to lack of interest."

I adopted Jeannie Slay immediately as a friend. This upset Christine to a degree. She accused me of going back on a familiar vow. I was on record in italics as saying I never wanted to meet anybody new, it was too much fucking trouble.

Over the next three days, before the Winter Olympics started, and before Nell Woodruff and the other SM troops arrived, I had dinner with Jeannie every night in the bar of the Emperor Maximilian Marriott. One evening we were joined by

Christine and once by Shag Monti, who pulled up a chair uninvited and babbled incessantly about the "stone foxes" in town and how he was "schizzing out" from all things "radical."

Darned if I didn't think Earth Dude had managed to score some discipline somewhere.

Christine began to tease me about Jeannie Slay. Christine said it was the quickest she had ever seen me invite someone into "my group." I argued that I didn't have a group, I had never had a group, I only liked to associate with people who were intelligent or entertaining as opposed to float-brains, and why was she complaining about it since she was part of my group?

At this moment, we were in the press center cafeteria having goulash soup and concrete bread. It was an afternoon when Jeannie had gone to the Olympic Village to obtain an interview with an American figure skater named Cherry Blaine, the USA's fondest hope for a gold medal.

"You're infatuated with Jeannie," Christine said.

"I like her, that's all."

"It's hilarious."

"You like her, too."

"I *do* like her, but I don't jump up and go for coffee every time she does. I don't try to eat every meal with her. I don't sit around giggling with her all day long."

"It's only because we agree on all the best movies, books, plays, musicals, and Confederate generals."

"I'm sure you and Jeannie agree that you're the best sportswriter in the country."

"Well, there is that."

"I love the way she looks at you. Like every time you speak, it's something she ought to memorize."

"I haven't noticed that look."

"This isn't like you, Jim Tom."

"I know what you're thinking, Christine. You think if I still worked for the *Fort Worth Light & Shopper*, she wouldn't have the time of day for me."

"Not unless you had something to give her that she could use in her column."

"I wonder if that makes her any different from anybody else in our business? She's better than that, anyhow. I can tell. Sure, she's ambitious. So what? All that means is, she's not sitting around on her butt like half the people in our office."

I lit a Winston to improve the flavor of the goulash soup.

"I'm sure her looks have nothing to do with it," Christine said.

"What does she look like? I haven't been able to get beyond her mind."

"I have to fax your column. Anything you want to fix before I send it?"

I had written a column about the last time I had been to a Winter Olympics in Innsbruck, the time I covered Klammer's downhill from a TV set in a convivial bar, which was the only way I could have seen it.

"Nope, it's their music now," I said. "I'm glad you've accepted Jeannie into the group. She's going to be hanging around a lot. We've figured out we're going to a lot of the same events this year."

"That will be fun for you. I can't wait for Nell to find out."

"Does Nell know Jeannie?"

"I don't think so, but I know what Nell will say."

"What?"

"That she's the same age as your son."

"Actually, she's four years older. She's thirty."

"She's still young enough to be your daughter."

"Everybody is young enough to be my daughter. What's this in my soup?"

I was holding up a blob of something strange in my spoon.

"It's meat," Christine observed.

"Why does it look like a brain?"

A moment passed. "Jeannie's married," I said. "She's happily married to a guy who works on the national desk at the *LA Times*."

Christine smiled. "In your own words, Jim Tom . . . nobody's married on the road."

"Nell will like Jeannie," I said.

"Nell will want her dead!"

13

MY CO-WORKERS ARRIVED ON SUNDAY MORNING, THE DAY OF the opening ceremonies, a day when America's athletes would defend their title as the silliest-dressed team in the Winter Olympics. If things went according to form, the Russians would parade into the ice stadium in their fur jackets and cossack hats, the French would be smart in their berets and tan military uniforms, the British would look chic in their blazers and golf caps, all of the other teams would look regionally appropriate, and then here would come the Americans in their white cowboy hats and astronaut suits.

Nell Woodruff rang my room at eight thirty that morning. She summoned me down to the lobby where she and Ralph Webber were having a drink—it was only 2:30 A.M. for them, body-time. Their jetlag was horrendous, the rest of the troops had gone to bed, but the news from the office couldn't wait, she said.

Forgetting about the slanting eaves in my room, I stood up and gave myself another minor concussion, then showered and shaved and went downstairs on the elevator that was large enough to accommodate three midgets if they hadn't eaten any starch lately.

I gave Nell a wet kiss and shook hands with Ralph, as he looked around the lobby for pussy.

They delivered the news, sometimes talking at the same time. All of the news was disgusting.

Lindsey Caperton had been promoted from assistant managing editor to executive editor, a title Bryce Wilcox had created for him. This meant that Lindsey was clearly No. 2 now, and if anything happened to Bryce, like a promotion up to the corporate floor, or a staff member murdering him, Lindsey was firmly in place to succeed him.

This move opened up a spot for another assistant managing editor, and everybody had a candidate they lobbied for. The most popular choice among the staff was Wayne Mohler, a good writer and well-liked fellow, who had just gone up to bed. Wayne and his wife, Marilyn, were two of my best friends. Bryce had given Wayne some consideration but Lindsey had talked him out of it. The position went to Drone Two, Reg Turner, the man who drank his lunches and pissed in his pants all afternoon and was rarely awake long enough to say anything other than, "Windy boy." Lindsey had obviously wanted Reg because Reg would be no threat to him.

The last news was that Bryce wouldn't be the only top-brass litterateur coming to Innsbruck. Les Padgett, founder and chairman of the board, and Fenton Boles, oily dwarf and CEO, were also coming along, the reason having nothing to do with sports but some cocktail party an international socialite was giving, some friend of Les Padgett's. The party was evidently important enough for the brass to be coming over on the company's Gulfstream Four.

It was probably a good thing Fenton Boles was making the trip, I said. An all-business, cutthroat pig like him couldn't possibly allow himself to be gone from the office more than a day or two. They would be out of Innsbruck in no time.

I sat around with Nell and Ralph until they both began to yawn, but this was long enough for Jeannie Slay to step off the elevator, as luck would have it.

Jeannie waved to me, beaming, and came toward our table.

Regrettably, Jeannie had chosen that day to wear a spiffy, brown-leather, short-skirted outfit with high heels, displaying a pair of legs that rivaled Nell's as the best in sports journalism. Something had been done to her caramel hair, as well. It was long and smooth and cascaded over one shoulder. She looked more like a fashion model than a deadline junkie.

"Whoa," said the keen-eyed Ralph Webber. "Who is *that*?"

"Jeannie Slay," said Nell. "I recognize her column picture."

Nell glanced amiably at me. "You know her?"

"We met here."

I stood up to bring a chair over to our table for Jeannie.

"All right," Jeannie said, smiling. "The *SM* troops are

here. You're Nell Woodruff and you're Ralph Webber. I'm Jeannie Slay.''

Wooden Dick held on to Jeannie's hand as long as he could.

Nell was smiling at Jeannie as she said, ''Your column on the Lakers was awesome—really terrific.''

''First rate,'' said Ralph, who hadn't read it. ''Full of energy. It really picked up speed.''

''Wow,'' Jeannie said. ''Nice to have an elite readership. You guys must be exhausted.''

''We are,'' Nell said.

''I'm fine,'' Ralph said.

''You did say nine thirty for breakfast, didn't you?'' Jeannie was looking at me.

''Uh . . . yeah.''

''I'm starving,'' Ralph said.

''Have at it, kids,'' said Nell, rising. ''I'm a vegetable.''

I hugged Nell. ''Glad you're here, babe.''

''Me, too,'' she said. ''What time is the opening ceremony?''

''One o'clock,'' I said.

''Am I going to miss much if I don't go?''

''Nothing,'' I said.

''Good. What time do we meet in the bar?''

''Five forty-two,'' Jeannie said, reciting a familiar command of mine. Nell didn't react.

''You don't write today?'' Nell said to Jeannie.

''No, we have a lead guy here. I'm just doing my three columns a week.''

''Nice assignment. Gives you a lot of free time.''

''Well,'' said Jeannie, giving me a playful poke, ''it's not as good a deal as old One-a-Week here.''

I walked Nell to the elevator as Ralph Webber took Jeannie by the arm and led her toward the coffee shop.

''She's stunning,'' Nell said.

''Yeah, she's a good girl,'' I said. ''We've kind of been loafing together.''

''No shit,'' said Nell, as the elevator door closed.

58

14

IF YOU CARE TO BET ON EVENTS IN A WINTER OLYMPICS, I strongly recommend putting your money on those athletes who have the fewest vowels in their names.

In the first week of the games, a flying Finn with an overdose of k's and n's won the Nordic jumps, those things where guys soar off a mountaintop and try to miss being castrated by the church steeple down below. Two indomitable Swedes with a payload of m's and g's stood apart from everyone else in the cross-country races. A cluster of Russian men and women, up to here in y's and v's, ran away with the speed skating medals. And the Czechs, led by a goalie with a full complement of l's and d's, won the ice hockey in a somewhat messy gold medal final in which they broke the noses of three Canadians.

I didn't envy poor Wayne Mohler's job of having to put all this in perspective for the magazine's lead-lead, but he pulled off a good story by concentrating on a Russian housewife who set five world records in speed skating, and to his credit, he never mentioned that a two-hundred-pound Toro mower couldn't have cut a swath through her facial hair. Part of his piece also had to deal with the flying Finn, but Christine obtained a very nice quote for him, which was, "I am a seagull among fish."

Nor did I envy Ralph Webber having to do the second lead on that business with the American ice hockey team, a group of collegians who came into Innsbruck hopeful of duplicating the miracle of Lake Placid. Our boys lost to Yugoslavia and then lost to Canada and were quickly out of the running for a medal. The theory was that these disappointments had something to do with our boys tanking their last game to Nigeria, which had never played hockey before, and then demolishing a restaurant on the Maria Theresienstrasse, for which six of them were jailed, and in the process beating up their coach so badly he had to be hospitalized.

America's failures demanded my column attention, so I actually went to the 20-kilometer cross-country race to seek further inspiration. This was an event in which we had never had an athlete finish better than fifteenth. This time, our best racer, a young high school history teacher from Vermont, came in twenty-seventh and collapsed in the arms of his wife, a high school English teacher, and vomited on her hiking boots.

I had my lead: "When the hills are alive with pain and suffering at a Winter Olympics, that's where you go to look for American athletes."

I didn't see much of any of my pals the first week, other than around the hotel bar at night. Christine was assisting Wayne Mohler. Nell was assisting Ralph Webber. Jeannie was going to as many events as she could and acting very excited about it, this being her first Olympics.

I mostly hung around the press center and caught glimpses of some of the action on TV while I drank coffee and visited with other writers. Boris Svetlov and I discussed the wholesale elimination of ragheads. I talked golf with a couple of British colleagues, Ian Malcolm of the *Daily Mail* and Derwent Hopkins of the *Daily Telegraph*. I passed the time with some good buddies among the American writers—Richie Pace of the *Daily News*, Dub Fricker of the *Florida Times*, Bubba Slack of the *Atlanta Journal*, Dave Rocker of the *Chicago Tribune*. They were as bored as I was and preferred to talk college football.

In the evenings in the hotel, I would establish an expandable headquarters table in the bar. The troops would come limping in and the night's journalism seminar would begin.

A sportswriting seminar in a bar is where you discuss who has the biggest shitheel for a boss, which papers will fold next, and which writers, among those not present, are the most overrated and ought to die of rectal cancer.

When we would get around to dining, we would all order a dish I had introduced to the kitchen staff. It was a steak tartare, well-done, with French fries on the side and bread to wrap around the well-done steak tartare.

In these combination seminars and dinners, Ralph Webber would always find a chair next to Jeannie Slay, even if he had to squeeze in and reshuffle everyone around.

One day in the press center, Jeannie said, "Ralph is a very attractive man, and very nice, but talk about a full-court press!"

That's when I was compelled to divulge his nickname, Wooden Dick, and caution Jeannie to keep guarding her flanks—Ralph was even money to fuck the Mona Lisa if he ever went to the Louvre.

She said, "You may want to tell him he has a severe case of the N.F.C.'s with *me*."

"No fucking chance?"

"Not with this cowgirl."

The two glamour events, Alpine ski racing and figure skating, were scheduled for the second week. I skipped the giant slalom and slalom for both the men and the women, knowing they would be won by boastful Italians and Austrian girl-boys. I continued to lounge in the press center, but one day I went shopping.

In a store on the Maria Theresienstrasse, I stumbled upon a six-hundred-dollar jacket that looked right for James Junior, I thought. It was a baggy thing of soft black leather with suede trim. It seemed to have lots of compartments for dope and cassettes.

The six-hundred-dollar price tag didn't slow me down. That was two dinners on the expense account—and I was in a photographer's league as a blank-receipt collector.

The store mailed the jacket to James Junior in Athens, Georgia, for me, and I enclosed a note.

"Yo, Captain Hipness: Hope this thread is bad enough to wear to a pizzafest. By the way, I've researched it. Most dudes 26 years old have graduated by then. Love. The Dad Unit."

I did go to the men's downhill, largely to root for Drin Hoxha.

Sadly, however, the dead-game little Albanian couldn't match his Lauberhorn feat. I must say he gave it a good try. In his desperate pursuit of Pepi Henkel's leading time, he took the last bump so recklessly, in clear view of everyone at the finish, he landed sideways and went into a sixty-mile-an-hour cartwheel and slammed into the little picket restraining fence at the end of the runout. By my watch, it took twenty-two minutes to remove his head from the lumber.

Pepi Henkel won the gold easily over Emile Louvois and everyone else. Louvois, in fact, finished seventh—he didn't even grab a face-saving bronze. So much for the man my magazine said was the best ski racer in the world.

Louvois' performance embittered the French press. Christine later translated a story in *L'Equipe* for me in which the writer said Louvois was a spineless fraud, repugnant to every French patriot, and the coach of the French team, long rumored to have homosexual acquaintances, should face an official government inquiry to answer for his insipid, neglectful leadership and *apres*-ski conduct.

At the finish of the race, Pepi Henkel was lifted onto the shoulders of his countrymen, as Wayne Mohler and Christine and I watched. Pepi was showered with bouquets of flowers. Adoring snowbunnies pawed at him. In the meantime, as I mentioned to Wayne, the Austrian throngs didn't seem to care much that Drin Hoxha would walk with a limp and sing soprano the rest of his life.

"Can I have that?" Wayne asked. He would have to write about the downhill in his lead-lead.

"What's in it for me?"

Wayne thought a minute. "I have a blank receipt from an Italian restaurant the other night."

"Date it tomorrow," I grinned. "I used up last night's today."

15

BY NIGHT, THE FIGURE SKATERS WERE TOE-LOPPING TOWARD their decisive long programs, and it was looking like the ladies' gold was going to come down to a vicious three-way battle between Tatyana Romanova, the Russian dreamgirl, Marika Luftner, a German lass with tanks for thighs, and America's Cherry Blaine, a fetching twenty-year-old of much experience but one who seldom landed upright when she attempted a triple, and whose stage mother was known to those who covered the sport regularly as The Cannibal of Colorado Springs.

I decided to devote my column to Tatyana regardless of the outcome, so for the price of two windbreakers—one blue, one khaki—Boris Svetlov arranged an exclusive interview for me.

Tatyana was only five-two and couldn't have weighed more than a hundred pounds. She was barely sixteen and reminded me of Audrey Hepburn's kid sister in *Sabrina*, although Audrey Hepburn didn't have a kid sister in *Sabrina*. Tatyana was already the class of the field in my estimation. I figured it wouldn't hurt to introduce my readers to a future world champion.

Boris took me to Tatyana's dressing room in the ice stadium and told her I was a very important writer from the United States. She batted her eyes at me and seemed to take on a special glow, and spoke surprisingly good English. In the column I spaced out her best quotes, which were:

"I want to come to America and drive sports car. I would like to be movie star. I want to see Disney World. I like rock stars. Are there many cowboys in Texas? I have been skating since I was two. I don't take my performance to the crowds. I leave it on the ice. When I am finished winning gold medals, I will have many boyfriends. How much does house cost in America with toilet?"

In the middle of the figure skating drama, the company's private jet landed in Innsbruck.

I ran into Bryce and the others as they were checking into the hotel one morning. The others were Les Padgett, Fenton Boles, and the lady Les brought along, a fleshy blonde actress named Donna Roach, of whom nobody would have heard if they hadn't seen her pour a tub of hot grease on a chef in *Psycho Waitresses*, an unintended comedy that I happened to see on a plane and sort of cherished.

"Hey, big guy," Bryce said, shaking my hand vigorously. "Everything under control?"

"Morale's at an all-time high," I said.

"You know Les and Fenny, don't you?"

I did know our founder and CEO from their occasional visits to the edit floor.

Diplomatically, I shook hands with Les first, he of the fat cheeks, thick lips, and slits for eyes. His suits never fit and his shoulders always looked as if they'd been attacked by armies of dandruff that came out of the cigar-colored hair he couldn't keep combed.

It was difficult for me to look at Les Padgett without wondering how there could be a God if this man was personally worth over five hundred million dollars. On the other hand, it was well for me to remember that Les had given Ed Maxwell the funds to start *The Sports Magazine* and more funds to sustain the first two years when it lost money, and remember, too, that he had always acted as if he liked me.

Les owned homes all over the world but he was originally from Murfreesboro, Tennessee, which was brought to mind whenever he spoke. "Jim Tom, how you doin', you old pisser-offer?" he said.

"Fine, Les. Somebody has to keep 'em honest."

"Well, you do *that*," he said, whereupon he whistled at Donna Roach, who was curled up on a lobby sofa. "Donna! Say hello to my pisser-offer. This is Jim Tom Pinch."

Donna raised up, waved feebly. I waved back.

"I think jetlag's got her," I said.

Les Padgett moved closer to me and whispered, "Jetlag, shit. A goddamn twenty-three-year-old girl can outsleep a Mexkin."

There was no need to ask Les how his wife was—he was always traveling with his next wife.

He whistled at Donna again. "Come on, honey. Let's go upstairs and see what our room suite looks like."

Les squeezed on Donna's ass as they walked to the elevator.

Fenton Boles showed no evidence of jetlag. In the mold of all CEOs and cutthroat pigs, he was clear-eyed and fresh-shaven. He was dressed in an Oxford gray three-piece suit, white shirt, quiet tie, and four-inch built-up shoes. He was stinking of mint.

His black hair was combed straight back, his complexion was dark. His eyes held the cold stare of a man whose only enjoyment in life came from counting dead bodies after a merger. Nobody had ever seen him smile.

"There's supposed to be a fax in my suite," he said. "Do you know if it's been arranged, Pinch?"

I wanted to say I'd been so busy with the Olympics I'd been neglecting my travel agency lately, but all I said was, "Nell Woodruff and Christine Thorne each have one I'm sure you can use."

"Who does?"

"Our researchers."

"What are they doing with fax machines?"

"It's how some of us file our stuff."

"Oh."

Fenton glanced at his gold Piaget, which was no larger than a baseball. "What time is it in New York?"

"Four thirty in the morning," I said.

"Damn." The CEO turned to Bryce. "Is the party tonight or tomorrow night?"

Bryce said the party was tomorrow night. "It's a command performance, Jim Tom. I hope you brought a sport coat. If not, buy one. You can put it on the expense account."

"Why do I have to go?" I said.

"Les wants all of us there."

"I have a blazer."

Old reliable was with me. The double-breasted black blazer I had owned for eight years. It traveled with me for just such harrowing occasions.

Fenton Boles said, "Tell one of those women I'll need her fax later today."

Bryce sent his bag up to his room with a bellman and said he wanted to have a talk.

You never knew what to expect when Bryce wanted to have a talk. He might want to say he was giving you a raise. He might want to say you were abusing your expense account. He might want to say you weren't giving him your best effort lately. He might want to tell you he was buying himself a Jaguar.

In this instance, he wanted to tell me he had gone out to the Coast last week to make a speech to advertisers and he had played Bel Air and Riviera.

On the first hole at Riviera, he said, he pulled his tee shot into the light rough, but the lie wasn't all that bad. He got the ball out of the rough with his Mizuno three-wood, pitched onto the green about twenty-five feet from the cup and two-putted for his par.

Shot by shot, he took me through the next three holes, which was where I said, "Bryce, if I have to go the full eighteen holes, I get a caddy fee."

He didn't hear me. He was feathering a five-iron at the fifth.

16

FOR YEARS, I HAD BEEN ON RECORD AS SAYING THERE WAS NO such thing as a good cocktail party unless you arrived conversantly drunk or pharmaceutically lit—preferably both.

I was forced to admit, however, that once I reached the castle on the outskirts of Innsbruck, I wouldn't have wanted to miss the party that was given by Les Padgett's playboy buddy, Baron Kurt Gerhard von Drechsler, who, as I learned in a conversation with Countess Silvia Tesa de Leopardo, was quite famous for his extravagant neckwear and killing bears from helicopters.

I never again expected to see as many sets of store-bought tits on so many contessas, or as many unemployed counts whose eyes were raging from just about all the cocaine any group of white men could handle.

It was regarded as something of a coup that Les got everybody from our magazine invited to the party along with Jeannie Slay—my spadework—whereas *Sports Illustrated* and the rest of the print and broadcast media got shut out.

Shag Monti and our other photographer, Hae-Moon Yoong, were even permitted to take pictures. In turn, this inspired Bryce to clear a spread in the magazine for a layout Dalton Buckley headlined, "High Style in the Tyrol."

If you ever saw that issue of *SM*, you must have burst out laughing at the shot of Prince Vanni Amado in his pale blue pajamas, unbuttoned to the waist, dancing raucously with a sullen twig of a woman named Yasmine Marina Fadila-Horowitz, of Houston.

Or the shot of the tanned and shaggily-bearded Count Enrico Clausonne de Rizzi in his polo togs and polo helmet, clinging to the arm of a bony girl named Gabby Tortella-Mimmo, both of them grinning outlandishly and pointing to their noses.

Or the shot of Booger Red Hawkins, the renowned real estate developer from Dallas and St. Moritz, in his western suit and Stetson, reaching for the six-shooters on his hips, only they happened to be cellular phones.

Or the shot of Baron Kurt Gerhard von Drechsler himself and his companion for the evening, Fritzy Erwina Krupp-Streicher, sitting astride a gigantic stuffed polar bear, each of them wearing an old Nazi field marshal uniform.

I chose a moment to ask Les Padgett where they might have found those uniforms.

"Hell, out of a closet, don't you 'magine?" he said with a grin, his slits widening. "Ger's a good old boy. Him and Fritzy only wore them things as a joke, thinkin' I might bring some Jews along."

"What's the story on Ger?" I asked.

"His granddaddy took Poland and his great uncle took Norway," said Les, laughing hard enough to wheeze.

"Who's his date?"

"Fritzy?" Les said. "Aw, some old rich gal. I can tell one thing by lookin' at her. No head."

He wheezed again.

I went to the buffet table and stood with Shag Monti while he worked on a pile of smoked salmon.

"Bad ride," said Shag, meaning he approved of the party. "Lot of jing in this house."

"Some of them only look like they're rich," I said.

Our girls were the best-looking women at the party—no contest. Even Donna Roach. They all showed up in understated attire. Pants suits among the long gowns and blinding jewelry.

I was standing near the back of the living room when Baron Kurt Gerhard von Drechsler stopped the music to make a presentation. Stopping the music for a while was a merciful thing to do. The music was being provided by a combo consisting of a bass, two accordions, and a man who could hold a fiddle bow in one hand and the tip of a carpenter's saw in the other and, somewhat phenomenally, make it sound like Julie Andrews.

The baron took the floor and spoke in French, German, Italian, and English as he introduced his nephews, Ludwig and Petey.

Ludwig and Petey were twelve and fourteen years old, respectively. They both wore white Armani jackets with the sleeves pushed up to their elbows, baggy pegged trousers, Reeboks, and they each had a spiked haircut. Insolent only begins to describe the look on their fresh faces.

As Ludwig and Petey stood there for everyone to admire, the baron proudly announced that in a forthcoming issue of *Clique*, an elaborate, oversized monthly magazine catering to high-rent Eurotrash, Ludwig and Petey would be listed among the Top Ten Playboys of the World.

Applause broke out.

Nell and Jeannie and I gazed at the contemptible little shits with disbelief.

"Torpedo, *los!*" said Nell.

"Six years on a whaler!" said Jeannie.

Nell and Jeannie gave each other a high five.

Later on, I accidentally wound up in a room of animal heads with Fenton Boles.

Fenton was forty-one. He held a law degree from somewhere. He was unmarried and lived in a penthouse apartment with his mother, but he was occasionally linked with fashion models and anchorwomen in gossip columns. It was rumored he had a press agent.

Struggling to make conversation, I made the mistake of saying I understood our magazine was doing well financially these days. I'd heard it from Bryce. Our circulation was two-point-five million, and ad pages were up.

"*SM* would be doing better if you print people had any sense of responsibility," the CEO said.

"Oh?"

"Lot of waste in edit," he said, sipping his club soda with

a lime. He shook his head grievously as he thought about it some more.

It crossed my mind that taking the company's Gulfstream Four to Europe for a cocktail party might be considered waste by some shareholders in TPG, The Padgett Group, but I didn't bring it up. I only lit a Winston and said, "I don't know anything about money, but I guess it costs a lot to put out a good magazine."

"Good magazine," he said with a sneer. "Typical edit reaction. Do you think anyone buys *SM* because of what you write, Pinch?"

"I know a few," I said. I wasn't actually sure that I did.

"You're a bridge."

"A what?"

"You're a bridge to get from one ad to another. It's all right with me if you edit people want to play your little game . . . if you want to think you put out a magazine of *quality* sports news, *quality* sports features, but *SM* is no different from any other magazine. It's an advertising package."

Scotch made me say it. "Maybe we could start a magazine of nothing but ads. We could call it *SC*, the *Sports Catalog*."

"Oh, sure, you need a product, a lure," he said, missing the joke, or ignoring it. "For Christ's sake, you edit people don't sell the book. You know what sells the book? An aggressive sales force. The one *I* put together. As for the product, I personally think we spend too much money on words and not enough on pictures. I'm talking to Bryce about it. *SM* needs to target the fourteen-year-olds better. There's a new generation of fourteen-year-olds every year. Their parents are sitting ducks for subscriptions. Their parents are the people who buy the cars, clothes, wine, cigarettes, insurance, travel, leisure time."

"They only read ads?"

"They may read some of your crap, I don't know."

"Thanks for straightening me out," I said. "All this time in the business, I've been thinking I wrote for grownups."

"To be blunt about it," he said, "you write for J and B and Winstons, and quite frankly, I wouldn't want to assess the value of your column if those advertisers ever decide to drop that inside back page."

I admit it. I was momentarily stuck for a response to an oily dwarf who didn't care about anything but bottom lines and had just informed me that everything I stood for and had worked for in thirty years of journalism didn't amount to a drop of piss.

But I resisted the temptation to end my career then and there by kicking the rotten little prick off his built-up shoes. Instead, I went for humor.

"Any openings in sales?"

He looked at his gold baseball Piaget. "What time is it in New York?"

"Three thirty in the afternoon."

"There must be a phone around here somewhere," he said, and walked away briskly.

I simmered for a moment. Then I left the animal-head room and went to a bar in the guns-and-swords room. Silvia Tesa de Leopardo was at the bar, asking for a refill of gin.

She commented on what a handsome group we were—the magazine troops—and how exceedingly clever it was that we all worked for a living.

17

MY HANGOVERS TEND TO HAVE A LIFE OF THEIR OWN. MY kind of hangover won't take yes for an answer, it makes my head feel like a hippopotamus slept on it, and the headache won't go away until it sees that it is hopelessly surrounded by Anacin tablets. The hangover didn't help things the next morning at breakfast when I had to look at Clipper Langdon in his burial-at-sea outfit. Nobody ever said it was gonna be easy.

Bryce arranged the breakfast in a private dining room of the hotel. As I had predicted, the big three of journalism, Bryce, Fenton Boles, and Les Padgett, were leaving that day, but not before Bryce introduced a gathering of the edit staff to our new publisher, the Clipper.

In attendance were the three writers, Wayne Mohler, Ralph Webber, and myself, plus Nell and Christine, plus our drone,

Dalton Buckley. The CEO and the founder skipped the affair.

Nobody had seen much of Dalton, other than at the cocktail party, where he had stood alone in a corner most of the night. I asked him what he had been doing.

Well, he said, he'd had this darn volleyball piece to close, and he'd been working on this other feature, quite a nice story about a lady golfer, although it needed reorganizing, so he had pretty much been confined to his room.

Clipper Langdon circled the table, warmly pumping everyone's hand. He said he was already acquainted with the Pincher and he was delighted to meet the Wayner, the Ralpher, the Dalter, the Crissybird, and the Nellybird. Behind Clipper's back, Nell stuck her finger in her mouth and pretended to gag, or do what my collegiate son would describe as talking to Ralph on the big white telephone.

Dalton asked Clipper when he was coming on board.

"Up to the Commodore," he said. "The Brycer's the man who unfurls the spinnaker."

Bryce said, "We'll tack for two or three weeks. Let you find your way around the main deck. Jimbo Creavy ran a heck of a flotilla, but he's earned another stripe. Fenton's taking him up to fleet."

"Jimbo will be a tough skipper to follow," Clipper said, "but I think I can keep all of our oars in the water."

I was the first to excuse myself from this dockside reunion. I left under the pretense of having to go watch figure skaters practice. But I didn't leave without giving Clipper a hearty handshake and saying I thought he was going to bring a lot to the regatta.

18

ON THE FINAL NIGHT OF THE FIGURE SKATING COMPETITION, the last event of the Winter Olympics, all of my friends were in the press section of the ice stadium to root for the American, Cherry Blaine, while I was there to root for Tatyana Romanova. This didn't make me anti-American. It made me selfish.

If the Russian dreamgirl won the gold, I wouldn't have to touch a word of my column. If she barely lost the gold, I would have to rewrite maybe a paragraph. But if she choked and fell, or wound up a dismal third, or worse, I would have to junk the whole thing and sub a new column on deadline.

It was a serious matter.

I sat with Boris Svetlov to be better informed about what was going on. We were on the row directly behind Nell, Christine, Wayne, Ralph, and Jeannie Slay.

Ralph intentionally dropped something on the floor, his Mont Blanc pen, and caused some confusion, and wound up sitting next to Jeannie.

Intensifying the drama of the evening was the order in which the girls would skate. The German, Marika Luftner, would go first, the American second, then Tatyana.

I can only say it was discomforting when the German girl was very good. She put together an undaring program but did it smoothly and the judges littered her with 5.8's on technical merit and a few 5.9's for artistic impression.

"This is not good," said Boris. "Tatyana will have to put in six triples."

Cherry Blaine then skated the performance of her life, without falling down, much to the pleasure of all my pals who didn't have to sub a column. Cherry took the lead for the gold with her 5.9's.

"This is not good at all," Boris said, as he reached in the

pocket of what used to be my navy blue windbreaker, removed a flask, and took a swig of vodka. "Tatyana must now put in the quad."

"Oh, shit," I said.

Even I was aware that no lady figure skater—and only one or two men—had ever hit a quadruple jump.

"Where will she put the quad?" I asked.

"In the beginning," Boris said.

Nell looked around, and said, "Ten dollars, no quad. She falls on her Kremlin ass."

I looked at Boris, as if to ask if he thought Tatyana could hit the quad under Olympic pressure.

"She has done it in practice," he said.

"You're on," I said to Nell.

"I'll take some of that," Jeannie said, glancing around.

"You've got it."

"Me, too," Ralph said.

"You're down."

Wayne Mohler wanted ten on it, as did Christine.

Now I had fifty dollars riding on a sixteen-year-old girl to land the world's first quadruple jump on ice, and a column riding on her overall performance. There *were* situations when figure skating could be suspenseful.

Out came Tatyana in her white costume to take her mark at the center of the ice, a trifle unsteadily, I thought. Her music began. It was an old Dixieland recording of "Sweet Georgia Brown."

Tatyana swooped away and went into her routine.

Within thirty seconds, she launched into a sprint, gathering momentum, flying around the rink.

I nudged Boris. "If she hits this, it's ice cream."

"What means ice cream?"

"The gold," I said.

Tatyana circled the rink again, then suddenly she did a little hop and went spinning into the air, about four feet above the ice.

One rotation, two, three . . . and four!

She landed perfectly and opened her arms and grinned at the crowd. The roars were thunderous.

"Yes!" I yelled.

"Bravo!" Boris shouted, leaping out of his seat. "BRAVO!"

Nell spun around. "You want to keep it down back there?"

For good measure, Tatyana then hit six triples perfectly and when her routine ended with a spinning-top thing, Boris said it was the most flawless performance he had ever seen on land, sea, or ice. The gold medal was hers.

Tatyana received a wall of 6.0's from all but a rotund German woman. This judge awarded her a 5.2 and a 4.8 and quickly fled the arena, which was smart of her because Boris was furious and planned to kick her senseless.

Some said the lead on my column was in poor taste. Others, Nell and Christine, for example, said it worked. It read:

"I don't usually make a habit of keeping candy in the pocket of my overcoat, but this was before I met Tatyana Romanova."

We all split in various directions the next day. Wayne and Christine were sentenced to Leningrad by Bryce, to do the definitive takeout—drone word—on Tatyana. Shag Monti went along to shoot. Ralph Webber and Hae-Moon Yoong were sent to Paris to work on a massive preview of the Summer Olympics. Dalton Buckley went to London to meet his wife, Nonnie, for a week's vacation. Nell and Jeannie and I boarded a train to Munich where we then caught planes to the States.

The three of us had a long lunch in the Munich terminal before Jeannie rode off on six moving sidewalks that would take her to her flight to LA by way of Chicago. Nell and I rode off on six moving sidewalks that would take us to our nonstop to New York.

Jeannie and Nell hugged a goodbye—they seemed to have become good friends. Jeannie kissed me lightly on the lips in Nell's presence, saying, "See you at the hoops, fella."

Nell and I got comfortable in our first-class seats, settling in with magazines, newspapers and paperbacks, and I suppose we were on about our third pre-meal cocktail when Nell looked over at me with a smile I didn't trust.

"Okay, asshole," she said. "About the precious little princess from LA."

THE SPORTS **SM** MAGAZINE

MR. ROLLIE AMBROSE
Editor, Nonfiction
Fust & Winslett Publishers
New York, N.Y.

Dear Rollie Ambrose:

Thanks for not letting your birds loose on the rest of Part One. Now to address the points in your note:

1. Yes, I'm going to take the reader to the Final Four and the Masters. That's coming up in Part Two.

2. Who cares what Bryce and the drones think? The fact is, they're getting off easy.

3. Cutthroat pig is not an overly harsh description of Fenton Boles. I doubt it will bother him now, anyway.

4. Don't worry about Nell Woodruff and Christine Thorne. Nell will only suffer pangs of nostalgia, and the book is going to do wonders for Christine's social life.

5. You say you have queasily counted an abundance of four-letter words in Part One and wonder if there might be an excessive amount. Goddamn it, I'm pissed off to hear this. In fact, I'm totally fucking mystified as to how all that shit got in there, and I intend to find the cocksucker who did it.

Onward,

Jim Tom Pinch

Jim Tom Pinch

PART TWO

MONEY-WHIPPED AND PLAYING HURT

19

THE ONE WEEK I WAS HOME BEFORE GOING OFF TO WATCH tall black scholars settle the issue of college hoops, I didn't do much but hang around the office and Fu's Like Us, or sit in the big easy chair in my apartment and eat chicken pot pies and watch the world coming to an end on CNN.

I worked on the fiction of my expense accounts. I wrote a column about Atlanta, happy venue of the Final Four. I threw away the forty tons of catalogs and junk mail that had accumulated. I established telephone contact with my son to let him know the banker was back in the country. I established telephone contact with Jeannie Slay to coordinate our social plans for Atlanta. I got drunk twice at Fu's and convinced Nell Woodruff, though not completely, that my interest in Jeannie was purely friendship. I turned down an offer from a charity group in Dallas to make a speech for free. I also gave some thought to why a man would live in Manhattan unless he held a suspicious allegiance to psychopathic cab drivers.

The weather in Manhattan in the middle of March was unpredictable—bright and invigorating one day, sleet and slush the next.

The first day I went into the office, a day of sleet and slush, two cabs were required to take me to midtown.

The driver of the first cab was one of those Arab-Haitian-Cuban individuals who spoke almost no English. He liked to attain speeds of eighty miles an hour over a distance of one block, then slam on the brakes, then speed up again, then slam on the brakes again, all the while screaming, "Mokka bocka rocka ca-lock!"

From experience, I knew this translated into, "I don't care if I live or die," so I jumped out after three blocks.

But then I climbed in a cab with Guido.

And I no sooner relaxed to look at *The Times* than I realized we were stalled in traffic when we were trying to do that impossible thing of getting across town in the East Sixties, and Guido was now in a shouting match with Carlo, who was behind the wheel of the cab next to us.

"Fuck you, buddy," Guido was saying.

"You know what you fuckin' are?" Carlo said. "You're a fuckin' asshole."

The passenger in the other cab was somebody's grandmother, I noticed. She was calmly reading the *Daily News*.

The dialogue between Guido and Carlo went on as follows:

Guido: "Gimme a fuckin' break, I'm tryin' to work here."

Carlo: "Yeah? Work on this, motherfucker."

Guido: "Who you fuckin' think you're talkin' to, you cocksucker?"

Carlo: "Hey! My dick, all right?"

Guido: "You want to fuck with me? Come on, fuck with me!"

Carlo: "You ain't worth fuckin' with, dicklip."

Guido: "Come on, fuck with me. I'll kick your fuckin' ass."

Carlo: "You'll kick *my* ass? You don't kick nobody's ass. I'll kick *your* fuckin' ass, you keep fuckin' with me."

Guido: "Hey, you fuckin' want to know somethin'? You're full of fuckin' shit, that's all."

Carlo: "Ah, go fuck yourself."

Guido: "Go fuck myself? Go fuck *my* self? You go fuck *your* self, asshole."

Carlo: "I'm sayin' fuck you."

Guido: "You're sayin' fuck me, right? Fuck me, is that it? I'm sayin' fuck *you*, you motherfucker!"

So it went until the traffic untangled.

It was good to be home.

20

ON ONE OF THOSE SHINING, GOLDEN DAYS THAT MADE YOU proud and even a little arrogant about being a New Yorker, I decided to walk to work but I might as well have gone to the opera.

At Lexington and 67th, I stood for a moment to watch two black dudes operate on the door handle of a parked Mercedes. A man in a suit carrying a briefcase happened along, stopped, and hollered, "Hey, what do you think you're doing?" One of the black dudes looked offended and hollered back: "Stealin' a fuckin' car—you got a problem with that?"

The man in the suit walked on, as did I. Nobody's car was worth dying for, nor was anybody's bicycle, moneyclip, neck-lace, shopping bag, or deli sandwich. Native New Yorkers learn this at birth. People who move to New York learn it within twenty-four hours or less.

I crossed 57th to Park Avenue. Here, I was treated to the sounds of a six-piece calypso band, a construction crew plun-dering the sidewalk with three airhammers, the bloodcurdling screams of a young mother trying to correct a horrid three-year-old, and an ear-splitting ghetto blaster belonging to a bunch of punks holding a seance in the entranceway of a va-cated shoe store.

The music blaring out of the ghetto blaster was without a melody, of course, and registered 9.6 on the Richter scale.

Strolling down Park in the Fifties was peaceful enough until I came upon the protest group. A dozen gaunt young men were marching in a circle outside the headquarters of the NBA. Some of them carried placards.

One placard read: GAYS CAN SLAM-DUNK TOO.

Another read: WE ARE NOT ALL SHORT.

I listened to their chant:

> "Hey, hey,
> What do you say?
> Where are the gays
> In the NBA?"

I laughed at first, but by the time I got to the TPG Building I was livid.

"Single-issue people," I said, storming into Nell's office. "Let the homeless eat the endangered species!"

I took a sip of the coffee in the mug on her desk and described the scene in front of the NBA headquarters.

She smiled but couldn't get a word in.

"We're hostages," I said. "In our own country."

I lit up a Winston. "I've had it with single-issue people, Nell. I'm sick of it. I've had it with the lifestyle police. I've had it with the taste cops. We're doomed. This country is doomed. I can't smoke a cigarette anywhere anymore without getting assaulted by wild-eyed nut cases. Murderers, robbers, rapists—they aren't murderers, robbers, and rapists anymore, they've merely got a problem with their *genes*. Alcoholics and dopefiends used to be called alcoholics and dopefiends, remember? Now they're *victims*. But a drunk driver can sue me for overserving him in my own goddamn apartment! A schoolteacher can't use a paddle on a spoiled brat. The schoolteacher is a child abuser! What's next year's trendy crime? All waste is hazardous, all hair-sprays are killers, all cholesterol levels are dangerous. People who oppose abortion are in favor of the death penalty—explain *that*. One bird-watcher can shut down a whole factory. Snarling, halfwit mothers want to ban Mark Twain from schools. A movie can't make money unless the body count is somewhere over a hundred. You can't watch a talk show on TV unless you're interested in battered lesbians. A corporate crook can steal a billion dollars and do six months in a suntan joint, working on his tennis. Did you know the gays were *your* problem? I sure as hell didn't know it was *my* problem that a lot of waiters in San Francisco like to get fucked in the ass. And I didn't know it was my problem, or yours, or anybody else's who has a steady job, that the people who can't find work lack *self-esteem*, instead of it being their own fault that they lack self-discipline. Maybe there's a mall somewhere that sells self-esteem. But if you want to know what really pisses me off, it's the fact that any careless remark or innocent remark or, God forbid, *humorous* remark, written or spoken, can be punished by chickenshit boycotts or lawsuits. We are seriously doomed."

I paused to light a cigarette. Nell said, "They're shooting a movie."

"What?"

"On Park Avenue. The protesters you saw. They're actors. They've been shooting over there for four days. It's some sort of comedy. You didn't see the trucks?"

"I wasn't looking for trucks. I was too busy thinking about an all-gay expansion team in the NBA."

"It's a movie."

"I stand by my statement," I said. "We're nearing the end."

21

THE EDITORIAL OFFICES OF *THE SPORTS MAGAZINE* WERE ON the eighteenth floor of the TPG Building, and there were those who said my view was the best of any senior writer. If you stood at a particular window of my cubicle in the northeast corner on a reasonably clear day, you could look down through a crease of daylight between two other buildings and feast your eyes on one eighth of the Rockefeller Center skating rink.

I admit it was an improvement over the view I had before I was money-whipped away from *Sports Illustrated*, although I had only moved to the east side of Sixth Avenue and one block south, a block down from Radio City. For fifteen years in my twentieth-floor cubicle at *SI*, I had savored the view of all the Venetian blinds in the building across the street.

SI's offices were in a skyscraper at 50th and Sixth that would always be known to me as the Time-Life Building regardless of how many dark mergers might be arranged in boardrooms where the white-collar criminals gather.

I wasn't exactly sure at the moment, things changed swiftly on Wall Street nowadays, but I think my old skyscraper was now known as the Warner Time Yoshihari DeutschCorp Building.

The landscape at *The Sports Magazine* hadn't changed all that much in eight years. All of the offices with windows were occupied by Bryce Wilcox and his bootlickers atop the masthead, by senior writers, senior editors—the drones—and the department heads of art, photo, production, finance, and so forth.

Everybody else was consigned to an interior space. Everybody else included Nell and the research staff, which was headed up by Molly Connors, a foolish girl who served as an undercover agent for Bryce and Lindsey, and all of the underlings in the copy room, art, photo, production, finance, and a middle plateau of individuals that were called staff writers, associate writers and editors, and who, incidentally, fell into two categories.

The middle plateau people were either young, promising, industrious, and talented, or they had once been young, promising, industrious, and talented but were now tired, lazy, dejected, forgetful, and seemingly content to languish in the discard heap.

Now and then, one of the middle plateau people would come into my office to look out of the window and see if it was raining or snowing or sunny outside, and the person would get around to asking me a question. He or she would want to know how he or she could get out of the discard heap.

I would have to tell them the same thing Ed Maxwell would have told them. That *SM* was a magazine, not a journalism school.

I would also paraphrase the Bogart line from *The Barefoot Contessa*: "If you can write, there are a few people around who can help you. If you can't write, *nobody* can teach you."

But to complete the landscape:

Bryce Wilcox resided in a large corner office, the southeast. Bryce had enlarged it to twice the size it had been when Ed

Maxwell sat there. Bryce could swivel around in his chair and see the upper one sixteenth of the Empire State Building.

The managing editor was flanked on one side by Lindsey Caperton, now our executive editor, and on the other side by Doug McNiff, still an assistant managing editor. Reg Turner, the newly appointed assistant managing editor, half-asleep in a pool of urine and breaking wind, was next door to Doug.

One floor below, on seventeen, was our live-wire publisher's office and all of Clipper Langdon's energetic ad salesmen along with Chipper Lewis and his energetic circulation personnel. It was a source of pride to some of us that we now had a Clipper and a Chipper to "sell the book," whereas *SI*, the competitor, struggled to get by with only a Don and a Mike.

The rest of the floors from the lobby up to the corporate tower were where the other magazines were located, not to forget the divisions of pet food, diapers, cable TV, what have you.

The fourteenth floor was the company cafeteria, famed for its gray meat, rude service, and the nickname Nell had given it: Eat Nam.

Which brings up the fact that many areas in the building and on our floor had earned nicknames over the years. The corporate floor had several: Disney World, the Banana Factory, Ozone, the Convalescent Center, Random Harvest.

The Bermuda Triangle was the glum southwest corner of our floor, spooky and dim. It was said to be inhabited by drones. Myself, I never went near it.

The Bat Cave was the corner where, when summoned, you went to see Bryce, Lindsey, or Doug.

The Cookie Store was finance. This was where you drew advance money for a trip and where you turned in your expense reports to Marge Frack, head of the department, who was sometimes known as the Exorcist. It was characteristic of most writers who traveled often to be three months behind on expenses, always owing the company twelve thousand dollars. Of course, you didn't actually owe the company twelve thousand dollars. After you submitted your expense reports totaling eighteen thousand dollars to Marge Frack, expecting her to disallow the usual three thousand in entertainment, you came out three thousand ahead, which was how you recovered all the money you forgot you spent.

Filling out an expense report was an absurd game you were forced to play. It was company dogma that you were asked to account for every dollar of every minute of every day while you were on the road. You had to list the daily cost of your hotel room, each meal, each phone call, each cab ride, each candy bar. Accounting vermin think up this shit so they will have something to do.

The bailout was that you weren't required to keep a receipt for anything under twenty-five dollars, thanks to the federal government. Therefore, if you didn't entertain anyone for business purposes, you could list breakfast, lunch, and dinner at twenty-four ninety-nine each. In my case, twenty-four ninety-nine also went down for toothpaste, newspapers, Kleenex, laundry, dry cleaning, Anacin, and anything else I could think of—every day.

But everyone needed to entertain to come out all right, or break even. When you entertained, you were required to list the person you dined with, the purpose, the place, the amount. It was my position that every breath I took outside the office was business-related. I would argue that a writer drew inspiration from everything around him. A total stranger in a bar, an insurance salesman, might furnish me with more information than any coach or athlete. It happened often. But you weren't permitted to entertain nonsports people, which is why the expense account game was even sillier. The company made you a fiction writer, a liar, cheat, and thief, although nobody thought of it like that.

One of my entertainment sheets from two years ago was framed and adorned the wall of Marge Frack's office.

Travel & Entertainment

DATE	PERSON—PURPOSE—PLACE	AMOUNT
9/7	Breakfast for T. J. Lambert, TCU football coach; discuss new offensive formation; Paris Coffee Shop, Fort Worth, Texas	$102.37

9/7	Lunch for T. J. Lambert, TCU football coach; discuss old offensive formation; Juanita's Restaurant, Fort Worth, Texas	$156.28
9/7	Dinner & drinks for T. J. Lambert, TCU football coach; discuss other Southwest Conference offensive formations; Sammie's Barbecue, Fort Worth, Texas	$298.10
9/15	Breakfast for Barry Switzer, ex-Oklahoma football coach; discuss role of black athlete in investment banking industry; Beverly Hills Hotel	$215.14
9/15	Lunch for Barry Switzer, ex-Oklahoma football coach; discuss influence of Al Capone on college football; Beverly Hills Hotel	$394.50
9/15	Dinner & drinks for Barry Switzer, ex-Oklahoma football coach; discuss NCAA's relationship to mass murders in USA; Beverly Hills Hotel	$394.35
10/3	Breakfast for Knute Rockne, former Notre Dame football coach; discuss college football recruiting; Four Horsemen Hotel, South Bend, Ind.	$201.75
10/4	Lunch for Knute Rockne, former Notre Dame football coach; discuss George Gipp's affinity for chest colds; Four Horsemen Hotel, South Bend, Inc.	$246.18
10/5	Dinner & drinks for Knute Rockne, former Notre Dame football coach; discuss why Four Horsemen were midgets; Ritz-Carlton Hotel, Chicago	$568.90

You would think that a man with as many corporate responsibilities as Fenton Boles wouldn't have time to bother with my expense accounts, but I was called up to Disney World on a Monday afternoon in late March, the day before I was scheduled to leave for Atlanta and the Final Four.

The CEO's office covered one third of the entire thirty-third floor.

It included a dining room, screening room, conference room, sitting room, health club, kitchen, and full bath. In the bath, a huge tub was situated on a dais in the center of a marble floor. The rest of the office was lushly carpeted and decorated with antiques.

It was known throughout the building that a decorator had done Fenton's office, and that the CEO had sent the decorator to London on three occasions to find just the right end-table for only thirty-seven thousand dollars.

One whole wall was floor-to-ceiling glass through which you could see most of the Empire State Building, nearly all of lower Manhattan, and on south to the Falkland Islands.

I was escorted into Fenton's office by Raymond, his secretary, a slender young man with tall hair, who offered me a piece of chocolate candy out of a box.

It was roughly a thirty-yard walk over the burgundy carpet from the door to the antique desk behind which the CEO was seated in his dark suit, white shirt, and tie, his back to one of the many paintings that hung on the walls.

I gathered all of the paintings were notoriously expensive, or why else would they have been so large, ugly, and stupid?

I sat down across from the CEO and noticed he was browsing over my expense sheets. I reached for a Winston, but without looking up, he said, "Not in here, please."

I put the pack away and studied a painting of what looked like the orange leg of a ballerina sticking out of a blue-and-white tiger's mouth while fish and birds consorted in a typhoon sky, but it could have been something entirely different.

"We have a problem," he said, finally.

"What kind of problem?"

"Your entertainment. It's way out of line."

"I know a lot of people," I shrugged. "I've been around a long time. I'm on the road more than half the year. I think a writer representing *SM* ought to pick up the check. I have receipts for everything. I *did* spend the money."

Fenton Boles said, "I wouldn't ordinarily waste my time on

something like this, but Lindsey thought it was important enough to bring to my attention."

"What the hell is Lindsey Caperton doing worrying about my expenses?"

"He's your executive editor."

"That's what I mean. Shouldn't he be more concerned about story ideas? Putting out a good magazine? Something crazy like that?"

"The budget is part of his charter."

"I think I'll let the budget write my column next week."

Fenton continued leafing through the reports. "Who is Boris Svetlov? I see where you bought him several dinners and drinks."

"He's a Russian journalist. He helped me with figure skating. He got me an exclusive interview with Tatyana Romanova. It cost me two windbreakers. I couldn't put the windbreakers on the report, so I made up the cost in entertainment."

"You falsified entertainment receipts?"

"I think of it as getting even."

"I see. Who is Dostoevski?"

He pronounced it Dee-dosty-dosky, actually.

"A Russian writer," I said. "Friend of Boris'. He helped, too."

Fenton looked at another name.

"Ivan Turgee-nof?"

"Turgenev," I said. "Another Russian writer. Very helpful."

I sat there waiting for him to get around to Hank Ibsen, Dottie Parker, Fred Henry, all the others, but he overlooked them.

"I'm going to give you a chance to do these over," he said. "Get them down to an acceptable level."

"I don't have time to redo them," I said. "I'm a writer, not an accountant."

"Fine," he said. "I'm cutting them in half. If you want to live like King Farouk, you can pay for part of it yourself."

He began to draw lines through the expense sheets.

"King Farouk," I said, softly. "I haven't heard that name in years."

He said, "I'm also obligated to tell you that this is your first official warning. It will be in writing to Bryce."

"My first what?"

"It's a new policy I'm instituting. I've worked with legal on it. An employee will be entitled to three official warnings over a two-year period. But after the third warning, management will have the right to dismiss the employee if it chooses to do so. In that event, the employee will leave the company with no financial benefits."

"I'd like to point out that my expense accounts aren't as high as they were three years ago."

"If I had been CEO three years ago, you would have been fired for negligence."

"*Negligence*?" I said. "I've never missed a column. I've never missed a deadline. Does Les know about this warning bullshit?"

"Mind your language, please."

He was making Z's on my expense sheets.

"Does Les approve of your warning policy?" I rephrased it.

"Les Padgett approves of any division in the company that shows a greater profit this year than it did last year. He doesn't ask how."

"I want to congratulate you, Fenton. Your warning system is going to be a great morale booster when word gets around."

"I'm not interested in morale, Pinch. I'm interested in looking after this company for the shareholders. That will be all."

Leaving the CEO's office, I overheard him speaking to his secretary on the intercom. "Raymond, call that fitness center in New Jersey. Ask them why my new walking machine hasn't been delivered yet. Remind them it's the one with speed control and an incline-adjuster."

I was in something of a rage on the elevator, wishing I had reminded the oily dwarf that my column sold a facing ad that brought in fifty thousand dollars in profit every week, but I was on warning—*me*, Jim Tom Pinch, great American, wonderful human being.

I went straight to the Bat Cave to see Bryce, to tell him he had better start looking around for a new executive editor because if Lindsey Caperton ever sent another of my expense reports up to Fenton Boles, I was going to stomp the piss out of the chinless prick.

Bryce wasn't in. Eileen, his secretary, said Bryce and Clipper Langdon were out of town. They had taken some clients down to Hilton Head.

I glanced in Lindsey's office, but he wasn't there.

I looked in on Reg Turner to see if he knew where Lindsey was. Reg was slumped at his desk. I asked him the question.

"Windy boy," said Reg.

"Never mind," I said.

There was no point in talking about it with Doug McNiff. Doug would only clear his throat and hum a Broadway tune.

I went around to Nell's office.

"I'm on warning," I said. "Fenton Boles has this new deal. Three warnings and you can be fired. I just got my first warning. Can you believe that shit?"

"Everybody is on warning," Nell said.

"What do you mean?"

"Fenton is putting everybody on warning. There are memos coming around. Eileen told me about it. Eileen says it's a scare tactic. A way to get everybody to shape up."

"The whole floor? Everybody at *SM*?"

"Everybody in the building, apparently."

I started to laugh. And I laughed all the way to finance, where I picked up a plane ticket and a six-thousand-dollar advance to go to the Final Four.

22

ATLANTA IS CONSIDERED TO BE THE GREATEST CITY IN THE world on a Friday night, and one of the greatest cities in the world on any other night, but this endorsement by and large comes from gentlemen who have a weakness for lively bars, tend to fall in love easily, and keep a brigade of divorce lawyers listed in their Rolodexes.

In my column, I offered Atlanta's Chamber of Commerce

what I thought was a good slogan to attract tourism: IF A HONEY CAN'T BREAK UP YOUR HOME IN ATLANTA, BUBBA, YOU JUST AIN'T STAYING OUT LATE ENOUGH.

I had been going to Atlanta for more than thirty years to immortalize and de-immortalize athletes—Georgia Bulldogs, Georgia Tech Rambling Wrecks, Atlanta Falcons, Atlanta Braves, professional golfers of one ilk or another, and I could testify that it truly is a city of fun-loving women: Homewrecker Megablondes, Showtime Mommas, Mall-Hair Helium Heads, Cool-Whip Killerettes, and Hurt-Somebody Partyqueens, all of whom seemed to be convulsively attracted to what is known to certain linguists as fuckage and suckage.

I had fallen in love with Janice in Atlanta while I was married to Earlene. I had fallen in love with Priscilla in Atlanta while I was married to Janice. Atlanta had been a learning experience, which was why I now considered the risk-reward ratio too high on the risk side to talk to a good-looking Atlanta lady for more than two minutes in a bar.

Being a generous fellow, I might offer to buy the lady a cocktail, but if I said anything to her after that, it would be that I was going to Bern, Switzerland, next week—I'd heard they'd found a cure for AIDS.

This remark would generally prompt the Atlanta lady to wrinkle her nose, and say, "Boy, I don't want to catch that shit again," and she would drift away to another part of the room.

None of this was a problem during the week of the Final Four. Jeannie Slay was around to protect me.

We both arrived on Tuesday night, four days before the first games, the semifinals, were played.

All four basketball teams, all of the NCAA officials, and most of the press, were staying in the same hotel downtown, the Summitorium. It was an enormous glass tower, probably no larger in square miles than Rhode Island. The hotel featured plastic foods of the world in a dozen restaurants that were integral parts of gardens, forests, indoor streams, and bird sanctuaries.

Each time I went back to Atlanta, I was struck by how much newer the city looked. "The heart of the New South can't have too many l'atriums," I said to Jeannie the first night, as we interrupted a tour of the lobby to have a drink under a waterfall.

"Mall wars," Jeannie said. "I thought they were over in America. California won."

Nope. Atlanta was back in it. The Final Four was going to be played only a mall away from our hotel in the new Georgia Malldome, which was connected to the new 85,000-seat Atlympic Stadiaplex, the new home of the Atlanta Falcons, Atlanta Braves, and Georgia Tech Rambling Wrecks. Upright old Grant Field on the Tech campus, the site of so many glorious football moments, had been converted into a student condo-mall, and Atlanta Fulton County Stadium, the old home of the Falcons and Braves, had been roofed and was now the South's largest Mall-mart.

Checking into the hotel was something of an athletic competition in itself. You had to plow your way through a lobby teeming with fans. The grown men and women with tiger paws painted on their faces were the Clemson rooters. The grown men and women with pigs on their heads were the Arkansas rooters. The grown men and women waving tomahawks and wearing Indian headdresses were the Florida State rooters. The grown men and women dressed like Husky dogs were the UConn rooters. The ears stood up on their furry caps. My immediate guess was that Clemson might have the most fans in town. Out on the street, completely surrounding the hotel, were hundreds of RVs.

I met Jeannie for breakfast on Wednesday morning. We ate in a bamboo-and-bird room amid Arkansas people hollering, "Woo, pig, sooey," and Clemson people hollering something you can't understand, I don't believe, unless you're from somewhere in rural South Carolina or dropped out of school in the ninth grade. It sounded like, "Yow gobba geeby, baugh!"

The media headquarters was in the grand ballroom on the mezzanine. We flashed our admittance cards to a husky policeman, who said, "Yawl come on in here now."

About twenty local volunteer ladies in polka-dot dresses and Scarlett O'Hara hats were seated behind a long table.

I thought I was trapped in a romance novel.

Jeannie went first. She introduced herself to one of the ladies.

"I'm so happy to meet you," the lady said. "I'm Margaret Hancock. Welcome to our wonderful city."

Jeannie said she would like to pick up her credential.

"Well, of course you would," Margaret Hancock said. "I am sure your name is on this list somewhere."

"*Los Angeles Times*," Jeannie said, hoping to expedite matters.

"That's not another one of those liberal newspapers, is it?"

"We've never been called the *Washington Post*," Jeannie said.

"Oh, my goodness!" Margaret Hancock said with a little jump. "Don't even *say* the name."

Jeannie looked over at me. I looked down at the floor.

"Here you are," the lady said. "It's right here in alphabetical order, after all." She turned to another woman behind the table. "Suzanne, you got *one* in the right place." Both women giggled.

Margaret Hancock went to a filing cabinet and took out Jeannie's credential, a large square of cardboard with Jeannie's photo on it, laminated in plastic, dangling from a chain.

I gave my name and publication to Margaret.

"*The Sports Magazine*," she said. "Is that in Seattle?"

"No, ma'am, we've moved to New York."

She jumped again. "You live in New York City?"

"When I'm not on the road."

"Well, I feel sorry for *you*."

I said, "Now, Margaret, I don't insult your town, why do you want to insult mine? You have a crime rate, too, I hear."

"That is nothing but statistics," she said. "I swear, people do anything they want to with statistics. The white people in Atlanta don't have any crime rate at all. You should put that in your newspaper."

"Magazine," I said.

"That's right," Margaret said.

Jeannie and I were each presented with a thick folder of Chamber of Commerce material and restaurant flyers. You throw this away as soon as you leave the desk, but not before you shake out all of the party invitations. Most of what the Final Four is all about are big, sprawling, ice-sculpture parties.

At any Final Four, as at any golf or tennis tournament, you don't leave the registration desk until you receive your graft. The volunteer ladies always hope you will forget to ask for it so they can take all of the graft home and give it to their kids and friends of their kids, but we asked for our graft.

Margaret brought us our shopping bags, in which we would find our official briefcase, windbreaker, baseball cap, clipboard, toilet kit, T-shirt, keychain, paperweight, moneyclip, ballpoint pen, and package of pralines.

We looked up the sports information directors, the SIDs, of the four schools to say hello and pick up media guides from them. Those of us who fell into the category of "national writers" were never too familiar with the rosters of the teams involved. We didn't cover the sport on a regular basis.

I knew all of the SIDs from the past. I introduced newcomer Jeannie around. She met Handy Soober, the helpful midget from Arkansas, Snail Chapman, the efficient beanpole from Florida State, Tony Newberg, the wiry pundit from UConn, and Murky Booker, the colorful spokesman from Clemson, who shook my hand, and said, "Yow gobba geeby, baugh?"

Handy Soober assured us that the Arkansas Razorback players were the finest group of scholar-athletes in the school's history. Every kid on the starting five was carrying a 3.6 in his studies. Some hard questioning revealed that they were majoring in something called Human Development.

Snail Chapman assured us that the Florida State Seminole players were the finest group of scholar-athletes in the school's history. Every kid on the starting five was carrying a 3.6 in his studies. Some hard questioning revealed that they were majoring in something called Weight-Lift Management.

Tony Newberg assured us that the University of Connecticut players were the finest group of scholar-athletes in the school's history. Every kid on the starting five was carrying a 3.6 in his studies. Some hard questioning revealed that they were majoring in something called Social Conditioning.

Murky Booker assured us that the Clemson Tiger players were the finest group of scholar-athletes in the school's history. Every kid was carrying a 3.6 in his studies. Some hard questioning revealed that they were majoring in something called Physical Beingness.

I asked Murky Booker one of the most important questions you can ask at a Final Four: where was the Hospitality Room?

He led us to an adjacent ballroom. This is where you can always find coffee, rolls, donuts, and an after-hours bar.

Murky visited with us for a moment before he needed to run off and worship at the feet of the CBS announcers.

"I tell you what," he said. "Gonna be a dogfight. You got your Climpsons, your Phlarr States, your Arksaws, and your UConts. It's gonna be hoss on hoss, is all it is."

Over coffee, Jeannie and I thumbed through the media guides and caught up on hoops.

Arkansas (29-0) was the favorite. The Razorbacks were led by an expert three-point shooter named Car Radio Bailey. The members of his supporting cast were considered excellent. They were Stereo Rogers, Safeway Mumford, Air-Duct Williams, and Clearance Hardy. Arkansas' coach, Bobby Reed Mix, was known as the kind of man you would want your son to play for.

UConn (28-1) was the second favorite. The champions of the Big East were led by Rondiel Washington, an agile six-ten forward who could score and rebound. The Huskies were thought to be the most "physical" team. Rondiel was joined in the starting five by Montiel Woods, Wendiel Smith, Rashiel Richardson, and Boonaro Shoolomfet, a seven-four freshman center of unknown nationality. UConn's coach, Luther Traynor, was a wily veteran who had only been placed on NCAA probation three times in his long career as a character-builder at six different colleges.

Florida State (25-3) was given a good chance. The Seminoles were a team blessed with height. All five starters were six-eleven—Cleveland Cott, Detroit Maynes, Topeka Byers, Racine Brown, and Galveston Beamer. The big question was how well Florida State's coach, Slippery Conway, would react to the pressure of the Final Four. He had come from a high school job in Reptile Cove, Florida.

Clemson (20-8) was the underdog, the Cinderella team. The Tigers had barely scraped by in every game throughout the regionals. They had all but stolen two games in the playoffs, one from a talented group of Duke premed students and the other from a talented group of Stanford prelaw students. Clemson had won each game in the last minute on what even the most impartial observers agreed were lousy, corrupt foul calls. Clemson had a starting five of showboat leapers and dunkers: Leondus Hicks, Dolphus Shaw, Rondus Oliver, Rayleedus Walker, and Potatus Fry. It was said of Clemson's lovable coach, Hayseed Gibbs, that he was the kind of man you would want to take with you on a hunting or fishing trip.

"I'm announcing it now," I said to Jeannie. "Potatus Fry is minc."

23

JEANNIE SLAY WANTED TO CHECK OUT HER ELECTRICITY Wednesday afternoon.

We walked across the glass-enclosed bridge leading from the hotel mezzanine to the Georgia Malldome. Halfway across the bridge we stopped to enjoy a view of Atlanta traffic. Six lanes of cars, bumper to bumper, were streaming in one direction, and six lanes of cars, bumper to bumper, were streaming in the other direction.

I described the action. "The ones going that way are hoping to find an exit ramp before they reach the Florida border. The ones going this way are hoping to find an exit ramp before they reach the South Carolina border."

"It's not even going-home hour," she exclaimed.

"No," I said. "If it was going-home hour, they wouldn't be moving at all. But everybody has a phone and a gun in the car."

"It's wonderful. Can we stay here awhile?"

The press facility was in the basement of the Malldome. Jeannie saw that she would have a phone near her seat and an outlet for her laptop.

Electricity didn't concern me. I would be writing on the

geezer-codger portable and giving my column to the SID of the winning team to fax to New York for me after the championship game Monday night. You couldn't trust the SID of the losing team to send a column for you. He would be in tears, headed for a bar. I noticed a wall of fax machines that could be used by those writers who didn't send on a computer, but I didn't get along very well with any fax machine but my own at home. All others tended to eat my homework.

Jeannie wanted to check out the electricity on the press row as well. She would require a phone and an outlet at courtside. We went out on the court and over to the press tables where she saw that an electrician had worked it out so that she would have to wedge her plug against a board and use her shoe to hammer it into the socket.

There were three tiers of press seats at courtside, the press tables running the length of the floor. Every year there are approximately one hundred writers who feel strongly that they deserve to sit on the front row, but the front row never accommodates more than seventy-five writers, and every year there are twenty-five bruised egos.

Jeannie and I were not among the bruised egos. Jeannie was new and had not expected a front-row position, and I had actually requested the third row. If you sit on the prestigious front row, your family and friends might catch a glimpse of you on TV, but it's the seat from hell when a game ends. The deadline writers behind you come vaulting over in a frenzied effort to grab players for quotes before the players can reach their locker rooms, and the writers don't care how many hands, arms, or typewriters they stomp on.

A few other writers were milling around, inspecting their own electricity. One of them, my friend Richie Pace of the *Daily News*, was complaining about his seat assignment.

"I don't *do* third row," Richie was saying to a flustered tournament official.

Richie didn't agree about the safety and tranquillity of the third row—his image was at stake—and now he was telling Dub Fricker of the *Florida Times*, "I'm taking your seat."

"You're not taking *my* seat, asshole," Dub replied.

"You're not a front-row guy," Richie said. "You've never been a front-row guy."

"I'm sitting where I'm assigned," Dub said.

In the fraternity, Richie Pace had more stature than Dub Fricker, but not physically. Richie was only five-five, a peppery fellow in horn-rims. But his column commanded a big metropolitan readership, he did a radio show, he freelanced magazine pieces, he wrote sitcom scripts. Richie was now about thirty-five but he had been a child star in sportswriting and still thought of himself as twenty-two despite the fact that he was married and the father of three. His wife, Joanna, was regarded as something of a saint for putting up with his ego. His column was one of the best in the country when he dealt with issues and personalities, but on Sundays, he called it "Mouthing Off" and became a three-dot lightning bolt, the old Jimmy Cannon stunt. "Never drink with a guy who follows harness racing." Dot, dot, dot. "Nobody could paint the slider like Dave Dravecky." Dot, dot, dot. "This guy Sampras goes to jail if he knocks another letter out of Lendl's name." Dot, dot, dot.

In contrast, Dub Fricker was a hulking, easygoing southerner of forty-five, a man losing some of his hair, and frequently a contact lens. He wrote his own column in a workmanlike style and didn't much care whether John McEnroe, Jack Nicklaus, Joe Montana, or Mike Ditka knew him by name.

Richie and Dub were both good friends of mine, and good friends of each other, but not today.

Richie said he was going to take up the seating problem with the NCAA's press committee.

"Go ahead," said Dub. "I hope nobody asks you what a box-andone is."

"I'm hit!" said Richie, clutching his chest, bouncing around. "I've been hit with expertise."

Richie was aware of an audience.

"I don't know hoops, do I?" Richie said. "Who named the four corners for Dean?"

Dub looked appalled. "You're not saying *you* did?"

"I took it national."

Dub burst out laughing. "You little prick, I've been to every Final Four since Howard Porter at Villanova. I covered Butch Lee, Walton, David Thompson, Magic . . ."

"I covered Magic!" Richie interrupted.

Dub went on. "Darrell Griffith, Isiah . . ."

"I did Isiah for *Sports Illustrated*," Richie said. "Cover."

Dub said, "It was such a good piece, they didn't hire you."

"I turned 'em down," Richie snapped. "They crawled. I hate it when people crawl."

"I guess that's why you were sucking their cocks in Albuquerque."

"You weren't in Albuquerque. You were *not* in Albuquerque. Albuquerque was Phi Slamma Jamma."

"You're not going to take credit for that, too, I hope."

"I took it national."

"Jesus!" said Dub, spinning in a circle.

"Admit it. You missed Albuquerque."

Dub said, "Okay, I missed Albuquerque. But only because some asshole at the paper thought up a budget crunch. I had to choose between Albuquerque and the Masters. You were sucking their cocks in Dallas, that's where it was."

"Grantland Rice," said Richie, pointing at Dub, glancing at Jeannie and me. "Outlined against his swamp-fuck column, the four Gators rode again."

"What's a diamond-and-one?" Dub asked.

"What's a diamond-and-one? *I* don't know a gimmick D, right?"

"Who ran the first zone-and-two?"

"Do me a favor, Granny," said Richie. "Isolate this on the J-man."

The finger.

Dub returned the finger. "Nice talking to you, Red. Stay outta my air."

Dub walked away. Richie came over to Jeannie and me.

"Who reads him?" Richie said. "He shits a load of grits three times a week, who reads him?"

"Who reads anybody?" I said with a shrug.

"He's history. I'm in his seat. Where are you?"

"Third row."

"*You*? Third row. It's Iraq."

"I don't mind," I said. "I know if I miss some nuance in the diamond-and-one, you'll tell me, right?"

24

IF YOU'VE EVER PLAYED THAT GAME CALLED TRY TO FIND THE Kid, you know what a rigorous task it can be. James Junior was only an hour's drive away in Athens, Georgia, and I had been expecting to hear from him, or simply have him turn up at my hotel. I had left several messages for him on his answering machine in his apartment, inviting him to come on over to Atlanta for as many dinners or drinks as he could work into his busy schedule. I had suggested he bring along some friends, if he was so moved, or his current squeeze, if he had one. I knew he was alive and well, although I could only faintly hear his voice on the phone above the rock music and the laughter of others in the background. His latest message to the world was: "Yo, you've reached the Heinous Hut. I'm running like a big dog. Gotta catch the Clue Bus. If this is Tina, the girl of my dreams I met last night, leave your number. We'll creep some brews and get lathered."

Just to satisfy my evil curiosity, I called the registrar's office at the University of Georgia to see if my son was, in fact, still enrolled. He had been known to take a semester off if the surf was up anywhere within a thousand miles of his campus. The woman on the phone said such information was confidential and could only be obtained with the written approval of the student. I called the School of Business to see what classes he was taking and when. Another woman on the phone gave me the same response. Today's college students had a good thing going.

There were other phone calls. Nobody at Rhett's Rec had seen him. Nobody at Belle Watling's Parlor had seen him. A bartender at the Peacake Lounge knew him but hadn't seen him in a night or two.

I thought I was fairly easy to find myself, but evidently it had been tough for James Junior. Saturday morning I found a hand-written note in my box at the hotel.

"Dear Dad:

"Sorry we keep missing each other. This is really a bogus week for me. Lots of tests and stuff. I will keep trying to hook up with you. Thanks for the jacket from Europeville. I hate to ask any more favors of you but there are a couple of things that would really help me out. I got this really shitty speeding ticket. I was only doing 62 in a 55-mile zone but this main-stream cop saw that my insurance had expired by two days. He nailed me with a $500 ticket. Can you believe that? I don't have that kind of money right now, but I am getting ready to go back to the Peacake part time as a bartender. I need a loan real bad. I figure I can pay you back in two months. Everybody around here is wired for the Final Four. I have these buddies who are big fans of yours. They read everything you write. I know it's kind of late to be asking, but I sort of guaranteed them you could get tickets for us to the championship game Monday night. You can leave the tickets and the money at the hotel desk. I will swing by and pick them up. If I miss you at the hotel again, I will look for you at the game. Thanks a lot, Dad. Love, James."

I hated the ticket business. I detested it with every fiber in my body. But a sportswriter can never get out of the ticket business, never in his whole life. A sportswriter is expected to be able to get tickets to something even if the event has been sold out for months, which was always the case with the Final Four.

People have the impression that a sportswriter's major job is getting tickets to things like the Final Four, the Super Bowl, the World Series, the Texas-OU game.

People don't understand why you would be a sportswriter, otherwise.

Once again, I was forced to become a begging whore to get the tickets for my kid. I went to Murky Booker, the Climpson SID. I needed this one, I said. He got me the tickets, though it took a few nervous hours, and the unspoken understanding between us was that I would write a favorable column about Climpson when he badly needed it.

25

HERE'S THE DEAL: BY THE TIME THE GAMES COME AROUND AT the Final Four, you're lethally bored from three days of going to dreary press conferences to find out if any player has failed a drug test, from loitering and gossiping in the hotel lobby with the nation's coaches in the hope of getting a scoop, an item, a quote. You're suicidally hung over from going to three nights of ice-sculpture parties and winding up each evening in the hospitality room, drinking eccentric brands of whiskey in the company of wobbling, nostalgia-stricken SIDs and lost-in-the-past sportswriters like yourself. This is where you remind the younger writers that you gotta play hurt. It's where you allow them to prod you into telling the same old tales of yesteryear. So you talk far too long about the days when all of the athletes and coaches in all of the sports were infinitely more heroic and infinitely more accessible, days when all the writers chainsmoked and no writers jogged or drank nonbeer, days when you could *hear* the words being made on the paper by the deadline muse that lived in your typewriter, days when this guy and that one wrote literature that still gets quoted today by young sportswriters with taste and a sense of history, whose ranks were growing a damn sight thinner each year, it seemed.

Then it's time for the basketball games and you are smack in the middle of the shrillest event in sports. It's worse than a Poll Bowl to see who's No. 1 in college football because it's indoors.

All four bands are right there at courtside blaring their fight songs in your ear, sometimes all four of them playing at once. The cheerleaders are doing their shrieking, tumbling, dancing, and hopping around, and the whole time you are trying to hear yourself think and keep track of Clemson's twelve-point run and look for the nuance in Florida State's diamond-and-one defense—and behind you are a dozen aggravated fans screaming at you to keep your head down and asking why the fucking press gets the best seats.

Then suddenly a game is over and writers are vaulting over press rows, stepping on table tops and kicking over phones to reach the floor and grab the scholar-athletes for deadline quotes before the scholar-athletes can get to the locker rooms, where they will be sequestered for thirty minutes, which will be too late for most stories, but this will be of no consequence to the mercenary NCAA, which will be busy counting the millions of dollars in rights fees it has received from network television.

The quotes from the scholar-athletes can usually be set in type and held from year to year. "We took them out of their game plan,". . . "We beat 'em in the paint,". . . "We wanted to run and shoot,". . . "Nobody can play us commercial."

There are two nights of this, the semifinal night on Saturday and the championship game on Monday. It's about 2 A.M. on Tuesday before you are through with your work and limp back to your hotel, but this is where you find a nice little surprise. The last party of the Final Four will be under way in a banquet room. Here, you find an open bar and steaming tables heaped with food—scrambled eggs, bacon, sausage, ham, steaks, omelettes, hash browns, creamed chip beef, waffles. You can have dinner-breakfast and watch a replay of the game on big-screen TVs that are positioned all around the room.

Each year, this is where the Sleazeball of the Year award is presented. It goes to the sportswriter who has most disgraced himself or herself during the week. It is voted on by those sportswriters who care to bother with it. One year it went to a girl from the *Boston Globe* for having been seen kissing the North Carolina State coach on the lips. One year it went to a writer from the *Washington Post*, a Duke graduate, for having been seen by the entire world on TV hugging the Duke coach after Duke had lost a close game. One year it went to a writer from the *Chicago Tribune* for complaining about "all the bitches" who were taking over his profession. The Sleazeball of the Year award is a piece of net cord on a plaque. Each year, the previous winner passes the trophy on to the recipient, and there are some speeches that nobody listens to. By then, everybody is exhausted and you sneak off to bed, knowing you'll see most of your pals again in a week at the Masters.

But in Atlanta there *were* the games, of course.

In the semifinals, it was Climpson against Arksaw and Phlarr State against UCont.

The Razorbacks led the Tigers from the opening basket and built a lead of fifteen points by halftime. Many Tiger paws were sitting behind Jeannie and me, and we overheard them wondering when their lazy fucking Zulus were going to wake up and get in the game.

The Climpsons began to hit from the outside in the second half, however. Potatus Fry took the Tigers on a twelve-point run late in the game and Climpson trailed by only two points with ten seconds to play, but Arkansas was in possession of the ball. The only strategy was for Climpson to foul intentionally, but as the precious seconds ticked off, no Climpson player wrapped up any Arkansas player like a fajita. I looked over at Hayseed Gibbs. His face was buried in his hands. This was when Potatus Fry stole the ball from the dribbling Car Radio Bailey and hit a three-point jumper at the buzzer. It was a dramatic victory for the Tigers, 73 to 72. A heartbreaker for the Razorbacks but a highlight film for the Tigers, who were suddenly in the championship game on Monday night for the first time ever.

Murky Booker raced onto the court and hugged Hayseed Gibbs, yelling, "Yow gobba geeby, baugh! Yow-yee damn, yooby!" The coach yelled back, "Yow-yee, oh pooty baugh doan fooky airboddy!"

The UConn-Phlarr State game was a walkover for the Huskies. Rondiel, Montiel, and Wendiel hit from everywhere, and Boonaro Shoolomfet swept the glass, and the Huskies coasted to an 85 to 72 win. No Phlarr State war chants were heard throughout the night around the hotel, but there were occasional howling dogs.

On Sunday afternoon, both teams practiced lightly and press conferences were held.

Luther Traynor, UConn's coach, held up a book at his press conference. It was a copy of *The Iliad*. The coach said he had found the book in Rondiel Washington's room and just wanted the press to see the type of reading material his kids brought with them.

Luther opened the press conference with what the press recognizes as the Mandatory First Lie. He said, "We're just happy to be here." He followed that up with the Mandatory Second Lie: "Regardless of the outcome, we just want the kids to enjoy the experience."

His team was loaded with character, Luther said, and the kids had overcome all kinds of odds this season, including those embarrassing accusations about date-rapes on the campus.

As for the championship game, Luther said, "They know what we like to try to do. We know what they like to try to do. They'll try to take away this. We'll try to take away that. Momentum will have a lot to do with it. If our kids play their own game, we'll be fine."

"Does that mean you think you'll win?" somebody asked.

"I didn't say that," the coach frowned.

Rondiel Washington was the most eloquent of all the UConn players.

He said, "See, we're goin' for numbra one, you know what I'm sayin'? We're not with losin'. We can't be with that. We ain't been with losin' all year, you know what I'm sayin'?"

Hayseed Gibbs came to his press conference in an orange suit with tiger paws painted on his cheeks. He carred a tin can and spit his tobacco juice in it as he spoke.

"We're just happy to be here," he said. "We just want the kids to enjoy the experience."

He was asked who painted the tiger paws on his cheeks.

"My wife did that," he said. "Purty, ain't they? My family's got a lot of Climpson in they hearts."

Hayseed got a laugh from the press when he said he would shake hands with Luther Traynor before the game, but if Luther said anything like, "May the best team win," Hayseed was prepared to say, "Shit on *that*—I want Climpson to win."

Potatus Fry entered the press conference in mirrored glasses, a beret, boots, suede jacket, and he carried a riding crop.

Potatus lounged back in his chair with the microphone in his hand, and said:

"I've been saving my commerciality for the big game, and Monday night is the big game, you know? The big game is where I become the missin' ingredient. Deceptionally, we'll stay in our D, but if they try to deployalize us with confusionness, we have the flexilazation to do other things. Tonight, I'll be restin' my brain and thinkin' about the productionality of my J's. I'll be having to hit my J's to keep them out of their zoneial tendencies. That's why I say I'm the missin' ingredient, you know? They'll be playing us with a lot of zealous but, you know, our zealousness can offset that. I'll be savin' my zealous for the last five minutes, understand what I'm sayin'?"

Win or lose, my column was going to be on Potatus Fry. I got part of it done Sunday afternoon but a distraction kept me from finishing it. That was the day T. J. Lambert called long distance from Fort Worth to tell me the tragic news about TCU, my alma mater.

26

THEM SORRY-ASS SONS OF BITCHES, T.J. WAS SAYING ON THE phone. Them low-rent fuckin' hypocrites. Them pissant, cheap-shot cocksuckers. Them goddamn shirt-liftin', slack-jawed, know-nothin' motherfuckers.

"Who are we talking about, T.J.?" I asked, plaintively.

"Them lightweight NC Double A's," he said. "Them butt-fuckin', dicknose candy-asses. You know what the NCAA is about to do, Jim Tom? They about to pull down their pants and shit all over us. It's a sorry damn world, is all it is."

It seemed that TCU had received an official letter from the NCAA saying that Texas Christian University's football program was under investigation for illegal recruiting practices. The school was accused of fifty-seven different violations. Another letter would be forthcoming that would provide more detail on the alleged violations, but for now, the university could prepare to defend itself against the major accusations.

The major accusations, according to T. J. Lambert, head

football coach, were (a) providing cash payments to prospective athletes, (b) providing cash payments to currently enrolled athletes, and (c) providing automobiles and cash payments to prospective and currently enrolled athletes.

"You know what this means, Jim Tom? It means them lightweight candy-asses could give us the death penalty."

I understood the seriousness of the situation completely.

The NCAA rules state that if a school is found guilty of major rules violations twice within a five-year period, it can be barred from playing football for two seasons. That's what the death penalty was about.

The death penalty, of course, was the worst thing that could happen to a university's football program. It could ruin your football program for a decade. The rebuilding process would be slow and painful. It could take at least ten years to recover.

And T.J. didn't need to remind me that four years ago, under his leadership, TCU had been found guilty of rules violations that had resulted in a two-year probation. The school had been banned from TV or bowl appearances for two seasons and had been forced to sacrifice fourteen scholarships.

None of us among the TCU alumni or boosters had complained too much about the probation, however. It had been worth it. Under T.J.'s leadership, the Horned Frogs' long-undernourished football program had been resurrected. T.J.'s recruitment of two exciting running backs, C. S. (Convenience Store) Roberts and Clitorrus Walker, had given TCU two straight 8-3 seasons. Convenience Store Roberts and Clitorrus Walker had taken the Frogs to the Peach Bowl and the Bluebonnet Bowl, and the city of Fort Worth hadn't been as elated about TCU football since the days of Sam Baugh and Davey O'Brien in the thirties.

It is an inarguable fact that universities prosper immensely through football successes. It's likely that nobody would ever have heard of Notre Dame if it hadn't been for college football. The same might be said of Southern Cal, Stanford, Nebraska, Georgia Tech, Michigan, certainly Oklahoma and Alabama, or even Yale, Harvard, and Princeton, if you wanted to go back far enough. Without football, as T.J. liked to say with contempt, "Them places wouldn't be nothin' but *schools*."

TCU was a good example. When the Horned Frogs suffered through twenty long years with losing teams, often going 1-10, the university couldn't even keep the grass mowed on the campus. But then came the touchdown runs of Convenience Store Roberts and Clitorrus Walker. And simply because of those two minor bowl appearances, a rich oil man named Big Ed Bookman and a rich real estate developer named Billy (Whip-Out) Murdock gave the school so much money, TCU was able to build a new dormitory, expand the communications building, put a wing on the library, buy new band uniforms, and hire a landscaping crew. Another good team or two and TCU might see a new science building and another dorm.

But now there was this problem with the NCAA, and T.J. was saying he felt so goddamn unlucky that if he sucked a dick he might find out he liked it.

"We in deep shit," T.J. said.

"How many players did you buy?" I asked.

"Me, personally?"

I stifled a laugh. "How guilty are we, T.J.?"

"Guilty is a word I don't like to hear, Jim Tom. You know damn good and well we ain't no guiltier than anybody else. There ain't a coach in major college football that don't bend the rules. When your opponent goes out and buys him a big, fast 'brother,' then you better get one who can catch him—or get fired."

I had first known T. J. Lambert when he was an all-pro defensive end with the New York Giants. He was a good friend of Billy Clyde Puckett's, the ex-TCU immortal and ex-New York Giant immortal for whom I had once written that book. T.J. was a throwback to the days when a man played the game for love instead of money, and nothing infuriated him more than a player who didn't give his all in every minute of every game. When he had maimed his last quarterback and his pro career was behind him, he went into coaching, first as an assistant at Mississippi State, then at Tennessee, his own alma mater. Billy Clyde helped him land the TCU job. It was after Wes Brisco, the worst coach in TCU history, was killed in the crash of a private plane on a recruiting trip to Alaska. T.J. tried to win by the rules his first five seasons as TCU's head coach, but he eventually realized this didn't work anymore. Angry people used to win football games. Not any longer. Today, football games were won by big, fast brothers and white boys on steroids.

"I understand the real world," I said to T.J., "but you must have done something to make the NCAA come after you. The NCAA doesn't really want to catch anybody cheating anymore. They're into TV and bowl money."

"You want to know why they're after us?" he said. "It's because ever now and then the buttholes got to act like they're doin' something to *police* the sport. We ain't Michigan. We ain't Notre Dame. We ain't Texas. We ain't Nebraska. We ain't Alabama. We're just turd-squat TCU. They can strap their 'selective punishment' on our ass and it looks like they're tryin' to keep the game clean. Don't make a fuck to the networks or the eastern sportswriters if TCU can't play football."

I said, "Somebody blew the whistle on you. Sombody went to the NCAA. All the NCAA knows is what somebody tells them. What happened?"

"I'll tell you what brought this up," he said. "I'll tell you exactly what brought this up. It's that kid I run off."

"Which one?"

"Parker Lee Boone."

"The wide receiver?"

"He *thought*. The little fucker couldn't hold on to a big tit if he heard footsteps within two miles of him. We tried him everywhere—wide receiver, running back, corner on defense, special teams. He liked contact about as much as a golfer."

"I'm sure he wasn't expensive at all."

"Aw, naw, not at all. I wish all them academic fuckers who are so *concerned* about the kids could know Parker Lee Boone. He was like all them other blue-chippers. He had a fuckin' agent when he was a junior in Tooler High. Cost us a Corvette Stingray. Cost us two wardrobes. He said he needed one for fall, one for spring. A coach ain't supposed to know this, of course. All a coach is supposed to do is tell somebody like Big Ed or Billy Murdock, 'I sure want that kid, but don't tell me how you get him for me.' Well, we got him, all right. Then I had the pleasure of watchin' footballs bounce off his jersey all last season. Then he came in my office last December and said he'd figured out why he had a bad year. His apartment was too small. He needed a bigger apartment off-campus. I broke his plate.''

"Right then?"

"That fuckin' day. He said I couldn't run him off. If I did, he would go to the NCAA and tell 'em what we gave him for coming to TCU. I called him a blackmailin' little prick and kicked his lazy ass out the door. Probably the worst mistake I ever made, Jim Tom, but I ain't been so mad since we played the dogass Jets in the Super Bowl.''

"That explains it," I said.

"He shopped himself around to three or four schools. Oklahoma State finally took him. I'm sure the NCAA has granted him some kind of chickenshit immunity to play ball up there while he tells lies about us.''

T.J. said there was something I could do to help him out. I could try to find out something about all of the members of the NCAA's infractions committee. My magazine had powerful investigative resources, he said. Maybe *SM* could find out that there were some queers and marijuana smokers on the committee.

He said, "Hell, you know teachers, Jim Tom. They all a bunch of liberal subversives—artsy-craftsy shitasses. I got to have me some ammunition to fight 'em with if they try to drop the death penalty on us.''

"What if we find out they're all honorable people?"

"Well, in that case," he said, "I'll just have to drop a fifty-pound can of perjury on the NCAA's ass. They'll have a hard time proving anything. We've run all the money through the church.''

27

I CALLED JEANNIE SLAY IN HER ROOM TO FILL HER IN ON MY alma mater's problems. Also to ask if she would like to join me in the hunt for a queer, lesbian, dope-smoker, or traitor to our country on the NCAA's infractions committee.

"At least TCU is trying," she said. "How would you like to root for my Tar Heels? It's like waiting for the biopsy. The only time I get excited is when they have Appalachian State on the schedule."

It was times like this, I said to Jeannie, when I wished college football would go back to the days of one platoon, leather helmets, high-top shoes. Only thirty players on a squad then, and all of them graduated. A school only needed two coaches, a head coach and a line coach. Everybody played on real grass. Of course, there was one awkward thing about the old days—all of the players were white.

"There is that," she said.

Jeannie said she had reserved a table for four that evening in the hotel's gourmet restaurant, the Chateau de Trellis. She had invited Richie Pace of the *Daily News* to join us. Who else did we want?

"I'll ask somebody," I said.

We agreed that gourmet restaurants were usually fraught with peril, but it would at least be a way to escape from the noise in the festive lobby for a while.

The TV was on in my room and *Desperate Journey* was nearing its conclusion. Errol Flynn and his flight crew had been trying to escape from Nazis for two hours. Some had been killed, others tortured. But now they had stolen a plane and Errol Flynn was at the controls. Errol Flynn flashed a big smile to his mangled crew, and said, "Okay, boys, now to Australia and a crack at those Japs."

I wrote down the line. Jeannie collected them, as did I. Stuck in the middle of a column in a press room, she had been known to turn to me, and say, "Wainwright, what does prognosis mean?" Bette Davis. *Dark Victory*. Finishing a column in a press room, she had been known to turn to me and recite the ending to *Deadline, USA*. Martin Gabel: "Hutchinson, what's that racket?" Humphrey Bogart: "It's the roar of the press, baby—and there's nothing you can do about it."

I phoned Nell Woodruff in New York. I wondered if Nell would like to join me in the hunt for a queer, lesbian, dope-smoker, or traitor to our country on the NCAA's infractions committee.

Nell liked the idea of blackmailing the NCAA.

"I'll put our stringers on it," she said. "If we come up with anything, what do we do with the information?"

I said, "We wait till they're ready to decide the punishment they're going to level on my fine Christian school, then we threaten to expose their sordid secrets unless they back off from the death penalty."

"I think I know of a lesbian on the committee."

"You do?"

"I heard her speak at a Women's Sports Federation banquet. Her name is Martha Callaway. She's the women's basketball coach at some college in the Midwest. Mt. Grimmall, or something like that."

"Figures," I said. "It's a natural bodily function of the NCAA for the Mt. Grimmalls to tell the Alabamas and Oklahomas what to do."

"If she's not a lesbo, she ought to be. She has a big, deep voice. 'My girls go on the court to kick some butt.' You wouldn't want to mix it up with Martha Callaway in a dark alley."

"It's a beginning," I said. "Be nice to find out she's having an affair with Denise, her point guard."

"I'll get the names of everybody on the committee."

"Maybe there's an old classics professor who's still doing acid. A doctor of religion who's going down on his grader. This is for the overall good of college football."

"I understand. How's the Sportswriter of the Year?"

"Jeannie?"

"No, John Lardner."

"She's good. This is her first Final Four. We've had a few laughs. So far, the highlight of the week was watching Richie and Dub argue over their press box seat."

"Jeannie wrote a funny column yesterday. It moved on the wire."

"What about?"

"A Clemson player named Potatus Fry."

"*What*?"

Pissed was what I was. "That was going to be *my* column."

"Well, there you are," Nell chuckled. "Now you have to disfigure her face."

28

STEAL A GUY'S COLUMN TOPIC ONCE, IT'S OKAY. CALL IT AN accident. Call it a breakdown in communications. But steal a guy's column topic *again*, you wind up in a cement quilt, tits or not.

I was explaining this to Jeannie as we had a drink under the waterfall before dinner.

She said, "I didn't want to write Potatus Fry—I knew you were—but I found out everybody else was writing him, so I had to go with it."

"Everybody wrote it?"

"Almost everybody. You can't really sit on something like Potatus Fry, can you?"

"What was your lead? One Potatus, two Potatus?"

"Please. Do I look like Richie Pace?"

"What was your lead?"

"I can't remember."

"You can't remember? You can quote Damon Runyon from nineteen twenty-eight, but you can't quote yourself from two days ago?"

"It's embarrassing to quote yourself."

"Not for Richie. What was your fucking lead, Jeannie?"

"I really can't remember it all. It was something about his vocabularyness."

The other person I invited to dinner was H.E.S. Bromley, Jr., *SM*'s college basketball writer.

Achee Bromley, as he was known, was a puffy, harmless-looking Harvard man with a slight stutter, a writer who bled profusely over his word processor. Monday night would be a killer deadline for him. He had been cloistered in his hotel room for four days, clacking away, trying to cover every angle of the tournament, writing the story upside-down, which was what the situation demanded. Achee had been given a line count of 2,400 words, and all but the top eight paragraphs needed to be written and filed before he would know which team won the championship game. Achee should have been used to this chore by now, but he wasn't. Tight deadlines rattled him. He had been known to plead illness on tight deadlines, causing panic in the office and forcing someone like Doug McNiff or Lindsey Caperton to come to the rescue of the story with the aid of the AP wire.

Over drinks, as he joined us under the waterfall, Achee fretted about the transition he would have to make from either Clemson or UConn to the bulk of the piece he had already written.

I suggested he fall back on the old standby in the ninth paragraph: "But nothing was more fascinating than the events leading up to the finals."

Achee said he was t-tired of u-using that.

I said if he didn't put it in, a drone would. He thanked me for reminding him, and seemed not to be in a fog for a while.

H.E.S. Bromley, Jr., was someone with whom I came in contact only twice a year, once at the Final Four and once at Wimbledon. His other beat was tennis. Like most of the writers at *SM*, he didn't live in New York. He chose to live in the vicinity of Boston. One of those Salems. Our writers were spread out everywhere. Cloyce Windham, the golf writer, who wrote mainly of the past except when it came to instruction, lived in Pinehurst, North Carolina. Stewart Mason Gardner, the college football writer, whose name alone might suggest that he knew nothing whatever about the sport, lived year-

around in Martha's Vineyard, that old hotbed of college football. Bumpy Tresler, the thoroughbred racing writer, who
wrote more often about his relatives among the owners than he
did about jockeys or trainers, lived in Lexington, Kentucky.
Kitter Morring, the track and field writer, who could make
almost any middle-distance runner express the ideas of Jean-
Paul Sartre, lived in Eugene, Oregon, the town that invented
jogging and no smoking. DeChane Moxler, the baseball writer,
who would argue that baseball was the only literary sport, lived
in Carmel, California. Pete Buttrick, the pro football writer,
who had once played tackle for Temple and thought he could
diagram plays better than Bill Walsh, lived in Buffalo. *SM* had
other far-flung writers who covered ice hockey, harness racing,
and the NBA, but I wasn't sure of their names—I had never
read a story about ice hockey, harness racing, or the NBA.
Actually, Wayne Mohler and myself were the only senior writers who still lived in Manhattan, although Ralph Webber was
just across the Hudson in New Jersey.

In another era of magazines, say, fifteen or twenty years ago,
every writer on a New York publication was expected to live in
or around Manhattan. Most of us enjoyed it even if we couldn't
afford it. We worked hard, drank hard, and sang George M.
Cohan songs as we bounced from one tavern to another. But
now in this age of fax machines and word processors, a staff
writer could live anywhere. People were out. Software was in.

The waiter arrived at our table in the Chateau de Trellis. He
looked as if he might burst with exalting news regarding the
nouvelle menu, but Jeannie didn't give him a chance.

"What colors do your steaks come in tonight?" she said.
"Can you show us something in black or a dark brown? That
would be without blue potatoes, of course."

The waiter said, "If I just might suggest . . ."

"No, you may not," Jeannie said, sharply. "We will all
have the split-pea soup, a New York strip medium, blue cheese
on the salad, and take the drink orders first."

We had discussed it beforehand. This was the safest order on
the menu.

"And what are we drinking?" the waiter asked.

"Bombay martini," said Achee. "Olive, n-no ice."

Richie Pace ordered an unleaded beer.

"J and B and water, tall," I said. "Hold the peppercorns."

"Same," Jeannie said. "Hold the hazelnuts in mine."

The waiter said, "How many of you would like a dip of our special raspberry yogurt in your split-pea soup?"

I think you could say I laughed the hardest at this insane question.

Food monopolized much of the dinner conversation.

Jeannie recalled one of the toughest things she had ever gone up against. It was the abalone-and-plum pizza in this movie-star hangout in Beverly Hills.

Achee Bromley spoke of a chic place in Dallas that offered a blackened l-lobster, radicchio, and tomato aspic sandwich on p-pita bread.

Richie went on at length about the horrors of Timothy's, a place in Scottsdale. He had taken his wife Joanna out to spring training for a week in the sun, and Timothy's had been highly recommended. He had started to worry when he opened the menu and read a message from Chef Timothy, who basically denounced the customers for being morons about food.

The main course had been bad enough—a chicken dressed in chintz. But then came the dessert, a plate on which a dainty puddle of turquoise cream hovered under a large brown wire cage made out of spun sugar. "Facemask," Richie said. "Intentional."

I said they could put all of that in the trenches and they couldn't defeat an entree that attacked me in a fern joint in San Francisco—a tiny raw squab, bleeding openly as it crouched in a field of sculpted, undercooked carrots.

Jeannie insisted on paying the check. She was on an expense account, too, she reminded everyone. I gave the waiter an extra ten-dollar tip. He gave me a blank receipt that would be worth three hundred dollars. This was the extent of my knowledge about economics.

We all stood around in the lobby for a few moments to watch Climpson's fans throw Kentucky Fried Chicken bones at the UConn fans.

I asked Richie how he and Dub Fricker were going to handle

the seating arrangement at the championship game. At the semifinals on Saturday night, Dub had generously given the front-row seat to Richie during the second game.

"I get the first half, he gets the second half," Richie said.

I didn't mention it to Richie, but the sportswriter seat war was going to be my column now that I had been scooped by the whole country on Potatus Fry. I planned to re-create their conversation of the other day, and somewhere in the column I would say we all remembered how Grantland Rice and Ring Lardner had slugged it out in the Comiskey press box to get a better view of the crippled kid and Babe Ruth pointing to the centerfield fence.

Jeannie and I rode up on the elevator, and I walked her to her room. I had no intention of doing anything more than walking her to her room, to protect her from the marauding and beer-can-littering Climpsons and UConts.

But after she unlocked the door, she suddenly slipped into my arms and initiated a long, thought-provoking kiss. Her body was pressed against mine, and I was alerted to a larger set of tits than I had envisioned. Meanwhile, she ran her tongue over my upper-right implant and all along my lower-left permanent bridge.

Recovering from the kiss, I said, "Do I take this to mean you're still happily married?"

Softly, she said, "To quote a wise old philosopher, Jim Tom—'ain't nobody married on the road.' "

I released her gently, and said, "You rascal, if you'd caught me in another life, we'd be parallel parked by now."

"We called it bone dancing at Chapel Hill."

She kissed me again. Longer, even more passionately.

I recovered again and fumbled around for a Winston and my Dunhill.

"This is not rejection, Jeannie," I said. "Okay? Think of it as Gregory Peck being strong for both of us."

"I'll think of it as cowardice."

"Right," I said.

She opened the door to her room and lingered in the doorway, one hand on her hip as she ran the other through her hair.

She said, "It *is* going to happen, you know."

"To a person of my staunch character?"

"Go to bed," she said, smiling sweetly. "You look foolish."

She closed the door behind her, and I fled clumsily down the hall.

29

IT IS NO SECRET TO ANY ENLIGHTENED PERSON THAT MOST college basketball players spend their time in slam-dunk labs and take a universal course called Motherfucker 101.

But as I was saying to Jeannie, I was still a strong defender of the athletic scholarship. If a kid could get into a university for being able to play the harp, an athlete should also have an opportunity to be exposed to college. How much room did athletes take up on a campus? Hardly any. You were only talking about fifteen basketball scholarships, and only ninety-five football scholarships. Was that a lot on a campus of fifty thousand students, like an Ohio State or a University of Texas, or even six thousand, like a TCU? Without these revenue-producing sports, a university couldn't support golf, tennis, baseball, track, swimming, or any other kind of minor sport, and when did a harpist or a math student ever bring in five million dollars to the alumni fund? Why should colleges be reserved for cocaine-dealing pledge captains and computer programmers learning how to steal on Wall Street? It happened to be an overlooked fact—something the chemistry professors loved to overlook—that a vast majority of basketball and football players *did* graduate. The most recent study I had seen proved that fifty-seven percent of all basketball and football players earned a degree as compared with only thirty-two percent of the rest of the student body as a whole, and this was the case at any university you wanted to name. As for the idea that our campuses were only "farm systems" for the pros, that was test-tube, iambic pentameter propaganda, or utter bullshit, to put it another way. Five thousand kids played major college basketball every year, and only fifty of them went to the NBA.

Ten thousand kids played major college football every year and only two hundred of them wound up in the NFL. What "farm system" were the naive nitwits talking about?

I said, "I don't want to live in a country that doesn't have athletic scholarships. There wouldn't be anything in it but computer freaks who fuck up my bank balance."

My lecture ended as we watched Potatus Fry do another behind-the-back dribble, piledrive down the lane, go up in the air and do a whirlygig three-sixty, levitate high above the UConn rim, and crash-dunk a basket.

Despite the bands and the yowling fans, we could hear some of the dialogue on the court, even from the third row of the press section, and when Potatus Fry trotted back down the court, he passed by us, flashed a smile to the writers, and said, "I *own* these dicks."

At this point, he did. He was taking Clemson on a 15 to 3 run to get the Tigers back in the game after they trailed at the half by ten and Hayseed Gibbs and Luther Traynor had thrown towels at each other. Now there were only five minutes left to play, the score was tied, and it didn't hurt Climpson's cause that UConn's Rondiel Washington was playing with four fouls.

It is said that a basketball game doesn't start until there's only five minutes to go. Some say two minutes. I say, in most cases, forty-five seconds. You can often see three time-outs and nine missed free throws in the last forty-five seconds.

The two teams swapped baskets for four more minutes and the arena was bedlam during a time-out with one minute to play. Dueling fight songs were in full throat from the bands, and down in front of us, tan-legged, honey-blonde cheerleaders were being tossed in the air. The coaches were shouting instructions to their huddled players, none of whom were listening and all of whom were begging to be given the ball.

Of equal interest was the drama on the front row of the press section, not too far from us. Richie Pace had refused to give up the front-row seat, so now Dub Fricker was sharing it with him. Each writer had one cheek on the seat, and I noticed some shoving and nudging of an irritable nature.

Forty seconds went by and the teams were still tied, as

Potatus missed a three-pointer and Rondiel blew a layup. Now, another time-out.

But as the Climpson players walked to their bench, they were forced to step over, and around, Richie Pace. Dub had thrown him onto the court.

Richie curled up in a knot to avoid being stepped on by the Climpson players. Then he stood up and rushed back to the press table, whereupon he grabbed what he thought was Dub's computer, raised it above his head, and smashed it on the floor.

Except it wasn't Dub's computer. It belonged to Bubba Slack of the *Atlanta Journal*. Bubba was furious. He grabbed Richie by the throat and dangled him in the air. Richie squirmed and flapped his arms. Dub was pissed at Richie, but he didn't want Bubba to choke him to death. He tried to come to Richie's rescue by jerking on Richie's arm and leg.

Other writers were now on their feet, cussing and shouting and pushing and accidentally unplugging one another's computers and phones.

The dispute was quieted by two Climpson players and three uniformed police, as most of it was being documented by two hand-held cameramen from CBS.

I couldn't have asked for anything better for my column. God loved me for not screwing Jeannie.

30

THE CHAMPIONSHIP GAME ENDED HYSTERICALLY. UCONN elected to hold the ball in the final twenty seconds and take the last shot. Hit the shot and the Huskies would win. Miss the shot and they would at least be in overtime. It was the smart play. Rondiel Washington took the last shot and hit it from the corner for two points. The UConn fans erupted into a horde of jubilant lunatics. Tony Newberg, the UConn SID, even jumped on top of a table and punched his fist in the air. But there was one second left on the clock, and in basketball, one second can be three-quarters of an eternity. Climpson called another time-out to plot its use of the final one second. The game clock wouldn't start until a Climpson player touched the in-bounds pass, so what Climpson had to do was obvious. Throw a long pass to midcourt and hope a Climpson player could catch it and get off a three-point shot before the buzzer sounded. Under the rules, the buzzer was the thing that signaled the official end of a game. The clock might show 00:00 but if the buzzer hadn't sounded, the one second wasn't up. Many logical people, including myself, didn't see how this was scientifically possible, but those are the rules.

History will record that it was Climpson's Rayleedus Walker who threw the ball in, a high pass to midcourt, and that it was Potatus Fry who leaped up and caught it. And Potatus never came down until he somehow spun around in midair and lofted a three-pointer that sailed high toward the ceiling and came down into the UConn basket, hitting nothing but net. The buzzer was definitely sounding while Potatus was in the air with the ball, and the question was whether the buzzer had begun to sound *before* he fired the desperate shot. The players and fans of both schools were celebrating. Either UConn had won the national championship by 82 to 80, or the Tigers of Climpson had won the national championship by 83 to 82. One zebra ruled the shot good, but another zebra ruled no goal. The third zebra made no judgment at all—he had apparently been looking at the tan legs on a honey-blonde cheerleader.

The zebras huddled for a moment, then wisely left the court before coming to a decision, fully aware that they would be mobbed and possibly even murdered by the losers. It was only after the zebras were in the safety of their dressing room and under armed guard that they issued a statement saying they agreed unanimously that the shot was good—Climpson had won.

When the announcement was made over the PA, the UConn players fell to the floor and wept. The Climpson players hoisted Potatus Fry on their shoulders. Simultaneously, Luther Traynor grabbed the PA mike and blabbered, "I protest this bullshit! This is highway fuckin' robbery!"

A group of NCAA officials met at courtside and decided there was too much chaos, including fights in the stands, to hold the usual presentation ceremony, the giving out of championship wristwatches to the players. This was announced over the PA.

Throughout the game, I had looked around the Malldome trying to spot my son. I never found him. He never found me. I had been tricked again. James Junior had only wanted the tickets for friends, to prove that he could get them. Nine times out of ten, this was the case when somebody implored me to get tickets for them to sold-out events. Another reason I loathed the ticket business.

Jeannie asked if I wanted to accompany her to the Climpson locker room. I declined. I never went into a locker room unnecessarily. Regardless of the team sport—basketball, football, baseball—a locker room was not the most alluring of sanctums. Frankly, I had never been in one—and I had been in hundreds—that didn't smell like all the dirty laundry in Bangkok.

But deadline writers also needed to go into locker rooms after such a wrenching ordeal as a game in order to make sports more vivid for their readers. It's the function of a reporter to document not only a team's ability and progress but also its character and thoughts, and this is sometimes done best by cornering athletes in a locker room before their tempers or festive moods have been dulled by time or homogenized by press-fearing coaches, whose numbers are legion.

No worry about Jeannie entering a locker room alone. First of all, she wouldn't be alone. Swarms of reporters would be in there, including a few other female writers, not to mention TV crews, boosters, relatives, hangers-on.

Women had been going into locker rooms for more than fifteen years, or ever since it became the law. Equal access. A lot of coaches and athletes still didn't approve of it. Once a year there would be the scandalous story, overblown by TV, of a woman sportswriter being barred from some team's locker room, or accusing some player of lewd conduct, which meant waving his dick in her face as he purposely paraded around naked, yelling motherfucker at somebody.

It was my experience that most athletes were modest. They didn't enjoy being disrobed in front of each other, let alone women. They found towels handy and some teams provided bathrobes. But there were those brothers and rednecks who occasionally liked to taunt female reporters, particularly if they sensed she was looking for trouble. The sharp female writer knew how to deal with it. There were three standard responses to lewd conduct, all of them having been originated by, I am proud to say, Nell Woodruff. They were:

1. "Gee, Butch, that would look just like a penis if it weren't so small."

2. "Hi, Pete. Sprinkle some water on that and it might grow."

3. "If you don't reel that thing in, Leroy, I'm going to tell your mother on you."

While Jeannie was in the Climpson locker room, I hacked out the top of my column, going with a lead that parodied Bob Considine's classic piece on the Louis-Schmeling fight: "Listen to this, buddy, for it comes from a guy whose palms are still wet, whose throat is still dry, and whose jaw is still agape from the utter shock of watching Richie Pace of the *Daily News* and Dub Fricker of the *Florida Times* duke it out over a press box seat at the Final Four."

I sought out Murky Booker, Climpson's delirious SID, and prevailed on him to fax the column to New York for me.

"How gobba geeby, baugh?" Murky said, as I shook his hand to congratulate him on the coveted national championship. "Recky UCont thankee for hoe scar down? Har, har."

This translated into, "Did I reckon UConn would thank them for holding the score down?"

SID humor.

I wandered over to H.E.S. Bromley, Jr. He was in his press seat, staring dazedly at the blank screen on his computer. He hadn't written a word.

He confided that the office was heckling him every ten minutes on the phone. First Lindsey Caperton had called, then Doug McNiff, finally Bryce Wilcox himself.

Where was his goddamn story? This delay was costing the magazine a fortune.

"I-I can't think, J-Jim Tom," he said. "My b-brain's gone."

I said, "Don't slobber over it, Achee. Send them anything. They're going to rewrite it anyway. They watched it on TV."

He said, "There's t-too many e-elements." His left eye began to twitch violently, and he covered it with his hand to keep it from falling out of his face.

I walked back to my geezer-codger Olivetti and typed up a lead for him. Nothing I would have written for myself but something I thought would appeal to Bryce. I wrote:

"The amazing Climpson Tigers became the national champions of college basketball last Monday night, although for most of the decisive game in Atlanta's Malldome they were lost in a Potatus field and looked about as appetizing as a cold, limp Fry without ketchup."

I took the piece of paper back to Achee, and said, "Here, send this, then tell them you've got the flu, they can pick up the play-by-play from AP."

The lead ran in the magazine untouched.

Later that night, up at the buffet in the banquet room, Richie Pace was presented the Sleazeball of the Year award for having been a brat about the press seating. His acceptance speech was quite bitter in tone.

31

My few days back in New York between the Final Four and the Masters were fairly uneventful, unless you want to count the hours I spent in Fu's Like Us, helping celebrate various things, or unless you want to count that I heard from all three of my ex-wives.

Christine Thorne returned from Moscow with word that the Russians still didn't know anything about dry cleaning. Her return was worth a night in Fu's. Christine brought me a present, a photo Shag Monti had taken of me with Tatyana Romanova, which Christine had asked Tatyana to sign. The inscription read: "To Tom Jim, my Amerika fiend—Tatyana."

Yes, the "r" was missing. Somehow it seemed better that way.

Another night in Fu's was devoted to toasting Drone Four, Travis Steed. After seven rejected manuscripts, Travis was finally getting a novel published. The demented editor-in-chief of an obscure publishing house had given Travis a fifteen-hundred-dollar advance for *Is That You, Durwood?* The book was said to be autobiographical and had something to do with his father going blind during Travis' boyhood days in Dover, Delaware. I couldn't think of anyone on the staff who intended to buy the book or make the slightest effort to read it when it came out, but one of our people bursting into hard-cover was big news around the office.

As for my three ex-wives, I opened their letters and dealt with the contents in the order in which I had been married to the ladies.

Earlene's letter said:

"Jim Tom,

"I don't know how many times I have to tell you this but I would appreciate it if your checks would arrive on time. Last month's check was 23 days late. I cannot make ends meet without the money you send me. Mr. Thompson says I may have to take a cut in pay because the economy in Fort Worth is so bad. Nobody is building any houses which makes it hard for us to sell any doors.

"Business is just terrible. Blake Lumber is closing and so is Tiller Electric. Snodgrass Furniture closed last week. It is going to be very sad to drive by there every day. My father and Mr. Snodgrass were good friends, if you remember. I will never forget the Halloween night in high school when Buddy White and A. C. DuBose and you broke out Mr. Snodgrass' front windows and you claimed you weren't there but I know you were, just like I know you were a lot of other places you lied about when I couldn't find you.

"I feel so sorry for Mr. Thompson who works so hard, and on top of everything, his wife is going in for surgery next week. It is not major surgery but it is surgery just the same. Aunt Iris had surgery again last month for her hip, and Uncle Elzie needs surgery on his back but he keeps putting it off because he says he can't afford to miss work at the barber shop.

"It is very unsafe around here now. Everybody I know is worried about it. I don't know where all the niggers keep coming from. I remember in Paschal that the only niggers we ever saw were the ones in the band at that place where we used to go dance. Mr. Thompson says it is football that makes the niggers multiply. I think he is right.

"I hope you saw James when you were in Atlanta. He told me you were coming there for a sports deal. When he came home at spring break I thought he looked thin. He says it is because he studies so hard. I am so proud he is going to get his degree. One of the great sorrows of my life is that I did not finish college and get a degree, what with all the opportunities for women today. I am sure you can guess what the other great sorrow of my life is. It had something to do with marrying a fart-face.

"Lord, I saw Rebecca Sue Ellis the other day at Neiman's (which if it ever closes, we are sunk for sure). She has moved back from Amarillo since Eddie Joe died in surgery two months ago. I almost did not recognize her. Well, she is no longer the stuckup queen of Paschal High and somebody you used to slip off with. She is just a little old gray-haired lady now, and ha, ha, ha, is what I have to say about it.

"Mr. Thompson still reads your magazine and says you do a good job. I said to him yesterday that I was happy to hear it because that was ALL you had in life!

"Earlene."

I wrote out three checks to Earlene and enclosed them with the following reply:

Dear Earlene:

Here are your checks for April, May, and June. This ought to see you through Neiman's for a while. The reason I was late last month is because I was in Europe with Rebecca Sue Ellis, screwing her brains out. That's why she looks so old now.

As a matter of fact, I never laid a glove on Rebecca Sue Ellis. We were never anything but good friends. I DID lay a glove on Linda Beth Coggins, but you know this because I seem to remember you catching us one night in the back seat of Gary Don Wheeler's Buick.

I am particularly grieved at the news about Snodgrass Furniture. I'll always remember the Swedish-modern coffee table he sold us. I was NOT with Buddy White and A. C. DuBose that night, and I guess it won't hurt anything after all these years to tell you that Dorothy Chatham can vouch for it.

I didn't see James in Atlanta, but he sounded fine when I talked to his answering service.

I'm glad to hear the economic downturn in Fort Worth hasn't interrupted everybody's surgery. I don't know what people in Fort Worth would talk about if it weren't for surgery and niggers. It seems like only yesterday that all the men I knew in Texas didn't talk about anything but money and pussy. Well, times change.

Cordially, Jim Tom.

The Earlene with whom I had once fallen in love was a peppy cheerleader, a stacked little brunette, and I could have sworn she had a sense of humor back then. Maybe she did, but not after James Junior was born on the day TCU lost to Baylor 35 to 7 and I was in a press box instead of in the hospital, stupidly not realizing that my son would be born two weeks early.

I would see Earlene now and then when I went back to Fort Worth. We would have coffee or lunch. I had always tried to stay on good terms with the mother of my son because, for all I knew, she could still hit a mirror on a dresser from forty feet with a cold cream jar.

It was about six years into our marriage, and shortly before the divorce was final, that I found myself in a sports bar in Atlanta with a pocketful of expense money. It was easy to meet Janice Williams with a pocketful of expense money and a by-line in a national magazine. Janice was twenty-four at the time, a terminal Chi Omega but a fun-loving killerette with long brown hair and a slinky way of moving around. Janice had gone to college in Tuscaloosa, so we spent three months fucking and talking about Bear Bryant and then got married to celebrate one of Alabama's national championships. To this day, I don't know why it took Janice four years to discover I didn't come from old southern money.

The letter from Janice said:

Dear Jim Tom:

How in the world are you? It seems like ages since Bubba Dean and I ran into you at that Sugar Bowl party. I am sorry Bubba Dean acted so peculiar that night, but I think I have finally convinced him that he did not have a thing in the world to do with you and me breaking up. Goodness, was it that long ago? I often miss New York. I still hope to get Bubba Dean to bring me up there sometime so I can go back to some of the old haunts. We can certainly afford it. Bubba Dean is now president of his daddy's investment firm, which allows Mr. Carpenter to play more golf. I know Bubba Dean would like New York if he gave it a chance but he says he has not lost anything up there with all those Jews. I have said to him, Bubba Dean, the Jews don't bother you in New York if YOU don't bother THEM, but he says I don't know anything because I'm a woman.

Jim Tom, the real reason I am writing this letter is to ask you for a BIG FAVOR. Next fall Bubba Dean is going to be co-captain and speakers' chairman of the Birmingham Quarterback Club and it would be a big feather in his cap if he could get a famous sportswriter like you to come down here and speak to the club. They will pay your plane ticket and hotel and a fee of $4,000! Or you could stay with us. We have a wonderful home at Shoal Creek. I would love to be able to arrange this for Bubba Dean. He is too shy to ask you himself. Please think about it and let me hear from you. Love Ya!

Roll, Tide! Janice.

P.S.—Don't believe anything you read in the papers about Bubba Dean's daddy. Mr. Carpenter assures us that it is all a political plot and the government has no case at all.

I wrote back:

Dear Janice and Bubba Dean:

I'm flattered by the generous offer to speak to the Birmingham QB Club, but I'm afraid I'll be in Johannesburg, South Africa, at that time. I hear it's the best place to go to have the surgery done. It's nothing serious but something that needs to be taken care of. Good to hear from you.

Fondly, Jim Tom.

Priscilla Tinsely almost didn't qualify as an ex-wife. I was only married to her for eight months, which was how long it took for her to meet Russell Biddison and discover that he was a widower worth twenty million and would die a lot sooner than me. Priscilla was a sultry blonde, a fleshy, shapely, husky-voiced female animal whose sex appeal was effortless—it must have been ingrained at birth. She was in her late twenties when we met, divorced from a house builder, selling spots for an Atlanta radio station. I had first seen her in the mixed grillroom at Peach Farm Country Club during the week of the U.S. Open golf tournament. She was surrounded by four golf pros, all of whom I knew, and one of whom, laughing and blushing, motioned for me to come over and join the group. I wandered over as Priscilla was winding up a story of some kind, and the first words I ever heard her say were, "But I never sucked *that* dick."

Her letter said:

Hi, Darlin'—

I thought the old shit had finally bought it the other day. We were playing golf at the club. (Can you believe I have taken up the fucking game? I blame it all on those line-call cunts who bummed me out of tennis.) Russell tripped over his Pole Kat 2 putter. That long thing that looks like a Swahili's dick? He fell into a bunker. I was about to kick sand over his scrawny butt but he popped up cussing and swinging at imaginary demons, spry as ever. He said he was going to sue the maniac who invented the putter—it could cripple somebody. False alarm, in other words. He is 82 now, for Christ's sake.

I wish we still lived in Rome, but Russell got this crazy idea that foreigners were trying to kill him. He decided he hated foreigners who were trying to kill him more than he hated our Congressmen who were trying to take his money away from him. I guess I shouldn't complain. I got a lot of good young cock in Europe.

I look wonderful for a woman in her fucking forties, and Jesus, does that piss me off. If the old raisin doesn't die soon, my rich little clit won't have too many good years left.

I know you are not likely to come out to Palm Springs for any reason, but you *do* go to LA and you could call, you prick. We could have a merry old grope for old times' sake.

Love on you, Priscilla.

I was always careful with the manner in which I answered Priscilla's notes, which came on the average of two a year. I had to assume that Russell might read my replies, too. This time, I wrote back:

Dear Priscilla:

Thank you for the get-well card. It was only a fake heart attack. I was out of the hospital in no time. I'm sure it was brought on by my exasperation with foreigners and Congress. I think I'm going to have to stop watching the news on TV or even reading newspapers.

It's great to hear you are playing golf now. You were always a natural athlete, as I recall. Best to Russell.

Sincerely, Jim Tom.

Nell Woodruff was familiar with my marital history. In Fu's, I showed her the letters from my ex-wives. She didn't know any of the ladies personally, of course, but she had seen photographs of them and she had read other notes from them.

Nell said, "I guess Priscilla's not teaching Sunday School classes anymore—there's no mention of it."

32

WRITING AN ADVANCE COLUMN ON THE MASTERS WAS USU-
ally no chore, as long as you didn't worship too long in the
"cathedral of pines." You spoke briefly of the dogwood, jas-
mine, azaleas, the wisteria vine that crawled up the stately tree
guarding the oldest part of the clubhouse—an *Aphananthe aspera*, hackberry family—and then of Amen Corner, Rae's
Creek, Sarazen's double eagle, Hogan, Snead, Palmer, Nicklaus, and you were outta there. This time, it took me a little
longer because I kept being distracted by the depressing thought
of Travis Steed having a novel published.

Before Travis became Drone Four under Bryce Wilcox, he
was a guy who had been nothing but an embarrassingly wordy
feature writer who passed himself off as a sensitive, caring,
probing individual. He was a man who often referred to himself, in all seriousness, as "this little boy from Delaware." He
would pound the reader with literary references and his unend-
ing search for the meaning of things, even in a story about a
middleweight prizefighter, who would not even have read a
comic strip unless it was printed in Spanish. Travis would
devote eight paragraphs at the top to a description of the prizefighter's eyebrows and how they hinted at something boiling
within the man's soul. There was something about the thick-
ness of the eyebrows, Travis would write, and the way they
reminded him of the dark ripples in a Steinbeck river. Didn't
they suggest an illumination of the spirit? And what of the
perfect curves of the eyebrows, one equidistant from the other,
as in the structure of a Henry James short story? Didn't they
signal an incalculable resolve? This man, this fighter, was
going to lift himself out of the life into which he had been born
and seek with his fists the things from society that other men
had lost and found there.

Travis Steed wasn't my kind of writer. If I ever described an
athlete's eyebrows, which I never had, I would be prone to say

they were on his *face* and appeared to be located, quite conveniently, just above his eyes.

I would wait with trembling for the publication of *Is That You, Durwood?* knowing Travis would spend the first five pages rambling on about the land, the haunting land, the ruthless land, the triumphant land, the land that bred an indisputable melancholy as you crossed the Delaware Memorial Bridge and headed south on I-95.

But Travis Steed was getting a novel published and I was only going to another sports event.

33

SOME PEOPLE HAVE THE MISTAKEN IMPRESSION THAT THE MASters is all about golf. That's wrong. The Masters is only about golf in Sunday's final round when the leaders reach the tenth tee and the usual unruly things begin to happen on the last nine holes. Before this, for four or five days, the Masters is about socializing under the trees on the lush green veranda of the Augusta National Golf Club, eating country ham and peach cobbler in the simplistic but cozy clubhouse, keeping an eye out for scabs and sores on all of the teenage hookers who have come to town to terrorize every public bar, and dropping in on some of the cocktail parties and cookouts that are held in all of the antebellum mansions that have been rented for the week.

One thing is true. The Masters is the first golf tournament of the year that matters to the press. In this sense, it's one of only four golf tournaments a year that matters to the press.

The Masters is one of the game's four major championships, although, curiously, it isn't the championship of anything, it is merely the most original and exclusive invitation tournament in the world. A golfer has to be somebody, past or present, to receive an invitation. The other three majors are the championships of something. The U.S. Open, always held in June, is the championship of the United States Golf Association, the British Open, always held in July, is the championship of the

Royal & Ancient Golf Society, and the PGA, always held in August, is the championship of the Professional Golfers Association of America.

These are the four big titles that the touring pro would like most to win, just once, for the financial opportunities that go along with winning a major are quite lucrative. Besides that, his name will enter the history books as someone more distinguished than all of the logo-clods who can't win anything more important than a Savings & Loan Classic, a Junk Food Open, or any of those other TV-shilled, corporate-sponsored events on the wearying PGA Tour that can put anyone with a quality education straight to sleep.

I was giving Jeannie Slay a crash course in the Masters—and pro golf—at the bar of the Magnolia Inn on Wednesday evening in Augusta. We had both arrived that day and had met in the towering, lecture-hall press center that borders the first fairway as we were being issued our credentials.

A Masters credential is a badge with your name on it that entitles you to enter the clubhouse, where nobody is admitted but contestants, press, and Augusta National members, who are recognizable by their green blazers. It also entitles you to go out on the sacred, flowery, pine-infested, immaculately kept golf course without being arrested, and to loll around on the veranda, standing under the *Aphananthe aspera* or the two huge water oaks with captains of industry, agents, managers, equipment salesmen, executives of golf organizations, famous contestants, family members of famous contestants, and colleagues among the working press. A Masters credential with clubhouse-veranda-golf course privileges is more valuable than a lung or kidney. Most of the forty thousand people who attend the Masters every year have never been inside the clubhouse or inside the ropes that protect the veranda from the rabble. Your average golf fan can buy a ticket to watch the practice rounds on Monday, Tuesday, and Wednesday, but for the seventy-two holes of the tournament proper, the rounds that are played on Thursday, Friday, Saturday, and Sunday, there are posses of Pinkertons around to make sure nobody is on the premises but season ticket holders and individuals with legitimate reasons to be there. A season ticket holder to the Masters is somebody who has always been one, who will never die. The Masters is the only golf tournament that is sold out every year. It is the toughest ticket in sports. I liked this about the tournament. People knew it was useless to ask me for a ticket to the Masters. Those people who didn't know it was useless and asked me got laughed at. I enjoyed explaining to people that there was no such thing as a Masters ticket.

Of course, I *could* get my hands on a clubhouse badge in a dire emergency, but I wasn't about to tell anyone how, not even Jeannie.

"Don't lose your badge," I said to Jeannie in the bar at the Magnolia Inn. "That's the first rule of the Masters."

"I won't lose my badge," she said.

"Where is it now?"

"In my purse."

"Show me."

She opened her purse and showed me her badge.

"Don't lose it."

"I won't lose my fucking badge," she said.

She put it back in her purse.

"Watch your purse," I said.

"I'll watch my purse."

"Never stand too close to a bumpkin in the gallery," I cautioned. "He'll rip it off, literally. He'll rip it off your sweater or jacket. I mean it."

"Let's say I lose my badge," she said.

"Don't."

"What would happen? I couldn't go to the press center, show my ID, and get another one? They throw me out? They arrest the *Los Angeles Times*?"

"You could get another badge," I said. "After you argue your case before the Supreme Court. Just don't lose it."

"I won't lose it! Jesus! It's just a golf tournament."

"No, it's not," I said. "It's the Masters."

I also gave Jeannie a crash history course in Augusta living. The Magnolia Inn, where I had insisted we stay, was a four-story hotel in an old neighborhood only two miles from the Augusta National Golf Club. It had been remodeled, redecorated, and strenuously overhauled in the past couple of years, and it now was as decent a place to stay as anywhere else during the Masters; at least it would be until the weekend when the big rectangular bar off the lobby would be overrun by drawling, intrusive fans who'd want to tell you about the shot they saw Jack Nicklaus hit at the third hole, even though Jack was no longer a threat to win the Masters—his glory days were behind him, resting back there with all of the cover stories I had written about him.

I had first stayed at the Magnolia Inn more than twenty-five years ago. Back then, your room would be one with the windowpanes shattered and pigeons sharing the dresser with you. The water groaned out of the faucet a dull orange. The mattress would have a gaping hole burned out of it. And the ceiling fixture would go off when you turned it on. The hotel had been known as the Confederacy's revenge on the Yankee press. But this hadn't made it any different from any other hotel in town. Augusta, Georgia, might have been the home of the Masters, and Bobby Jones might have built his dream course there, and the town might have been a well-regarded spa back around the turn of the century, but Fort Gordon had long been on the outskirts of the city and Augusta was still retaining the ambiance of an old army town.

I asked Jeannie if she would like to go downtown some night and see a stripper dance with a boa constrictor. No thank you, she said.

Did she care for a tattoo?

Not just yet, she said.

I explained that for a few years the derelict hotels had encouraged various members of the visiting press to get together in groups and rent private homes for the week of the tournament, just like the captains of industry or the Arnold Palmers. You might have to put up with alarming portraits on the walls, gruesome furniture, and a desperate search for whatever plate, saucer, or kitchen utensil you were looking for, but you would enjoy water coming out of the shower that was the color of water, and you would have shelter from the pigeons.

"Why is the Masters here?" she asked, intelligently.

"Bobby Jones couldn't find the land he could afford in Atlanta," I said. "He found it here—an old nursery. He tried to recreate Sunningdale, his favorite course overseas—it's in a suburb of London. He outdid it, is what he did, but first he had to reverse the nines. Not many people know it, but in the first Masters in 1934, the front nine was the back nine. Jones then realized the front nine was more dramatic and ought to be the finishing nine. Four holes, ten through thirteen, are probably the greatest stretch of holes in golf. Not probably. They are."

"Why?"

"Scenery . . . danger . . . shot quality . . . history. If you fancy clichés, you can call it Amen Corner. That's the nickname for ten through thirteen. Herb Wind, a sportswriter, gave Amen Corner its name. Grantland Rice gave the Masters its name."

"What's your contribution, old-timer?"

"I might have been the first guy who said the Magnolia Inn was the Confederacy's revenge on the Yankee press."

"Thanks for the column." Jeannie smiled.

"Xerox me a copy. What did Jeannie Slay mean by this?" She looked confused.

"Old joke," I said. "Guy's stuck for a column one day so he tore Red Smith off the wire and put a line on top of it—what did Red Smith mean by this?"

"It'll grow on me," Jeannie said.

"The joke?"

"Journalism."

34

JEANNIE WAS HAVING THE BELUGA OF CHEESEBURGER AT THE bar and I was having the noisettes of BLT when some of the other writers came straggling in. Some came from the press center where they had been punching out advances and columns, others came from sleaze bars where they had been checking out the debutantes, and still others came from Calcutta auctions, which is to say private homes where the names of contestants were raffled off to drunken bidders. I had once participated in the Calcuttas, but every time I would buy a Jack Nicklaus or a Seve Ballesteros, it would be a year when a logo-clod would win the Masters, and every time I would buy two or three logo-clods, at a bargain price, it would be a year when Jack Nicklaus or Seve Ballesteros would win. I also used to devote a night or two to a tour of the sleaze bars, but this was back when you could find some soft country music instead of a heavy metal reenactment of Gettysburg, and long before you needed to worry about all of the diseases that might be lurking in every cocktail glass. Now, I never left the premises of the Magnolia Inn, except to go to the golf course in the daytime. Friends said I was aging gracefully.

Richie Pace, Dub Fricker, and our own Cloyce Windham were among the writers who joined Jeannie and me at the bar. Other writers, in groups of threes and fours, were spread out around the bar. Richie and Dub had patched up their spat from the Final Four and seemed pleased to have been immortalized in my column, although Richie wasn't altogether thrilled at my description of his ego being so large it made midtown Manhattan look like Nogales.

"People forget I have a typewriter, too," he said at the bar, a warning to me to be on the lookout for some future three-dot jolt in his Sunday column.

Mocking Richie's style, Dub Fricker said, "In a town called New York, there's a team called the Mets, and they play a game called baseball."

Richie glared at him, and said, "The Gators won the toss and elected to receive."

Cloyce Windham had been telling the bartender to start the turn with his left shoulder and keep his right foot square and never try to hit a six-iron more than 145 yards, as Hogan recommended, but now Cloyce suggested we all put twenty dollars in the pot and pick a player who would finish best in the Masters, winner take all.

"Good idea," said Richie. "I hate golf. Anything to make it interesting."

"If you hate golf, why are you here?" Jeannie asked.

"That's why I'm here," Richie said, looking around as if to ask how anyone could fail to understand that.

Cloyce Windham didn't believe that Richie or anyone else could hate golf. Golf was life. His life, anyhow. Cloyce was now in his sixties and had never thought about anything, talked about anything, written anything, or read anything that didn't pertain to golf in his whole tweed-suit, golf-playing life. He had written about golf for *The New Yorker* and *Sports Illustrated* before he had become *SM*'s golf writer. He had personally known Jones, Hagen, Snead, Hogan, Nelson, Demaret. He had been going to the Masters and all of the other majors for forty years. He had written books about golf courses, golf heroes, and golf instruction. He had even written a memoir about his life around golf twenty years ago, a book titled *Golf Between the Ears*, which was still available in paperback and was held up as a classic among people who worried about the hip turn and the overseeding of bent grass.

Earlier in the day, I had run into Cloyce in the press center and he had immediately said, "I don't quite know why they changed the slope of the green at thirteen. Drainage, I suppose, but wasn't it more interesting when they could play to the flag? The new mound at fifteen helps. Defines the tee shot. By the way, I went around the front nine with Bobby Joe Grooves today. Lazy hands, if you ask me."

Cloyce only admired golfers who had a "quiet grip," as he often said in his stories.

I never failed to read a Cloyce Windham story, but I sometimes wondered if anybody else did, outside of Bryce Wilcox and a few other faithful golf sickies. I frankly read them to be astonished at what the magazine would publish.

Cloyce had no sense of line count, couldn't write to fit if his life or seven-wood depended on it, and didn't even try to write to fit—"A writer should be allowed to clear his throat," he would say.

So Cloyce would invariably write three thousand words on a tournament when the layout called for two thousand words, and since he was impossible to edit at the top, a drone would have to jump in at the bottom and somehow get the name of the winner in the story along with a hint of how and why the winner might have won. The story would then come out reading as if it had been co-written by a historian back around 1927 and an AP man dictating the outbreak of a war by telephone.

Often, Cloyce would ramble on for fifteen hundred words, or six pages of copy, before he would get around to mentioning the event he was covering, no matter how captivating the event had been or how suspensefully someone might have won it.

Around the office, everybody had a favorite Cloyce Windham lead. Some liked his essay on slow play the year Nicklaus dramatically captured his sixth Masters. Others liked his reflections on Charles Dickens the year Nick Faldo won a British Open. My own favorite went back to Curtis Strange winning a U.S. Open in heroic fashion. Cloyce's memorable epic began:

"Ben Hogan was born on Aug. 13, 1912, and this is an important date indeed for those of us so vitally interested in clubhead speed and other rhythms of the golf swing. I cannot forget the first time I saw Hogan's clubhead (a five-iron, I believe, on the 16th at Merion in 1950) travel through the shot with such irresistible speed that it went far past the ball before it came up in that lovely, unforgettable arc which so separated Ben from all others, except, perhaps, Bob Jones."

Where was Curtis Strange and the U.S. Open? Forty-two paragraphs down. I counted.

But Cloyce Windham was golf and we were all honored to be in his presence, even if his tweed suit smelled like a stable.

35

IN A SERIES OF COIN FLIPS, RICHIE PACE GOT FIRST CHOICE IN the betting pool and chose Wilbur Lovey, the big blond, long-hitting Australian lout. We all scoffed at Richie's selection. Wilbur Lovey was popular with the galleries because of his booming, 300-yard tee shots and the golden hair that hung down his neck, but he had never won a big championship and had consistently shown a tendency to collapse under pressure. In fact, the Australian press, which had once hailed him as a national treasure, had now nicknamed him "Wilting Matilda."

"The lout is a choking dog," I said to Richie.

"He's due," said Richie.

"He's been due for five years."

"This is his year."

"Based on what?"

"His hair is longer."

Jeannie went next and took Mark Peel, the leading money winner, but that wasn't her logic. Her logic was that Mark Peel was slender and looked good in his clothes.

"Bad choice," I said.

"Why?" Jeannie said. "He wins."

"He wins Dorals. He doesn't have the heart for a major. He doesn't have the game for Augusta. Too many sidehill lies, and the greens are slicker than cum on a gold tooth."

"That fast, huh?"

"I'll tell you what Mark Peel likes to do for fun. Watch his kids turn over glasses of milk in Marriott dining rooms."

"I hate my pick," Jeannie said.

Dub Fricker went with a proven winner, Wiley Sullins. Wiley was a big, muscular redneck from east Texas who had played football and golf at Rice, though how he had managed to get into a fine academic school like Rice was something of a riddle. Wiley wore a wide-brimmed straw hat and was well liked by the press because of his rural humor. Wiley had almost won the Masters a couple of times, and it was Wiley who had come into the interview area a year ago and told all of us he had figured out why his alma mater, Rice, wasn't any good in football anymore—niggers didn't want to be astronauts.

We waited forever for Cloyce Windham to study a pairings sheet for Thursday's first round. He was giving careful thought to his selection. None of us wanted to take a Ballesteros, Faldo, Strange, Crenshaw, or Norman. The marquee names hadn't won anything big in three years—they were too rich, too interested in picking up fifty grand in corporate outings.

Cloyce settled on Bohn Maggard, a handsome stylist, a proven quantity, maybe the next great player, but a streaky fellow whose temper often got the best of him.

"Quietest grip on the tour," Cloyce announced.

"You can have him," said Richie Pace. "One bad bounce and he's down the road."

"Ah, yes," said Cloyce, sipping his vodka martini. "No game affords a greater scope for folly than golf."

"What the fuck does that mean?" Richie wanted to know.

Cloyce tactfully said, "It means, dear boy, that golf, like no other game, can foolishly impair the properly concentrated mind."

"I have no quarrel with that," Richie said, giving me a look.

With last choice, I took Bobby Joe Grooves.

I explained that I wasn't taking Bobby Joe Grooves because I wanted to root for a logo-clod, but I had a hunch that this might be a year for another logo-clod to win, and Bobby Joe Grooves was king of the logo-clods, lazy hands or not.

Bobby Joe's golf bag advertised Creel's Lite Beer, the sleeves of his golf shirts advertised Mid-Life Insurance, the pocket of his golf shirts advertised Baker's Car Rental, and his visor advertised Hal's Prime Steaks. He became even more unsightly when you looked at his pencil-thin mustache, vacant eyes, pouting mouth, and baggy slacks. As for his personality, he went back and forth between being the dullest interview on the golf tour and that rare combination of someone who's loud and wrong at the same time.

"Just what we need Sunday night," Dub Fricker said.

"I'm only out here to make a living for my family," Richie said, quoting Bobby Joe Grooves.

"The Masters is just another golf tournament," Dub said, quoting him again.

"Is that what he says?" Jeannie said to me.

"Uh-huh," I said, nodding, "but normally, he's not that interesting."

36

SITTING AROUND WAS AN ART THAT MAY HAVE BEEN POPU-
larized by novelists with writer's block, but I liked to think I
had helped refine it over many blissful years on the veranda at
the Masters.

You can't just sit around anywhere, of course, and expect it
to be a pleasant experience. Nobody ever enjoyed sitting
around a hospital, loading dock, funeral home, or textile mill.
I would even suggest that you couldn't enjoy sitting around in
some lady's apartment if you didn't know exactly where her
husband was.

A friend of mine once said the trouble with sitting around
was you never knew when it was over. That wasn't true at the
Masters. Sitting around was over on Sunday afternoon when
the contenders reached the back nine, as I have stated. That's
when the tournament would be won or lost, and you would find
it necessary to go to the geezer-codger typewriter, or whatever
machine you used, and try to make sense of it.

But unless you worked for a daily paper, you got to sit
around a lot on Thursday, Friday, and Saturday, eating, drinking, smoking, chatting, reminiscing, not caring who was doing
what on the golf course or on the big scoreboards where numbers were going up and coming down continuously. For me,
nothing mattered till Sunday night deadline.

At this Masters, my sitting around began the same way it
always had. Breakfast upstairs in the grillroom of the oldest
part of the clubhouse. Country ham, red-eye gravy, eggs over,
biscuits, coffee, newspapers. Same old table by the window
that looked out on the wisteria vine creeping up the huge *Aphananthe aspera* and beyond it to the pines and hills of the golf
course.

Then, more coffee on the balcony outside the grillroom,
once the press room for Granny Rice and the boys. Visits with
players coming and going, writers coming and going, green

blazers coming and going. Some solitude and the occasional glance down on the veranda to wonder what unlucky contestant had married that speed-trap bimbo with the prisoner-taking eyes.

Eventually, it would be time to move down to the veranda proper. Lunch. Tea and snacks later on. The whiskey drinking would start around 4:30. In the meantime, I would keep watching the numbers on the scoreboard and interpreting the roars from out on the golf course—a mammoth roar that lingered could only be Nicklaus, Watson, or Ballesteros doing something wonderful. Birdie at two if it came from that direction. Birdie or eagle at fifteen if it came from another direction. A piddling roar was meaningless. Bobby Joe Grooves could have saved a par. Arnold Palmer could have hitched up his trousers.

As a younger man, I had walked the course countless times, following Arnold, Jack, some relic of the past, some personal friend on the tour. There was a definite path to take, which I mapped out for the newcomer, Jeannie Slay. Up the right side of the fairway at the first hole, down the right side of No. 2, but not all the way. Cut through the pines to the third green and fourth tee. Skip No. 5, which runs along the back side of the property, along a ridge. You only have to come back down the hill again. There's a joke that Augusta has a seventeen-hole golf course—nobody goes to the fifth hole, not even contestants. From the fourth tee, you go to the sixth green, then up the seventh fairway. Skip No. 8, uphill all the way, because the ninth comes back to the clubhouse. Down the right side of the decorative tenth, a serious cathedral of pines. Move along the right side of the eleventh. Peer over at the dangerous twelfth, toughest par three in the world. Move along the right side of the gambling thirteenth, genuflecting at the bank of azaleas. Skip No. 14, a dreary but rugged par four, because the fifteenth comes back to you. Watch the shots over the dyed-blue ponds at fifteen and sixteen. Now trudge to the clubhouse or press center to catch the finish on TV.

On Thursday, I was sitting on the veranda when Wilbur Lovey finished with a 66, six under par, and took the first round lead by three strokes. Everybody caught his press conference but me. I knew he would call every writer "pard" and want to talk about the golf course he was designing on a lava bed in Hawaii.

Richie Pace passed by my table on the veranda and said, "My guy could have had a 59. He missed six putts under ten feet."

"You'll have to be nimble on Sunday," I said, "to step over his vomit."

Jeannie sat with me for a while and asked questions. Golf wasn't her strength.

"What's a controlled fade?" she asked.

"A slice that's been to church," I grinned.

She wrote something in her spiral notebook.

"A slice is a thing that goes over that way?" she gestured.

"Right."

"And a hook goes this way?"

"Usually very quickly. You can't talk to a hook."

"What do you mean?"

"A hook has overspin. It goes left to left—and when it lands, it looks around for the worst possible place to stop. If a hook can't find a really rotten place to wind up, it keeps rolling till it does."

"A hook has a *mind*?"

"No, it's just an evil, psychotic piece of shit that hates golfers. With a slice, you can say, 'Get down, baby, whoa,' and it might do that, but when you hit a hook, all you can say is, 'That's right, bitch, hook some more.' Your weekend golfer hits hooks and slices. The touring pro thinks he only hits draws and fades. Hogan said he would rather let a cobra crawl around inside his shirt than hit a hook."

"In his press conference, Wilbur Lovey said he overpured it on twelve. What's that?"

"A touring pro never hits a bad shot, never makes a mistake. Was he in the back bunker?"

"Yes."

"He's trying to say he hit too good a shot—he overpured it. But he probably had too much club. Put a water lock on it. Pros three-putt, it's the unfair pace of the greens. If they're not stiff, an idiot set the pins. If they miss a fairway, they got a bad bounce or hit a sprinkler head. Most of their poor iron shots

come from bad lies. They're in a divot, they had a flyer, there
was nothing under the ball but crust. Very few of the pricks
ever finish college, and very few of them ever went to class
when they were *in* college, but once they get on the tour,
they're brain surgeons.''

"Mark Peel had a 69," Jeannie was happy to report.

"I know. He three-putted one and birdied eight on the front.
He reached thirteen and fifteen in two, got his birdies, and he
birdied seventeen. Saved a good par at fourteen."

"How do you know all that? You haven't been off the veranda."

"I have a scoreboard," I said. "I know which way the
wind's blowing. I know how fast the greens are. I know where
they put the pins every day. I have a wristwatch. It took a long
time for his score to up on fourteen."

"What's Bobby Joe Grooves doing?"

"He's one-over through twelve," I said, glancing at the
scoreboard. "But he can get in with a 71. He can reach thirteen
and fifteen today with a five-iron—he's stronger than laundry."

"He'll be five shots back. No good, huh?"

I said, "Jeannie, I'm only going to tell you this one more
time. The tournament hasn't started yet."

"I'm sunburned," she said, looking at her pink shoulders
and arms under the shade of the umbrella at my table.

"I'm not," I said, motioning to a waiter.

37

THE DANGERS OF SITTING AROUND, AT THE MASTERS OR ANY
other golf tournament, are numerous, for there are well-
meaning but lacerating bores on all sides of you, always ready
to pounce.

At breakfast on Friday morning, a radio man from somewhere in North Carolina insisted on taking me through Bohn
Maggard's back nine of the day before, shot by shot, hole by

hole. Bohn Maggard had shot an even-par 72, so it wasn't as if I was hearing about Hogan's 67 at Oakland Hills. The man also had a few things to say about Bobby Joe Grooves' five-iron to the fifteenth, which had skipped across the water after he thinned it out of a divot.

Out on the balcony that morning, I then was forced to listen to a golf architect go on at length about C-115 decline, the newest fad in bent-green disease. I knew nothing of agronomy and nothing of course maintenance, or cared. The only three words I knew were overseed, underseed, and verticut, and I wasn't entirely sure why or when they were necessary. Grass was either long or short in places, it nearly always grew back, and most of it was green. That's what I knew about maintenance.

It was only a wild guess, but I said to the architect that maybe a bent green wouldn't catch C-115 decline if it weren't mowed so short.

"You know, you may have something," he said.

A little later on, down on the veranda, I was assaulted by an equipment man and heard about wedges with sixty-degree loft angles and five degrees of bounce, about shorter-than-normal bore-through hosels, narrower flanges, flatter soles, U-grooves with investment casts, perimeter weighting, medium-square toes, melanite finishes, titanium shafts, and dyadic something-or-others.

"That's all pretty interesting," I yawned. "What do you know about mild steel?"

"Do what?"

"Mild steel. They're talking about it over there." I pointed to a group of gentlemen I'd never seen before.

He looked concerned.

"Better listen in," he said, and scurried away.

Cloyce Windham trapped me and described in great length how Nicklaus had mastered the chop shot out of thick, high grass. By gripping the club lower and applying constant pressure on the grip, Jack was accelerating the clubhead instead of relying solely on gravity, you see?

"I'm so relieved," I said.

The rest of Friday and Saturday passed without much happening in the tournament. The course was playing tough because of the slick greens—they're rolling at 10.5, Cloyce had said with a look of pandemonium. Wilbur Lovey followed up his opening 66 with rounds of 73-72, but he held the 54-hole lead at 211, five under par, by four strokes over Bohn Maggard and Bobby Joe Grooves. Wiley Sullins was six strokes back, but he was "cognint of the fack," as he said in his press conference, that he wasn't out of it, not if he could "scorch the fucker" with a low round on Sunday, get to the house, and let everybody behind him shit a big old turd.

Inconveniently for Jeannie, Mark Peel was out of it. On Saturday, he blew to a 78, but at least this gave Jeannie a column in which she compared him with many of history's choking dogs, from the Spanish Armada to Michael Dukakis.

With a possible column interest in Bobby Joe Grooves, I thought I'd better make an effort to talk to him Saturday afternoon. I found him in the players' dining area just off the downstairs locker room. He was alone at a table, having a lite beer, staring off into space.

Like a lacerating bore, it is the prerogative of a member of the press to sit down uninvited with a touring pro at a tournament, particularly if he's in contention.

"Mind if I talk to you a few minutes, Bobby Joe?" I said, politely, sliding into a chair with a J & B and water.

"I gotta go practice," he said.

"This won't take long," I smiled.

We knew each other slightly.

"You're in a good position," I said. "Wilbur goes under the ether, Bohn doesn't make a move, you're in there."

"Fuckin' greens," he said. "I ought to be twelve under. How 'bout thirteen? Is that a pile of shit? I just looked at the fuckin' ball, it went fifteen feet past. They ought to bulldoze this fuckin' place."

"You don't like the Masters?"

"Piss on the Masters."

"Be nice to win it."

"You guys write about the majors all the time. You don't have to play in 'em."

"I've played the course. I love it."

"What do you do when you're above the cup on sixteen?"

"Three-putt."

"You better fuckin' believe it. People don't want to watch that."

"Bobby Jones thought you ought to be punished for being long."

"Fuck Bobby Jones. He wasn't out here trying to make a living for his family."

"Lot of history around here."

"Fuck history."

"Fuck Ben Hogan, too?"

"Shit," he said. "They talk about how good Hogan was. I'd like to see what he'd do out here *today*. We got a hundred and fifty guys on the tour who could bring Hogan's ass."

"You don't actually believe that, do you?"

"I said it, didn't I?"

"What's important to you, Bobby Joe?"

"Where?"

"In golf."

"Money list," he said. "That's what you sportswriter assholes can't understand. Put me up there on the money list, pal. You can have all that other shit."

"You don't care if you never win a major?"

"Fuck majors, man. Majors are for the press. You know the only thing good about the U.S. Open? The fuckin' money, pal."

"How many times have you gone to the British Open?"

"Once. One time in that fuckin' zoo. You won't catch my ass over there again. It's campin' out, man. My fuckin' hotel room didn't even have a shower!"

"I better let you go practice," I said, getting up. "Good luck tomorrow."

"I don't need luck," Bobby Joe said. "I need to get my putter out of the shithouse, is all. If I make some putts tomorrow, you can stick a fork in these other fuckers—they're done."

38

JEANNIE DIDN'T LOSE HER BADGE TILL SATURDAY NIGHT.

She discovered it was gone shortly after she met me in the bar at the Magnolia Inn. I had been at the bar for two hours alone, long enough to put five J & B's down my neck and poke around at the medallions of fried catfish I'd ordered for a snack. I had gone straight to the bar from the course while all of the ink-stained wretches plugged away at their deadlines. Actually, I was only alone at the bar part of the time. A red-faced man in a Schlitz cap sought me out to inform me that Arnold Palmer was the greatest American since Dwight Eisenhower. Arnold had autographed his cap. "Arnold's good about that," I had said to the man. "You bet he is," he replied. "I ain't hardly nobody at all." A stoop-shouldered man in an alpaca sweater and railroad shoes sought me out to tell me how the gold graphite shaft had put the sunshine back in his life, although it might have been responsible for his recent divorce.

When Jeannie took her seat on the bar stool, I didn't see the badge on her hip, where she had been wearing it. I asked where her badge was. She felt around and said, "Uh-oh."

After feeling around some more on her blouse and skirt, she emptied her purse out on the bar. No badge.

"Great," I said, sarcastically. "I had Saturday in the pool."

"I had it when I left the course," she said. "I had it in the car."

"Who came back in the car with you?"

"I came alone."

"Did you go to your room before you came in here?"

"No."

"Was there anybody on the elevator with you?"

"Two or three fat people. They were talking about Auburn football."

"That's it," I said.

"Goddamn it," Jeannie moaned. She felt around on her blouse and skirt again, and looked around on the floor.

"I started to tell you yesterday to take the badge off your hip," I said. "You wear your goddamn badge over your heart, like I do mine. You always know it's there, out of the corner of your eye."

"Where is *your* badge now?" she asked.

"Right here in my pocket. You take it off at night, but you don't leave it in your hotel room when you go to dinner. The maids will steal it. I told you not to stand too close to anybody, didn't I? Especially a fat guy from Auburn."

"Maybe it fell off in the car."

"It's not in the car," I said. "The Auburn guy got it on the elevator. He stood next to you, right?"

Jeannie looked around at the other customers in the bar. "Naturally, I don't see him anywhere."

"Of course not," I said. "He's having dinner at Hardee's, celebrating. He'll change the name, be on the veranda tomorrow."

Richie Pace wandered in, moved up to the bar with us.

"Guess what?" I said. "Jeannie's lost her badge."

"Bodges?" said Richie. "We ain't got no stinkin' bodges."

Jeannie said, "Alfonso Bedoya. Don't fuck with me on movies, Richie."

She turned to me. "You're enjoying this, aren't you?"

"No, it's too stupid to be funny."

"*I'm* stupid because some asshole stole my badge?"

"It was careless."

"You've never lost anything, have you?"

"Never," I said emphatically. "I've never lost a credential, passport, driver's license, credit card, moneyclip. Nothing important. It's too inconvenient."

"What'll we do?"

"*We?*"

"I'll go to the course with you tomorrow. You'll help me get another credential."

"They won't let you in. They'll ask to see your badge at the gate. You're history. Archives, as my son would say."

"I can't get in the golf course?"

"No."

"I can't tell the guard my badge got stolen and I have to go to the press room to get another one?"

I laughed. "He'll say, 'Honey, I've heard that one before.' And he has—about five hundred times."

"You're saying I can't go to the tournament tomorrow?"

"You can watch it on TV in your room."

"This is bullshit," Jeannie said.

We were interrupted by a man in a rain hat and faded pink golf shirt with the emblem of Swamp Creek Country Club on it.

"Jim Tom Pinch," he said.

"Guilty," I said.

"You probably don't remember me," he said.

"You're probably right."

"Hell, no reason why you should—we ain't never met."

"What can I do for you?"

"Not a damn thing," he said. "It's what I can do for you."

"What would that be?"

"I got the winner for you. Who it is, is Bohn Maggard."

"He's right there," I said.

"Want to know why?"

"Why?"

"Me."

"You?"

"I've taught that kid everthing he knows about the golf swing. Hell, I give him the flashlight theory. Naw, he was out there on the range at our club one day, and I seen what he was doing, and I told him about the flashlight. Boy, he's got it on a string now."

I wasn't about to ask the man about the flashlight theory, but Richie Pace couldn't resist.

The man took a golf stance, as if he was addressing an imaginary ball.

"The flashlight's in your chest," he said. "The beam of the flashlight shines down on the right half of the ball. You look at that beam, you follow it with your right eye, and you hit through that beam. That's all there is to it."

"Bohn Maggard," said Richie. "Flashlight guy."

"You betcha," said the man in the rain hat. "That flash-light's right there in his chest, where I put it. Yes, sir."

"Thank you," I said, turning away.

Mercifully, the man left us and returned to his own side of the bar.

Jeannie left the bar for ten minutes, to look for her badge in her car.

"You weren't wrong about her badge," Richie said. "You knew she'd lose it before the week was over. I knew it. Dub knew it. They knew it in Lisbon."

"I know," I sighed. "I was wrong about something once, but it's been so long ago, I can't remember what it was."

When Jeannie returned, badgeless, as I expected, I made a speech.

"You don't lose your credential," I said. "You NEVER lose your credential. You don't lose it at the Super Bowl, you don't lose it at the World Series, you don't lose it at Wimble-don, you don't lose it at the Masters. You don't lose it ANYWHERE—it's too much fucking trouble."

There were tears of anger in Jeannie's eyes.

She had just walked up the dirt path through the woods from Keenan Stadium where the Tar Heels had lost a heartbreaker to Duke. This self-sufficient, industrious young woman from a fine old family in Winston-Salem had been beaten out for homecoming queen by a listless, vapid Chi Omega. Men pre-ferred listless and vapid beauties over a girl who bought her own beer at Spanky's, who liked her privacy as she read the newspapers every morning in the Carolina Coffee Shop. Her date had stood her up at The Arboretum. Should she throw herself down The Old Well on the campus at Chapel Hill or bang her head against Silent Sam, the statue of the Confederate soldier? Life sucked.

"Here," I said, taking a badge out of my pocket. I handed the badge to Jeannie, a badge with the name of "Mrs. Jim Tom Pinch" on it.

It was a clubhouse guest badge. I had once brought Janice to the Masters. I no longer had a wife but they didn't know this at the Masters, so I still picked up a badge for my wife every year. It was always good to have a spare in case of an emergency, like this. Granted, there were years when "Mrs. Jim Tom Pinch" had been an Augusta cocktail waitress—a Kitty, Diana, or Vikki—but those years were as far back in the past as Janice.

I said to Jeannie, "This will get you in tomorrow. I'll talk you past Tiny on the door of the press center. We'll get you another press badge."

Tiny was the 300-pound cop who had been keeping non-writers out of the press room at Augusta for twenty years. Tiny did his job well. The Masters wasn't like the U.S. Open or the PGA, where volunteer club members allowed their adolescent sons, daughters, nieces, and nephews to go romping through the press tent. I had known Tiny a long time and he knew me, or Jeannie would still be in trouble.

Jeannie looked at the guest badge for "Mrs. Jim Tom Pinch."

"You bastard," she said. "You've had this in your pocket all night."

"All week," I said.

"I don't think I like you anymore."

"You like that badge, though, don't you?"

"I *do* appreciate it, yes."

"Give it back to me."

"*What*?"

"I'll keep it for you till tomorrow morning. I don't want you to lose it before the night's over."

Jeannie slammed the badge down on the bar. I put it back in my pocket. "What are you drinking?" I said. "I've got a check going."

"I'm sure they won't serve me," she said with a look. "I don't have a badge."

39

UPSTAIRS AT MY TABLE IN THE AUGUSTA NATIONAL CLUB-house on Sunday morning, I was about to embark on my eggs, country ham, red-eye gravy, and biscuits when Sylvester, one of the waiters, called me to the phone. As I went to the phone, I told Sylvester not to let the wisteria vine grow while I was gone, and if an equipment salesman or course designer tried to sit at my table, kill him. I thought the call might be from Bryce Wilcox, stupidly suggesting I get my column in before I knew who won the Masters, but it was from James Junior. My son was in Athens but he said he could be in Augusta by noon if I would leave a clubhouse badge for him at the main gate. I said, "James, if you were already in town and handcuffed to me, I might be able to get you a badge, but you and I both know the badge is not for you, it's for some buddy of yours, and you're not going to trick me again." Bummer, he said.

I said, "Where the hell were you at the Final Four?"

"Aw, man, I was ragged out. I'd made a donut on this economics quiz, and the professor said I could take it again, so I had to study."

"How are you?"

"Everything's cool," he said. "Dad, thanks for the jing, I really appreciate it. Dad, you know what? I think I've found something I'm really interested in. Might change my major."

"You're supposed to be close to getting a business degree."

"I know, man, but I started thinking about it. I mean, like, what happens? I get a business degree and I go to work for this company. I'm a nine-to-five dude, right? The rest of my life."

"That's what most people do, James."

"You don't."

"I chose a different kind of profession, but I work hard at it. I may not work nine to five, but I work a lot of times when I don't want to. Nights, holidays, that kind of thing. I travel a lot

155

when I don't want to, as you must surely know by now. It's the nature of the business I chose."

"I don't know, man. I just can't see me in a suit and tie, doing that nine-to-five gig. Pushing paper. Some zipperhead telling me what to do in a four-wall job."

"It's called life, James. You get a degree, you get a job, you work hard, you make money, you get married, then you have your own kid who stays in college eight years."

"I'm changing my major to archaeology."

"*Archaeology*?"

"It's great. I know this dude who does it."

"Does what?"

"He does archaeology."

I said, "James, listen to me a minute. It'll take you two more years, maybe three, to get an archaeology degree, which by the way will be worthless unless you have a master's, and then you'll need a doctorate, and all that will take six more years, and then you'll only be qualified to work in a museum, which also has four walls."

"Naw, Dad, you go on digs. This dude goes to South America. You find a lot of Indian stuff."

"Then what?"

"Then you go to Egypt."

"You also starve to death," I said. "Archaeologists don't make any fucking money. Did the dude tell you that?"

"Money's not everything, Dad."

"No, it isn't, except when you don't have any. Have you told your mother about wanting to change your major?"

"Yeah, I kind of like mentioned it."

"What did she say?"

"Aw, man, you know. She said dinosaurs or something and started crying."

"She didn't say it was my fault?"

"No."

"Good. James, I have to go. We'll talk about this some more. I'm glad you checked in. You all set for a summer job?"

"I'll be tending bar at the Cake."

"The Peacake Lounge?"

"Right."

"Is it a good joint?"

"It's okay. It'll Sue-out on you, but we get a good crowd."

"I love you. Take care."

"Love you, too, Dad. Who's gonna win the tournament?"

"The Australian goes south," I said. "Somebody will pick it up off the ground."

40

MY SON, THE STARVING ARCHAEOLOGIST, AND HIS FATHER, the broke and shriveled-up sportswriter, were on my mind for most of the first nine holes of the final round of the Masters, as Wilbur Lovey increased his lead to six strokes with two long, brainless birdie putts. The Australian lout was paired with Bohn Maggard in the last twosome, and just ahead of them were Bobby Joe Grooves and Wiley Sullins. I was in a cluster of writers that included Jeannie, Richie, Dub, and Cloyce Windham as we followed both groups, taking the well-worn path. I was thinking that if James Junior stayed in college six more years, I could pay for it by writing some more nitwit books for athletes and coaches in my spare time, and maybe going on the lecture circuit in my spare time, and possibly I could reach the age of sixty and see him graduate before I died. Finally, I gave up thinking about it when the leaders reached the tenth tee. "The tournament starts now," I said to one and all. "Good," Jeannie said. "I was hoping it would start before it was over."

Wilbur Lovey crushed a big drive down the tree-lined tenth fairway. The crowd thundered approval, but he hit his approach shot into a greenside bunker on the left, and then bladed the shot across the green and had an impossible chip coming back. But just as I was predicting a double bogey, or worse, he holed out the chip shot to save his par. "I don't believe this shit," I said.

On the eleventh, where water beckoned to the left of the green, Lovey flat pulled his iron shot from the middle of the fairway, and it headed for the pond for certain, but on the second bounce, the ball struck the flagstick and stopped a foot from the cup for a gimme birdie. He was now seven strokes ahead of the field with only seven holes to play. "I *really* don't believe this shit," I said.

"It's destiny," said Richie.

"Destiny doesn't swing the fucking golf club," I said.

"Can we go type now?" Jeannie asked.

"Not yet."

"You'll tell me when?"

Cloyce Windham said, "I rather like this chap's preshot routine. He never deviates from his normal preparation. He always allows his weight to rock from his heels to his toes and back again, and he has that little kick with his right knee toward the target. Quite a wonderful swing trigger, if you ask me."

Cloyce had just finished that last sentence when Wilbur Lovey hit a seven-iron fat at the twelfth, and the ball found the water, far short of the green. Huge groan from the crowd, a little minuet from me.

I nudged Jeannie.

"The tournament just started," I grinned.

Wilbur Lovey walked down to the edge of the hazard and played his third shot at the par three hole. It was a scooped wedge that splashed into the water again. Another groan from the gallery.

"You wimp dog!" said Jeannie, who had her column all planned on the Australian.

"Wilting Matilda," I said.

"Get tough, Wilbur!" Jeannie hollered.

Wilbur Lovey got his fifth shot over the water and on the green, but then he three-putted for an eight. Suddenly, he was only two strokes ahead of Bohn Maggard and Bobby Joe Grooves, who were playing even-par golf, and Wiley Sullins, who was shooting two under on the day. It was anybody's Masters.

Wilbur hurt his tee shot at the par-five thirteenth, a big one that got him around the trees and put him in shape to go for the green in two. The crowd tried to revive him as he walked to his ball.

"Come on, Wilbur! . . . Lotta holes left, baby! . . . You can do it, Wilbo! . . . Yee, ha!"

But it was here that Wilbur half-topped his three-iron, and the ball ran into the creek fronting the green. He was quickly en route to a double bogey seven.

"Get some backbone, Wilbur," Jeannie urged.

Wilbur Lovey followed up this exhibition of spineless golf by three-putting the fourteenth for a bogey, then hitting a four-iron into the water at the fifteenth. Another double bogey. From an awkward downhill lie and from behind a tree, there had been no chance for him to clear the water, but evidently he wanted to make certain he had no possibility of winning. He had dominated the tournament and the headlines for three days. He had led the tournament by a comfortable margin through sixty-five of the seventy-two holes, but now he was going to finish fourth or worse. He was aptly named. Wilting Matilda.

"The water *again*?" Jeannie cried out, as Wilbur's ball darted into the pond at fifteen. "He's a fucking sea turtle."

Up ahead of Wilbur Lovey and Bohn Maggard, the twosome of Wiley Sullins and Bobby Joe Grooves quietly birdied the thirteenth, and while Wilbur was screwing up the thirteenth, Bohn Maggard cold-jumped a two-iron and reached the green in two and sank a curling ten-footer for an eagle three. He assumed the lead by one stroke.

"Column," said Richie Pace. "The shot that won the Masters."

"You're an impulsive child," I said to Richie.

Promptly at the fourteenth, then, Wiley Sullins struck a crisp six-iron to within eight feet of the flag and holed the putt for a birdie, and he was tied with Bohn Maggard for the lead.

"Playoff," said Richie.

Now to the fifteenth. Wiley Sullins and Bohn Maggard both reached the par-five green in two with long irons that carried the water, but Bobby Joe Grooves had nailed a four-iron that radared the flag and left him with a three-foot putt for an eagle. When Sullins and Maggard each three-putted, missing birdie opportunities, and Bobby Joe drained the eagle putt, Bobby Joe was the new leader.

"Column," said Richie. "The shot that won the Masters."

We faced a moment of truth here. Should we go to the clubhouse or the press center and watch the finish on TV or stay out on the course?

"It's two cigarettes from here to the clubhouse," I said. "We'll miss two holes."

Jeannie asked another question: "How do you write all this when you've got chronic fatigue syndrome?"

The par-three sixteenth hole demanded a dangerous carry over more water, and the flag was in a taunting place near the water on the left, in a hollow below a horribly slick undulation. Bohn Maggard put a five-iron on the green but above the cup and he three-putted from twenty-five feet, whereupon he angrily threw his ball in the pond. At this same hole, Bobby Joe Grooves, fresh from his eagle at fifteen and looking confident, played a nice iron onto the green, but he too was above the cup, fifteen feet away. He barely touched the putt but it trickled down the slope and rolled ten feet past the cup, and he three-putted for a bogey. Bobby Joe didn't throw his ball in the water but he turned his visor sideways, crossed his eyes, and blew spit bubbles. It was the most endearing thing he had ever done in front of a gallery.

This left an opening for Wiley Sullins, who had put his shot on the green but *below* the cup, ten feet away. He sank the putt for a birdie two—and now *he* was the leader by one. It was Wiley Sullins by one stroke over Bobby Joe and by two strokes over Bohn Maggard. At this point, Wilbur Lovey was only trying to stay out of the way. Over a stretch of the last four holes, four different players had led the Masters.

"It's too big for me," Dub Fricker said.

The lead didn't change on seventeen, although there were three separate mini-dramas. Bobby Joe's drive caught a limb on Ike's Tree, a big hackberry that rises up on the left side of the fairway. He was forced to play a long iron to the green but he overpured it, and only a remarkable chip from ten yards behind the green and a gritty twelve-foot putt saved the par for him. Bohn Maggard fought back with a prodigious drive and a cunning seven-iron that gave him a six-foot birdie putt, which he made. In the meantime, Wiley Sullins had to rescue himself from the bunker in front of the green with an explosion shot out of a buried lie and an eighteen-foot putt that somehow found the cup. With one hole left to play, it was Wiley by one shot over Bobby Joe and Bohn Maggard.

"I hate golf," Jeannie said. "Every hole is a novel."

Everybody's wheels came off on eighteen. Bohn Maggard drove wildly into the woods on the right. Bobby Joe drove into the woods on the right but he wasn't as deeply in the trees. Wiley blasted an unwise tee ball that went too far and wound up in the fairway bunker on the left side. On this uphill finishing hole that went back toward the clubhouse and veranda, it became a question of who could save par and who couldn't.

Miraculously, Bohn Maggard chipped out of the woods and played a seven-iron onto the green and staggered in a twenty-foot putt for his par. Bobby Joe Grooves saw an opening in the trees and punched a four-iron out that ran up to the front edge of the putting surface. He had a forty-footer for birdie. Wiley Sullins hit a terrible shot out of the bunker, barely plopping it out of the sand, but he recovered with a beautiful six-iron that put him on the green with a ten-foot for his par. Bobby Joe narrowly missed on his long birdie attempt and then took forever to line up the four-footer coming back. He looked at it from all four angles and discussed it with his caddy. Then he made it. So it was all up to Wiley Sullins now. If he missed the ten-foot putt, there would be a three-way playoff, starting at the tenth tee, sudden death.

It was starting to get dark, thanks to the slowness of the play, chiefly because of all the trouble Wilbur Lovey had encountered. "We could be here tomorrow," Dub remarked. True. If there was a playoff and nobody won it before dark, it would be continued the next day. And what if play was rained out tomorrow? The Masters could last till Tuesday.

For the press, there was more riding on Wiley Sullins' putt than the Masters.

Wiley lined up his putt from behind the ball and talked it over with his caddy, a black man named Mercy. He straightened his wide-brimmed straw hat and took a couple of practice strokes. And he calmly rapped the putt into the heart of the cup. Wiley Sullins was the Masters winner. He high-fived his caddy.

"Yes!" I said, as the putt dropped.

"You like this redneck asshole?" Richie asked.

"I like *anybody* over a playoff."

We all handed Dub Fricker a twenty-dollar bill—he had won the pool. "I was never worried," Dub said.

"By the way," Cloyce commented. "Lovely shot after he came out of the bunker. No tightness in the upper body. His hips and legs behaved quite correctly, as I saw it."

We all traipsed down to the press center and got Cokes and coffee and egg salad sandwiches. The news-lead people were punching furiously on their word processors—it was a clack factory. The winner and losers would be brought in for interviews, but while we waited for this, I wandered around, pestering writers on deadline.

"It was a day like any other day," I said to Bob Green of the AP, who didn't look up from his poetry.

"Wiley Sullins, comma," he smiled.

I stood behind Dave Rocker of the *Chicago Tribune* for a second.

"Outlined against *what*?" I said, peering at his computer screen.

He ignored me.

I stopped Bobby Joe Grooves at the door to the interview room, to congratulate him on a brave effort.

"Fuckin' sixteenth green," he said. "All that fuckin' hole needs is a windmill. You won't see my ass back here till they change that son of a bitch."

"You'll be back," I said. "It's the Masters."

"Fuck the Masters."

"You're talking about Bobby Jones."

"He was crippled, wasn't he?"

"Jones?" I grinned. "Yeah, well . . . you know. He was confined to a wheelchair in his last few years."

"That's what I thought," Bobby Joe said. "Fuck that crippled cocksucker."

A half-hour later, Wiley Sullins sat behind a microphone in

the traditional green jacket of a Masters winner. A hundred writers listened intently, asked questions, and made notes.

Essentially, Wiley said, the day proved a dog don't piss on the same man's shoe all the time. He said he'd proved a big turd could float. He said he was so tired, he couldn't cornhole a big-ass goat, but he was happy as a nigger with three dicks.

Somebody asked Wiley about the putt on the last green. Did it break left, right, or was it straight in?

"Straight as a Indian goes to shit," he said.

Cloyce Windham never bothered with player interviews. He believed that what he had to say about a tournament was more interesting. Cloyce went to his hotel room and labored all night on his story, in longhand on yellow legal pad. If you saw the piece in *SM*, then you know Cloyce devoted most of the piece to the 1937 Masters in which Byron Nelson made up six strokes on Ralph Guldahl at the twelfth and thirteenth holes, by going 2-3 to Guldahl's 5-6. Cloyce told me later that he had woven this in with Wilbur Lovey's collapse but a drone had taken that part out, thus the story read as if Cloyce hadn't been anywhere near Augusta all week.

Jeannie, Richie, and I all finished our columns at about the same time, around nine thirty at night. Jeannie wrote about Wilting Matilda's escapades in the water. Richie wrote of how Wilting Matilda gave the Masters to Hal's Prime Steaks who gave it to Wiley the Redneck. I liked to think I took the high ground. I pointed out that amid all the chaos of the final hour, Wiley Sullins had shot three under par over the last seven holes, had fired a last-round 67, low for the day, after all, so in that sense, nobody gave him the Masters.

I did mention, however, that in the end, it came down to a confrontation between two sophisticates, Bobby Joe and Wiley, and that the gentleman whose eloquent phrasemaking had most reminded me of Winston Churchill had won out.

Richie Pace bolted for his rented car to drive the two-hour expressway to Atlanta, spend the night in an airport hotel, and catch an early flight to New York in the morning. A Yankee-Red Sox game tomorrow would have a crucial bearing on the American League pennant race, he thought, even though baseball season was barely under way and they would be playing games for the next seven months, or seven centuries, I could never remember which.

"It comes as no surprise to this reporter that you don't like baseball," Richie said.

I said I liked it okay before the players all wore leotards and were paid sixteen million dollars a year for scratching their nuts.

Jeannie and I returned to the Magnolia Inn. We showered and changed quickly and met in the bar. The bar was crammed with bumpkins, replaying the Masters, describing to one another the shot they saw old Jack Nicklaus hit to the seventh. We got drinks and took them out on the porch and sat down in wicker chairs where it was quiet.

"One more time. Thanks for handling the badge case," Jeannie said.

"Don't ever do that to me again."

"Thanks for the lore, too. I couldn't have covered the tournament without you."

"Sure you could."

"Not as well."

"You wrote well, did you?"

"My office thinks so. Jim Tom, I have to confess something."

"You wrote better than I did?"

"No, it has nothing to do with work. It bothers me because . . . well . . . I've never crossed a man who rode with me."

A line from an old Western movie. *Rio* something.

"What bothers you?"

"I'm not really married."

It wasn't easy to be expressionless but I tried as I looked at her for a long moment.

"What happened to Craig on the national desk?" I said.

"There is a Craig on the national desk—I've dated him—but he's not my husband."

"Why did you tell me you were married?"

"I tell every man I'm married for the same reason I have an unlisted phone number at home."

"I'll work on that for a minute."

"It's safer."

"So," I said, still expressionless. "You're not married."

"No."

"Have you ever been married?"

"No."

"Have you ever been in love?"

"In college—like everybody else. But he was a Kappa Sig and I wasn't rich enough for him. I haven't been in love since. Till now." She reached over and took my hand.

I said, "Jeannie, you can't be in love with me. We've only known each other three months. We've been to three sports events together. I'm not a truck driver and you're not a waitress. I'm old enough to be your daddy. We live three thousand miles apart. We're both deadline junkies. I swore off the love thing a long time ago. You're a dynamite lady, Jeannie. Christ, you've got it all—and I know *you* know I think that. Believe me, there's no woman, no girl—no woman-girl—I'd rather hang out with, but . . ."

"Good!" she said, rising, still holding my hand. "Let's go up to my room and talk about it some more."

"Oh, shit," I said, faintly, struggling up out of the chair.

"What?"

I smiled as I said it. "Do we want to live in Devon or Sussex?"

THE SPORTS SM MAGAZINE

Mr. Rollie Ambrose
Editor, Nonfiction
Fust & Winslett Publishers
New York, N.Y.

Dear Rollie Ambrose:

Your response to Part Two is not as disappointing as your response to Part One, but it's close. How in the hell could I have been more involved in office politics when I was on the goddamn road covering the Final Four and the

Masters? There is plenty of office politics to come. Kindly let me tell this the way I lived it.

Meanwhile, here is a list of words you have inserted in Part Two that I have taken out because I haven't used these words since I gave up teaching at Amherst: cancerously, avouch, damask, unequivocally, elegiac, frenetic, juxtaposition, bibulous, rapacious, proclivity, resilient.

You need to stop being so rapacious in your editing and I unequivocally think you should switch to a more bibulous breakfast cereal before you damask yourself permanently.

I'm sorry you feel "cheated," as a reader, because I didn't describe an erotic love scene with Jeannie Slay. I'll check with her and see if it's all right in some future chapter if I have her get naked, hop on a bed, spread her legs, and scream, "Oh, baby, stick your big warm cock in my honey jar and fuck me, fuck me, fuck me! What is your name, anyway?"

Onward,

Jim Tom Pinch

Jim Tom Pinch

PART THREE

IF GOD DIDN'T WANT A MAN TO COVER SPORTS EVENTS, HE WOULDN'T HAVE GIVEN HIM WHISKEY AND AIRPLANES

41

THE MONTH OF MAY IS A DULL TIME IN SPORTS, AS FAR AS I'M concerned, because the only two events of national interest are those where horses and cars do all the work. Think about it. Humans are only subliminally involved at the Kentucky Derby and the Indy 500, and I dare you to try to say subliminally fast if you've been drinking. All the same, I must confess that I would rather go to the Derby and Indy than have a thyroid problem.

That lead on a column I wrote after I came back from Augusta prompted a note from the oily dwarf.

"To: Jim Tom Pinch

"From: Fenton Boles

"That was a tragic column and I am sorry Bryce saw fit to publish it. In case you didn't know it, car people buy ads. F.B."

I wrote back the following:

"Dear Fenton:

"I would like to invite you to go to Indy with me later this month. I will take you to the hospital in the infield and show you some people being treated for injuries endemic to automobile racing—a man with part of a beer can lodged in his teeth, a girl whose big toe has been bitten off by a pig, a woman who has been shot in the hair-curlers by a man in a baseball cap that

says 'What Are You Looking At, Shithead?,' and a little boy
who has had three pennies and a French fry stuffed down his
ear. I apologize for not knowing these people are advertisers.
Jim Tom.''

I wanted to get out of going to the Derby this time. For one
thing, Jeannie wouldn't be covering it. In California, they
don't recognize the Derby as anything special—they have Santa
Anita and Hollywood Park. For another thing, it looked like an
ordinary year for three-year-olds. There was certainly no Secretariat out there anywhere.

I went into Bryce's office and suggested that I could write a
Derby column off TV that might be as good as the one I could
write if I went to Louisville, where I would have to watch the
race on TV anyhow in the press box—you can't see the Derby
from anywhere in Churchill Downs.

Bryce was very busy. He was pouring over the annual report
of an exploration company, one of his investments.

''You're putting me on, big guy,'' he said. ''Why do all
those people go to the Derby every year if they can't see the
race at Churchill Downs?''

''To get drunk and bet,'' I said. ''All they want to know is
the result. They can get a glimpse of the race, depending on
where they're sitting or standing. The start. The finish. A turn.
Nobody sees the race.''

''You're not really going for the race,'' he said.

''I'm not?''

He explained that Clipper Langdon, our publisher, wanted
me there. Clipper was taking a half-dozen mega-clients to the
Derby on the company's G-4. A house had been rented for the
weekend. I would fly down commercial on Friday, stay in
the rented house with the mega-clients. There would be a Friday night cocktail party, a catered dinner at the house. They
would ask me sports questions. I would tell funny stories. It
would be good for business.

''I don't do that shit, Bryce.''

''It's no big deal.''

''It's an *outing*,'' I said. ''People get paid for outings. I
ought to get five grand for putting up with guys in green slacks
and pink blazers.''

"In a sense, you're getting paid," Bryce said. "Fenton's approved it. He'll take you off warning if you do this. I acted as your agent."

That was that.

I flew to Louisville Friday afternoon, the day before the Derby, and took a cab to the rented house. It took the cab driver an hour and a half to find the house; he had never heard of the development, a new one, which was called Paddock Hills. The streets had such names as Seabiscuit Lane, Bold Venture Drive, War Admiral Circle.

The house was a two-story Colonial, a tract mansion as new as the sod that had just been put in the yard—that morning, I suspected—an art known to real estate developers as Green Side Up.

That evening, I got stroke-drunk on J & B—there was no other way to cope with Timmy Rathbone of Q & H, Biff Robinson of R & P, Tippy Donahue of B & M, Dippy Riley of B & A, Bunky Trace of P & B, and Rip Bellemy of ModeTech Industries.

Slack check: two green, two red, two yellow. Shirt check: two pink, two blue, one white. Blazer check: three pink, one white, one red, one green. Clipper Langdon went with his bright blue slacks, red-and-white-striped button-down shirt, no tie—this was casual—and a maroon blazer. I was definitely underhued in my khaki pants, white golf shirt, and navy-blue windbreaker.

Clipper introduced me to all the great guys, the Timmer, the Biffer, the Tipper, the Dipper, the Bunker, and the Ripper.

Through most of the cocktail hour, I kept going to my room upstairs to talk to Nell Woodruff on the phone. I had prearranged for Nell to call me long distance three times between six thirty and eight o'clock, on urgent editorial business.

"What's going on?" Nell asked during the first phone call.

"It's gala," I said. "Biff and Timmy are discussing three-acre zoning in Connecticut. Tippy's wife plays in a croquet league. Bunky knows the names of all the waiters at Le Cirque. Rip has a big red nose to match his coat and wants to know where the hookers are."

"Where *are* the hookers?"

"They'll be here later, if they can find the house. I called the bartender at the Back Stretch Lounge. He remembered me from my tip last year. He said he might be able to scare up a couple of Junior Leaguers."

"I didn't know that was part of your job description."

"I didn't either, but Clipper brought it up."

"How's Clipper?"

"He's heavily into white wine and demographics."

"I'm editing your column this week," Nell said.

"That's great, babe."

My two weeks in New York between the Masters and the Derby had passed all too quickly, as New York time does. I'd written a couple of columns ahead, worked on expenses, as usual, argued with my bank about overdrafts, talked to Jeannie on the phone a lot, talked to Earlene on the phone and listened to her cry about dinosaurs, and made the handyman in my building rich for taking care of a plumbing and an electrical problem. I had also spent a good amount of time with Nell and had noticed that she was pointing her life in a new direction. She was dressing more like an executive—tailored suits and dresses and heels. She said if she was going to become an editor, she would have to start going after it, and a new image was part of it. Bryce had begun to throw her the odd edit job lately—a column, a book review, a slow-closing feature. She was moving ever closer to dronedom. Now Bryce had thrown her my column this week, largely because of an emergency. Dalton Buckley would be out of the office over the weekend. His wife was playing in a C-team tennis match and Dalton was worried about the line calls. Nell was filling in.

"The indicators are all there," I said to her. "You'll be a drone before the year's out."

"I better be," she said. "I told Bryce something better happen soon or I'm going to quit."

"You can't quit," I said. "What would you do if you quit? Go to *SI?* It's no better over there."

"I'll move to Sioux Falls, South Dakota, and marry a tractor salesman."

"That'll get even with 'em."

"What do you think you might write about?"

"Who knows?" I said. "I can't write about jockeys. All a jockey ever says is, 'I heet de horse.' I can't write about owners. Owners are all in the son business or the wife business, and I'm not about to drive all the way to Lexington to hear somebody lisp. I can't write about trainers. All trainers talk about are the two horse and the four horse. Maybe I'll write about the state drink."

"The state *drink?*"

"Most states have a state flower or a state animal. Kentucky has a state drink."

"That would be your mint julep?"

"Right."

"I'm not sure I know exactly what it is. I've heard of it all my life, but I don't think I've ever been drunk enough to order one."

The way to make a mint julep, I said, was to dissolve granulated sugar in water until it turned to oil, dump in a murderous portion of bourbon, and add a freshly picked leaf of a mint.

"What does it taste like?"

"A rare combination of cough syrup and jockey piss."

"Well, no wonder people like it," Nell said.

The catered dinner was served at a long dining-room table with Clipper Langdon at one end and me at the other, facing a large portrait of a Confederate general looking apprehensive about something. I yearned to be staying downtown in the renovated Seelbach Hotel, fending off a different cast of strangers in the oaken bar.

The mega-clients were on coffee and cognac when Clipper rang on his glass, said a few words about *SM*'s place in the world, and then asked me to stand up and be brilliant.

I stood up and said, "So . . . that's about it. Any questions?"

The mega-clients stared at me.

"I come from humble origins," I said.

Biff asked Rip to pass the cognac bottle.

"Who's going to win the Derbo?" Timmy Rathbone bellowed out.

"The what?"

"The big horsey-do tomorrow."

173

"You must mean the traditional Run for the Roses—the eighth race at historic Churchill Downs on the first Saturday in May."

Purely from reading the newspapers, I knew Scanty Clad was the favorite with Carlos Monriquez up. I knew Listen Close was the second favorite with Julio Rodriquez up. I knew a good longshot was Sultans Dream with Jesus Vasquez up.

"It will definitely be an animal," I said.

"You guys," Clipper chuckled. Then he said: "Tell the gang about the horseplayer, Pincher." He looked around at the mega-clients. "This is hysterical," he promised.

"He hasn't told us who's going to win the Derbo-rama," Timmy Rathbone said. "Some of us might want to make a little wageroo."

"Scanty Clad, I suppose," I said. "He'll have the smallest jockey, not that a small jockey can't pull an elephant if the economic situation calls for it."

Tippy Donahue leaned over to ask Dippy Riley what elephants had to do with anything. Dippy Riley shrugged—he had no earthly idea.

"Betting on animals can become a serious illness," I said, and I quickly told the story about the horseplayer who ruined his life at the track. The fellow had once had a profitable business, a big home, a wife, kids, a boat, four cars, memberships in country clubs, but one day he had nothing—he'd lost everything on slow horses. Now he was living in a seedy rooming house on Queens Boulevard, but he was still going to Belmont or Aqueduct every day. A friend ran into him at Belmont and asked how he was doing. "Great," he said. "I'm ahead for the year."

Clipper was the only one who laughed.

"The guy's lost everything at the track but he says he's ahead for the year," Clipper said, convulsively. "Killer story."

"Ahead of who?" Rip Bellemy asked, glancing around the table. "Did I miss something?"

I plunged into the story about the sportswriter who was also a degenerate horseplayer. He'd made a sizable bet on a colt that actually died on the backstretch in a race at Saratoga—

collapsed and died, yes. The sportswriter saw the news of it on the wire machine in the office.

"Jesus Christ," the writer yelled out, as he looked at the wire copy. "I had this horse!"

Two of his co-workers were watching him.

"How'd you have him?" one of the co-workers asked.

"To live," the other one said.

The mega-clients stared at me again. Even Clipper Langdon was looking at me quizzically.

I swallowed half a glass of J & B.

"What do you do, Pinch?" Rip Bellemy said, finally.

"What do I *do?*"

"Yeah. I mean, I know you're a writer, but . . . is that all?"

"That's about it," I answered, lamely. "I write words . . . sentences . . . paragraphs. Quite a few paragraphs at times. A lot of sentence putting-togetherness, paragraph-wise."

"I have a question I think we would all be interested in," Timmy Rathbone said. "What horse has won the most Kentucky Derbies?"

A tidal wave of fatigue swept over me.

"Mind if I sit down?" I said.

"Zap it right down," somebody said.

I sank into my chair, lit a Winston.

"The Kentucky Derby is a race for three-year-olds," I explained. "A thoroughbred can only run in it once."

"You're joking," Biff Robinson said, challengingly.

"No," I said, meekly. "It's sort of been that way since . . . oh, eighteen seventy-five, I guess."

"What a crock," Timmy said.

"Yeah!" Dippy said. "What if the Giants could only win the NFL once?"

"Exactly," Bunky Trace put in. "What if Babe Ruth could only win one World Series? What if . . . what about *this?* What if Jack Nicklaus could only win one Masters? I mean, seriously, folks."

"I wouldn't care to live in that world," Biff Robinson stated.

"You have a point," I said.

"So, Pincher," Clipper said. "You like Scanty Clad, do you?"

"I think he can go a mile and a quarter," I said.

"Why would he only run a mile and a quarter?" Tippy asked.

"Why would he only go a mile and a quarter? That's how long the race is."

Dippy Riley said, "Pretty funny distance, if you ask me."

I said, "If you think that's funny, what about the Preakness? They run a mile and three-sixteenths in the Preakness."

Biff Robinson raised his eyebrows. "A mile and *three-sixteenths?*"

He wheeled around to Clipper Langdon. "Boy, this is some nutty sports event you've brought us to, Clippo. I'm talking Walnut City, baby. The Big Pecan, *n'est-ce pas?*"

42

A MOMENT LATER, I WELCOMED THE SOUND OF THE FRONT-door chime, even though it played a strain of "My Old Kentucky Home."

"I'll get it," I said, clambering past Clipper, relieved that my performance was over.

Clipper moved the mega-clients into the den where they could relax, keep drinking, and admire the art on the walls, a mixture of modernistic sports prints and curious, gilt-framed landscapes in which tiny electric lights shined ingeniously on the bridges leading from temples to gardens.

I opened the front door to find Micki and Misti.

Both girls were about eighteen years old, I judged. Both wore seriously short mini-skirts, high heels, and low-cut knit tops that bulged with their tits. Streaks of orange ran through Micki's blonde punk haircut. Misti was a brunette with ten pounds of eye shadow around her green eyes. They were both chewing gum. They both smelled as if they had been dunked in a tub of cheap perfume.

"This better be a good party," Micki said. "It took us two hours to find this fuckin' place."

"You gotta want to get here," Misti said.

I escorted the debs into the den. Clipper met them with an ingratiating smile. "Good evening, ladies. May I get you an *aperitif?*"

"A pair of what?" Micki said with a squint.

"What would you like to drink?" I interpreted.

"Diet Coke," Misti said.

"Dr. Pepper," said Micki.

Clipper marched to the bar in the corner of the den to get the drinks.

"Gentlemen," I said to the mega-clients, "this is what the Kentucky Derby is really all about. These Tri Delts just happened to be in the neighborhood. They're from fine old southern families. I understand they're both majoring in economics."

"Let's cut the shit," Micki said. "Who wants to get fixed up first?"

The mega-clients were all sizing up the debs. Two of the mega-clients were counting their money.

Misti moved close to me, and said, "How 'bout you, baby doll?"

"Sorry," I smiled. "War wound."

"You *look* cock dead," she said, rudely.

That seemed like a good exit line for me. As Micki and Misti chose laps to sit on, I ambled into the foyer. Clipper Langdon followed me and stopped me at the staircase.

He shook my hand with sincerity.

"This is great, Pincher. Beautiful. I'm talking beaux-coup whameroo. You sold mucho ads for us tonight. Fenton is going to be very pleased."

"Tell the gang I'll be with them in spirit," I said.

Halfway up the stairs on the way to my room I heard the boisterous voice of Rip Bellemy as it rang out from the den.

"Two hundred for the one that looks like my daughter!"

43

RULE ONE: LOCK THE BEDROOM DOOR. RULE TWO: HIDE THE money. Rule Two was in case Micki and Misti were agile enough to try to crawl out on the roof and come in through my window. I hid my moneyclip in my loafer.

I made a couple of phone calls before I sent Sominex and Maalox into the ring against four Anacin.

First, I tried to call Jeannie in LA, but all I got was her recorded voice, which said: "Hi, I'm not in right now, but I should be back from the voyage by tomorrow night. I don't care if Jerry's wife won't give him a divorce. It's like I told him yesterday, 'Jerry, why ask for the moon? We have the stars.'"

I called Nell after that. We must have talked for twenty minutes. I gave her a full report on the mega-clients.

"It's a great thing," I said. "After thirty years in journalism, I've wound up a pimp."

"Ad guys are the real pimps," she said, in an effort to comfort me.

We laughed about some things involving the office troops. Dalton Buckley had done it again on a baseball cover: YANKS FOR THE MEMORIES. Charlotte Murray had complained to Bryce about the odor in Reg Turner's office. Bryce said there were limits to what a managing editor could do, and Reg's kidneys and bowels didn't come under any heading he could think of. Wayne Mohler broke a lamp on Lindsey Caperton's desk in an editing dispute. Wayne had written a feature on a Boston Celtic, and Lindsey had made more than the usual number of needless changes in it. Lindsey had changed game to melee, basket to bucket, excitement to hoopla, championship to gonfalon, and dog to pooch, among other things.

"Dog to pooch," I said. "When they write the history of *SM*, that will be the title."

I woke up at midmorning to find the house empty. No dead bodies, thankfully. I had arranged for a limo and driver to take me to Churchill Downs, wait for me during the day, then take me to the airport after I was through typing. It would cost five hundred dollars, but I figured it was the least Fenton Boles could do for me for selling all those ads.

Churchill Downs is about five miles from downtown Louisville in a neighborhood where, if you aren't careful, you can be taken prisoner and held hostage in a mobile home.

The driver let me out at the clubhouse entrance. I was immediately saddened by the sight of so many trees and flowers missing. They had been removed to make room for all the hospitality tents.

Hospitality tents are the same everywhere. Companies lease them in order to entertain mega-clients with food, drink, and TV sets on which the mega-clients can watch their commercials interrupting and demeaning the sports events that are being televised. Clipper had invited me to partake of the hospitality in *SM*'s tent. He had given me a little button that would see me past the security guard on the door. I said I would probably be too busy to join in the fun. I had been 0-for-hospitality tent for the past six or seven years. The last time I had been in one, at the U.S. Open golf championship in Tulsa, the vice-president of a brewery had taken me all eighteen holes of a pro-am in which he had been paired with Bobby Joe Grooves.

Even my pals among the network sports announcers avoided hospitality tents. Not that I had many friends among the sports announcers. The business hadn't bred that many Jack Whitakers and Howard Cosells, Pat Summeralls and Dave Marrs. TV sports announcers bore no resemblance to network news people. Network news people, your Dan Rathers and Tom Brokaws, were hard-working, enlightened, well-informed guys. But TV sports announcers for the most part were uninformed, unenlightened dolts. They were talking heads, anchor monsters, who shilled shamelessly for whatever event they were broadcasting. Your average TV sports announcer had never seen an athlete who wasn't a legend, had never met a coach or manager who wasn't a genius as well as a devoted family man, and had never witnessed a sports event of any kind that wasn't going to have a dire effect on the Palestinian question. If a TV sports announcer saw a mammoth nuclear bomb falling toward a stadium, he would grin at the camera and blithely say to his audience, "Here comes the Big Mammoo, folks—talk about second effort!"

Out of curiosity on my way to the press box elevator, I took a side trip to the "hostility" tents to peek in the door at *SM* and see if all of Clipper's mega-clients were alive and well. They were. The Timmers and Dippers were all holding mint juleps. The room was ablaze with their apparel. The Ripper was hugging on Micki and Misti as he introduced his nieces to someone I presumed to be a fellow CEO.

"The country is doomed," I said to the guard on the door, as I ducked out of sight and continued to the press box.

Not many of my close friends in the sportswriting fraternity were at the Derby. There never were at a horse race. Thoroughbred writers were a special sect. They studied numbers, knew how to translate the bewildering agate in *The Racing Form,* and were ever striving to hit a trifecta.

Bubba Slack and Dave Rocker were in the box, but they had become horseplayers for the day and were too busy with their homework for idle chitchat.

Having nothing better to do, I squandered a couple of hundred on the first seven races. I only bet on longshots. Why bother otherwise? My methods of selection would have been harshly criticized by racing writers. I bet the nine horse in a race because nine had been Sonny Jurgenson's number with the Redskins. Nine ran last. I cagily bet on a colt whose jockey wore purple and white silks because those were TCU's colors. He ran sixth in a field of seven. So it went.

To my way of thinking, there was only one good way to make a big bet on a horse race. This was the way I had done it at Saratoga one afternoon. Back during the glory days at *SI,* Ed Maxwell and I had gone up to Saratoga for the Travers, purely for pleasure. We had been the house guests of a rich friend of Ed's, a man well connected in thoroughbred circles. We had sat near all of the owners' boxes. During the post parade for the Travers, Ed's rich friend had said, excitedly, "Oh, gee, the grandmother's here." He had pointed to an elderly little gray-haired lady being helped to her seat by her

cane and two lisping grandsons. "Bet Flying Justice," he had
continued. "Flying Justice is ten to one but they're going to
turn him loose today. The grandmother doesn't come out to see
her horses lose." Ed Maxwell and I had scrambled to the
parimutuel windows. Ed had bet a thousand, as I recall, and I
had bet everything in my pocket, about four hundred dollars.
Flying Justice had won by eight lengths.

When the twelve thoroughbreds came onto the track for the
traditional Run for the Roses, and a band struck up "My Old
Kentucky Home," a moment guaranteed to make two hundred
thousand people shed a tear, if you believed the sports announcers on TV, I borrowed a pair of binoculars to look around
for a grandmother. Every owner's box seemed to have one, so
there went *that* logic.

Scanty Clad was now 4 to 5. Listen Close was down to 3 to
1. Sultans Dream was even down to 7 to 2. Simply to have a
rooting interest in a sports event which had been written about
for two months and would only take two minutes, I put a
hundred dollars of *SM* expense money on a 17 to 1 shot named
Drillers Hat, oil prices being stable at the moment. Drillers Hat
might hold my attention until he hit a dry hole on the far turn.

Suddenly, they were off.

Drillers Hat came out of the gate with no bumps and moved
quickly to the rail. He was ahead by two lengths when the
horses came past the grandstand the first time. Drillers Hat held
the lead around the first turn. He upped the lead to three lengths
around the second turn. He increased his lead to five lengths on
the backstretch.

The track was fast but the pace was extremely slow, and I
couldn't decide if this was in his favor or not.

Horses started to come at him on the far turn but he didn't die
until the top of the homestretch. His sprint was over. He was
standing still, but so were the big favorites, Scanty Clad, Listen Close, Sultans Dream.

Maybe it was my suspicious nature, but as I observed it, I
didn't think the riders on Scanty Clad, Listen Close, and Sultans Dream were using their whips with any great dexterity.

And now here came a chestnut colt named Big Job, a curious
30 to 1 shot. Big Job moved to the middle of the track as the

jockey flogged away at him. Big Job galloped into the lead by a length, then two, then three. Behind him: statues.

Big Job galloped under the wire, a winner by five lengths. Two other obscure horses were second and third. Drillers Hat lumbered home a distant last.

Watching Big Job cross the finish line, I was astounded that I hadn't noticed him in the post parade—the nine horse with the jockey in purple and white silks.

Big Job's winning time was 2:04, a woeful five seconds slower than Secretariat's Derby record. In fact, it was the slowest Derby time in thirty-five years.

A mint julep would go down faster. Column lead.

44

MUCH TO MY FASCINATION, ON THE ONE HAND, AND SOMEwhat to my embarrassment, on the other, the only two things any of my friends around the office wanted to talk about when I got back to New York were the rumor and the romance. I hesitate to use all caps here but everybody in our small world thought these things were, well . . . BIG.

"It's big," Nell said on this night in Fu's Like Us, referring to the rumor.

"Very big," said Christine Thorne, who was home for a while after traveling the countryside with Kitter Mooring, our intellectual track and field writer, helping him prepare features on Summer Olympic athletes who would transform the morals and customs of the modern world. I had known as many track and field athletes as Kitter Mooring. They were basically a pack of steroid-shooting hypochondriacs, but to the sensitive, perceptible Kitter Mooring they were majestic figures, driven by celestial fires, with a loftiness of soul that could only be compared with Rousseau's.

"It's big?" I said.

"Big," Nell promised.

"Huge," said Christine.

The rumor was also wild and crazy, though completely absorbing. It was so rampant now throughout the building that nobody could remember exactly how it got started, nor did they care. They only hoped and prayed it was true.

The rumor was about Fenton Boles and Lindsey Caperton.

"They're pinned," Nell said with a gleam.

I said, "You don't mean . . . ?"

"Yes! Did I say it was big?"

"I love it," Christine said.

Ralph Webber was in the bar, just back from a trip to the Coast where he had done a piece on the Dodgers. Through a phone call to an assistant manager of long-time acquaintance, I had managed to get Ralph into the Beverly Hills Hotel, where he had never stayed before, and Wooden Dick had shown his gratitude by taking Jeannie Slay to dinner three nights in a row and trying to fuck her. He may well have, and I wouldn't find out about it until Jeannie and I had an argument someday. If I had to bet big money on a guy to score a sport-fuck or a friendship-fuck, I would bet it on Wooden Dick. But Jeannie claimed she had kept him at a distance. It was unfortunate, however, that one of the tools she used to keep him at a distance was to confess to him that she was in love with *me*. Now Wooden Dick had come home to share this news with Nell, Christine, Wayne Mohler, and Bryce's secretary, Eileen Fincher, with whom Wooden Dick needed to exchange information in order to keep up with his salary level in relation to everyone else's. This was the romance my friends wanted to discuss—particularly Nell—on more solemn occasions, but right now, we were talking about The Rumor, and Ralph was saying, "Lindsey goes up to thirty-three for lunch an awful lot. They frequently have lunch in Fenton's office. Just the two of them."

"Lindsey's an accounting mole," I said. "Not to defend him."

"Well," Ralph said, slowly, suggestively, "I think it might be a little more than that."

"I've known it all along," Wayne Mohler said. "I've seen the way they look at each other."

"You're disqualified," I said to Wayne. "You hate Lindsey more than anybody."

"You hate Fenton more than anybody," he came back.

"Hey, listen," I said. "Nobody wants to believe this more than *I* do."

"Watchband," Nell said. "Lindsey wears a blue suede watchband. I rest my case."

"Doesn't anybody know how this got started?" I asked, up and down the bar.

Christine said, "I know how *I* think it started. Bryce's secretary was up on thirty-three one day. Eileen was talking to Raymond, Fenton's secretary—and we *know* about Raymond, don't we? Eileen heard Raymond make a dinner reservation for two at this restaurant in SoHo. 'Yes, two gentlemen,' she heard Raymond say. Eileen knows the place. Ladies are *not* welcome, she says."

"Did Eileen tell you this?"

"No, she told Marge Frack."

"Did Marge Frack tell you this?"

"No, she told Wayne."

Marge Frack, the Exorcist, did Wayne's expense accounts for him and they would split the profits. I came out better doing my own.

I turned to Wayne. "How do you know the dinner reservation was for Fenton and Lindsey?"

"Because Reg Turner saw Fenton and Lindsey getting in Fenton's limo after work, and I remember what day it was, distinctly. It was the day Lindsey changed dog to pooch."

"How could you forget?" Nell laughed.

"That's right!" Wayne said, vehemently.

Ralph Webber said, "Let's not forget the way Lindsey walks. Ever noticed? When he's in a hurry? His feet don't touch the floor."

"Let's not forget he has a wife," I said. "The charming Paula."

"That frumpy little charity-working bitch?" Nell said. "He married her for cover."

"They were high school sweethearts, weren't they?"

Wayne said, "She helped him through algebra—the least he could do was marry her."

Christine said, "I would like to remind everyone that neither one of them is athletic. Fenton works out on his machines, but they don't play golf, they don't play tennis, they don't ski, they don't swim, they don't play handball. They don't even bowl."

"That part's good," I said. "I'd rather work for fags than bowlers."

"All I know is, it's going to be a great day," Wayne Mohler said, drinking to it.

"What day is that?" Ralph asked.

"The day one of them shoves a light bulb up the other one's ass and they can't get it out."

"Does our medical cover that?" Nell wondered.

Sometime around midnight, Jimmy, the Chinese bartender, announced last grand-final call. The man who said all things in moderation didn't know about whiskey, smoking, or sportswriting. Wayne went home to his wife, Marilyn, up on 88th and First Avenue. Ralph saw Christine home in a cab with the usual thing on his mind. I saw Nell home in a cab, but we wound up in an all-night Greek restaurant near her Murray Hill apartment on 39th Street.

We sat there for two hours, eating half the menu, drinking coffee, reading the early editions of the *Times* and *Daily News*. Near the end of our sit, Nell finally brought up the romance.

She said all of the same things to me that I had said to Jeannie. Cross-country relationships don't work. I might as well be involved with an *actress*, for God's sake. Writers should never be attracted to other writers. That was fatal. Look at Sinclair Lewis and Dorothy Thompson. Look at Lillian Hellman and Dashiell Hammett. "Who else?" I said. "A lot of people," she said. And what about the age thing? When I would be in my 60s, Jeannie would be in her 40s. When I would be in my 70s, Jeannie would be in her 50s, still sexually active. "When I'm in my 80s," I interjected, "I'll be dead and my kid will still be in college." Nell said she adored Jeannie personally. Jeannie was fun and talented and attractive and all that. Who wouldn't like her? But why couldn't it stop right there—with *like*? She said, "I'm your closest, dearest, warmest friend, so I'm obligated to say these things to you."

Nell shook a Winston out of my pack on the table and I lit it for her.

''There's one more thing,'' she said, ''and I don't know why in the world you don't know it by now.''

''Don't hold anything back.''

''*I'm* in love with you.''

I knew her well enough to see in her look that she was serious. ''Woogeeba,'' I mumbled softly. A nonword. A sound.

''That's it?'' she said. ''A gorgeous, witty, wonderful woman, a dynamite lady by anybody's definition, tells you she loves you, and that's all you can say?''

I opted for humor. ''You'll have to fight for me.''

''I'm going to,'' she said, convincingly. Which was scary.

I walked her to the entrance of her apartment building. Two awkward blocks in which nothing was said. It was starting to drizzle lightly. The streets were empty of potential muggers. Muggers don't like inclement weather.

''You don't have to wait,'' Nell said, as she stood outside the entrance and she pressed a buzzer to wake up the night doorman.

I put my arm around her to give her a standard goodnight kiss. But she turned it into something else. I suppose it ought to go into the record that I had never been kissed and standing-up hunched like that before by a good friend, and certainly not by an editor. When the night doorman appeared, we were still entangled and doing tongue things to each other that we had never done before, in all the years we had been close friends.

We finally released each other and I couldn't think of anything to say that wouldn't sound misleading or evasive or stupid, but Nell was alert.

She grinned slyly, and said, ''Gosh, Mary Ellen, you've let your hair down and taken off your glasses. Is it really you?''

I laughed, gave her a little wave, and walked away to look for a cab through a blur of confusion and amazement. All of a sudden, everybody was in love with me.

45

RICHIE PACE CALLED UP TO SAY THE POLO COLUMN CERTAINLY enriched *his* life.

In a week when I should have been writing a column about a Pittsburgh Pirate slugger who hit ten home runs in three days, Bryce Wilcox ordered me to write a polo column. The reason Bryce ordered it was because Fenton Boles told him to order it. And the reason Fenton told Bryce to order it was because Les Padgett, our founder, had been introduced to polo-watching by his buddy, Baron Kurt Gerhard von Drechsler, who played polo, and Les had mentioned to Fenton that he kind of liked the sport now that he understood it better. It wasn't rich man's soccer, he had said. It was closer to croquet on horses.

Les had gone down to Argentina for a month with the baron, primarily to look into some Nazi real estate as an investment for TPG. A month in Argentina was long enough for Les to marry and divorce Donna Roach, the brainless actress, and then marry Fritzy Erwina Krupp-Streicher, the young woman who had been the baron's date at the party in Innsbruck.

The baron had apparently been happy to get rid of Fritzy, who at the age of twenty-seven had already gone through her own inheritance and was now going through his. Les and Fritzy were going to live in New York, London, Palm Beach, St. Croix, and Murfreesboro, and Fritzy was planning to redecorate our entire building. Her taste was impeccable.

I learned all this from Fenton Boles.

The CEO called me up to thirty-three to give me a raise, personally, rather than let Bryce do it. Along with the $20,000 raise came a stock option. A person from finance would come around within a day or two to have me sign something.

"Just say yes and sign it," Fenton said, as I sat across from him at his desk and fitfully refrained from smoking. "You won't understand it if you try to read it. You're getting two thousand shares of TPG at seventeen and a half. The stock is selling for thirty-five and three-eighths today, but it's going to be worth more, a great deal more, I think. My advice is to hold it for a year or longer.''

I did some math in my mind and realized I needed thirty-five thousand dollars I didn't have to buy the stock, but before I could mention this, Fenton said, ''Any bank will loan you the money to buy the stock. If you have a problem, tell them to call me.''

''Why are you doing this?''

''Clipper filled me in on the fine job you did at the Derby. It was a splendid example of the kind of cooperation we need between the edit floor and the sales floor, the kind of cooperation Bryce and I strongly believe in.''

To be aligned with sales went against everything in my nature. An ad guy would sell our cover to Chrysler if he could get away with it. He would sell my typewriter to Xerox if he could get away with it. But nobody had sold my words to anyone, which was why I accepted the raise and the stock option. I still was holding on to a sliver of integrity.

''Where is our next hospitality tent?'' I asked.

Fenton said, ''We'll have one at Wimbledon for sure. I don't know beyond that.''

The CEO was in such a good mood—for him—I took a chance on running something by him. ''As long as you're passing out favors today, I want to ask one,'' I said. ''It's not for me. It's for somebody else at the magazine. Nell Woodruff is in line to become a senior editor, and we can really use her in that capacity, but Bryce has been too busy to get around to it.''

I was proud of my diplomacy, leaving the impression that Bryce was busy at magazine duties. If Bryce was busy at anything, it was his golf game.

''Nell Woodruff is a woman,'' Fenton said, as if he was reminding me of a fact I had overlooked.

''True,'' I said, ''but believe me, she's more capable than any editor on the floor, and think about it for a moment from the stockholders' point of view.''

''Equal opportunity,'' said Fenton. He was quick. Nobody could say the oily dwarf wasn't quick.

''Absolutely,'' I said. ''I'll tell you something else. Nell

Woodruff is assistant m.e. material. Down the road, I think she's managing editor material.''

"Hmmm," Fenton said, the wheels turning. He picked up the phone on his desk. "Raymond, get me Bryce Wilcox." Then: "Bryce, Fenny. Nell Woodruff. Brightest female on your staff? That's what I think. Let's elevate her to senior editor as of next week. I might just add that in my view, she could be assistant m.e. material down the road. Glad you concur.''

I left the CEO's office thinking about the extraordinary impact a pimp could have on magazine journalism.

What impact my column had on poloists as a group, I never heard. What I wrote was:

"It is a known fact that the pastime of polo has never aroused much interest among dockworkers or, for that matter, sportswriters. Even back in the 1930s, when it could be said that polo peaked in the United States—largely, I think, because Jean Harlow went to polo matches in clinging white dresses—most people without hyphenated names had a tendency to look upon the sport as croquet on horseback.

"Polo is a tougher game than that, however, one in which the Maharaja of Jaipur once sustained a lingering bruise on his left hip, for which an opponent was dropped into a pit of cobras.

"You may ask where polo came from. Some historians insist polo was invented by the Persians 4,000 years ago, when horses were the size of sheep dogs and the riders often stubbed their toes on the ground in the middle of a wild, crazy, dizzy, overheated chukker, a chukker being one of eight periods of play which lasts seven and a half minutes and was named for Chubby Chukker, the East Indian who wrote 'Twist Around the Curry.'

"Why polo should have been popular with Persians has never been satisfactorily explained. My own guess is that they wanted to get their sheep dogs outdoors and off their rugs, which would be worth a pretty penny someday.

"It seems more likely, however, that other historians are correct, that polo actually got started in India in the 1860s as an outgrowth of 'wild riding' exhibitions in and around the town of Punjab, where you can pick up a townhouse for a song in today's market, I hear.

"In Punjab one day, a group of servants got the notion to

entertain the British army officers in this fashion rather than wait around to be belted, flayed, and yelled at for more gin. That day, one of the servants on horseback was seen swinging at a ball with a long stick. One of the army officers asked what the ball was. 'Pulu,' he was told by someone. This was East Indian for willow root, out of which the polo ball is made.

"The British army officers were uneasy with the word 'pulu,' believing it to sound too much like an intestinal disorder, so they pronounced the word 'polo,' whereupon they chose up sides and had a go at it. The game was quickly transported to England where the Hurlingham Club became the Yankee Stadium of polo. A decade later, the sport arrived in America, in Newport, R.I., and out on Long Island, where a gathering of idle sportsmen saw it as a way to get out of the house, although this didn't always work.

" 'Where are you going, dear, and why are you dressed so peculiarly?'

" 'I'm going to play polo.'

" 'Not today. Polo has gone to Europe with her mother, and if you see that hussy one more time, I'll take you for every cent your father has.'

"Patriotism helped the sport become popular in America. The International Polo Challenge Cup was thought up—polo's version of the nerve-wracking America's Cup yacht races—and suddenly dockworkers everywhere wanted us to win that cup, which the good old USA did throughout the 1920s and 1930s.

"In those days, our top players had such names as Devereux Milburn, Harry Payne Whitney, Monte Waterbury, Laddie Sanford, Winston Guest, Stewart Inglehart, Michael Phipps, Tommy Hitchcock, and Cecil Smith. It was clearly a sport of the people.

"A serious poloist—and I know one personally—will tell you that the horses are the real athletes. They have to know how to turn, twist, resume speed, sustain pain, cuts, jolts, duck mallets, and not mind contact—all the things sportswriters have to know.

"I looked it up. The greatest polo horses in history were named Brown Fern and Gay Boy. Imagine my surprise, then, to discover that polo inspired nouvelle cuisine."

I did hear about the column from Les Padgett.

He called long distance from somewhere as I was in my office, toiling on expense reports. Nothing wrong with an $87 dinner receipt you couldn't fix by putting a two in front of it.

Les said, "Jim Tom, you old pisser-offer, how you doin'?"

"Fine, Les. I hope the polo column didn't piss you off too much."

"Naw, hell, I thought it was interesting. Was all that shit true?"

"As a matter of fact, yes. I did a little research."

"You didn't make up pulu?"

"Nope."

"Pulu," he cackled. "I can't wait to drop that on the baron."

"Congratulations on getting divorced and married again," I said, as nicely as possible.

"Aw, well, you know. A man's got to do what a man's got to do."

"You gotta play hurt."

I thanked the founder for tolerating the polo column, and he left me with an insight into his future plans.

"Foreign women," he said. "I'm stickin' to foreign women from here in. If this Nazi don't work out, I'm goin' for a chink. A chink will rub your back and she don't wear but one dress."

46

SELF-EXAMINATION, I HAD ALWAYS THOUGHT, WAS FOR PEO-ple who didn't need to get a column ahead, but I could take it in small doses. Usually I indulged in it during air travel if the movie was about the shattering of glass and the demolishing of automobiles, or if the novel I had bought because of the sexy jacket was about a sensitive family in rural America dealing with the larger issues of life. The movie would be tuned out after the first car wreck, and the novel would be tossed after the literary-minded daughter appeared on page three and wanted to

talk about workers' comp insurance. Self-examination would
kick in and last through two cocktails, and I would always
reach the same conclusion. I had been misunderstood by every
woman I had ever been attached to. Not just my three ex-wives
but all of the women I had taken out and then not taken out over
the past ten or fifteen years—Sharon, the network news producer; Connie, the book publicist; Sheila, the boutique owner;
Sarah, the inveterate shopper; and others not worthy of comment. Of all these, Sharon Falls had lasted the longest. We
were on and off for five years despite her unquenchable appe-
tite for sit-down dinner parties and her desire to know every
single person on the globe. I had liked Sharon and thought we
were getting along okay until I found out in a discussion that I
was an inattentive bastard and about as thoughtful as a crusta-
cean. A week later, she moved in with a Norwegian brain
surgeon. The last I heard, she was linked with the governor of
Montana.

Nell Woodruff was undoubtedly right about me, I had decided. I had this attitude about life and the world in general that
most women found maddening in the extreme and impossible
to change. Nell gave it a Noel Coward name: habitual nonchalance.

On the flight to Texas, I wondered if Nell might be the only
woman who might know how to deal with my terrible afflic-
tion, but after the second cocktail on the plane, I didn't think
about it anymore. I thought about a column.

47

ALMOST ANY MAP WILL SHOW YOU THAT IT ISN'T NECESSARY
to go through Fort Worth to get to Indianapolis from New
York, but T. J. Lambert had wept and cussed on the phone
again about them goddamn shirt-liftin', jock-twinkin' NC Double A's and said my poor old alma mater needed my advice
badly.

TCU had received the detailed accounts of the NCAA's

fifty-seven charges of illegal football recruiting and other rules violations. The chancellor, Dr. Glenn Dollarhyde, the athletic director, Rabbit Tyrance, and T.J. were in a frenzy as to how to respond and what course of action to take. They thought I could be of some help.

I rented a car at D/FW, drove downtown, and checked into the Worthington for a two-night stay. I hadn't been back to the old hometown for a year. It was in my mind to drive around and relive some memories, eat some barbecue, maybe visit with Earlene, but maybe not, drop by the *Light & Shopper* to see who had died and see if there was still a burrito in the lower right-hand drawer of my old desk.

But the first thing I had to do that afternoon was meet with the chancellor, the athletic director, and the head football coach. I drove out to TCU, which was still a small university of only six thousand students, but as I circled the campus to look at the football stadium and all the buildings where I had cut so many classes, I was flabbergasted by the sight of all the cars. The Quad was full. The stadium parking lot was full. When I was a student thirty-five years ago, only fifty people owned cars and most of them wouldn't start without a push. Now it looked as if every student had come to school with two cars—one for day, one for night. They couldn't all belong to running backs.

I parked in a spot reserved for a vice chancellor behind the Ad Building and went up to the second floor to the chancellor's office. In the outer office, I noticed that the chancellor's priorities were still in place. On the wall were portraits of Sam Baugh, Davey O'Brien, and Billy Clyde Puckett, three of TCU's gridiron immortals. No longer a portrait of Shake Tiller, however. The Frogs' all-time receiver had been taken down. I gathered it was because Shake had never contributed to the alumni fund, or it could have been because the chancellor had seen the last movie Shake had written in Hollywood, a campus comedy called *White Punks on Dope*.

Chancellor Dollarhyde, Rabbit Tyrance, and T.J. all greeted me with a handshake and a hangdog expression. The chancellor was wearing his purple blazer and purple tie. Rabbit was in a business suit. T.J. was in a white golf shirt and slacks. T.J.

looked thinner than when I had last seen him. He was still a big man but he wasn't the brute he had been as an all-pro defensive lineman. He was losing some of his sandy hair but none of the anger on his freckled face. He still looked ready to butt his head against a locker and holler, "Let's get them summitches!"

We talked briefly about how I had been, where I had been, where I was going—Indy—what I had written lately, and the chancellor out of nowhere asked if I knew a Gus McCalip in New York City. Gus McCalip, it seemed, had made a fortune in the computer business, and somebody had recently discovered that he was a TCU graduate. The chancellor was wondering if I knew him so I might be of some help in bringing Gus McCalip into "the TCU family." I didn't know Gus McCalip, I said, but I was happy to know TCU had another wealthy alum—somebody besides Big Ed Bookman and Billy (Whip-Out) Murdock.

T.J. said, "There ain't gonna be a TCU if we don't dig our ass out of all this NC Double A shit."

For my benefit, the chancellor read through the fifty-seven alleged violations, most of which were absurd, as is generally the case with the NCAA. Things about keychains being illegally provided for the girlfriends and sisters of prospective athletes, illegal cheeseburgers being bought by boosters for presently enrolled athletes, illegal phone calls being made by athletes on the football office telephone, illegal automobile rides being provided by assistant coaches transporting recruits from their high schools to their homes, illegal even during blizzards and tornados, and illegal T-shirts being given to prospective athletes during campus visitations. Fifty-two of the fifty-seven violations were of this nature.

I watched Rabbit Tyrance squirm and nod with anguish at the weight of these grievous sins as the chancellor read them out. Of course, he would. Rabbit Tyrance, the athletic director, *was* the NCAA. He was on the NCAA's ethics committee. He was part of the out-of-control bureaucracy and hypocritical organization that made these silly rules. You couldn't expect a committee of NCAA officers to go off on an all-expense paid trip to a golf resort for three days and not come back with a new keychain rule. The NCAA's manual of conduct was now 537 pages thick, and no coach could understand it, even if he bothered to read it.

It was so easy to cure most of the things that were supposed to be wrong with college football. I preached about it two or three times a year in print. Make freshmen ineligible again, as they had been for a hundred years before the 1970s. That would give freshmen a fighting chance to find out where the classrooms were. To be eligible for the varsity, make the kids take—and pass—old-fashioned courses like English and history instead of Physical Beingness and Weightlifting II. That *would* seem to tie in with education. Give the athletes spending money above the table—$100 a month, $200 a month, subsidized by the alumni and boosters—so the kids could buy their own cheeseburgers. Thousands of people who loved to complain about the "ills" of college football didn't realize it, but a football player on scholarship wasn't allowed to have a part-time job during the school year, as all other students could, including all of the cocaine-selling pledge captains of all the worthless fraternities. Further, the rulesmakers could return to one-platoon football, as the game was cheerfully played for a hundred years. It hadn't seemed to hurt all of the Tom Harmons, Doak Walkers, and Johnny Lujacks to have played offense *and* defense. This would cut the scholarship load in half, and yet there would still be All-Americans, polls to determine national champions, bowl games, stadiums filled on Saturdays—and TV. But no. To do all this would eliminate too many NCAA committees. And the schools in major conferences and the big-time independents were fearful there wouldn't be as much TV and bowl money available. Today, the educators at universities with winning programs not only ran the NCAA, they went around grasping for TV and bowl money with one hand while feverishly fanning themselves with the other as they pretended to fret over academic integrity. These were the true phonies, the terminal hypocrites. The only realists were the football coaches. They were forced to buy players to survive in a world they didn't create.

I'm afraid I made Rabbit Tyrance a little uncomfortable by saying all this again in the chancellor's office, after which I told them what to do about their problem.

"You're dealing with hypocrites, so why should you be the only honest patsies in America?" I said. "Drag the procedure out as long as you can. You can drag it out a year. Conduct your own in-house investigation into these matters, which, I need not say, will uncover no wrongdoing. Then throw the infractions committee a bone. Once they investigate you, they have to find *something*. Be horrified to discover a thousand-dollar payment to a kid, from an overzealous booster. It will be a display of honesty. You're making an effort to clean up the program. Maybe you'll get a probation, but you can live with that. But don't confess, ever—and I mean never—about the big money and the cars. Not unless you want to get the death penalty and bury yourself for ten years."

The chancellor said, "I don't know anything about any money or cars. I was never in a room where such things were discussed."

"I wasn't either," the athletic director said.

"Me neither," said T.J.

I laughed as I looked at T.J. "How did Convenience Store Roberts and Clitorrus Walker get here?"

"They wanted engineering," T.J. said.

"I didn't know TCU had an engineering department."

"Geology," T.J. said.

"Geology?" I was still smiling.

"Maybe it was communications."

"Tell me about the church," I said.

T.J. looked at Rabbit. Rabbit looked at Dr. Glenn Dollarhyde. The chancellor looked at T.J.

"I don't know anything about it," the chancellor said. "I wasn't in town when it was discussed."

"Neither was I," Rabbit Tyrance said.

T.J. explained about the church. A way had to be found to put money into the hands of prospective athletes and currently enrolled athletes without leaving a paper trail for a potential NCAA investigator. That was if T.J. was going to have a competitive program. Big Ed Bookman had come up with the church gimmick, although it was rumored that Big Ed borrowed the idea from a Baptist booster associated with Baylor, or maybe it was a Methodist booster associated with SMU. The thing was, a church didn't have to show its financial books to the NCAA in the event of an investigation. Perfect. Big Ed Bookman and Whip-Out Murdock could donate money to the church, even take a deduction, and the church would be the paymaster for the studs. T.J. had gone to Dr. E. R. Pettibone, the minister of the University Christian Church, which was across the street from the campus and affiliated with TCU, and had asked Dr. Pettibone if he would like to have the honor and privilege of being the Horned Frogs' paymaster. Dr. Pettibone was a big fan of TCU football but not that big. He had asked T.J. to pray with him. What for? T.J. was only talking about trying to win some fuckin' football games. What was this prayer shit? Dr. Pettibone had ushered T.J. out of his office, telling the coach to seek some emotional guidance. T.J. had gone to Big Ed Bookman, at a loss for what to do next. Big Ed had said fuck it, we'll start our own church. That's when Big Ed had bought a building near the campus, a decaying movie theater, and had it converted into the Worth Hills Christian Church, Rev. Donald (Fatty) Owens presiding. Fatty Owens was a former TCU tackle who had been called to the ministry after serving three years in Club Fed for mail fraud. TCU's football players were now attending services regularly at Worth Hills Christian Church, although most of the spooks, T.J. said, would pick up their money and leave before the sermon and the singing started.

Dr. Dollarhyde blushed, cleared his throat, shuffled papers on his desk. "I didn't hear this conversation. My calendar says I was out of the city today."

"So does mine," the athletic director said.

The research T.J. had asked my magazine to do on the NCAA's infractions committee had turned up nothing, I said to everyone. None of the stringers had been able to uncover anything embarrassing in their private lives that might be used as blackmail. The members of the committee were all leading drab lives as law professors, chemistry professors, art history professors. Martha Callaway, the women's basketball coach at Mt. Grimmall, *was* a confirmed lesbian—her nickname was "Buck"—but everybody at her college was aware of her sexual preference, as was everybody in the NCAA. She was a good coach with a winning record and everybody admired her courage and openness at living her life the way she wanted to live it. She was "married" to an automobile worker named Francine, and she was a tough-minded individual, as evidenced by the fact that she had once struck a probing reporter so hard with a large leather dildo the young man had suffered a slight concussion.

"Stall as long as you can," I said to the group. "That's the best advice I can give you. I understand you might have a good team this season, and the prospects look good for the year after."

T.J. said, "Between you and me, I'm sittin' on a powder keg."

"Good," I said. "If you're real good—I'm talking about a Top Ten team—you might even get out of this without a probation. You'll become a TV attraction and the networks won't want you on probation."

T.J. jumped up out of his chair, looking greatly encouraged. "Goddamn, I think we got it whipped. Let's go get some barbecue and drink some whiskey, Jim Tom."

48

THEM TWINS, T.J. WAS SAYING. THEM TWINS WAS WHAT WAS going to do it for TCU next season. With them twins, TCU was going to line them all up and lay wood on their ass.

We were well into our drinking at the bar of T.J.'s choice. We had already laid to waste the barbecue, having eaten the ribs at Sammie's and then the sliced sandwiches at Angelo's. Now we were in The Cadaver Room, a hideout bar near All Saints Hospital. College football coaches throughout the nation, as I had known them, all had a secret bar somewhere in the city or campus town, a place where they could drink and relax and not be bothered by wives or fans or the press.

I had spent the first half of my life in hangouts like The Cadaver Room, drinking, eating potato chips, playing the pinball machine, listening to salesmen complain about their unreliable customers, listening to highbrow conversations about niggers, spicks, Jews, A-rabs, queers, and '57 Mercury Cougars.

Behind the horseshoe bar was Wanda, a voluptuous cowgirl bartender, a woman in her forties, who looked as if life had only done her two favors and she didn't expect much else.

As an added attraction, six off-duty nurses were crowded around a booth in the back of the room. They were swilling margaritas, letting out whoops, and playing the same song on the jukebox. A country male vocalist named Marty Epps was singing, "His Boil Was So Big, All the Girls Called Him Lance."

One of the nurses came over to the booth where T.J. and me were drinking and talking. She asked if anybody wanted to waltz.

"We're senior citizens," T.J. said.

"Senior citizens is good dancers," said the nurse, who was a trifle plump for my taste.

"Some are," T.J. said, "but we got them senior citizen rules we have to live by, you see?"

"What rules is that?"

The plump nurse left us alone after T.J. recited the three rules that senior citizens must live by.

1. Never pass up an opportunity to take a piss.
2. Never trust your first hard-on in the morning.
3. Never trust a fart.

Our privacy ensured, T.J. went back to the twins, the juco running backs.

The coach pronounced their names O-ron-gelo and Lim-on-gelo. This was how the twins themselves pronounced their names, but the correct spelling, I learned, was Orangejello and Limejello.

Orangejello and Limejello Tucker were both six feet three, weighed two twenty-five, and were faster than rent.

The twins came from Milburn Junior College over in East Texas. Before that, the jucos had achieved academic excellence at Mosquito Lake High School outside of Dallas. They had been signed and sealed for Notre Dame, Oklahoma, Texas, and UCLA—all four—until Big Ed Bookman and Billy (Whip-Out) Murdock got involved with their checkbooks.

"How did they come by those names?" I asked.

T.J. said he had asked their mother the same question. The explanation was, she had been working at a Winn Dixie when the twins had been born. She would have named them Winn and Dixie, but that's what she had named their older sisters.

"I gather they're very religious."

"They don't never miss church," T.J. said.

I said I was looking forward to seeing Orangejello and Lime-jello wearing the purple next fall.

T.J. said, "Son, Orongelo and Limongelo is gonna lay wood on their ass. All I got to do is keep air in the football."

49

THE NEXT MORNING I CALLED EARLENE AT THOMPSON'S WINdow & Door Frame to see if she might care to have lunch somewhere in a crowded place. It was my policy never to meet Earlene alone in a dark corridor or visit with her too long in private—she might be packing a cold cream jar.

Earlene asked what I was doing in town. I told her. She said she had read in the *Light & Shopper* about TCU being under investigation for what she described as "paying niggers." It was her fondest hope, she said, that TCU would get the death penalty because she hadn't forgotten how I had been at the TCU-Baylor football game the day James Junior had been born.

"How could you forget or forgive?" I said on the phone. "It was only twenty-six years ago."

She suggested we meet at Herb's Cafe, which would be convenient for her. Herb's was near her office and she would only have forty-five minutes for lunch. Mr. Thompson's restructuring in the midst of Fort Worth's economic downturn had left her with three jobs.

"If there's no business, why are you busy?" I asked.

Her explanation was that while there was no door business, owing to the lack of new construction, there was still window business, owing to the increase in crime. The sale of windows and handguns hadn't been excessively affected by Fort Worth's faltering economy, which was into its fifth year.

I asked if Herb's Cafe still served a catcher's mitt and called it a chicken fried steak.

"I have to go now," she said. "My fax is pingin'."

"Please, God, let it be a door," I said, and we hung up.

After examining the *Light & Shopper* over room service breakfast, I dismissed the idea of dropping by the newspaper. It wasn't the same newspaper. Red and blue streaks swept across the front page above the fold. Yellow and green boxes jutted out here and there. All of the section fronts were tinted rose, violet, beige. The weather map had apparently overflowed. It wasn't just greening in the Midwest and yellowing in the Northeast, it was blueing in sports, orangeing in metro, and threatening to red like the dickens in lifestyle. I didn't recognize any of the by-lines, even in sports, where every writer was talking about the Dallas Mavericks, who weren't even in the NBA playoffs. Back on the front page, I couldn't tell if there was a lead news story or not, amid the jumble of features, although it may have been the pink one under the tangerine headline that said GERMANS CHANGE HELMETS.

I drove around town for a while before I met Earlene.

The old South Side neighborhood where I had grown up, once a nice middle-class part of town with shady streets and well-kept lawns, was looking more different than ever. Rusted kitchen appliances were sitting in front yards. Cars were up on blocks. Weeds were thriving. The neighborhood had been zoned commercial, I gathered, after seeing a sign on Mrs. Watkins' house that advertised palm reading by Pauline. Hard to believe it was the same neighborhood where I had found an old Remington typewriter in the attic of our house and had decided at the age of ten that I intended to be a journalist so I could wear a press card in my hatband like Clark Gable did.

My folks were long departed. My daddy, Tom, a carpet salesman when he wasn't gambling on the golf course, had died of a heart attack twenty years ago after losing $500 he didn't have to Quick-Putt Moody and Rear-Door Gibson on the back nine at Goat Hills, and my mama, Louise, had died of a broken heart two years earlier because my daddy had played a lot more golf than he sold carpet. It was just as well that Louise and Tom Pinch hadn't been around to watch the neighborhood deteriorate, as all neighborhoods do when people take flight from blacks and Mexicans and Catholics and chain-smokers and anything else they think they are supposed to fear. Louise and Tom would die again today, I thought, if they could see that our house on the corner had become a Korean grocery store, that Mrs. Beauchamp's fine old two-story house in the middle of the block had been turned into Grady's Paint & Body, and that Mr. and Mrs. Chapman's house with the fish pond and gardens had been torn down completely and had been replaced by a deserted Whataburger.

The rich guys in Fort Worth were supposed to be in financial trouble, too, if I could take the word of TCU's chancellor, because of a few slimy bankers who were now in prison and a few grubby real estate developers who were now living in the Cayman Islands. I would be the first to admit that I didn't know very much about the financial world. Recession, inflation and deficit were words that made me appreciate the remote clicker on the TV. As I drove around the rich-guy neighborhoods, I did notice a "For Sale" sign in the yard of every other mansion, but I also noticed the parking lots were full at all of the country clubs. Until the country clubs were emptied of gin rummy players and noontime drunkers, all of whom were still living on granddaddy's oil and cattle money, there was no real cause for panic, I decided.

For a while, society murders were a growth industry in Fort Worth, if not in all of Texas. I drove along what had become known as The Fort Worth Murder Trail. It wasn't anything the Chamber of Commerce liked to brag about, but it was something every visitor to the city seemed to enjoy more than the Kimball Museum or a tour of the old stockyards. I drove by the mansion where Ronnie Hinds shot and killed his wife, Heather, so he could marry Patricia Carldon. I drove by the mansion where Polly Seymour shot and killed her husband, Ed, the rich dentist, when she caught him making a porno video with two fourteen-year-old girls from Paschal High. I drove by the mansion where Ollie Bob Bowman shot and killed his father so he could inherit the family drilling company. I drove by the mansion where Virginia Rense shot and killed her husband, Rodney, because he used to make her hang up her clothes. I drove by the mansion where Kathy McCaffrey shot and killed Frank McCaffrey, the rich car dealer, so she could marry, and support in the style to which he had become accustomed, Darron Pinckney, the artist. All of these upstanding citizens had pleaded not guilty to these murders, and in trials that had been talked about all over Texas, Horse Race Hamrick, the famous criminal lawyer from Houston, had miraculously got them off. I was acquainted with Horse Race Hamrick slightly, through sports, and he didn't like to see it put that way—that he got them off. "They were found innocent by a jury of their peers," he would insist, with a wink. The last time I had bothered to inquire about the murderers, I had been informed by somebody at the *Light & Shopper* that they were all doing quite well. They were still living in Fort Worth and could be found almost any day, either out at one of the country clubs or shopping at Neiman-Marcus.

As I drove past the last murder mansion, I glanced at my watch and realized it was time to go meet Earlene. Coincidence, I called it.

50

I ORDERED THE CATCHER'S MITT AND EARLENE ORDERED A diet salad. I said, "A diet salad's not food. A diet salad is what food eats." Earlene glared at me and asked for her money. I wrote her a check. She folded the check and put it in her purse.

We were lucky to grab a table in the dining room. This was the noon rush hour at Herb's and the catcher's mitt with pintos and fries and cream gravy was the day's special at $3.19. There had been a line waiting for a table, but Earlene was a good customer and Robyn, the barmaid, had seen her come in. Robyn had gestured to Alma, the hostess, and Alma had seated us ahead of a heavy-lidded man in a wheelchair being looked after by a frail woman in hair-curlers and a neckbrace.

In another era, I could have slipped the line if Herb Macklin had seen me come in, or if the old barmaid, Juanita Hutchins, had seen me come in. But Herb had retired to his farm in Jacksboro, and Juanita had gone off to become a country singer and songwriter. Juanita's photo was framed and hung on the wall. The photo was inscribed with a line from one of Juanita's hits: "Life don't owe me a living, but a Lear and a limo ain't bad."

A lot of us liked to claim we had been drinking in Herb's during the nights when Juanita had written some of the songs that made her famous. Things such as "Rendezvous Rhonda, the Motel Queen," and "He Didn't Need Algebra to Think Up a Threesome."

Earlene seemed to be holding up well despite her life of torment. A few lines around the eyes and neck, but she had kept her shape and had dodged the gray hair that had evidently attacked Rebecca Sue Ellis.

"What did you say to James about archaeology?" Earlene asked, as I cut off and shoved aside the third of a catcher's mitt that a dinosaur couldn't have chewed.

"I said it sounded expensive and I couldn't see a big payday at the end of it."

"I'll tell you what I told him. I told him it was utter bullshit, he could get his butt in gear and graduate with a business degree, and get a job like any other white man. I knew I would have to handle it."

"I'm trying to handle it in my own way."

"You never handled anything important in your whole life."

"I handle the typewriter pretty well."

"I don't want you to give James another nickel till he graduates."

"I only loan him money when he needs it. He paid me back once—part of it."

"I mean it, Jim Tom."

"I know you mean it. You've always meant everything you ever said."

"What is that supposed to mean?"

"It means you've always been a direct person."

"Tryin' to talk to you is hopeless. You love to get off the subject."

"The subject is our son, right?"

"It *was*."

"I know that."

"It is just like that business with Linda Beth Coggins."

"What's James got to do with Linda Beth Coggins?"

"James doesn't have anything to do with Linda Beth Coggins. *You* did."

"When?"

"One of those *many* nights and days when I needed you and I couldn't find you anywhere."

"Are we talking about high school now?"

"Of course, I'm talkin' about high school. Why would I be talkin' about Linda Beth Coggins if I wasn't talkin' about Paschal? Linda Beth Coggins is dead."

"She is?" I was actually surprised to hear this.

"She died two years ago in surgery. She went in for an appendectomy and never came out, and Dr. Dexter, that old fool, had the audacity to show up at her funeral. It was a wonderful funeral. All of the old DBS's were there. I saw Dorothy Chatham for the first time in years. She looked too thin, if you ask me. She and Bobby Lee still live in Wichita Falls. She had hip surgery last month."

"I didn't know Linda Beth died. I'm sorry."

"Oh, I would be, too, if I were you."

"You never forget anything, do you, Earlene? I seem to recall that I went out with Linda Beth for a while because you said we should date other people."

"My mother said that."

"You listened to her."

"I didn't *do* it."

"You could have."

"But I didn't—and you couldn't wait to do it!"

"Does it really matter now?"

"Yes, it does. It matters because things matter in life, but I don't expect you and your typewriter to know anything matters, including the future of your son. Nothing ever mattered to you but something you had to write.''

"Which you never read."

"Be sure you bring *that* up."

"I take it back."

"I would like to know when I had time to read anything when I was raising a child, and keeping house, and tryin' to look after my mother, especially after she had back surgery, and tryin' to look after Aunt Iris after her gallstone surgery, and all the time being worried sick because my daddy was so overweight and fightin' diabetes to boot? But I couldn't expect you to understand that, or even think about it—not if it interfered with a Cotton Bowl game!''

"I have a better idea about it now," I said. "How's your social life, Earlene? Going out with anybody?"

"What business is it of yours?"

"It's none of my business—forget I asked."

"I do see someone occasionally. I'm not a hermit."

"Mr. Thompson . . . ?"

"Where did you hear that?" She looked stunned, frightened.

"I didn't hear it anywhere."

"I want to know what you've heard!"

"I haven't heard anything. Where would I hear it in New York? It was a guess. You work together. You've been working for him for years. I just figured . . ."

Earlene cut me off, saying "Otha Thompson happens to be the nicest, gentlest, most considerate man I have ever known. He is thoughtful in ways you would never dream of, and he is a saint to put up with his wife's migraine headaches the way he does, and if it gives him a little bit of enjoyment in his life to take me out to dinner, or to a movie, after we leave work, I don't think it's a very big crime!''

"I certainly don't, either," I said, controlling a smile.

A man stopped by our table as he was passing through the room. A tall fellow in his sixties. If I had ever known him in my Fort Worth days, I couldn't remember it.

"Jim Tom Pinch," he said.

"Guilty."

"Ace Woodall," he announced. I shook his hand in a robot

fashion, and quickly wished I hadn't. Ace Woodall tried to crush it.

"I haven't seen you around lately," he said.

"I haven't been around lately."

"On the road, huh?"

"Yep."

"How you, little lady?"

"Fine," Earlene said, reaching for her ice tea.

"This is Earlene . . . ," and my voice trailed off into a word that sounded like "thorserpish." I wasn't sure whether Earlene was going by Pinch or Thornton, her maiden name, these days. She had been back and forth on it.

"How's everything down at the paper?" Ace Woodall asked.

"Pretty colorful."

"The New York Light and Shopper, I call it."

"Do you really?"

"If it's about niggers or Jews, they'll print it, won't they? Heh, heh. How's old Big 'Un Darly? I haven't seen him around lately."

Big 'Un Darly had been the sports editor of the *Light & Shopper* for thirty-five years. He had hired me out of college. I had replaced him as sports editor when he retired. Big 'Un would be in his eighties now, and the last I heard, he had moved back to Claybelle, a little town twenty-five miles southwest of Fort Worth. What I remembered best about Big 'Un was his habit of pouring cream gravy over his watermelon at the Piccadilly Cafeteria and his strongly held belief that if you addressed any black person as "Yuryee!" the black person would answer promptly.

"Big 'Un's somewhere," I said to Ace Woodall.

"Aw, hell, I still pick up your rag once or twice a week. I keep up with you fellows. What do you think about that nigger deal out at TCU?"

"I don't know much about it."

"I went to Texas A & M myself."

"A & M's a good school. Lot of tradition."

"Well, it was—before they went coed on us, but . . . the old world keeps changing. Good to see you again."

Ace Woodall moved on to the back of the dining room and joined a table of businessmen. For a moment, I'm afraid I lost a grip on my habitual nonchalance.

"Gee, it was good to see old Ace again," I said. "I guess I just barely missed him at the library earlier. It always makes you feel good to run into somebody who's been reading the column you haven't written in twenty-three years. Jesus. I just hope I can get out of this town without getting physically hurt."

Earlene looked at me as she would a paraplegic. "Amazing. Totally amazing."

"What is?"

"That you never change. That something like what that man said is the only thing that can get a rise out of you."

"It's my profession, Earlene."

"It's sick, is what it is. I have to go back to work."

I threw a twenty-dollar bill on the table, tipping twelve dollars on an eight-dollar check. My contribution to the city's depressed economy.

I walked Earlene to her car, which was a new white compact something-or-other. I didn't risk a comment on it.

No goodbye kiss from Earlene as usual. No hug. Not even a handshake.

She unlocked her car and got in and started it and pushed down the window. She said, "You are going to be a lonely and bitter old man, Jim Tom, and I pray to God I live to see it!"

She ignored my grin and friendly wave as she backed the car out of the parking spot and sped away.

My mind was already made up to leave town a day sooner than I had planned. I drove downtown to the hotel and went up to my room and grabbed my canvas overnight bag and the geezer-codger portable. I went down to the lobby and checked out. I gave the valet parking attendant twenty dollars to turn in my rented Lincoln for me. I hopped in a taxi. At the D/FW terminal, I told the girl behind the American Airlines counter to get my ass to Indianapolis, Indiana, and I didn't care how many stops I had to make—as many as possible, I hoped. That way, I could get off the plane for a few minutes and smoke a fucking cigarette in this land of the free, as it used to be known.

51

UNLESS YOU UNDERSTAND THE INTIMATE RELATIONSHIP BE-
tween a universal joint and a left axle—and I had never come
close—you can grow weary of the Indy 500 pretty fast. You
start growing weary of it long before the wall of sound hits you
in the forehead and the acrid smell and taste of fumes wrap
around your senses. The weariness starts the first day you're in
town for Race Week and realize you have to fight an endless
weave of traffic from your downtown hotel to the Speedway,
the old Brickyard. The Speedway is only three miles from
downtown, but it takes an hour to get there because of the
traffic, and the traffic mostly consists of bikers in black leather
vests with knife scars on their bellies and drunken Winnebago
pilots holding up signs that say, "Free Beer If You Show Us
Your Tits."

That's how I remembered it, and that's what I was telling
Jeannie in my hotel room at the Holiday Inn.

We had both arrived that night, two nights and a long day
before the race. I had called her from the lobby to let her know
I was there, and she met me in my room with part of a Domino's pizza and two Cokes out of a cold-drink machine.

Jeannie gave me a kiss and said she loved me and had missed
me terribly. I said I didn't know about her plane, but mine had
stopped three times and I was exhausted, and besides that, I
was going to wind up a bitter and lonely old man, and what
kind of dog should I get?

"You are *not* an old man, and stop acting like one," she
said.

She went on to say that her father was sixty-eight years old,
could pass for a man of fifty, and consistently shot in the low
70s at his country club in Ashville, and *his* father, her grand-
father, was eighty-nine and still smoked two packs of cigarettes
a day.

"Age is all in the mind," she said. "We have a long life ahead of us."

"The next two days will shorten it considerably," I said.

I went to sleep on one of the twin beds in the room while Jeannie sat up and watched movies on TV. Once during the night when I got up to take a leak, Jeannie was sitting cross-legged on the other bed, laughing and smoking, as Hugh Marlowe was speaking up to Bette Davis, saying, "It is about time the piano learned it did not write the concerto."

"*All About Eve*," Jeannie said, grinning with delight.

"I know," I replied, sleepily. "I am Addison DeWitt. I am nobody's fool."

I awoke to an empty room the next morning, but there was a note by the phone, which said: "Lonely and Bitter: I'm in the coffee shop with newspapers. Love, Margo."

By the time I got down to the coffee shop for breakfast, Jeannie had read all the papers.

"A Marlboro Penske Chevrolet is going to win," she said. "They have the best setup."

"I wouldn't be surprised," I said.

"What is a setup?"

"A setup is what wins a car race. The winning driver always says, 'We had a good setup.' A setup has to do with the chassis, the fuel, the tires, the pit crew, and all the universal joints and left axles."

"You don't know shit about cars, do you?"

"I know three makes of cars—Hertz, Avis, and limo."

"How are we going to write about this?"

"Same old way. We ask somebody what happened."

52

WE DROVE OUT TO THE BRICKYARD THE DAY BEFORE THE RACE to get used to the grit that would lodge behind our eyes and also to pick up credentials. As we crept along with the bikers and Winnebagos, I cautioned Jeannie not to experience a false sense of encouragement when she saw the first "Speedway" sign.

"This sucker is huge," I said.

It took us thirty minutes just to move halfway around the service road to the press entrance, and another twenty minutes after we were on the looping road that went past the eighteen-hole golf course, the fire station, the hospital, the museum, and several other small brick buildings, all of which were contained within the infield.

"The track goes around all this?" Jeannie said.

"Right. All this plus two Third World nations."

We found a parking space near the museum and stood in line for an hour to pick up the credentials, listening all the while to auto racing writers talk about grip, wing adjustments, wrench men, and Turn 4's.

Back to the car after the credential ordeal to loop around some more and find the press building. Jeannie was astonished to discover that the press facility for this famed event was so small, so dowdy, so spartan, and decorated in Early American latrine.

I called her attention to a big chalkboard on the wall. It was there to shed light on all of the cars in the race—the make, model, driver, team owner, chief mechanic, etc.

"We live by this chart," I said. "It tells us that Bobby Ray Erickson is driving a Lotus he bought from Roger Penske."

"Is that important?"

"It depends on how he gets killed."

I led Jeannie on a tour. The press building was near the car stalls. We meandered among the stalls where all the crews were working on their setups.

"Tricky overalls," Jeannie observed.

We walked down a narrow road leading to the track itself.

"Hey, yo!"

The yell came from behind us and we leaped out of the way as a crew pushed a whining car past us. The car exploded and sped away, making a noise you could feel in the back of your throat.

We strolled along gasoline alley behind a chain-link fence and watched pit crews doing one thing or another to brightly colored, decal-splattered racing machines.

Jeannie commented on the Penske logo, which was all around us, on all the yellow trucks and oil cans. It's impossible to escape the Penske logo at Indy. You see it in your sleep.

Jeannie gazed around the infield with horror. There were cars and people as far as we could see, and the infield was already running with rivers of vomit, beer, grease, and smoke. You can't see from one end of the infield to the other. Only a faraway glimpse of the rising turns on the two-and-a-half-mile track, above the hamburger stands and beer tents. It's the worst vantage point for any sports event in the world, but I assured her there would be two hundred thousand people there tomorrow, waiting for a car to hit a wall and a driver to burn to death.

We went through the tunnel under the track to the grandstand side of the Speedway and climbed a small, open-air tower, a rickety old structure. To our left, I pointed out the last turn, a steep curl before the short straightaway to the finish line, and to our right, I pointed out the first turn. That's all you can see of Indy, even from the press box.

"Where is the rest of the track?" she asked.

"It's way down there and way around there and then they come back here."

"What am I doing here? I could see it better at home on TV."

"Yeah, but you wouldn't get a blistering headache or have the exquisite taste of fuel on your tongue."

We attended Jimmy Burt Logan's press conference later in the day. Jimmy Burt Logan would be driving one of the Marlboro Penske Chevrolets. He talked about the aerodynamic edge he would expect to have if his crew could fine-tune the wing adjustment. He talked about a minor ignition problem. He talked about an exhaust pipe correction. He talked about his "groove."

While I drank coffee in the press room, Jeannie went off to corral Jimmy Burt Logan after his press conference, to see if she could get something out of him nobody else would have. She came back in forty-five minutes.

"Scoop?" I said.

"Uh-huh. Big one."

"What?"

"He likes his setup."

53

As Jeannie and I caught up on our lives over dinner at our Holiday Inn that night, there were a couple of things I neglected to mention. I didn't tell her about the TCU church that was hemorrhaging money for college football players. No newspaper person needed to know about such a thing, not even one who thought she was in love with me. More than once in the past, I had shared something confidential with a newspaper friend—a Richie Pace or somebody—and the newspaper friend had found the information too irresistible not to print, and I had wound up in quicksand, barely able to lie my way out of the ugly situation. I also saw no useful purpose, for the moment at least, in telling Jeannie that another woman, Nell Woodruff, thought she was in love with me. I was full of secrets.

Jeannie had a secret, too, but it was one she shared with me. TV was interested in her.

"In what way?" I asked.

"On camera."

"Local?"

"Network. CBS."

"Are we talking Edna R. Murrow here?"

"The Edna R. Morrow of sports."

"You're not interested, I trust."

"I'm interested enough to keep listening. The money could be outrageous."

"You're a writer. A damn good one. Good writers don't go into television. A bad writer does, but a good writer doesn't. Fuck the money."

"Fuck a half-million dollars a year? Maybe more? Fuck a possible million dollars in three years?"

"That's beyond outrageous."

"They like the way my mouth looks. They say it's all in the mouth."

"Who's talking to you from the network?"

"This executive producer in New York. They're looking for a woman."

"They're always looking for a woman. They keep hoping to find one who knows the difference between baseball and badminton."

"He says I'm their number one choice. I told him no three times on the phone, then he flew out to LA and took me to lunch."

"At the Bel Air."

"Right. Then he took me to dinner."

"At Morton's."

"Right. That's when I called an agent. A woman named Sonya at ICM in LA. The executive producer took the agent to lunch . . ."

"At The Palm."

". . . right, and Sonya says the guy didn't even blink. She thinks we can do better."

"Because of your mouth."

"*And* my mind."

In the gravest possible tone, I said, "Jeannie, can you really see yourself on the sideline at the Georgia-Florida game, telling America what gator-tail tastes like? 'And now back to you, Jim Nantz.' "

"They want me for more than that."

"About fifteen years ago, CBS offered me twice as much as I was making at *SI* to sit on a tower at golf tournaments. I was tempted, but in a sobering moment, I realized I didn't want to say 'Let's go to fourteen' the rest of my life. If I'd taken the job, I would have been better off financially for a few years, but I would also be dead by now. I would have drunk myself to death.''

"They want me to do in-depth features, on the NFL . . . all kinds of things.''

"In twenty seconds or less.''

"I can change the system.''

"Nobody changes the system. The system changes *you*.''

"I can live in New York if I want to.''

"If you do that, you better ask for more money. When do they want you?''

"Not till fall.''

"Good,'' I said. "That gives you three happy months before they change your hair and make you look like a housewife in Toledo. There's this hairdresser who works for all the networks. His job is make every woman on camera look stupid. I'm sure he gets his inspiration from the Miss America pageant.''

"I haven't made up my mind. That's why I'm talking to you about it.''

"Up to me, huh? I talk you out of it and for the rest of your life, I'm the guy who cost you a million dollars. I talk you into it, and I'm the guy who fucked up your hair.''

"You know how much I love what I do, Jim Tom. It's going to break my heart to leave newspapers. But Jesus, the money.''

"There's really no choice,'' I said. "You have to go for the money.''

"You wouldn't.''

"I'd like to think I wouldn't, but I've never been money-whipped that bad.''

54

THE CARS WERE WHINING BY SO FAST, WE COULDN'T MAKE out the decals. We were up on the rickety tower with grit in our eyes and so much fuel on our tongues we couldn't taste the Coca Colas we were holding. The band had already played "Back Home in Indiana," and somebody on the PA system had already said, "Gentlemen, start your engines," and there had already been the pileup on the first turn that had put ten of the thirty-three cars out of the race. Nobody killed. Just fires and twisted metal. A person was handing out Xeroxed sheets of lap reports and average speeds, and down in gasoline alley, the occasional car was coming in for a pit stop and tires were flying in the air. Some driver had hit a wall on some turn we couldn't see. Some favorite was fading because of a broken exhaust pipe. Another driver had withdrawn because of an ignition problem. Jimmy Burt Logan was in the lead through sixty-eight laps in his Marlboro Penske Chevrolet, although the only way to know this was to look at the tower scoreboard in the infield. "Had enough?" I said to Jeannie.

"Press room," she said.

We watched the next hour and a half on TV in the press room, drinking gasoline coffee and nibbling on cheese things. The cars kept going around the oval, and some astute racing writer informed us that Antonio Cherma's water pump had failed.

An internal announcement in the press room alerted us to the drama of the last few laps. Jimmy Burt Logan was only a third of a lap ahead of Theo Stoddard in his Lola, and both drivers had a pit stop scheduled but they might try to skip it—it was all up to the tires.

The astute racing writer told us he liked Stoddard's chances.

"Stoddard's going after it," the racing writer said, directing our attention to the Lola on TV. "He's low in the turns. Look at that! He's slipping the grass on Turn 3. He's drifting out and skimming the wall on Turn 4."

"Did you see that?" Jeannie asked me.

"No," I shrugged. "All I can see is my headache. It looks like Christmas lights cavorting with Penske logos."

"Logan knows he's leading," the astute racing writer said. "Roger is telling him on the radio, but sometimes a driver doesn't know it, or believe it. Last year, the computers went down and the race turned into high-tech chaos. Rick Mears won the race and didn't know it."

"We ought to go watch the finish live," Jeannie said.

"You go," I said. "I'll be right here."

Jeannie went back up on the rickety tower.

Everybody in the press room was standing up and crowded around the TV sets as Jimmy Burt Logan's Marlboro Penske Pennzoil Miller Time Goodyear Chevrolet whined into the final lap with Theo Stoddard's Lola on his tail.

It had come down to where Stoddard would try to pass Logan, *if* he could pass him, and whether one or both of them would be killed, in which case Red Harrison in a Lotus, now in third place, would win the 500.

Stoddard didn't try to pass Logan until the last turn, the steep curl leading into the straightaway to the finish line and the checkered flag.

Stoddard was the low car but trailing by just a little too much to have the right of way. Jimmy Burt Logan wouldn't back off. Suddenly, their wheels touched—and Stoddard's Lola went into a bizarre spin. The Lola banged into the wall, lost a tire, and went spinning into the infield.

Jimmy Burt Logan's car swerved and wiggled in the middle of the track, but the driver held it steady and came under the flag shaking his fist in the air, in triumph. Moments later, he glided the Penske car down Victory Lane with tricky overalls crawling all over it.

Meanwhile, in the infield, Theo Stoddard had climbed out of his car, slammed his helmet to the ground, and was kicking the Lola and having a cuss fight with his crew.

Jeannie came rushing back into the press room. "Did you see that? Fantastic! I saw it live!"

"Good for you," I said.

She then frowned and said, "What the fuck happened?"

We wrote through most of the internal announcements in the press room. Periodic bursts of information, such as the fact that Jimmy Burt Logan led the race for ninety-two laps, including the last twenty in succession, and that he maintained an average speed of 187 miles per hour.

Presently, it was announced that Jimmy Burt Logan was in the interview room, another unimpressive structure a few steps away. Jeannie went to hear his thoughts. I didn't. When she came back, I asked her to give me his best quote.

"He said they had a good setup."

Jeannie wrote about the last lap. I wrote about the wall, saying that through the years, the wall had won more Indy 500s than A. J. Foyt, Wilbur Shaw, and all of the Unsers combined. I concluded by offering a suggestion on how to make automobile racing more interesting and prove who the best driver was, really.

Two-way traffic.

55

TO BE HONEST ABOUT IT, I WAS GLAD JEANNIE LABORED OVER her Indy column for six hours, straining every muscle in her upper body in an effort to sound authoritative. She came back to the hotel too tired to do a mattress thing.

I had showered off the grit and was drinking alone in the bar when Jeannie walked in. All she wanted, she said, was a long soak in a tub and a good night's sleep.

I looked at her on the bar stool next to me and I knew it was Jeannie Slay, ace columnist, but I kept visualizing this person I would see sometime in the future on TV. A strange girl, deplorable hairdo, different makeup, a frilly sweater she would never have picked out for herself, her eyes shifting from the camera to the teleprompter.

What a waste of talent, I thought, but I didn't bring up the subject of TV again, and neither did she. We both knew there would be plenty of occasions to discuss it later. Over the next couple of months we were going to be in many of the same places—at the U.S. Open, Wimbledon, British Open, Summer Olympics.

We were probably going to be at the fight, too, in August. It was beginning to look as if the gangsters had worked out all of the details for Rhino Ray Thomas, the heavyweight champ, to meet Nelson (Pork Chop) Perkins, the top contender. Rhino and Pork Chop had been ducking each other for two years, but they had been staying in the news by knocking out drunks in the ring and getting arrested for wife-beating and shoplifting. Reports in newspapers were now saying they were finally going to collide in August, in either Las Vegas or Atlantic City. The venue, I presumed, would depend on where the nation's cocaine dealers would decide to hold their annual convention.

Jeannie kissed me goodnight and limped to the elevator. We would have an early breakfast and go to the airport together. I drank a while longer, until the bikers came in, then I went to my room to call the office and see if my column had made it through the maze of drones with only minor cuts and bruises.

Sunday night after the dinner break was never a good time to try to reach anybody in our office. Most of the staff would have gone home, leaving things adrift until Monday noon. Some would be at Fu's, but they would have been there since the middle of the afternoon and wouldn't have the slightest notion of what I was talking about.

I tried several extensions—Nell's, Christine's, Bryce's, even Lindsey Caperton's—but got no answer. I finally found Wayne Mohler in the copy room. He was doing two things. He was doing what he could to keep the weeping Miriam Bowen from committing suicide over her daughter's failure to get accepted by The Spence School, but mainly he was changing his story on a Chicago Cub outfielder back to the way he had written it.

Wayne was a crisp, clear writer who needed less editing than any of us, but this didn't matter to a drone.

"Have you seen my column anywhere?" I asked Wayne.

"No," he said. "I'm fighting my own comma war."

Skeleton staff tonight, Wayne said. Bryce was still down at

Pine Valley on an outing with clients, and Lindsey Caperton had gone to the theater. Lindsey and Paula had been invited to join Fenton Boles and Fenton's mother at a black-tie opening of Stephen Sondheim's new musical, *Rebecca of Sunnybrook Farm*.

"Where's the gang?"

Wayne said Nell and Charlotte Murray had gone somewhere to eat Mexican food and hadn't come back, and Christine and Wooden Dick were at the Hilton, doing what they usually did on Sunday nights. "Doug's here," he said. "I'll switch you to Doug."

Doug McNiff cleared his throat loudly and said, "Rather an interesting race. Sam has quite a nice beat on it."

Sam Crumby was *SM*'s motor sports writer that I had never actually laid eyes on. It was said he lived in Long Beach. His stories sort of appeared out of a void.

"What kind of beat did Sam get?"

"The business about the chassis. It was a new chassis, the PC-93 Lullaby, that made the difference."

I said, "Doug, I don't know that we ought to go overboard on that. After four hundred and ninety-nine and two-thirds miles, there wasn't a half a car difference between the Penske and the Lola."

"Quite right," Doug said. "Just that tiny bit of aerodynamic difference. Sam explains it in rather marvelous detail."

I gave up. "Who handled my column?"

"Reg Turner caught it."

"Did the windy boy do any serious damage?"

"Not at all. He only had to cut one paragraph, I believe."

"Which one?"

"The first one, but it reads quite nicely."

56

NOT MUCH OF AN EXCUSE WAS EVER NEEDED TO HAVE A POUR-
ing in the office. The pouring was a cocktail party toward the
end of a workday to which everybody was invited and at which
everybody would drink out of coffee mugs, plastic cups, or
even a brown leather loafer if there was nothing else available.
The departure of a dear employee, either through retirement or
to a better job, was an excuse for a pouring, as was someone's
return from illness, someone's pregnancy, or Valentine's Day,
or Robert E. Lee's birthday, or the assassination of a tyrant
somewhere in the world, or the fact that there were only twenty-
three more shopping days before the Super Bowl. Pourings
were supposed to be happy occasions, a time when staff members could be on an equal footing with their bosses—discuss
the boss' habits and manners and not let the staff member's
shoddy salary and current assignment go unspoken. Office romances developed at pourings and office romances could be
shattered at pourings. Many women would often burst into
tears before a pouring was over, and many a male commuter
would often miss his last train to Long Island before a pouring
was over. Lamps and chairs would often get broken at pourings
because very few drones were good dancers. Many of my
friends and associates enjoyed pourings. Wayne Mohler, for
instance, always saw a pouring as an excuse to shove Lindsey
Caperton into a corner and call him an insufferable prick. Ralph
Webber always embarked on a pouring with great anticipation,
and he would nearly always come away with a piece of ass.
There were a few of us, however, who never stayed very long
at these social functions, sharing the view, as we did, that they
were unmitigated hell.

The pouring for Nell Woodruff started in Bryce Wilcox's
office. It was on a Monday in the late afternoon at the end of
the first workweek in June. The last parenthesis had been inserted in the last story of the closing issue, and Bryce was

particularly pleased with the week's cover, a startling closeup of two NBA armpits. Photo credit: Hae-Moon Yoong.

The announcement of Nell's promotion had come around earlier in the day in the form of a memo from Bryce, which said:

"To: The Staff

"From: The Managing Editor

"I am delighted to announce that Nell Woodruff is being elevated to the rank of Senior Editor, effective immediately. She will be a roving department head, working on all major sports, and working closely with myself, the Executive Editor, and the Assistant Managing Editors on ways that will continually improve the appearance and content of our book, which, I might add, is in very good health these days, thanks to the efforts of all of you as well as America's ever-growing fascination with what I like to call The Wonderful World of Sport.

"It goes without saying that Les Padgett, chairman of the board of TPG, Inc., and Fenton Boles, our chief executive officer, join me in expressing extreme pleasure that a FEMALE staff member can be rewarded with this promotion.

"Please join me in my office at 4:30 this afternoon for a pouring to wish Nell good luck in her important new assignment. B.W."

Nell was a popular person and the moment the memo hit the in-boxes, she was inundated with phone calls from around the floor and found herself receiving guests who wanted to congratulate her.

As I arrived in Nell's office to give her a kiss, Christine was already there.

"You fucked him," Christine said.

Nell laughed. "I didn't. Honest."

Christine broke into a smile and gave Nell a hug.

I said, "Babe, you know what this means, don't you? It's raw power. The memo all but says you're the next assistant m.e. Great victory for writers. We have somebody to fight the parenthesis wars for us."

"I'll be in there slugging."

"What's the salary?"

"I can't say it out loud. I'm too embarrassed."

"A hundred and twenty-five?" I said, guessing.

"Close."

"My God," Christine mumbled.

"A little under a U.N. hooker, but not bad," I said.

"Nope, not bad," Nell grinned. "Now I can almost afford my apartment rent."

57

NO EDIT PERSON UNDERSTOOD HOW OUR MAGAZINE GOT printed nowadays. It had something to do with computers, laser beams, satellites, and my own suspicion about a conscientious little gnome out of MIT who lived full-time in a graphics screen and could only be heard to raise his voice when it was time to feed him more microchips, or peanuts.

Still, the managing editor's mock-up room, next door to his office, was an important place. It was a big, carpeted room with no furniture and one wall of windows. Here, Bryce Wilcox would approve or disapprove of layouts and cover tries that would be brought to him by someone from the art department. Lindsey Caperton would usually be at Bryce's side.

"What do you think?" Bryce would ask Lindsey, as they studied a proposed cover.

"The red looks a little harsh to me," Lindsey would say.

"I kind of like it," Bryce would say.

"I mean harsh in the best sense of the word," Lindsey would respond.

The mock-up room served two other important purposes. It was a place where Bryce could practice a full golf swing with his metal driver, and it was always the main bar for a pouring.

A couple of staff people would usually volunteer to be bartenders at a pouring, but pourings were mostly help-yourself affairs with everyone plunging into the whiskey and ice that would have been put on card tables. At the pouring for Nell, the volunteer bartenders were Billy Fain, a kleptomaniac who worked in the mail room, and Charlotte Murray, our overpaid researcher.

"What can I fix your honky ass?" Charlotte asked me. I was among the first arrivals.

"I'll just have a dirty coffee mug of J and B," I said.

I asked Charlotte what she had been working on lately. She said she had been down to Alabama to help our college football authority, Stewart Mason Gardner, prepare a feature on the new head coach at Tuscaloosa. It was Charlotte's first trip to the Deep South. The story wouldn't appear until early next fall. Blubber Daniels was the eighth head coach Alabama had hired since Bear Bryant died. "What did you think of Blubber Daniels?" I asked. She said, "He asked me if I had any brothers who could run a four-two forty."

The trip to the Deep South had not been a pleasant experience, Charlotte said. The accents terrified her, and what exactly was it you were supposed to do with grits?

She said, "I got my black butt outta there after three days—before I wound up half-mast on a magnolia."

Bryce trapped me early on, to tell me about the third, fifth, eighth, thirteenth, and eighteenth holes at Pine Valley. I had been down in that part of New Jersey on numerous occasions to play Pine Valley, and I was quite knowledgeable about the course, but this didn't stop Bryce.

"Third hole," he said. "Four-iron. Two feet right of the cup. Hell of a shot. Didn't even breathe on the putt but I had twenty feet coming back. Some greens, huh? Fifth hole? Driver. Short. You can't get there. What about the eighth? Is that a great short hole? Driver, wedge . . . front bunker, but I got it up and down. Thirteen's the best par four in the world, big guy. Nailed a two-iron. Front edge. Killed the drive on eighteen. Put a five-iron left-front. The pin was back-right. Had to three-putt, right? Holed it. Is that any good? Stayed in the Pine Lodge. Not a bad way to travel. I'm applying for membership. They say the waiting list is five years, but why wouldn't they want the managing editor of *SM*? *I* would. I figure I'm in. One year, two at the outside. I'll have Winged Foot and Pine Valley. Is that any good?"

"What's good for golf is good for the magazine," I said.

"Got to get you back in your cleats, big guy. Come up to Winged Foot next weekend. We'll get Clipper and somebody else."

"I'll be at the Open," I said.

"Oh, that's right. Merion. Good track. Lot of poa last time I played it."

"I'm sure they've corrected it by now."

Most of the pouring-goers were greatly impressed that Fenton Boles and Clipper Langdon dropped by for a short time. I was standing with Nell and Christine when Fenton shook Nell's hand and said, "Well deserved. I believe this makes you the only female senior editor in our magazine group. I hope it will be a sign of encouragement to our other female staffers." The oily dwarf turned to Christine. "You're . . . ?"

I said, "This is Christine Thorne. You met in Innsbruck. She's another one of the bright spots around here, female-wise. Bryce has her in mind for chief of research, if he ever gets around to it."

"Hmmm," said Fenton, and I thought I could see the wheels turning again.

The chief of research at present was Molly Connors, a treacherous little bitch whose incompetence was only overshadowed by her agility to report everything she saw and heard in the office to Lindsey Caperton. Everybody was lobbying to get Molly removed and transferred to another job within the company. Pet food would have been good.

The CEO drifted into a corner and was instantly encircled by Bryce, Clipper, and Lindsey.

"Thanks for the flagrant plug," Christine said.

"I hope it helps more than it hurts," I said. "You never know around here."

A little later, I was motioned into the hallway to join Fenton and Clipper and their plastic cups of Perrier. I heard a reference to ModeTech Industries and another murmured remark about a nonpublic common stock, I think it was. Financial stuff. Wall Street garble.

Fenton said, "Just to bring you up to date, Pinch. We've decided to have a hospitality tent at the U.S. Open. Naturally, we want you to be involved in the, uh . . . hospitality."

I slumped. "You know, Fenton, there are a lot of people who are better at hospitality than I am. I don't know a soul in Philadelphia. I haven't been there in ten years, not since the last time the Open was at Merion."

Clipper said, "Oh, I think a fellow of your ingenuity will come up with something. Rip Bellemy is looking forward to seeing you again, Pincher."

"He is?"

"Rip Bellemy is very important to us right now," Fenton said.

"Why?"

"That's nothing for you to be concerned about."

"Rich guy stuff?"

"You guys," Clipper smiled.

Fenton said, "You might want to start thinking about Wimbledon, too. Hospitality-wise. I'm a strong believer in planning ahead."

To the CEO, Clipper said, "I'd love to take the Ripper to England on the Gulf Four if Lester's not using it."

"We'll see when the time comes."

Fenton asked if I had been in touch with a bank. I had. A banker had been pleased to lend me thirty-five thousand dollars on my signature alone to buy TPG stock.

"You'll see a nice profit," Fenton said.

"It'll be the first time I've ever made a good investment," I said, "other than take the seven-and-a-half and Penn State over Notre Dame."

I was still standing with the CEO and the publisher, as if I was a member of the fraternity, when Lindsey Caperton slithered up, and said, "Fenny, I called Christopher and told him to hold the table—our reservation is for seven o'clock."

"Fine," Fenton said.

It wasn't lost on a few others at the pouring that Fenton Boles and Lindsey Caperton left together.

Presently, there were several signals that it was time for some of us to leave the pouring and move downstairs to Fu's. Wayne Mohler had started to dance with Marge Frack in Bryce's office. One of Christine's roommates, Rachel, had wandered in and was now in a quiet corner in an ardent conversation with Wooden Dick. Word filtered back that things were getting lively in the art department. Ronnie Zander, the art director, was said to be smearing poster paint on the bare tits of some girl nobody had ever seen before. And the weeping Miriam Bowen was on her hands and knees with her head in a wastebasket. She had been there for an hour, with nobody much caring. She wasn't weeping or nauseous. As usual, she had passed out.

Nell and I didn't stay very long at Fu's. This was *her* night, she said, and she wanted to do what *she* wanted to do. Which was go to her apartment, just the two of us. She would cook bacon and eggs for us, and we would sit and talk, or not talk. I could nod off, if I felt like it, and she would stare at the wall and think about her vision of what the magazine should be after she became managing editor someday.

Nell hugged and kissed everyone goodnight at Fu's, including Jimmy, the bartender. We got into a cab driven by a member of the PLO, and I somehow made him understand that he should drive slowly and there would be a bigger tip in it if we could smoke.

"Marrock ca-lock," he said, which I took to mean that we could smoke because he didn't complain about it.

Nell's apartment was massive by the standards of New York single people. Two bedrooms, large living room, small dining area, stand-up kitchen. It was fully carpeted and simply but nicely furnished with pieces from auctions. There was no view but she had a working fireplace. And it was freezing in there. In the summer, she kept the window units at iceberg temperature so she could use the fireplace. She now lit a fire out of two designer logs, as I fixed myself a drink. She also turned down the lights before she went into the bathroom.

I was plopped down on the sofa near the fireplace when she came out of the bathroom, completely nude.

Jesus fucking Christ, is what I thought, as she slowly came toward me in the flickering light. There I was, feasting my eyes for the first time on her drapeless body—her long legs, flat stomach, centerfold breasts. All of it flawless, to be redundant, and holy shit, besides.

She knelt on the carpet in front of me, squeezed between my

legs, and smothered me with a gnawing kiss. Instinctively, I think you could say, I began to caress one of her perfect lungs while running my other hand over her smooth back.

"W-what are we doing here?" I stammered, idiotically.

"The situation clearly calls for a surgical strike," she said, softly if militarily, and with that, she was calmly and somewhat professionally unzipping my pants.

Of course, the term surgical strike was familiar to me from reading newspaper quotes from Pentagon officials, but I don't suppose I had ever appreciated the phenomenal devastation a surgical strike could produce if it was carried out properly.

Not until that night.

58

THE MERION GOLF CLUB ON PHILADELPHIA'S MAIN LINE IS an elegant and historic place where the ghosts of Bobby Jones and Ben Hogan loiter among the oak, beech, and gum trees, and I was wishing I had been around to see Jones complete the Grand Slam at Merion in 1930, or Hogan complete his comeback at Merion in 1950, as I sauntered into the *SM* hospitality tent with Jackie, Debbie, Staci, Justine, and Kimberly.

This was a Saturday afternoon around one o'clock in the middle of June. It was the third day of the U.S. Open but my first day at Merion. I was supposed to have arrived at this sports event by Wednesday night, but Nell and I had been too busy for five days, playing characters in one of those ever-popular, falling-in-love montages you see in the movies.

Nell and Jim Tom have lunch at the Central Park zoo. Dissolve to Nell and Jim Tom having drinks at the River Cafe. Dissolve to Nell and Jim Tom looking at puppies in a pet shop window. Dissolve to Nell and Jim Tom poking around in the Village. Dissolve to a surgical strike.

Nell had released me for a couple of hours on Friday night to recruit the killerettes for *SM*'s hospitality tent.

It wasn't that hard, as it turned out. I had sought the advice of a friend who worked in sports publicity at one of the networks. He said to go into the bar of any of Manhattan's swank hotels around six o'clock and I would step in a minefield. I scored in the first hotel I tried in the upper Fifties. I won't mention the name of the hotel here, to avert a legal problem, but that was where I met Jackie and Debbie, and they had rounded up Staci, Justine, and Kimberly for me.

The recruits were all shapely adorables of the finest quality, if I say so myself. All in their late twenties, well dressed, personable, good-natured, each one a high-rent lady who could easily pass for one of those hair-tossing girls in a shampoo commercial.

Jackie and Debbie were sitting side by side at the bar. From five stools away, I passed a note to Jackie on a cocktail napkin. The note said: "I am trying to write a song for a Broadway musical. You look like you can help me out. What rhymes with home entertainment?"

Jackie looked me over, borrowed a pen from the bartender, and sent back the answer. "Jackie."

I passed her another note. "Jackie, my treasure. This could be a very expensive musical. Is your girlfriend in the home entertainment business, too?"

Her reply: "No. Debbie is a nuclear physicist. Can't you tell?"

I knew I had stumbled onto quality merchandise when Jackie spelled nuclear and physicist correctly.

The three of us moved to a table to have another drink and discuss what I had in mind for them. I gave them my real name and showed them my column picture in an issue of the magazine to prove that I wasn't an undercover vice cop. Jackie and Debbie said they loved golf and they loved Philadelphia and they thought they might know three other ladies who loved golf and Philadelphia as much as they did. Debbie went to a phone and recruited Staci, Justine, and Kimberly.

As I promised, I collected the ladies in a stretch limo the next morning, picking up Jackie and Debbie at their apartments in Sutton Place, and Staci, Justine, and Kimberly at their apartments in the Sixties and Seventies on Park Avenue.

The limo was equipped with a bar. I fixed Bloody Marys for

everybody. Jackie fixed her own, saying, "A Bloody Mary doesn't work unless you can see through it."

All the way to Philadelphia on the turnpikes, I listened to conversations about Chinese silk screens, antiqued walls, Bill Blass, Ralph Lauren, and ranch property in Aspen, Sun Valley, and Santa Fe.

But now we had entered the hospitality tent and I was receiving applause from Clipper Langdon and Rip Bellemy.

Jackie quickly cased the tent. "Great, no Arabs."

Rip Bellemy introduced himself to Jackie—she would have been my choice, too—by handing her five hundred-dollar bills. "Here you go, baby," he said. "This will tide you over till I can get to the stock certificates Monday."

"Well, aren't you nice?" Jackie said, sweetly, taking the money and slipping it into her shoulder bag.

Other mega-clients latched onto Debbie, Staci, Justine, and Kimberly, pairing off, heading for the bar, the sumptuous buffet spread, or a table, the gentlemen in their floral trousers and pastel sports coats, the killerettes in their glued-on Madison Avenue jeans.

Clipper shook my hand. "Outstanding, Pincher. Are they all . . . ?"

"Yep."

"You mean girls who look like this are . . . ?"

"Yep."

"But they could be fashion models . . . movie stars. They could be *wives*."

"Trophy wives. I'm sure they'll all be married to CEOs someday."

"Pincher, you don't know what you've done for the magazine. You have walked in here with two million dollars' worth of advertising! I am personally going to see that you get one hell of a bonus at the end of the year, compadre."

"I don't feel very good about it, frankly, but I'm a strong believer in staying employed."

"It's commerce," he said. "Commerce comes in many different forms, *n'est-ce pas*?"

"I guess it was easier than getting two on the fifty for the

Super Bowl. You'll see that the ladies make it back to New York, will you?''

"Not to worry, El Capitan. They will all be granted diplomatic immunity. I, uh . . . I might just pick out one for myself.''

"Kimberly talks the least. She's the blonde in the six bracelets.''

"Gotcha.''

I went over to say goodbye to Jackie, to assure her that she and her friends had lived up to the highest standards of customer satisfaction.

"Don't run off, sweetie," she said.

"I have to go to work," I said, "but you know what we say about golf, don't you?''

"What's that?''

"There's nothing more boring than a golf tournament in the daytime.''

59

JEANNIE SLAY AND RICHIE PACE WERE HAVING COFFEE IN THE lounge of the press tent. They were as grumpy as everyone else around. The press and contestants are always grumpy at a U.S. Open. It's a grumpy event.

The golfers are always grumpy because they detest the course. They detest it the moment they arrive and can't see anything but weeds and exotic plant life bordering the pinched-in fairways and surrounding the marble-slick greens. The players always accuse the United States Golf Association of setting up the course to make them shoot high scores and look foolish to the fans. The USGA responds by saying it is only trying to protect the ''integrity'' of par and ''identify'' the best golfer of the week, and, meanwhile, ''Play away, gentlemen.''

The press is grumpy because of the way it is always treated by the USGA. The press is invariably headquartered at a scroungy hotel, which is never near the course, the parking passes will only get the writers as far as an area to catch shuttle buses, and most of the air-conditioned rooms of the clubhouse are always off-limits to the writers. Every year the press howls about its treatment and every year the USGA's officers say the inconveniences are a small price for the press to pay for the Open to be held at one of the country's fine old courses, a Baltusrol, Oakland Hills, Oakmont, Winged Foot, Pebble Beach, Southern Hills, or, in this instance, Merion.

I had been baffled for years by the sponsors of golf tournaments. They like to do everything within their power to make the touring pros happy in terms of lodging, food, drink, courtesy cars, baby sitters, travel arrangements, free medical advice, whatever, but the touring pros are never anything but rude and unappreciative and only interested in the million dollars in prize money they have a chance to win that week. Somehow, the touring pro got it in his mind many years ago that it was a federal law, if not a religious commandment, that he should be treated like royalty because of his ability to hit a golf ball. At the same time, the sponsors of most golf tournaments are careless and thoughtless about the members of the press, considering them necessary evils, even though it's the sportswriters who help sell the tickets and glamorize the event and the players. A curious thing. But no more curious than a long-standing attitude on the part of contestants, sponsors, and public alike, deriving, I think, from utter stupidity, that simply because some surly clown on the PGA Tour can hit a high fade with a two-iron, he is qualified to speak out on ways to solve all of the nation's social and economic problems.

Time to recycle that column, I was thinking, as Jeannie greeted me with a hug and kiss in the press lounge.

"Of all the golf tournaments in all the world, you had to walk into this one," she said.

Jeannie had been forewarned that I wouldn't be at Merion until Saturday. I had called her long distance from Nell's apartment, while Nell was asleep, and had pretended to be calling from Athens, Georgia, where I had gone to see how my son was doing after his traffic accident. He was going to be fine. At the moment, I didn't think it would be in anyone's best interest—namely, mine—to confess to Jeannie that Nell and I had been starring in a romantic comedy about a gynecologist and his patient for five days. I wasn't sure how I was going to deal with the confusing situation, although I had thought I might just buy a dog and do nothing.

Jeannie asked if I had been to the press hotel yet. I said no. She said I was in for a taste of pure luxury. The hotel was an hour away in King of Prussia, Pennsylvania. The traffic was dense at all hours. The hotel had sandpaper for bathroom tissue. It had a bar of soap the size of a domino. The hotel restaurant didn't serve past 10:00 P.M., which made it impossible for any newspaper person to get back from the course in time to eat there. The hotel bar was featuring a piercing rock band that never took an intermission. She and Richie and Dub Fricker and a few other writers had been dining at a McDonald's on the way home from Merion every night. Some of them had been entertaining themselves by taking their drinks out to the parking lot and sitting on curbs at night while others had been shooting down spaceships on the electronic game machines in the lobby. But the worst thing about this Open was, well, the Open. She locked her arm in mine and pulled me into the working press area and pointed at the big leaderboard on one wall. Richie Pace followed.

"Who *are* these people?" she said.

Until you came to the name of Bobby Joe Grooves, down in tenth place, the Open was being dominated by a cast of nobodies. Poor old Merion. No Jones or Hogan this time. The leaders through thirty-six holes were all second-class citizens from the PGA Tour.

"What we need," said Richie, "is a good marksman with a deer rifle."

Somebody named Stan Ponder was the leader and he was being pursued by other faded shirts and Ping caps.

Most of the marquee names—Ballesteros, Faldo, Strange, Norman—had missed the cut, and those marquee names who hadn't missed the cut, Mark Peel, Wiley Sullins, and others, were too far back to matter.

"I defy you to tell any of the leaders apart," Jeannie said. "They all wear the same white cap, they all finished eighth at

Memphis, they all live in Orlando, and they're all married to the same wife, who used to be a stewardess."

Richie said, "You know what this Open is? The yellow pages. Your sink's stopped up, you call Stan Ponder. Your roof leaks, you call Mike Teague. Your Plymouth needs a valve job, you call Billy Don Herring."

"I read your column yesterday," I said.

"See the line about speech impediment wins Open?"

"I didn't get that far."

"You didn't go to the bottom?"

"The phone rang."

Jeannie said, "I need lore. My column's begging for mercy. Hear it?"

"I can do lore," I said.

We were on our way out of the press tent when we bumped into Cloyce Windham. He had been out on the course with his chair-stick and binoculars. He was sweating badly in his tweed suit. There were traces of a pimento cheese sandwich on his checkered shirt and wool tie.

"By the way," said Cloyce. "I rather like this Stan Ponder. He's quite stable over the four-footers. He keeps his forearms nicely balanced and his ball-to-target alignment is very consistent."

"That's great," Richie said. "Maybe you and the boring asshole can have dinner sometime."

Cloyce burst into laughter, covering his mouth with his hand. "Yes, I *do* forget about the problems of you daily people."

I said, "See you later, Cloyce. We're going out to follow Olin Dutra."

Cloyce laughed again, appreciatively. Olin Dutra had won the '34 Open at Merion.

We walked halfway down the eighteenth hole outside the gallery ropes. "Right about here," I said. "Out there in the middle of the fairway. This is where Hogan hit the one-iron. He had two-twenty to the middle of the green. He needed a four to tie Mangrum and Fazio. He blistered it . . . got his four . . . won the playoff the next day. This was only a year and a half after the car wreck that almost killed him. Ben gave everybody a great quote that week. 'Write about my golf, not my legs.' "

"You couldn't have been here," Jeannie said.

"No, I was only thirteen. I was a delivery boy for my aunt's drugstore. But I was listening on the radio."

"Why?"

"*Why?* I was growing up in Fort Worth. Ben Hogan and Byron Nelson were from Fort Worth. If you didn't know about Hogan and Nelson by the time you were six, they put poison in your oatmeal."

"What were you delivering for the drugstore?"

"Syrup of Figs and Ex-Lax, mostly."

I took them down to the eleventh hole near the "Baffling Brook," the stream that guarded the green on three sides. The classic drive-and-pitch hole. Imitated a thousand times by architects since Merion was built in 1912. We stood behind the green and watched two or three groups of nobodies play the hole. In the meantime, I lore-whipped Jeannie and Richie.

This was the last competitive hole Bobby Jones played—the hole where he closed out Eugene Homans in the U.S. Amateur final of 1930, wrapping up the Grand Slam. A special Marine detachment had been assigned to protect Jones from the eighteen thousand fans, a huge crowd for those days. Four years later, Gene Sarazen made the eleventh even more famous. In the final round of the '34 Open, Sarazen was leading comfortably until the eleventh. Here was where he misjudged his pitch shot. The ball splashed into the "Baffling Brook." It cost him a triple-bogey seven, and yet he lost to Olin Dutra by only one stroke.

"I have enough," Richie said.

"So do I," said Jeannie. She tugged on my arm. "Take us to Missouri, Matt."

60

NOT EVERY GOLF TOURNAMENT STARTS ON SUNDAY. I LIED. And this U.S. Open championship never started at all, Jeannie was quick to remind me. However, I think the press was grateful to Stan Ponder. The colorless robot won the Open so easily, by six strokes, that all of the writers could start on their prose far ahead of deadline, and this was considered a blessing by those who had been held captive in the press hotel for five days. Stan Ponder won with monotonous rounds of 70, 71, 70, 71 for a two-over par total of 282. In Sunday's final round, no one drew within five strokes of him at any time, and the only moment he flirted with trouble was when he tripped and almost fell coming out of a portable john at the fourteenth hole.

The winner's interview in the press tent was spellbinding.

Question:	"What was the key moment, Stan?"
Ponder:	"I'm not sure."
Question:	"What was the best shot you hit all day?"
Ponder:	"I don't know."
Question:	"What does it mean to you to win the Open?"
Ponder:	"It feels good."
Question:	"Doesn't it feel better than winning at Greensboro?"
Ponder:	"That felt good, too."
Question:	"Did you think you had a chance when you came here?"
Ponder:	"You never know."
Question:	"Did any player give you a tip that helped you this week?"
Ponder:	"I don't think so."
Question:	"Do you have any hobbies, Stan?"
Ponder:	"Not really."
Question:	"Was your wife in the gallery today?"
Ponder:	"I saw somebody that looked like her."

Question: "How will you celebrate tonight?"
  Ponder: "Watch a little TV, I guess."
Question: "Does it give you a special kind of satisfac-
             tion to know you've won on the same golf
             course where Jones and Hogan won?"
  Ponder: "When was that?"

I spent two nights at the hotel in King of Prussia, Pennsylvania, escaping Jeannie's advances under the pretext of staving
off the flu. The freezing temperature in Nell's apartment *had*
given me a sniffle.

Otherwise, as sportswriters often do, we devoted a lot of
time to talking about where we were going instead of where we
were.

We were going to Europe, was where we were going—to
Wimbledon, the British Open, the Summer Olympics in Paris.
I would barely have enough time to return to Manhattan and
pack for six weeks and draw four hundred million dollars in
travel money and get a column ahead before the trip would be
upon me.

I normally looked forward to going to Europe—anywhere in
Europe other than Germany and Austria. Most of Europe was
romantic and sentimental and bathed in the kind of history that
appealed to me, in contrast to South American history, which
was all about scorpions and banana republics, or Asian history,
which was all about dragons and chopsticks, or the history of
India, which was all about guys in bedsheets tripping over
cobras. In Europe, I had been known to sit in sidewalk cafes
for eight or ten hours at a time, watching Nicole and Dick
stroll by.

But there was this minor problem now. Nell Woodruff, *SM*'s
new roving senior editor, had assigned herself to all of those
events with Bryce's full approval. Over the next six weeks,
there would be other friends and associates around, but Nell
was looking at it like she and Jim Tom Pinch were going to
Europe together, and meanwhile, Jeannie Slay was looking at
it like *she* and Jim Tom Pinch were going to Europe together,
which left me wondering how I was going to make it to the
month of August without becoming a eunuch.

61

PROTOCOL IS EVERYTHING AT WIMBLEDON—EVERYTHING
that is not a Pimm's cup, a bowl of strawberries, or a fatheaded
line call on break point. There are those journalists who say
Wimbledon is the most wretched event in the world to cover,
and others who have an unreasoning love for it. The attitude
depends on how you feel about seniority and tradition. It is,
from start to finish of the fortnight, a logistically impossible
place to work, endlessly frantic and frustrating, and in the
middle of all the tiebreaks, rainouts, and IRA bomb scares, the
old wing commanders who run things will sit around and sip
their sherry and nod and smile and say, "I think it's all going
frightfully well, don't you?"

Overlooking the fact that I wanted to punch out a Wimbledon official once a day, my first week in London was a delight.
Nell and Jeannie weren't coming over until the second week of
tennis, and the *SM* hospitality tent wasn't going to open until
the second week of tennis, so I was there with Christine
Thorne, Richie Pace, and Dub Fricker. Good friends. No com-
plications.

We ate good food in some of our favorite restaurants and
drank in some of our favorite pubs, and even watched a little
tennis, mainly on the outdoor courts where matches were going
on all around us and where we were shrewd enough to recognize the future stars of the sport.

Early in the week, before the grass courts turned into brown
dirt littered with chugholes, we were onto Courtney Duncan
and Lars Svanstrom. Courtney Duncan was a fourteen-year-old
girl from Naples, Florida, precious now but soon to become
another teenage monster. She was puppydog cute with big
round chocolate eyes and a winning grin, and she somehow
remained photogenic despite her backhand grunt, her line-call
pout, and her double-fault tantrums. Lars Svanstrom was a
handsome eighteen-year-old blond god with a powerful serve,

the latest in a line of Swedish lunkheads. They would both do very well at this Wimbledon, as you may know, but of course the players always have it easier than sportswriters at Wimbledon.

It all starts with your arrival, and one by one, Christine, Richie, Dub and myself all went through the same thing. You take a taxi from your hotel—in my case, the air-conditioned Hyde Park Hotel in Knightsbridge—and have the driver let you out on Church Road at Gate 8 of the All-England Lawn Tennis Club. There, you plow your way through the queue that has been sleeping on the sidewalk overnight and show the two bobbies on the gate your letter affirming that you have a credential waiting for you.

But the letter is not enough to get you in. So you smoke two cigarettes and study the orange, purple, and green hair on some of the punks in the queue while a bobby goes to round up a "liaison person" who will take you to the press building. The press building is fairly new but it has been built to look a hundred years old. It is painted dark green, like everything else, and is already showing signs of growing ivy on the walls. Wimbledon does ivy the way Manhattan does bricks.

Up to the second floor. Down a narrow hallway blocked by foodcarts and feverish Italian writers jostling each other to get somewhere. Past a door to a room for "British Tennis Writers Only." This is where you can find Ian Malcolm of the *Daily Mail* and Derwent Hopkins of the *Daily Telegraph* if you're looking for daytime drinkers.

Go to a window and wait in line for a drab British lady with a clipped accent to do you the very great honor of presenting you with your laminated plastic badge with your photo on it, to be worn around the neck every waking moment unless you want to be sent to the Tower of London.

Check out the creaking rooms in another hallway where you can find the guys and gals who work in public relations and publicity for the ATP and Virginia Slims–Kraft Foods. They are as vital as an agent for IMG. They are the only people who can give you any background material on any of the players. They alone know that Courtney Duncan's mother, Rita, is a former go-go dancer, and that Courtney's father, Roy, who put the first tennis racket in her hand when she was two, has been unemployed for the past twelve years.

Now to the press cafeteria to see if the sausage rolls, pork pies, cucumber sandwiches, and kidney things look as dreadful as ever. They do, but the price has gone up.

Then to explore the players' tearoom, a key spot, but this requires a special pin embossed with the Wimbledon logo—the flying W. So it's back to the credential window to get the tearoom pin from the drab lady with the clipped accent, after standing in line with other pin-getters from Japan, Poland, Romania, Yugoslavia. Then back down the stairs, go outside, walk down the main boulevard of the grounds, past the front of the Royal Box entrance, go back indoors and up a flight of stairs to be greeted by an unctuous Wimbledon official outside the tearoom. He must scrutinize your badge for five minutes to make sure you haven't manufactured it yourself with your Wimbledon badge-making kit that you bought at Fortnum and Mason.

"Thirty minutes only, please," he will say. "We *must* respect a contestant's privacy—there's a good chap."

The unctuous Wimbledon official in his dandruff-splashed green blazer will make a note of your badge number, for you are not allowed to enter the players' tearoom more than three times during the course of a single day. He will further look at his watch to clock the thirty minutes of your visit.

The tearoom has a bar and snacks and large glass windows and a long, wide balcony from which the players may survey matches in progress on some of the outside courts. The balcony offers a good view of the No. 2 court, the jinx court, the upset court.

"It slopes," Martina Navratilova once swore after almost losing a match on the jinx court to an unseeded Russian.

Onward to see if you can remember where the one restroom is located. One. To accommodate three hundred members of the world press. Down the stairs, along a hallway, up some stairs, down another hallway, ever cautious to stay to your left if you're going *that* way, ever cautious to stay to your right if you're going *this* way. "Ah, yes, there you have it," a helpful Wimbledon official will say.

The restroom is where it always was, and the same four Japs, three Spaniards, and four Germans are waiting in line.

Finally, the hike to appraise your seat in the press section of the Centre Court Stadium. Down the stairs, through a hallway, around a corner, back up some stairs, showing your badge to other Wimbledon officials along the way. "Do *not* go to your left, thank you very much."

As usual, my seat was in the upper rafters of the press section, fifty yards, approximately, above the Royal Box with a corner-of-the-court angle from, approximately, a hundred yards away.

And I would again be sitting between a Serbo-Croatian and a Nigerian.

62

My predicament with Nell and Jeannie, or Jeannie and Nell—I hadn't seen the latest AP rankings—didn't seem to be of the slightest concern to any of my other close friends. When I confided in them individually, either back in New York or now in London, all of them expressed a somewhat impudent view of the matter and only agreed on one thing: it wasn't a moral question.

The Christine Thorne View: I didn't deserve either one of them.

The Wayne Mohler View: Take the one with the best-looking mother. That's what they were going to look like someday.

The Richie Pace View: Forget Jeannie. How could I be in love with somebody who wrote better than I did?

The Dub Fricker View: Switch to Christine. Bigger tits.

The Wooden Dick View: There really ought to be a way to keep fucking both of them.

63

IT HAD BEEN MY OBSERVATION THROUGH THE YEARS THAT most heroines of women's tennis went to the net about as often as Vesuvius erupted. Chris Evert, queen of the baseliners, once played a match at Wimbledon that lasted longer than a page of Proust, and by the time it was over, nobody could remember the name of her opponent. The classic exception was Martina Navratilova, the occasional exception was Billie Jean King, and now the latest exception was Courtney Duncan, star of stage, screen, kindergarten, skin cream, clothing, shoes, and rackets. By the end of the first week, Courtney's serve-and-volley game had made her the darling of this Wimbledon and my column was one of only hundreds that were written about her.

Serving briskly, grunting on her two-hand backhand, and charging the net at every opening, Courtney eliminated four seeded ground-strokers, and as was the case with Tatyana Romanova back at the Winter Olympics, I suddenly needed another interview with an athlete who had been born during the Jimmy Carter Administration.

I would have asked Christine to get the interview for me, but Christine was primarily at Wimbledon because of her language skills and she was busy assisting H.E.S. Bromley, Jr., dealing with Czechs, Germans, Russians, and Frenchmen.

After Courtney smoked a baseliner named Leonora Schaller, the No. 4 seed, in two sets, I approached the child star's mother to see about setting up a one-on-one.

The mother, Rita, no longer looked like a go-go dancer, incidentally. She looked more like a sunburned prison matron who had been turned loose in Harrods with a valise full of her daughter's endorsement money.

We were standing in a pathway between two of the outdoor courts when I introduced myself to Rita and said I would like to have twenty minutes with Courtney at the time of her choosing in the players' tearoom. "You can be present if you wish," I said.

"I am present at *all* of Courtney's interviews," the mother said. "If you want to write about something, you should write about the courtesy car situation and the practice court situation."

"In what way?"

"Our courtesy car was ten minutes late this morning. That is inexcusable."

"Sorry to hear it."

"Have you tried to arrange a practice court at Wimbledon?"

"Not in years."

"It's ridiculous. This tournament is very poorly run. Wimbledon could take a lesson from Amelia or Boca, if you want my opinion."

"The interview won't take long."

"Courtney will see you for fifteen minutes at four seventeen this afternoon. Please confine your questions to tennis."

"Gladly."

"Who did you say you write for?"

"I'm Jim Tom Pinch. I have a column in *The Sports Magazine*."

"Oh, yes. *SM*. That's where H.E.S. Bromley, Jr., works, isn't it?"

"Yes."

"He's a complete imbecile."

"But he means well," I said.

I arrived in the players' tearoom at four seventeen, but Courtney Duncan and her mother weren't there. By four forty-seven, they still hadn't come in. I had used up one visit.

I went to the Wimbledon official on the door and explained my problem. Would he mind starting the clock over? He raised an eyebrow as I studied the hair in his nose.

"Quite out of the question," he said.

"I guess I'll go back in."

"Very good," he said, looking at his watch. "Your second visit begins . . . now."

Thirty more minutes passed. I was having another cup of coffee in the tearoom when the Wimbledon official came up to my table. "Terribly sorry. You shall have to leave, I'm afraid."

"Let's start the third visit," I said.

It was a quarter after five. I was willing to gamble on Courtney Duncan and her mother showing up in the next five or ten minutes. Nothing like a little suspense.

"Third visit, it is. If you will just go outside and come in again."

"Go outside the door and come back in the door again?"

"Keeps it tidy, you see."

"You're serious?"

"Quite serious."

I got up and walked outside into the hallway. "Maybe I'll just wait here till the player shows up," I said. "That way, I won't squander my allotted time."

"Quite impossible. Must keep the hallway clear."

"Fine," I said. "Third visit coming up."

"At . . . five twenty-two. Thank you very much indeed."

Going back into the tearoom, I somehow restrained myself from asking him how England had ever won a fucking war.

Courtney and her mother came in and joined me at five thirty-one. After I got them each a cup of tea, and after the mother apologized for their lateness—a TV person had detained them—I, a man of fifty-four, a man with thirty-four years experience in journalism, was left with fourteen minutes to talk to an American girl in the eighth grade.

"So, Courtney," I said, "that was a very good performance against Leonora Schaller."

"Yeah, really."

"You beat the number-four seed."

"Her groundies weren't working today. She didn't really have all of her weapons."

"I think your aggressiveness took them away. Her lobs didn't bother you either."

"No, her lobbies were off, and my ovies were on."

"Fun, huh? Fun to play somebody with no groundies and no lobbies?"

"Yeah, really."

"So you're in the quarterfinals. Looks like you'll play Ursula Kutcher."

"Wow, right."

"What do you think about that?"

"She's a ledge."

"A what?"

"She's a legend. It'll be neat to play her."

"So, Courtney. What's it like to have a six-million-dollar contract with IMG?"

Her mother said, "That's not a tennis question."

"Sorry," I said. "Have you had any time to see London, Courtney?"

"It's cool," Courtney said.

"Where all have you been?"

"We went to the Hard Rock, and . . . this really fun pizza place, and . . ."

"Westminster Abbey," her mother said.

"Oh, good," I smiled. "Everybody should see Westminster. What did you think?"

Courtney shrugged. "Lotta little dead dudes."

64

At the start of Wimbledon's second week, the computer industry became my friend. Nell and Jeannie both arrived that Monday morning on different flights. They both checked into the Hyde Park. They both went through the trauma of getting their credentials. But Jeannie was forced to spend most of her first two days and nights in London straightening out her electricity problem. The modem she brought didn't fit the English phone jack, so she all but tore apart the All-England Lawn Tennis Club hunting down and bribing the one little old man on the premises who could furnish her with the right equipment that would enable her to file her stuff. In turn, this gave me some much-needed time alone with Nell. I had decided that the only way around my current predicament was to throw myself on the mercy of Nell's court.

That first night, while Jeannie was thrashing around at Wimbledon with her modem problem, I took Nell for a drink to The Grenadier, a pub within walking distance of our hotel. The Grenadier was in a mews at the corner of Wilton Crescent and Old Barracks Road. London pubs all claim to have a history. If Oscar Wilde didn't drink there at one time, Jack the Ripper did. Supposedly, The Grenadier was the place where the Duke of Wellington had told his officers he was going to kick the little French dude's ass. Nell thought the pub offered all of the atmosphere anyone could hope to find in London, given the fact that half the clientele looked as if it had been parachuted in from P. J. Clarke's.

From there, we went to dinner at Motcomb's. Another short walk, over near Lowndes Square. Table in a dark alcove in Motcomb's cellar. Romantic. The ideal setting to ask Nell to do this thing for me.

I waited till we had finished the Dover sole and the wine and had gone back to whiskey to bring it up.

The way I tried to say it was:

"Babe, listen, I have a favor to ask. It's a big one. It's probably the biggest favor I've ever asked anybody. I ask it because I don't know what else to do at the moment. I ask it because I'm practically, almost the same thing as in semi-love with you, and because you're also my best friend. It's going to sound like a strange thing to ask, but . . ."

"I know what you're going to say."

"You do?"

"Of course I do."

Nell's look was convincing.

"How do you know?"

"Because you're a gutless, cringing, spineless member of the male population."

"Don't you just hate it when you go out to dinner with somebody like that?"

"You want me to act like there's nothing going on between us when we're around Jeannie."

That was it.

"Something like that," I said.

"We mustn't hurt the poor thing, must we?"

"I'm not worried about hurting her. I don't think you can seriously hurt anybody who's young . . . attractive . . . talented . . . American . . . white . . . not crippled . . . gainfully employed. At least, you shouldn't be able to, unless you can fly airplanes through their head, and that's not the case with Jeannie."

"What *are* you worried about?"

"I'd like to keep her as a friend."

"So I'm a coconspirator in letting her down easy, is that it?"

"Works for me."

"How long do we coconspire?"

"How long can you play the game?"

"How much longer do you want to keep fucking her?"

"I don't fuck her. She fucks me."

"How long?"

"I don't know, babe. Not all that long. We'll see how it goes. I just mainly want the pressure off. She's not in love with me. She's in love with success, but that doesn't make her a bad person. She's going into TV anyway."

"You're kidding."

"CBS wants her."

"She's too good a writer to go into television."

"That's what I said, but the money's obscene."

"On camera?"

"On camera—in sports. Our girl on the sidelines. Our girl in the studio. 'How 'bout those Dallas Cowboys, Jeannie Slay?' "

"God."

"And to think you like her."

"I *do* like her. I just wish she'd find another columnist to bat her eyes at."

"She'll find an anchorman. Or a network president. She hasn't decided to take the job, but I think it's a lock. They want her before football season starts. So you'll play the game for a while?"

"I'll try. But only because I've got the best part—the closet mistress."

"Right," I said. "She gets the Cuisinart, you get laid."

65

THE BIG DIFFERENCE BETWEEN NEWSPAPER SPORTSWRITERS and magazine sportswriters is that newspaper sportswriters are always working and never have much of a social life, whereas magazine sportswriters have to contend with the constant guilty feeling that they really don't work for a living.

I leaned heavily on this difference in dealing with my boudoir predicament. Wimbledon was a grim working week for Jeannie, one that kept her out at the complex most of every day and late into every evening. Meanwhile, all I had to do was choose a column topic and decide which two hours of which day I would devote to writing it, and all Nell had to do was observe, coordinate, and at some point "preread" my column and Achee Bromley's lead before the copy was sent to New York by whatever electricity was available. In other words, Nell and I had plenty of time on our hands, and we even spent some of it on our feet, fully clothed, at Wimbledon.

But there was time for Jeannie, too. Like four late dinners at an Italian restaurant near the Battersea Bridge that for years had catered to lame and halt journalists returning from Wimbledon. Nell and I met Jeannie, Richie Pace, Dub Fricker, Christine, and Achee Bromley there on those nights. Nell and I would get to the restaurant ahead of everyone, and I would arrange for a large round table. Jeannie and the others would come trudging in. I would give Jeannie a kiss and seat her next to me, and Nell would take a chair across from us. The first night this little playlet occurred, Richie and Dub followed me into the men's room at the earliest opportunity. I had no choice but to explain to them the role Nell had agreed to play and ask for their wholehearted cooperation. Beg, actually.

"Nell is a great American and a wonderful human being," Richie said.

"Yes, she is," I nodded.

"You gotta play hurt," Dub said.

That same night, Christine followed Nell into the ladies' room and was given the same information. I realized what Nell had told her because when Christine returned to the dinner table, she tossed me the sort of momentary look that she would a gutless, cringing, spineless member of the male population.

It was an absurd situation, I more than realized. By now, almost everybody in the upper echelon of the sportswriting business, from New York to LA, knew that Jeannie and I were an item while, at the same time, only Nell and I and Christine and Richie and Dub and Wayne Mohler and Ralph Webber knew that Nell and I were an item. As I saw it, the situation clearly called for more drinking and smoking than normal.

The drill after these dinners was for Nell, Jeannie, Christine, and me to go back to the Hyde Park Hotel and have more drinks in the lounge. There, we discussed journalism, New York, LA, movies, even tennis.

I always retired to bed first. One night I pleaded a sore throat. One night I pleaded a phone call to my son. One night I pleaded a stiff back. One night I pleaded exhaustion.

On the night of the stiff back, Jeannie called me in the room.

"How do you feel about daylight precision bombing?" she asked.

"The losses will be heavy but when you factor them into the overall picture, it won't look so bad to the chief."

"There'll be a briefing in my room in ten minutes."

"You'd better come down here."

Jeannie came to my room in a nightgown with nothing under it.

We kissed and she said, "You've been avoiding me. Is it because of the TV thing?"

"I haven't been avoiding you," I said. "Things are just, you know, hectic."

Her nightgown fell to the floor and we moved to the bed. "Some of them will be dancing at the Savoy tonight and some of them will still be in Germany," she said.

Later, as we lay in bed, Jeannie said, "I love Nell. She's a great girl, isn't she?"

I was staring at the ceiling as I said, "Best friend *I* ever had."

66

THE TROUBLE WITH HOSPITALITY TENTS IS WHO THEY ARE for. I can't remember whether that was Nell's line or Jeannie's. Doesn't matter. I'm stealing it.

The hospitality area at Wimbledon—marquee tents, the Brits call them—was on the back side of the grounds, at the opposite end of the outdoor courts from the Centre Court Stadium. Very exclusive. Engraved invitations only.

All of the tents were carpeted and strewn with fresh flowers. Tables were arranged with fine linen, china, crystal, silverware, waiters, waitresses, TV sets. All of them served good food and drinks throughout the days and nights.

SM's tent was in the middle of a long row of tents that were sponsored by IMG, BMW, NBC, ITT, ITV, GUR, and other members of the corporate alphabet. Caviar Lane. Smoked Salmon Avenue.

When the *SM* tent opened on Monday of Wimbledon's second week with Clipper Langdon as the genial host, I dropped by to say hello and pick up a batch of engraved invitations to distribute among friends. And debutantes, Clipper reminded me. But we wouldn't need the debs until the weekend when Rip Bellemy arrived.

"Why is Rip Bellemy so important?" I asked Clipper.

"Between you and me?"

"Sure."

"Deep graveyard?"

"Of course."

Clipper lowered his voice to a whisper. "TPG is in the process of acquiring ModeTech Industries."

"Does the Ripper know this?"

"Oh, he's very much for it. Fenton and the Ripper have been working on this for quite a while."

"Why does TPG want ModeTech?"

"Well," Clipper glanced around to make sure no one was eavesdropping, "we don't really want ModeTech—we want Nudom. Nudom is ModeTech's largest and most profitable subsidiary."

"What is Nudom?"

"You've never heard of Nudom?"

"I'm a sportswriter." Bit of a shrug.

"Nudom," Clipper whispered, "is, among other things, the world's largest manufacturer of condoms."

"Oh, *that* Nudom."

"Fenny hasn't said this in so many words, but *my* guess is we'll spin off ModeTech's other subsidiaries and only keep Nudom. Ripper makes a bundle in stock, we increase our earnings *and* our stock goes up. Hell of a deal for everybody."

"Nobody loses?"

"Well, I suppose in the long run, somewhere down the line, a few little machinists in one of ModeTech's other companies will lose their jobs, but that's life in the private sector, isn't it?"

A couple of days later, I called on my two British journalist pals, Ian Malcolm of the *Daily Mail* and Derwent Hopkins of the *Daily Telegraph*, to help me arrange the "hospitality." I invited Ian and Derwent for drinks in the writers' cafeteria and bought them each a bottle of the best red wine available.

Ian and Derwent were both weary-looking gentlemen in their forties, each losing a bit of hair, each wearing suede shoes, each with his tie loosened. They were among the better writers and drinkers in Great Britain. Men of the world.

After an exchange of laments about the boredom of Wimbledon, I brought the subject up.

"You need slatterns, do you?" Ian said.

"Yes," I said. "But high quality—for advertisers."

"Thank God the primeval urges haven't left us all."

Ian glanced at Derwent. "I rather think Nan and Daphne could accommodate the lads, don't you?"

"Diabolical, I must say," Derwent said.

"You don't agree?"

"I do, rather."

"Who are Nan and Daphne?" I asked.

Ian related that they were low-level editorial assistants for *Racquet World,* an English tennis monthly, but they weren't above accepting "gifts" for certain favors. They weren't all-out professionals, Ian said, but were quite useful on the whole.

"Are they good-looking?"

"A bit Covent Gardenish," Ian said, "but well-equipped with the proven intellectual inadequacies."

"I'll have to see them before I drop them on the clients," I said.

"Well," said Derwent, "they're sitting right back there, aren't they?"

Nan and Daphne were having tea at another table. Two young girls jabbering. They looked mischievous enough. The redhead was a definite 1-900, the blonde a certified 911.

"They'll do," I said.

Ian walked over to Nan and Daphne's table. The three of them chatted for a moment, then he brought them over. We were properly introduced. Up close, Nan and Daphne still looked acceptable, although I was slightly alarmed by the small fever blister on Daphne's upper lip. Such a thing would be the Ripper's problem, however.

I said to the girls that it was my understanding they liked to meet interesting gentlemen at social occasions. I handed them two engraved invitations. Nan was the redhead, Daphne the blonde.

"We do it for money, if that's what you mean?" Nan said.

"Saturday," I said. "Let's say around noon. Tent number seven. Present your invitations to the guard on the door and ask for a Mr. Langdon or a Mr. Bellemy."

"The marquee tents?" Daphne said. "Bit stuffy, aren't they?"

"Not this one."

"What shall we wear?"

Ian said, "Something you can slip out of rather gingerly, I should imagine."

"You'll meet some very wealthy gentlemen," I said. "You'll probably wind up with a flat in Chelsea and a Jaguar."

"I say!" said Daphne, excitedly. "Just for doing it?"

Shortly before noon on Saturday, the day of the women's

final, I took Nell, Jeannie, Christine, and Richie Pace to the *SM* tent for champagne and caviar, but also to make sure that Nan and Daphne showed up.

Clipper Langdon, looking very Bond Street, met us at the door with a glass of champagne in his hand. He gushed with the happy news that *SM* was out-tenting everyone. He had done a tent patrol and no other tent could boast of as many attractive couples, as many CEOs—five—a member of the Nobel Prize committee, a film producer, and a British TV comedian.

"Which one's the Nobel guy?" Richie asked.

Clipper pointed out a tall, well-dressed Swede at the buffet table, heaping strawberries into a bowl.

"I'd like to meet him," Richie said.

"I don't think they have a category for sports columnists," I said.

Richie went over to speak to the Nobel guy anyhow.

At this moment, Rip Bellemy approached us, drink in hand. It was only noon but the Ripper was already gasolined.

"Pinch, you've done it again, you old hard-on. I'll take all three. What's the tariff, honey?"

"I beg your pardon!" Nell said, taking a step backward.

"Five hundred for the tits," Rip said.

Now Christine took a step backward.

I said, "Rip, excuse me. I'd like to introduce you to Nell Woodruff and Christine Thorne. They work at *SM,* and this is Jeannie Slay with the *LA Times.*"

"Yeah, yeah, fine," said the Ripper. He pulled out a wad of bills. "I got a limo outside and a suite at the Dorchester. First one to get her tongue up my ass gets a bonus."

Clipper Langdon stepped in to help me out. "Good old Ripper. Always on the ready. Heh, heh. This isn't them, my man. Your nieces haven't arrived yet."

"This isn't them?" Rip was weaving, squinting.

Jeannie was staring at the Ripper's cream-colored sports coat, orange polo shirt, and lime slacks.

Jeannie said, "Who's your tailor, Baskin-Robbins?"

Rip didn't hear it.

"The debutantes will be here in a minute," I said to the Ripper. "Have another drink."

"Shit, my heart's broken," he said.

"We'll fix it," I said.

"How many we got coming?"

"Two."

"What are their names?"

"Mergers and acquisitions."

"Heh, heh," Clipper laughed. "The Pincher. Always in there with the lines." Clipper patted Rip Bellemy on the back tenderly and led him to the bar.

We took a table and were brought champagne, caviar, smoked salmon, cream cheese, and scones. We looked around the tent at the handsome guests, at the men in blazers and ties, the women in flowery dresses. I nodded across the way at Ian and Derwent, who were sitting in a corner, each with his own bottle of champagne and a mound of caviar. Richie rejoined us with word that the Nobel guy was in the room purely by accident—he had been looking for the IMG tent.

Presently, Nan and Daphne were standing in the doorway. In the long history of Wimbledon, it's doubtful if the All-England Lawn Tennis Club had ever seen such short mini-dresses and such wild, jagged hair.

Nan's mini-dress was gold and white; Daphne's was purple and yellow. Their spiked heels were five inches high, and their eyes had been done by a landscape artist. They looked like two overgrown wildflowers from a strange, distant planet.

"There they are, folks," Richie said. "Alice Marble and Helen Wills Moody."

Nell looked at Nan and Daphne, then at me. "You did this?"

"I seem to be moving more and more into PR work," I said.

I watched the Ripper fasten his lecherous eyes on Nan and Daphne and stumble toward them.

We seized the moment to take our leave. I waved to Clipper. He gave me a thumbs-up sign and a big, grateful smile.

We passed by Rip and the girls on the way out.

The Ripper had taken out his wad of money again and was stuffing bills into the bosoms of Nan and Daphne.

"Hundred dollar bills make young girls horny," Rip said to me with a stupid grin.

"Best to the wife," said Nell, slapping the Ripper on the shoulder.

We were walking down Caviar Lane, heading for the Centre Court Stadium, when Richie said, "What were their names?"

"Nan and Daphne," I said.

"Right," said Richie. "I *thought* I remembered them from Cambridge."

67

THE LITTLE DEAD DUDES OF WESTMINSTER ABBEY WERE already in my column lead, so naturally I was rooting for Courtney Duncan to win the whole thing at Wimbledon. The precocious fourteen-year-old had indeed become an official teenage tennis monster, not just with the help of her mother, but by hammering Ursula Kutcher and Ann Stern in big upsets to reach the finals against the defending champion, Maggie Ramsey, the rangy Australian lesbo with the slowest serve since McEnroe. Two other reasons, as I saw it, to be in Courtney's corner.

A nice thing about women's tennis is that the matches never last very long. The women only play the best of three sets, and it is a rare engagement that goes longer than an hour and a half. Martina used to polish off her opponents in anywhere from thirty-seven to fifty-two minutes and, in so doing, earn the eternal gratitude of every deadline writer on the premises.

Courtney started off in the final as if she was out to break one of Martina's speed records. With her groundies, lobbies, servies, and ovies all clicking, Courtney won the first four games of the first set, much to the roaring approval of what I gathered was a predominantly heterosexual crowd.

As it happened, I was prevented from keeping a sharp eye on some of this action, owing to my seat between the Serbo-Croatian and the Nigerian in the Centre Court Stadium. Just as the match started, a press release was distributed, and since the release was awkwardly written, it caused some confusion among the two reporters. The press release said:

"The Wimbledon committee wish to alert you to the fact that Mr. Sean McSean of Germ Warfare is expected to appear in the Royal Box today."

From my vantage point, I couldn't actually get a good look at Sean McSean in the Royal Box, but I was reasonably sure he was the one seated next to Princess Diana in the caftan and pith helmet with a parrot on his shoulder.

"We must vacate the stadium," the Nigerian said.

"No, it's okay," I smiled.

"But it says to be used, the germs."

The Serbo-Croatian, who spoke no English, was already babbling into his phone.

"No precautions are being taken," the Nigerian said. "The public should be announced. It is the work of the IRA, do you think?"

"You don't understand," I said. "Germ Warfare is a rock group. Music? Rock music?"

"This is most bad, to make music while he spreads the germs."

That, I couldn't argue with.

"The press release is poorly worded," I said. "Germ Warfare is like the Beatles."

"The Beatles are here?"

"No, no. Sean McSean is here. He's sitting down there. He's a musician, like the Beatles. No reason to panic."

Having said that, I honestly didn't think there was a reason to panic, not unless somebody tried to hook me up to a cassette player and make me listen to one of Germ Warfare's hits.

The Nigerian and the Serbo-Croatian spent the entire match screaming into their phones with great urgency and keeping their attention focused on the Royal Box in anticipation of some sort of terrorist act, but then again, maybe they were talking about the tennis and the mere fifty-seven minutes it took for Courtney Duncan to dispose of Maggie Ramsey, 6–4, 6–0.

The crucial point in the match came when the games were 4-all in the first set. Maggie Ramsey hit a backhand passing shot down the line, a shot that would have given her the game and a 5–4 lead. It was close. I thought the ball was in, and the linesman called it in, but Courtney disputed the call.

She jogged up to the chair umpire, Wing Commander Swanson, and wrinkled her nose and gave him a hurt little look, as if to say, "Oh, darn it, I wanted that point." Whereupon, the chair umpire overruled the linesman.

"What? WHAT?"

You could hear Maggie Ramsey all over the stadium as she charged the chair umpire. All over worldwide TV as well, I was sure.

"You're giving that little bitch the point?"

"Resume play, please," said the umpire, calmly.

She hurled her racket at a net post. "You pommy twit! You fuckin' asshole!"

The Australian woman did not win another game, she was so thoroughly distraught. She broke two more rackets. She refused to curtsy to the Royal Box on her way out of the stadium. Instead, she gave the Royal Box the finger.

This made for a splendid front-page picture in what is known as the popular press, the London tabloids, all of which were inspired to go with the same headline: UP THE ROYAL BOX.

"Shameful display," Derwent Hopkins said. "Convicts, you see."

In Courtney's press conference, she announced that she was going to produce her own line of tennis fashions very soon. IMG, her agency, had it in the works. She admitted there was truth to the rumor that she had signed a six-figure book contract. The autobiography of a fourteen-year-old was something for all of us to mull over. But despite her wealth, Courtney said she definitely planned to enter the ninth grade in the fall. She felt an education was important. The school in Naples, Florida, would fax the homework to her in Monaco.

68

OBVIOUSLY, I WOULDN'T HAVE SUFFERED THE INDIGNITY that occurred if I hadn't gone to the men's final on Sunday. The only reason I went was because I had nothing better to do. The column was in. I had no interest in the outcome. I had written Boris Becker so often I could have been wearing lederhosen, and Lars Svanstrom, the handsome young Swede, had lost some luster after it became evident that, like most Swedes, he was almost completely devoid of the gift of speech.

Throughout the days that Lars had been in the Wimbledon limelight, after knocking off Sampras, Lendl, and Chang, his interviews had ground the press into the floor.

He spoke in a strained slowness that made you move to the edge of your chair and want to reach up and tug at the words.

"Hmmm . . . yes," he would answer a question. "Hmmmm . . . no."

If Lars uttered a complete sentence, it might require a long moment for him to get it all out, but it was a moment to be savored.

One day, he said: "I am . . . prepared . . . physic . . . ally, but . . . I am not so . . . prepared . . . mmmmm . . . MENT . . . ally."

There was the one instance when Svanstrom's interview was spiced up by the appearance of his father, a large man in a red beard, who banged his fist on a table, and said, "I CREATE this boy! I PRODUCE him!"

The men's final was a study in theatrics, to say the least. It went five sets, included three tiebreaks, and required five hours and seventeen minutes to complete, by which time Becker's knees and elbows were bleeding scabs.

Becker's diving, lunging, and rolling about on the now-barren turf of Centre Court kept the crowd in an uproar throughout the long afternoon. To my mind, Becker's loss of blood alone made him the deserving winner, not that tennis wouldn't be hearing more from the young Swede in the future.

I missed seeing the best point of the match live and only caught it later on the television replay. This was a long rally in the third set in which Becker retrieved four lobs and three overheads while Svanstrom retrieved his own impossible array of shots from both corners of the baseline before Becker finally won the point by diving for a dropshot and somehow returning it crosscourt with topspin.

What happened was, I had badly needed to relieve myself, and I hadn't wanted to endure the agony of going down the stairs and up the stairs, and down more stairs and up more stairs, and then waiting in line at the only press urinal.

I successfully begged a Wimbledon official to let me use a more convenient john upstairs near the press section, a john strictly reserved for bigshots.

The problem arose when another Wimbledon official, an old ex-squadron leader with white hair and a white mustache, came into the restroom as I was standing at the trough.

"Out!" he said, gruffly. "Out this instant!"

"I'll only be a moment," I said.

"Absolutely no press in here!"

"Right," I said. "Be finished in a second."

"This is quite impossible!"

"I know, but . . ."

"I *do* have the prerogative to revoke your credential!"

"I understand, but . . ."

"Stubborn, are you? Well, sir, we shall make short work of this, you needn't wonder!"

That's when he grabbed my arm and spun me around. And ignoring what was happening to the front of his green blazer, gray trousers, and shoes, he dragged me to the door and slung me out.

I didn't complete the job I started out to do, or get zipped up, until, grievously, I was out there in the hallway with the Duke of Kent staring at me.

There was nothing I could do but smile blandly at the Duke, and say, "I think it's all going frightfully well, don't you?"

69

THAT EVENING WHEN WE ALL GATHERED FOR ONE FINAL WIM-
bledon dinner at the Italian restaurant near the Battersea Bridge,
I again sat next to Jeannie, and Nell again sat across the table
from us, and Richie and Dub and Christine again held their
admirable tongues and disguised their troublesome glances.

In the rich tradition of our profession, we talked mostly
about where we were going instead of where we were or where
we had been. In sportswriting, there is a statute of limitations
of six months before you can talk about where you have been.

We were all scattering the next day. Nell and Christine were
going to Paris to start getting everything organized—hotel
rooms, cars, drivers, credentials, restaurant reservations—for
SM's coverage of the Summer Olympics. Everything was sure
to be fouled up in Paris, and it would take Nell and Christine
a week or longer to straighten out the details. The Olympics
were starting right after the British Open, which was where
Richie and Dub and I were heading after three days of playing
golf ourselves in Scotland. Jeannie was staying over in London
for three more days to go to the theater, then she was going to
join us at St. Andrews. And immediately after the British
Open, the four of us would hop over to Paris for the Olympics.
At dinner, we all laughed about how this was a swell way to
make a living if you didn't have to write.

Jeannie had worked on me to skip the golf with Richie and
Dub and stay in London with her and go to the theater, but I
explained that squeezing in a few rounds of golf in Scotland
every year was a tradition as well as a treat. She reminded me
that I hadn't brought along my clubs. That was also a tradition,
I said. Lugging golf clubs to Europe was a pain in the ass. I
always bought a cheap set on the expense account, then gave
them to my caddy when I left. Two dinners covered it.

She said she was sorry I was going to miss out on soaking up
some culture at the London theater. I told her it would be

tempting if there were any new Stoppards or Grays around, but I wasn't about to shorten my life by sitting through *Gunga Din*, the latest effort by Andrew Lloyd Webber, or *Inside the Third Reich*, the new musical from Boublil and Schönberg.

Though I didn't confess it to either Nell or Jeannie, I was very much looking forward to those three days in Scotland without the girls around. No intrigue. No lies to tell. Maybe the squirrels would stop having a convention in my stomach.

Before dinner was over that night, I was prevailed upon to tell the restroom story twice, leaving out no significant detail. It got better the second time when the old ex-squadron leader became Sir Cedric Hardwicke.

Well, as I said, at least the incident gave me a fitting epitaph for my tombstone someday. HERE LIES JIM TOM PINCH. HE LIVED. HE TYPED. HE ONCE PISSED ON WIMBLEDON.

THE SPORTS SM MAGAZINE

MR. ROLLIE AMBROSE
Editor, Nonfiction
Fust & Winslett Publishers
New York, N.Y.

Dear Rollie Ambrose:

I am thrilled—thrilled beyond words—to hear that you participate in one of those rotisserie baseball leagues and that baseball is your "passion." I do not, however, see how I could have "batted in" something about baseball in Part Three, since I didn't go to a single fucking game until the World Series.

It would be a comfort to me if my editor had noticed that Part Three ended in July and could put this together with the fact that the World Series wasn't played until October, yet again.

There will be some baseball in Part Four but I want to

warn you that the game will only have a cameo role. This is not to say that I don't understand why all you intellectuals like baseball. I most certainly do understand it. After all, it is a game in which the most exciting thing that can happen is a home run, and this relates to the publishing business. The batter (writer) hits the ball (book) over the fence (reader's head) and the novel only sells 527 copies, but this gives it the perfect batting average for a precious literary award.

Having said that, I can now look forward to God striking me down with amyotrophic lateral sclerosis, better known as the Lou Gehrig disease.

The answer to your question about why nobody from *Sports Illustrated* is in this book is simple. I've been gone from *SI* a long time. I don't know any of those people anymore. They jog, they don't drink, they don't smoke, they don't hang around, you never see any of them on the road. Once a week, they slip into their Muppet costumes, put out the issue, then disappear again.

Onward,

Jim Tom Pinch

Jim Tom Pinch

PRISONERS IN JOCKDOM

PART FOUR

PRISONERS IN LOCKDOWN

70

THE MESSAGE WAITING FOR ME AT THE DESK WHEN RICHIE and Dub and I checked into the hotel in Scotland was from Bryce Wilcox, and only two things about it were disturbing. One, the managing editor was upstairs, not in New York, and two, he had confiscated my suite.

I had arranged for that very suite on the corner of the Marine Hotel in North Berwick months in advance. I loved that suite. I had stayed in it three times in the past on other golfing trips. From the big curved window in the living room, you could look down on part of the intriguing if antiquated North Berwick course, creeping right past and right up against the hotel, or out across the bay, the Firth of Forth. But now my boss was in the suite, and the hotel clerk informed me that the only other space available for me was a broom closet on the ground floor next to the elevator with a window looking out on the street. These were the types of rooms Richie and Dub had reserved, being on newspaper expense accounts.

I immediately picked up the house phone and rang Bryce. "How's the view?" I asked.

"Hey, big guy, what's up? I heard you needed a fourth—zapped on over. Nonstop to Prestwick, hired a limo. Played Gullane today. Four over on the front, two over on the back. Nice course. I made a dinner reservation in the dining room for seven thirty. North Berwick tomorrow? What's our tee time? Have you arranged Muirfield? Who cares, right? I'd just as soon play here every day. Crenshaw says North Berwick is his favorite Scottish course.''

"You haven't answered my question.''

"Guy with the most braid gets the suite. Old rule. Cocktails at seven, okay? Hell of a Wimbledon, huh? Hear about Cloyce?''

"What about Cloyce?''

"Bleeding ulcer. He's in the hospital in Pinehurst, but he's all right. His wife says he'll be laid up for a week or two. You'll have to handle the lead *and* write your column at St. Andrews, but that's no hill for a climber, right? Piece of cake.''

"To coin a phrase. Do I have a researcher?''

"No can do. We're over budget on the Olympics as it is. Who do you like at St. Andrews? I like Curtis. We had him down to Kiawah for a sales outing two weeks ago. He's got it on a string and his putter's working. See you at cocktails. I'm putting a new grip on my seven-iron.''

Although I was already overgolfed, I asked Richie and Dub if they wanted to go over to the North Berwick pro shop with me. I needed to buy a set of clubs, see that we all had caddies, and make sure there would be no problem with our tee time tomorrow.

My pals said they would rather take naps. The hassle at the Gatwick and Edinburgh airports, with so many Americans coming over for the British Open, and the two-hour drive from Edinburgh to North Berwick on the wrong side of the road, with me behind the wheel, had shredded their nerves.

I said, "Bryce tells me I have to do the lead at St. Andrews. Cloyce Windham has a bleeding ulcer. I guess Farrell beating Jones at Olympia Fields is what did it to him.''

"Hardly seems fair for you to have to work for a living,'' Richie wisecracked.

71

OVER THE NEXT THREE DAYS, WE PLAYED NORTH BERWICK twice and Dunbar once, and the golf was eventful only in the sense that Bryce went from a macho eight to a martyred sixteen as he wallowed in the heather and whins and put more balls in the bay and bounced more balls off the old rock walls than a dozen caramel-chewers pulling their own carts.

Mr. Golf, as Richie referred to Bryce behind his back, lost all bets every day but blamed his poor performance on the ankle he twisted slightly on a sandhill the first day out, and possibly those new stiff shafts in his irons had something to do with it. My own view was that he might have played better in the unseasonably warm Scottish weather if he hadn't almost suffocated to death in his dazzling, multicolored wardrobe of double-ply cashmere turtlenecks.

On Thursday, after we played golf that morning, Richie and Dub and I motored on over to St. Andrews. It was the first day of the British Open, and Bryce, in the true style of a magazine managing editor, chartered a private jet to London and flew home on the Concorde. Legitimate expense. Golf research.

One night while Bryce was still in Scotland, however, I got him alone for a while in the hotel bar after dinner, after Richie and Dub took the despondency over their pitch-shot grounders and boomerang tee shots up to bed.

I purposely enticed Bryce into more cognacs than he would normally have in order to get him talking about something. I wanted to try to better understand that Wall Street stuff involving TPG and ModeTech Industries.

Whatever was going on, it had something or other to do with me becoming a procurer for Rip Bellemy, and that was another thing. I wanted Bryce to know I was resigning from the bimbo business.

It wasn't hard to lure Bryce into a conversation about Wall Street. If anything interested him as much as golf, it was the giddy world of tender offers, leveraged buyouts, and debt-financing.

We talked for a couple of hours, with Bryce straying off onto golf occasionally and me asking questions to bring him back to the subject in which I was interested. Over and over, the point he relished making was that Fenton Boles was a slick operator, a genius, and a man who could give any other CEO in the country two-up a side.

I learned a great deal that night.

The whole business with TPG and ModeTech started when Clipper Langdon was accidentally introduced to Rip Bellemy one evening at the ground-floor bar in "21." In the course of their conversation, Bellemy happened to mention that Nudom, a subsidiary of ModeTech, was now the world's largest manufacturer of condoms, and that Nudom was also on the brink of developing an instant abortion pill.

This was back in March, when Clipper had just become the publisher of *SM*. Clipper took this information about Mode-Tech, and Nudom, back to Fenton Boles as fast as he could skate. But if the Ripper's intention was to trick TPG into investing heavily in ModeTech, and thus drive his stock up, Fenton Boles saw it as a larger opportunity for everybody concerned.

Fenton quickly contacted Barney Levine, a friend of his at the investment banking firm of Tweed, Hazard & Risk. Fenton asked Barney to look at ModeTech and see if it wasn't ripe for a takeover. Only if certain things could be done, Fenton was told, and only if Rip Bellemy wanted to play along.

Fenton then invited Rip Bellemy and Barney Levine to a secret lunch in his grandiose office at TPG. Rip and Barney went to the lunch in disguises and used the service elevator in the building, which was how high-level meetings were sometimes done. At the lunch, Fenton asked Rip how much he was in love with his company, how much of an obligation he felt to his stockholders.

Silly question. Rip Bellemy obviously said he didn't love his company or his stockholders as much as he loved pussy, yachts, villas, and the sixty million dollars he would insist on in the form of a gold-platinum-emerald parachute if TPG took over his company.

This was where me and the bimbos had fitted in, according to Bryce. I had helped keep the Ripper happy, well-fucked, and on friendly terms with TPG while Fenton was negotiating him down from sixty million to fifty million.

Next, for its usual fee of one hundred million dollars and a piece of the action, Fenton hired Tweed, Hazard & Risk, which was known for specializing in high-risk debt-financing, to underwrite a junk bond issue that would enable TPG to buy ModeTech. This explained why ModeTech's stock went into a nosedive.

If I had cared to notice over the past three months, I would have seen ModeTech's stock plunge from 47½ to 9¼. That's because Barney Levine orchestrated it through the use of bogus balance sheets, doctored income statements, and the revising of earnings estimates significantly downward. The scheme was to push ModeTech's stock down to the price that TPG, or Fenton Boles, the chief executive officer, would agree to pay for it.

In doing this, Barney Levine made even more money for Tweed, Hazard & Risk. The firm sold the stock short all the way down. And, of course, when TPG's stock soared upward with the eventual announcement that TPG was buying Mode-Tech, specifically Nudom, Tweed, Hazard & Risk would make more money by riding TPG to the sky.

A hundred million dollar fee wasn't enough for the investment banking firm. Investment banking firms like to eat from a big spoon. It's what they teach at Yale, Harvard, and Princeton.

So it was win, win, win. Rip Bellemy would walk away with fifty million for wrecking his company. The big payoff for Fenton Boles would come when the jovial Les Padgett would approve a gigantic bonus for the CEO at the end of the year—it would be in the millions—for bringing the moneymaking Nudom under the TPG umbrella and spinning off all of Mode-Tech's less profitable companies, which would put hundreds of people out of work, but so what? Barney Levine would receive a bonus up in the millions for making Tweed, Hazard & Risk fatter. There would be a promotion and a bonus for Clipper Langdon—his finder's fee. And there would be something in it for Bryce Wilcox. He had brought Clipper "on board," after all.

All this insider stuff was hugely unethical, of course, not to mention that it was about as legal as armed robbery, but it wasn't uncommon in the world of high finance. It was, in fact, why a Fenton Boles and a Barney Levine had obtained their MBAs in the first place. It was why most gangsters in today's doomed world carried an MBA instead of a violin case.

But that night in the hotel bar when I casually said to Bryce that these dealings sounded to me like they came under the heading of stock manipulation, he only laughed. It wasn't called stock manipulation at all, he said. It was called shrewd.

"It's the American way, big guy."

"I know that march," I said. "Sousa, right?"

72

THERE IS AN OLD SAYING THAT THERE ARE THREE KINDS OF British Opens: those played in Scotland, those played in England, and the one played at St. Andrews. The championship rotates to a different course each year. One year it might be played in Scotland, at Troon, Muirfield, Turnberry, or Carnoustie, and the next year it might be played in England, at Sandwich, Birkdale, Lytham, or Hoylake. But every six or eight years it goes back to St. Andrews, and that's when the 140-year-old championship, the oldest tournament in golf, takes on a keener aura of elegance and importance, for St. Andrews is the birthplace of golf and the headquarters of the Royal & Ancient Golf Society. The Old Course, created by nature, famed for its double greens and subtle difficulties, sits in the very center of the old university town, bordered on one side by smoky-gray buildings and rising spires and on the other by St. Andrews Bay and what has become known as the *Chariots of Fire* beach. The Old Course is the place where it is said that the first Scottish shepherd swung the first crook and hit the first pebble into the first rabbit scrape, thereby inventing the game.

More lore for Jeannie Slay, who was desperate for a column.

We were sitting next to each other at a working table in the press tent in the late afternoon on this Thursday in the middle of July, the first day of the championship. That morning, Jeannie, all cultured up from the London theater, had taken the shuttle from London to Edinburgh and had rented a car and had driven the hour and a half to St. Andrews, had dropped off her bags in her room at the Old Course Hotel, had toured the town, toured the course and all of its legendary obstacles—Hell Bunker, the Valley of Sin, the Swilcan Burn, the Principal's Nose, the Road—and was now trying to write a scene-setter. Richie and Dub and I had arrived a little later in the day and had checked into the same hotel.

Being a friend of mine sometimes paid a dividend. When the British Open is played at St. Andrews, a lowlife sportswriter can't usually get a room at the Old Course Hotel, which is wonderfully convenient as it sits adjacent to the seventeenth fairway, the Road Hole, and is only a short walk to the pubs, woolen mills, antique club shops, and bookstores of the town as well as the press tent and the R & A building behind the first tee and eighteenth green. The R & A had again reserved all the rooms two years ahead of time for itself and the contestants, but since IMG, the worldwide sports agency, represented half the players in the field, IMG had access to rooms, and if you knew an IMG agent and knew where some of his bodies were buried, as I did, you could threaten him to release some of the rooms. That's how I got four rooms for us. I was, as you may have guessed by now, an avowed enemy of inconvenience.

"A shepherd's crook is a long stick?" Jeannie asked above the clacking of her Tandy laptop.

"Aye, laddie."

On the geezer-codger portable, I was getting my own column out of the way early so I could cover the tournament proper, as Bryce had ordered. In the column, I surrendered to fantasy. I became the shepherd who invented golf and I explained why: in the future, rich people would need a game to play and a topic with which to bore their friends when they weren't avoiding taxes and stealing money from the poor and middle class.

British Opens can be tiresome the first two days, even at St. Andrews. The first two rounds, before the field is cut after thirty-six holes, can go on forever—the combatants don't finish play until nine or ten at night, and invariably the leaders will be among the late finishers, which means that the press can't get dinner until midnight, and only then in the R & A "club tent," the only place open by then. It was always amazing how good a pork pie or sausage roll could taste at that hour, if you dabbed it in mustard and chased it down with a lager or a glass of Glen Morange whiskey, which was the nearest thing to J & B I had ever uncovered in all of my Scottish travels.

At some point, I reminded Jeannie that the list of men who had won at St. Andrews was illustrious. It included J. H. Taylor, James Braid, Bobby Jones, Sam Snead, Bobby Locke, Jack Nicklaus, Seve Ballesteros, and Nick Faldo. Jeannie and others among the press were delighted when this turned out to be another of those occasions. After a South African nobody led the first round and an Australian nobody led the second round, Ballesteros gained control of the championship. On Saturday, Seve took advantage of a warm, windless day to demolish the Old Course with a nine-under 63. "Na' wind, na' golf" is what the Scots say about links courses, and St. Andrews was defenseless.

Two Americans, Wiley Sullins, the straw-hatted Masters winner, and Ben Crenshaw put up a valiant chase, but the Spaniard staved them off in Sunday's final round, bailing himself out of trouble time and again with inventive shots, recovery shots that only a player of great imagination can produce. Seve shot a 73 on Sunday, but that was good enough to bring him home by two strokes over Sullins, and by three over Crenshaw.

Most of the final-round drama centered around the Road Hole, the seventeenth. This is one of the most demanding par-four holes on earth, and it's even tougher when you're trying to win a British Open. It is a long hole, a dogleg to the right that demands a skillful fade from the tee to a narrow patch of fairway, then as deft a long-iron as you can launch to an uninviting green that's protected by a steep bunker on the left and a chunky little paved road on the right. Uniquely, the road is in bounds, in play, as it separates the upraised green from the true boundary, a low rock wall that looks old enough to have been built by a Roman real estate developer.

Playing a hole ahead of Ballesteros and trailing the Spaniard by only two strokes, Wiley Sullins rapped in a long putt for a birdie three at the seventeenth, but then he made a disastrous bogey five at the easy eighteenth when he underhit his approach shot and three-putted from the Valley of Sin, the deep swale in front of the green.

So it was Ballesteros' championship to win or lose when he reached the seventeenth tee. He was clinging to a two-stroke lead. He promptly put himself into trouble again, as he had all day, when his drive sped through the fairway and wound up in calf-high grass. Somehow, with a four-iron and the strength that most golfers don't possess, he slashed the ball out of the weeds and it ran up near the green. But that's where he encountered more trouble. The ball kept rolling and trickled down onto the road. Anything could have happened on his third shot, but Seve nipped the ball perfectly off the pavement with a pitching wedge. The ball ran up to within twelve feet of the flag—and he sank that putt to save his par. That was it. His drive, pitch, and two putts on eighteen were without suspense. He could enjoy that triumphant walk from tee to green, bathing in the prolonged cheering and applause that always greet the winner.

In his mass press interview, Wiley was his usual eloquent self. "When I birdied the Road Whore," he said—that's what he called it—"I thought I might win this fucker, but my satchel flew open on eighteen."

Ballesteros came in later and went through his round in his splintered English, acting as if all the recovery shots he had hit were simply routine. The final two holes didn't seem to be any different from all the others. He said, "Seventeen, Dry-yur, four-idyurn, picking weg, one pudd. Eighteen. Dry-yur, picking weg again, two pudds."

Seve did say he enjoyed the stroll up the eighteenth.

I thought it was a magic moment and tried to address it in the lead of the story I filed to New York. The lead read:

"As long as a man has to go for a walk on a golf course, there is hardly a better place than straight up the last fairway at St. Andrews, where one is surrounded by 500 years of history and embraced by the buildings of the old town itself. It looks as if it might be even more fun the way Seve Ballesteros does it occasionally. Seve made the walk again last Sunday, winning another British Open, with 40,000 warmly sentimental Scots creating enough noise to have drowned out the roar of a squall howling in off the North Sea."

That's not what ran in the magazine, however. Not after Lindsey Caperton got his grimy little paws on the copy.

It was around midnight when Charlotte Murray called me in my room from New York. The phone woke up Jeannie as well. Jeannie had invited herself in for a sleepover, but sleep was all we had been doing. She and Richie and Dub and I were programmed to rise at dawn to drive to Edinburgh, catch the shuttle to London, fly on to Paris.

Charlotte first asked some of the standard researcher questions—what was a four-iron, what was heather, what was a pork pie, how many times a year was the British Open played? I didn't become flushed with anger until she casually mentioned that the word "conquistador" was in my lead.

"Wait a minute," I said. "What the fuck is 'conquistador' doing in my lead?"

"You didn't have it in there?" Charlotte asked.

"No. Do I look like a guy who would put 'conquistador' in his lead?"

"Lindsey *did* say he did a couple of things to pep it up."

"Read me the lead," I said, lighting a Winston.

She read it to me. My story now began:

"Guess what, amigos? Severiano Ballesteros, Spain's swashbuckling conquistador, is once again the big tamale in pro golf. Last week in a taco-flavored British Open at St. Andrews, Ballesteros (who is from Santander, Spain) ate the whole enchilada and it was 'Adios, muchachos' to his nearest challengers."

For a moment, I fought off the urge to vomit.

"God DAMN that cocksucking motherfucker!" I yelled into the phone, as Jeannie sat up in bed with alarm. "The big tamale? The whole enchilada? With MY name on it? Are you fucking *kidding* me?"

I knocked over a chair. "Charlotte, tell that chinless son of a bitch something for me! I mean it! Tell him when I get back to New York, I'm gonna get a glass-bottom car so I can see the look on his fucking face when I run over him!"

I slammed down the phone and would have kicked a table leg if I'd been wearing shoes. It was like that in journalism sometimes.

73

IT DIDN'T TAKE LONG FOR ME TO REALIZE IT WAS EASIER TO love Paris in the springtime than it was in the summer during an Olympics. There were fifteen thousand athletes and ten thousand sports officials from seventy-three nations in the city along with a hellacious number of tourists. It seemed obvious to me that they all wanted to walk, sit, drink, and dine exactly where I wanted to walk, sit, drink, and dine. This gave me my first column from France, if nothing else, a column about the Paris in which Jake Barnes and Brett Ashley wouldn't have been caught dead, even if Jake had been to Fort Worth and had undergone successful surgery for his war wound.

Christine had arranged for all of us to stay at the Hotel Etoile, which was two blocks from the Arc de Triomphe. The Etoile wasn't the Crillon or the Ritz but it was comfortable, it had a bar and restaurant, and it was only a twenty-five-minute drive out Avenue Foch to most of the Olympic venues in the Bois de Boulogne.

The first night in Paris, while I was still bitching about Lindsey Caperton, I assembled our little group—Nell, Christine, Jeannie, Richie, Dub, myself—with the idea of taking everyone to dinner at a place I didn't think anyone would have discovered. It was a bistro called Roger La Grenouille—Roger the Frog—over on the Left Bank. I had known it from other trips to Paris.

It was a warm, still night, so we walked. We walked down the Rue de Rivoli, past the Louvre, over the Seine on Pont Neuf, stopping to admire the big willow that hangs down in the water. Logo willow. Then we walked up a slight hill to the Rue de St. Andre des Beaux Arts, a narrow winding street of muted lights, bistros, shops.

When we reached Roger the Frog, there was a line waiting for tables that stretched halfway down the street. Christine recognized some of the people in the line as members of the British equestrian team, the Yugoslavian water polo team, the Romanian gymnastics team, and the German fencing team.

"Cozy spot," said Nell. "Shall we put our name in the hat for a table in November?"

I quickly thought of a backup. We walked from there to the Ile de St. Louis, the island in the Seine that's connected to the Ile de la Cité. The cathedral of Notre Dame was lit up. "I didn't know they had a church, too," Dub Fricker remarked. The place to dine on the Ile de St. Louis was A Taste Du Vin, but the line waiting outside included members of the Australian rowing team, the Greek wrestling team, the Argentine trap-shooting team, and the Turkish weight-lifting team.

"I want to go home," Jeannie said. "I want my mama."

We walked back to the Etoile and ate dinner in our hotel. That was it for me, I said. I realized the scenery was more interesting and the nightlife more amusing on the Left Bank, but the quaint revolutionaries would have to get along without me this time. I would be content to stay in my own district, stroll the Champs Elysees and drink with the Eurotrash in the sidewalk cafes or stroll the Rue du Faubourg de St. Honoré and look at embassies, bakeries, jewelry stores. Surely, I said, I could find plenty of places near the hotel where I could just as easily pay $14 for a Scotch and water.

There are only four sports that matter in a Summer Olympics. They are track and field, swimming and diving, boxing, and gymnastics. Everything else is canoeing.

Over the next two weeks, we produced our normal share of heroes and heroines in those sports and endured our normal share of disappointments, especially in the boxing ring. There, three of our fighters beat the wobbly-leg, flying-mouthpiece slobber out of two Cubans and a Russian but lost gold medal decisions because of disgracefully inept judges from Eastern European and Middle Eastern countries. Six of our black fighters did win golds by taking the precaution to knock their opponents out after they had beat the wobbly-leg, flying-mouthpiece slobber out of them.

We produced our usual boy swimming star from California, Stevie Francis, who swam the same event six times and won six golds. We produced our usual girl swimming star from Indiana, Shirlee Cook, who swam the same event four times and won four golds. New world records were set in every event, as new world records are always set in every swimming event.

We produced our usual boy diving star, Drummer Grace, a handsome lad. He won both the springboard and the platform events, or what I called the high and the low, or what Jeannie called the four-flip and the two-flip. You probably didn't read anywhere that Drummer Grace carried around a teddy bear and introduced the toy to various people as "My friend, Mr. Jablonski."

We produced our usual girl diving star, Patsy Ventana, who won both events by a slim margin over a midget from China. Christine did some digging and found out that two Caucasian judges had given Patsy higher marks than she may have deserved because they had once traveled to Peking and still remembered the fishheads they had been served for dinner.

In the gymnastics arena, we produced our usual array of Siamese cats who held their own with the Russians, Chinese, and Romanians. Our leading Siamese cat was a sixteen-year-old blonde from San Diego, Ginger Buster, who vaulted, balance-beamed, and floor-exercised her way to three golds. Ginger waited until she won the third gold to announce that she had signed a contract to endorse a low-fat breakfast cereal.

All of these events were a mess to cover, for much of it was going on simultaneously in the vast Bois de Boulogne, and there were reports of poor Wayne Mohler and Christine Thorne dashing about trying to capture a swimmer, diver, boxer, or

Siamese cat for an exclusive quote, and other reports of Shag Monti and Hae-Moon Yoong dashing about with their Nikons sputtering.

At the same time, the track and field events were taking place in the 70,000-seat stadium the French had built in the Bois de Boulogne. *SM*'s well-read and intrepid Kitter Mooring—he of the shaggy hair and earnest expression—was on top of this, when he could work it into his busy jogging schedule and his research of Dostoevski and other sources to find huge ideas to put in the mouths of the athletes, even the East African tribesman who dominated the distance events.

Kenya's Abu Phutu won the 5,000-meter run by four seconds, the 10,000-meter run by ten seconds, and the marathon by four minutes, and never looked tired.

I listened in on Abu Phutu's press conference after his victory in the marathon and clearly heard him say, "Gooka, ma tocka . . . unpala monga."

Some of us were very much surprised, then, when we read in Kitter Mooring's story that Abu Phutu had said, "The sport of running is for all of humanity, and I will run as long as man seeks to worship that which is beyond dispute."

I ran into Kitter Mooring a couple of times in the stadium. Once, he was a bundle of nerves as the 20-kilometer walk was about to begin, and another time, he was transfixed by the javelin prelims.

My job was to write columns. After writing that first column on Paris, I wrote one on Robbie Morrison, our sprinter who won the 100, 200, and anchored our winning 4 × 100 relay team, all with ease. A powerful black Adonis from Houston, Robbie Morrison ran a 9.90 in the 100, breaking Carl Lewis' world record. He ran a 19.69 in the 200, breaking Pietro Mennea's world record. And the relay team ran a 37.71, breaking the world record of a previous USA quartet. But the most interesting things about him were that he refused to stay in the Olympic Village, preferring the Napoleon suite at the Crillon, and he competed with more jewelry on his person than the wife of a Texas oilman. It was exclusive in my column that the Dallas Cowboys had paid for the suite. The Cowboys had drafted Robbie as a wide receiver in the spring.

The day I visited with him in the suite, I asked him what he thought of amateur athletics.

"Shit," he said, derisively.

I asked him if it were true that the Cowboys had given him a six-figure bonus to sign with them.

"Add a fuckin' zero and you got it, baby," he said.

I did the last Olympic column on that duel between the two lady sprinters, our own Effie Tims and Russia's Lyudmila Bykova, who were not only the two fastest women in the world but the prettiest, despite the steroid rashes on their backs. They both ran the 100 and 200, and they both anchored the 4 × 100 and 4 × 400 relays.

A lot of things added to the intrigue of the competition between the two ladies. Effie Tims was a curvaceous little Diana Ross look-alike, most conceded, and Lyudmila Bykova was a taller, sinewy Meryl Streep look-alike, most conceded. They had never raced against one another before, and both had flirted with Florence Griffith-Joyner's world records in the 100 and 200.

Boris Svetlov, my friend from Innsbruck, had come to Paris with a third chin and without having had my khaki windbreaker cleaned since February. He was willing to wager all of the caviar he had brought on Lyudmila, against my cash. I took Effie Tims in all four events, at fifty bucks a pop.

"You have made an unfortunate wager," Boris said. "Your girl is top-heavy."

"You have not given it enough thought, my Russian friend," I said. "My girl's tits will win the photo."

The events were spaced out over four days of the Olympics. They were stride-for-stride thrillers, everything that was expected of them.

In the 100-meter dash, Effie came out of the blocks quicker than Lyudmila, by a step, and in lanes that were right next to each other, they roared down the track. The Russian girl made up most of the step, and if the race had gone another ten yards, she might have won, but Effie beat her by half a tit at the tape, in a new world record of 10.41 seconds.

In the 200-meter dash that was run on a curve, Effie and Lyudmila again drew parallel lanes, one and two. Effie again came out quick at the start, but Lyudmila soon churned to the front by a stride. Effie made up the stride on the straightaway, and over the last fifty yards they were a total blur, inseparable, until Lyudmila won it by the width of a blonde forelock. The time was 20.37, nearly a full second better than Flo-Jo's world record.

In the 4 × 100 relay, or what used to be known as the speed relay, Effie received the baton on the last leg with a half-step on Lyudmila, thanks to her teammates, and she held that lead all the way to the tape. It was another world record, cracking a mark that had been set by German damsels.

It was rare to find sprinters who could also run a 400, but Diana Ross and Meryl Streep were no ordinary athletes. In their last clash, the 4 × 400 relay, or what used to be known as the mile relay, Lyudmila got the baton for the final lap with a five-yard lead on Effie, thanks to her superior teammates, but Effie closed the gap by the time they were blazing down the opposite side of the track from the press box. Effie pulled ahead going into the third turn, but Lyudmila regained the lead coming off the last turn, and the Russian had more left at the finish. She won by a yard. Both teams broke the world record by two seconds.

After that race, the two girls locked arms and took a ceremonial lap around the track, enjoying a standing ovation. Boris and I had split. I had two tins of caviar; he had a hundred dollars.

Effie and Lyudmila insisted on conducting their final press conference together. There, they announced that they were moving to Hollywood and would soon be starring in a feature film for Disney. It was an adventure film about two female athletes who bring about the collapse of the Berlin Wall.

"We've seen the script," said Effie. "It's a very good first draft, but of course it's only a first draft."

"We think it ought to be more than just another buddy picture," Lyudmila said, in perfect English.

74

IN ALL OF MY RELATIONSHIPS WITH WOMEN, I HAD ALWAYS done everything possible to avoid a spat. I hated spats almost as much as I hated infantile editors. I would lie, cheat, and steal to avoid a spat and justify it on the grounds that spats were bad for my work. Shouting, cursing, and lecturing went along with the spats I had known, and I didn't agree with the theory that spats were healthy because they let you get the anger out of your system. Spats never solved anything that I knew of, but maybe I had never been a part of a good one.

Another thing about spats. There was never a good time or a good place to have them. A person was either eating, drinking, working, thinking, or sleeping, and why would you want to interrupt any of those things for something like a spat?

The spat with Nell Woodruff occurred toward the end of the first week in Paris. From the moment I arrived, I had detected a coolness in Nell, but I hadn't dealt with it, of course, knowing that if I ever said, "What's wrong?" it might start a spat.

But one afternoon Nell asked me to go around the corner from our hotel to a Eurotrash cafe on the Champs Elysees so we could "talk."

I knew what this meant. I had never known a woman who wanted to "talk" who couldn't work herself up to a spat.

As soon as the waiter brought the coffee, Nell said, "I'm being a fool."

"What do you mean?" I said.

That's another reason I was bad at spats. I had this habit of asking questions I already knew the answers to.

Nell said, "You know damn well what I mean. I was a total numbskull in London, playing that game with you and Jeannie. Here I am, the woman who loves you, and I agree to let you keep sleeping with her any time you please. Then I let you go off to Scotland to keep sleeping with her—and I'm supposed to act like it doesn't bother me. Christine is doubled over, laughing at my stupidity.''

"Is Christine the problem?"

"No, Christine is not the problem—don't be evasive. *You* are the problem."

"I thought you did a wonderful thing. I'm trying to preserve a friendship."

"Fuck your friendship!"

"I was afraid it might come to that."

I didn't say the over-and-under number was seven days and I'd bet the under.

"It's time for you to tell Jeannie about us. I might add that it's past time for you to stop screwing her."

"I'm not screwing her."

"It's past time for her to stop screwing you."

"We didn't do anything in Scotland."

"I don't believe you."

"Maybe we hugged."

"You hugged. Isn't that sweet?"

"It's better than fucking, isn't it?"

My smiles were having no effect.

"I want you to tell her about us immediately, and I don't give one shit if her little heart gets broken. If you don't tell her, I will."

"I think you ought to tell her."

Nell glared at me. "No, on second thought, you don't get off that easy. You have to tell her."

"I'm going to."

"When?"

"Pretty soon."

"Would it be in this millennium?"

"You really are great," I said. "You can't help being funny even when you're mad."

"Did it make you happy to humiliate me in front of Christine . . . Richie . . . Dub?"

"Don't forget Wayne and Ralph."

"I haven't. Wayne calls me Saint Nell."

"What does Wooden Dick say? You must have talked to him on the phone."

"You're the new wooden dick, buddy. He's been de-throned."

I tried to take her hand. She jerked it away.

"There's not another woman in the world who would do what I did," she said.

"No question about it," I said. "That's why I feel like an asshole."

"At last, we agree on something."

"Can you give me a few more days?"

"Of talking or fucking?"

"I'll tell her before we leave Paris. I just want to work it out where we can all stay pals. Jeannie adores you."

"Oh, God," said Nell. "I'm so moved to hear that, I don't know what to say."

She left me sitting there and evaporated into the throngs on the Champs Elysees. I ordered another coffee and sat there awhile and tried to think of any men I knew who enjoyed spats. I couldn't think of any.

75

A FEW NIGHTS LATER, ON AN EVENING WHEN THERE WAS nothing happening in the Olympics but weight-lifting, Greco-Roman wrestling, decathlon events, and the odd horse jumping the odd hedge, I made a reservation for Jeannie and myself in the chic dining room of the Lancaster Hotel. The restaurant was in our neighborhood, the kind of place where you might see high-level diplomats or a prima ballerina and her keeper. The room required the use of my trusty double-breasted black blazer, my one pin-collar shirt, and my one necktie, but this was a special occasion—the evening when I intended to straighten out my disruptive and, some might say, disreputable private life.

Jeannie looked tremendous with her hair flowing over one shoulder and her eyes sparkling and decked out in the eggshell mini-frock by Yves St. Laurent she had picked up in Place

Vendome for only eighteen hundred dollars—hardly a young woman for whom you would want to burst into a chorus of "Goodbye, Old Girl."

If I only had my health back, I thought.

I sidestepped all personal conversation through the pea soup, the plain omelette, the grilled sea bass, the green salad, and the vanilla ice cream, nimbly waiting for a slug or two of after-dinner Scotch to make my presentation, without slides or charts.

I began slowly, somberly, saying, "Jeannie . . . I want to talk to you seriously . . . on the subject of you and me, and . . . well . . . other people."

"About you and Nell?"

There was even the hint of a smile as she said it.

"What do you mean?" I said, helplessly.

The thought went through my mind that if I ever got around to counting, accurately, the number of times I had said "What do you mean?" to a woman, it would come in at around five thousand six hundred and thirty-two.

"It's okay," Jeannie said, convincingly. "I've been waiting for you to fess up. I've been hoping it wasn't true, but when you put on a tie tonight, I knew for sure it was. Do you love her?"

"How long have you been waiting?"

"Oh . . . since the first night we all had dinner together in London. I mean, that was the tip-off."

"How?"

"Well, when a woman who's your oldest and closest friend suddenly goes out of her way not to sit next to you, or stand next to you, or even exchange words with you, it's sort of an indication that something might be going on."

"Pretty slick, weren't we?"

"Do you love her?" Jeannie repeated.

"I guess so. I suppose I have for a long time."

"She's wonderful, you know?"

"That's what *she* keeps saying."

"She is."

"So are you."

"Thanks, pard. I'll have some more wine. A vat of anything will do."

I motioned to a hovering waiter. He came promptly. I ordered another bottle of Chateau de $97.50. He brought it promptly. We both lit cigarettes.

"I have some news," Jeannie said. "I've taken the job with CBS."

"You had to," I said, unsurprised. "When do you start?"

"I'll cover the fight in Vegas, and that's it for the old laptop. I have to be in New York the last week of August for an announcers' 'seminar.' "

"Will you move to New York?"

"They say I don't have to. I can't decide."

"We'd love to have you. The money still obscene?"

"Uh-huh. Six-fifty a year. Three-year contract."

"Wow."

"Yeah."

"The question is whether you want a beach house in Malibu or a Park Avenue apartment. You'll knock 'em dead, Jeannie. In a year, you'll have both, and a full-time limo." I lifted my glass. "Here's to the richest person I know outside of a hospitality tent."

She said, "Here's to the man who made me want to become a sportswriter."

"Thanks," I said, "but you're a hell of a lot better at it than I was at your age."

"I know," she grinned.

We drank and talked a while longer and then walked back to the Etoile, holding hands, like friends.

We glanced in the bar of our hotel to see if any of the troops were around. All of them were—Nell, Christine, Richie, Dub, Wayne, even Shag Monti. All of them were pretty drunk, or getting there, except Shag, who was stoned. He had scored some discipline.

"Cheese it," said Richie. "Here comes Rick and Ilsa."

I said, "She's not wearing blue and the Germans are reunified."

I whispered to Jeannie, "Is it okay if we tell 'em about TV?"

"Yeah, I can take it," she said.

To the group, I said, "The new announcer for CBS Sports would like to buy a round of drinks."

All heads turned to Jeannie.

"Hello, everybody," Jeannie said. "My name is Mrs. Norman Maine."

"You did it!" Christine said. "All right!"

"I need a loan," Dub said.

Wayne Mohler spoke into his cocktail glass, to achieve an echo effect. "I'm here on the sideline with Bevo, the University of Texas mascot. Bevo is a two-thousand-pound longhorn steer but he speaks very good English, and he's just told me he hates Oklahoma Sooners more than he hates Texas Aggies. Back to you, Jim Nantz."

"Yep, sold out," Jeannie said. "But, oh, bubba, the money."

"Tubular," Shag Monti said. "Go for the jing, man."

Jeannie and I worked our way down to Nell's barstool. Nell was sitting apart from the others, drinking as she looked over one of Kitter Mooring's cerebral files.

"Live around here?" I said to Nell.

"Go fuck yourself," she said.

I looked at Jeannie. "Told you she'd be in a good mood."

Jeannie said, "Nell, I didn't know how you felt about what's-his-name here until London. I had no idea. But everything's fine. I just want to say I'm out of the lineup."

"Well, *that* won't be any fun," Nell said, acidly.

"Of course, what he deserves is for both of us to turn dyke," Jeannie said. "Did you bring any hiking boots along?"

Nell was forced to laugh.

Jeannie gave me a friendly pat on the shoulder. "Thanks for the grub, pard. I think I'll take it to the shed."

She left.

Nell didn't speak for a moment. She swigged her drink and pretended to read Kitter Mooring's cerebral file. I smoked, waited.

She finally wheeled around on her barstool. "I want to tell you something while you're standing there looking so smug and self-satisfied. I'm not *really* as big a fan as you think of all this goddamn civilized behavior.''

"It is incredible," I said. "We aren't even French."

Nell remained cool and detached over the last four days in Paris, but by the time the Olympic flame had gone out and we were on the flight to New York, she had begun to warm up, and once we were back in the office she was bringing me coffee.

76

I LEFT PARIS REGRETTING THAT THE MAGAZINE HADN'T SPON-sored a hospitality tent at the Summer Olympics. That's because every day when my taxi or hired car neared the Bois de Boulogne, literally dozens of yapping hookers would leap out from under trees or off of benches and try to stop the car and other cars. They would whoop and cackle and hike their legs and throw open their coats and capes to reveal their menacing lingerie. It would have been fun and might have helped rid me of my pimp guilt if I'd had the opportunity to fix up Rip Bellemy with a vicious transvestite.

But revenge was mine, anyhow. When I returned to Gotham, I found out from Clipper Langdon what had been going on lately up in Greenwich, Connecticut, where Rip and a good many other mega-clients lived.

It seemed that Nan and Daphne, the London debs, had dropped a lethal gang of crabs on the Ripper. The Ripper had transmitted them to his wife, Pauline. Pauline was filing for divorce and determined to take Rip for a pretty penny, but she had also passed the crabs on to Nick the Carpenter. Nick the Carpenter had given them to Timmy Rathbone's wife, Lanette. Lanette Rathbone had given them to Ted the Bartender. Ted the Bartender had dumped them on Tippy Donahue's wife, Michelle. Michelle Donahue had shared them with Frederic the Dentist. Frederic the Dentist had allowed them to crawl onto Dippy Riley's wife, Connie. Connie Riley had transferred them to Bunky Trace, who had given them to Sheila the Waitress, who had given them to Randy Morris at P & D. As yet, the little devils were still marauding, and nobody knew where they might strike next.

I went to sleep with a smile on my face for a couple of nights, knowing I had been somewhat responsible for the fact that Greenwich, Connecticut, was clawing itself to death.

77

THE BIG, GARISH PRESS CREDENTIAL FOR THE HEAVYWEIGHT championship fight at Caesars Palace had a slogan written across it: "Aug. 20—Rhino Ray Thomas vs. Pork Chop Perkins—Once And For All!"

August 20 was an important date, but not as important as August 17, the day I arrived in Vegas. Waiting for me at the hotel desk was an urgent message to call Nell in New York.

I went up to my pink and orange room, ordered a BLT from room service, and then called Nell. The news she urgently wanted to share with me was that Fenton Boles and Lindsey Caperton had been rushed to the hospital that very morning, as I was boarding my flight.

Bryce Wilcox had gone to check up on them. Fenton and Lindsey were not out of the emergency room, but they were both suffering from the same mysterious ailments—stiff bellies, temperatures of 105, and semidelirium.

Nell said the doctors didn't know what to make of it as yet, but Bryce feared a plague of some kind and had sent around a memo telling everyone on the staff that if they experienced the slightest symptom of something wrong, they should go straight to the medical floor or, better still, to their own personal physician.

"Shellfish," I said, wittily.

"Thank you, doctor. I just thought you ought to know about it in case you start feeling peculiar. I'm fine, but people are trying to develop sniffles and coughs and difficulty breathing around here."

"I don't think I need to worry," I said. "I didn't kiss either one of them before I left."

"Interesting it's the two of *them,* don't you think?"

"Very."

"God knows where they go, who they see, or what they do when they get there."

"You don't suppose Dennis and Rodney have given them the A-word, do you?"

"I hope not. I wouldn't even wish that on Fenton Boles and Lindsey Caperton."

"No, I wouldn't either. I do hope they suffer a lot, though. What's everybody saying?"

"Everything from the A-word to the yuppie flu."

"Jeannie gets in tonight."

"Good. Tell her hi and hands off, bitch."

"Our demeanor will make you proud."

"How are the slots?"

"Tightly wound."

"How's the blackjack?"

"Hit eleven, stay on twelve. I only lost two hundred on the way to my room."

"How's your room?"

"Pink and orange."

"Are you betting on the fight?"

"I may make a small wager with Jeannie on who writes the best column on deadline. Keep me posted on the plague."

"I will. I love you."

"Same here."

"*Same here?*"

"I love you, too."

"No, don't say it like you're saying it to a stewardess, say it like you're saying it to *me.*"

"I love you, Theresa. I've never loved anyone the way I love you. Did I say 'Theresa'? I meant . . ."

But Nell had hung up.

78

HERE'S THE DEAL ON PRIZEFIGHTS: MORE LIES ARE TOLD BEfore a heavyweight championship fight than at any other sports event. Fight managers for some reason are more paranoid than pro football coaches. It could have something to do with the fact that a fight manager is a four-foot-tall Italian with hair like Albert Einstein, or it could have something to do with the fact that the fight manager fears that his tiger may have bet on the other guy and intends to go Dixie when the bell rings. Where the two fighters are staying is always a state secret, and so is what they are eating, what they weigh, what color trunks they will wear, and what they are doing to pass the time, other than being surprisingly bopped by a sparring partner on occasion. It is very big and quite exaggerated news if a fighter gets hit, or even grazed, while sparring. At the press conference, the fighter will not talk about anything but his shape and quickness and how ready he is to drop his opponent and "settle this thing" and "shut everybody up," at which point the manager will pat him and say, "Ain't he beautiful?"

This was the rhythm of the Thomas-Perkins fight for two days while Jeannie Slay and Richie Pace and Dub Fricker and I lost money at blackjack and couldn't find any Sinatras in town to go see and refused to go see Bobby Berosini and His Dancing Orangutans or Valerie and Her Trick Doves.

One night we did venture across the street from Caesars to a common man's hotel-casino where we could watch fat guys in double knits sweat at the dice tables.

"How do you win at craps?" Jeannie asked.

"Bet Don't Pass," I said, "but you have to bet Don't Pass your whole life, and that's no fun. It's more fun to bet on shooters and lose."

Dub said, "Some of my happiest times out here were spent at the crap table, losing two thousand dollars."

"In twenty minutes," Richie said. "Smart money ignores

290

the tables, goes for the debutantes. Vegas has the finest in the world.''

''Incoming,'' Dub said, alertly.

On the prowl was a twenty-year-old Sophia Loren, Amarillo variety.

''Somebody's daughter,'' I remarked.

Jeannie said, ''Dear Mom and Dad, I'm taking a heavy load this semester but my grades are looking good.''

I might interject here that Jeannie and I were well behaved throughout the Vegas stay. Just two old journalism chums. Richie and Dub were my witnesses, or, to put it another way, they were Nell's spies.

Tension started to build at the weigh-in, which was the morning of the fight.

The weigh-in was in a ballroom at Caesars, and both fighters arrived with cumbersome entourages. The twenty guys in the entourage of Rhino Ray Thomas, the champ, all wore matching T-shirts and shades, as did the champ's manager, Rudy Verregamo. The twenty guys in the entourage of Pork Chop Perkins, the challenger, all wore matching leather jackets and gold necklaces, as did the challenger's manager, Cookie D'Angelo.

A large, cold-eyed gentleman stood out from the rest in both entourages. Rhino Ray's head bodyguard was named Booty and his little brothers, Pooty and Scooty, were his helpers. Pork Chop's head bodyguard was named Dewey, and his two main helpers weren't any kin but they were named Huey and Stuey.

Jeannie and I approached Booty at the weigh-in and got him aside for a second, where Jeannie asked him what, as a bodyguard, he was mostly concerned about.

''Them balla-point pens, you know?'' Booty said. ''Them aug-raff seekers, you see? With them balla-point pens? Yeah. They can be stickin' my man in the hand. We be watchin' out for that shit, you know?''

Rhino Ray Thomas was being guaranteed eleven million for the fight, win or lose, and Pork Chop Perkins was being guaranteed six million, win or lose, but there was the usual highly staged commotion at the weigh-in, all for the purpose of trying to increase the pay-per-view audience on cable TV.

The champ had the more impressive build, remindful of Ali in his prime. Pork Chop didn't have that nickname for nothing. He was larger than Rhino and meaner-looking in the eyes, but his waist was no stranger to French fries and Häagen-Dazs Butter Pecan.

"You be goin' to medical school, Porky Pig," said Rhino. "You be needin' the entire-ah student body to sew up yo' face after tonight."

"Listen to the man," Pork Chop said. "Man talkin' doo-doo."

"Keep 'em apart, keep 'em apart!" shouted Cookie D'Angelo, grabbing his tiger. Much rustling around ensued and then calm was restored and the fighters kept glaring at each other.

"Hey, Porky Pig! You ever heard of Draculer?"

"Say what?"

"You lookin' at Draculer right here. I'm gonna suck yo' blood tonight, baby. Draculer ready for you!"

"What you talkin' about, motherfucker? You be suckin' my fiss, is all."

We spent that afternoon at the pool. Jeannie stretched out in the sun in a bikini while Richie and Dub and I sat in the shade of the poolside bar and watched shoe company executives from New Jersey and music moguls from Hollywood hit on her.

I considered doing a little preliminary work on the column, but decided it ought to be a fair fight. This was Jeannie's farewell performance on her Tandy laptop, and we had made a hundred-dollar bet on who would write the best lead on deadline. Richie and Dub would be the impartial judges.

Around 4:30, we went upstairs to our rooms to clean up and slip into our typing costumes. We all met downstairs in the lobby cocktail lounge at 5:30. We knew it would take a half-hour to push our way through all the dope dealers and high-rollers in the casino and around the swimming pool and tennis courts and reach the open-air arena on the back lot of Caesars.

There must have been two hundred entrepreneurs milling about in their velvet jumpsuits and sneakers, each one wearing a gold pendant on which his name was engraved. Among the names I read on pendants: Deion, Crank, Eddie Snow, Stardust, Hit Man, Corinne, Louie, Pony, Roof Top, Bernice, Superfly, Dread.

It had often occurred to me that if the Feds were serious about their war on drugs, they might want to attend a championship fight sometime.

We all set up shop in the airplane-hangar press room next door to the arena. My geezer-codger portable was on one side of Jeannie's electricity. Richie's and Dub's computers were on the other side. We drank coffee, smoked, lounged around, gossiped with other writers as they came in to make work preparation. Writers always tried to act blasé at big events, but they knew they were in for their own form of combat with their deadline muses.

"I'm going to miss it," Jeannie said.

"Not after your first paycheck," Richie intoned.

Two hours before the fight, we all wandered into the arena and down to ringside to watch the crowd fill up the bleachers and choice seats. It was always surprising to see how many wise old prizefight authorities there were in the Hollywood community. We watched as actors in Dodger caps and Laker jackets leaped into the arms of ex-champions of the ring and hugged on them until the ex-champions untangled themselves.

It was forty-five minutes before fight time and the ring announcer was introducing the usual lineup of celebrities when we all heard the loud shriek.

"Whoa! Jim Tom!"

We all looked around.

Clomping happily toward us was a paralyzing sight—a tan, meaty blonde with a big grin in high heels and a low-cut yellow Spandex bodysuit, a woman Richie Pace later described as the Motor Trend Car of the Year.

It was my third ex-wife.

79

PRISCILLA PRACTICALLY STRADDLED ME AND GAVE ME A SLURP-
ing kiss as she jubilantly told me how pleased she was to see
me and how pleased she was to tell me the old shit had finálly
died.

Three days ago, Priscilla said. Russell had been practicing
chip shots in the backyard of their home at La Quinta, and he
had just hauled off and toppled over from a stroke. Their chink
houseboy, who was basically a Hawaiian, she said, had found
Russell an hour later. Russell had been cremated and she had
sprinkled his ashes over PGA West, which she thought was a
kick, since the old shit had never even made a bogey there,
much less a par.

"I'm the richest bitch you know," she said. "Do I look
good or what? Who are these people, darlin'?"

Jeannie and Richie and Dub had been studying Priscilla with
awe and amusement. I introduced them.

"I know you," Priscilla said to Jeannie. "I read your crap
in the *LA Times*. Which one of these assholes are you fucking,
honey?"

"At the moment, none of them," Jeannie smiled.

"Don't let it go to waste, hon. Your donut's not worth a shit
when you're dead. Damn, it's good to see you, Jim Tom. What
are you doin' after the fight, darlin'?"

"I have to write."

"What are you doin' after that?"

"I'm going back to New York."

"Well, we have to get together, sweetie. When am I gonna
give you any head?"

Richie said, "I'm calling Nell."

Jeannie and Dub giggled.

"Who's Nell?" Priscilla asked. "You haven't gotten married on me, have you, darlin'?"

"No. Nell's my psychiatrist."

I was trying to remember the last time I had seen Priscilla. I was sure it was before her body had been slightly thinned by cocaine and her face had been slightly puffed by whiskey. But she still looked plenty okay.

"You don't have to rush back to New York," she said. "Come to Palm Springs for a few days, darlin'. I've got this big house. I've got my chink to wait on us. We can lay by the pool. We can play golf. We can play with my money. We can play with my clit. Whatever."

There was a tall Robert Redford clone standing behind Priscilla, holding her sable, and now he cleared his throat, as if he thought it was time for him to be introduced.

"Oh, this is Dutch," Priscilla said.

"Dutch Carruthers," the clone said, stepping forward.

Priscilla said, "Dutch thinks he's an actor. If they'd put his dick on the screen, he'd make a fortune."

Richie asked Dutch what films we might have seen him in.

"I have some projects in development," Dutch said. "My last picture was a little cult thing called *Psycho Waitresses*."

"I saw it," I said. "Donna Roach was in it."

"Nice kid, Donna."

"I'm sorry. I don't remember what part you played."

"I was the chef. The guy in the kitchen? The one they tied down and poured the hot grease on?"

"We better get to our seats," Dub said.

Priscilla gave me another slurping kiss. "Good to *see* you! I want you to promise me you'll come to Palm Springs, sweetie. We'll have an old-fashioned fuck-a-thon."

Priscilla hooked onto Dutch's arm and they walked back up the aisle to their two-hundred-dollar seats.

Jeannie was staring at me. "So that was the third missus, huh?"

"You gotta play hurt," I said.

"Terrifying."

"Tell me about it."

"I'm calling Nell," Richie reiterated.

"I'm calling the police," Jeannie said.

"DOWN IN FRONT!" a gangster hollered.

80

A SLOW ROAR IN THE CROWD BLOSSOMED INTO CRAZINESS. The band blared out a marching tune. Then here came Pork Chop Perkins, the challenger, in a red robe with a red hood over his head, his entourage having swollen from twenty to thirty. Pork Chop climbed into the ring, off came the robe, and he began to dance around, flicking jabs into the air and rehearsing uppercuts. He didn't wave at the crowd—he looked too angry. Now the band struck up a different tune, one of those old themes from *Giant* or *Red River* or *Quo Vadis*—I always get them mixed up. And here came Rhino Ray Thomas, the champ, whose entourage had also swollen from twenty to thirty. The champ climbed into the ring, slipped out of his white robe and danced around with a big smile, applauding himself.

Richie explained boxing to Jeannie.

"The challenger is the one in the red trunks and black shoes. The champion is the one in the white trunks and white shoes. When the bell rings, they will try to hit each other."

"Why would they do that?" Jeannie said.

The bell rang for the first round, and the fighters circled each other as their managers bellowed from the corners. Rudy Verregamo yelled, "Jab, jab!" Cookie D'Angelo yelled, "Move, move!"

The fighters kept feinting, bobbing, circling, glowering.

The first punch was thrown at exactly one minute and seventeen seconds of round one. A light jab from the champion that looked as if it might have touched Pork Chop on the cheek.

The challenger staggered backward, bounced against the ropes, and fell to the canvas with a resounding thud.

Rhino Ray Thomas raised his gloves in victory and pranced to a neutral corner.

"Oh, please," said Jeannie. "Give me a *break*."

The challenger rolled over on the floor and seemed to glance around as the referee, Artie Deleconte, stood over him, counting. Pork Chop raised himself to one knee as the referee kept counting.

Half the crowd, those who had bet on the champion, cheered wildly. The other half, those who had bet on the challenger, booed, hissed, and threw cushions, cold drink cups, popcorn boxes, five-dollar chips.

Just as the referee counted to ten, Pork Chop got to his feet, but the ref waved his arms—the fight was over. Pork Chop frowned and protested. Cookie D'Angelo jumped into the ring and attacked the referee. Booty and Dewey, the two head bodyguards, stormed into the ring and squared off. But police now filled the ring and restored order.

"It's always been *my* favorite sport," Richie said.

We moved hastily to the airplane hangar for the press conference.

At first, there was much quarreling between the two camps, cursing and shouting across the room, as reporters sought quotes and insight from the managers, handlers, bodyguards, and others in the entourage.

The promoters, Kinky Zarem and Freddie Lorenzo, threatened each other with pistols. Kinky fired a blank into the ceiling.

The two fighters came in and took seats behind microphones on a dais. They had dressed. Pork Chop was wearing a red pirate's shirt, dark glasses, and white golf visor. The champ was wearing an orange satin warmup jacket, dark glasses, and a Yankee baseball cap.

A man in a tuxedo with a deep tan and a snow-white pompadour sat between them to moderate.

"Draculer bad," the champion said. "Draculer was *clean* tonight. Draculer be illin', you know? Draculer strike like lightnin'."

The challenger demanded a rematch. He complained about the referee's "fast count." The fight shouldn't have been stopped, he said. He could have continued. Pork Chop went on, "Yeah, you know, I felt a jab, but it wasn't like I lost my luggage."

We moved to our writing machines and donned our cleats.

The two leads that Richie and Dub were obliged to judge were as follows:

"By Jim Tom Pinch.

"When a heavyweight earned six million bucks the other night in Las Vegas for getting knocked out by a wisp of fresh air, I was reminded of a Hemingway novel, The Bum Also Rises."

And:

"By Jeannie Slay.

"TRANSYLVANIA—Here in Count Dracula's castle, which bears a creepy resemblance to Caesars Palace, I am still looking for the punch that knocked the wreath of wolfsbane off Pork Chop Perkins' head."

I gave Jeannie the hundred. Even I agreed she won.

81

I RETURNED TO NEW YORK TO FIND THE TPG BUILDING under siege. Not from the mysterious plague that had put Fenton Boles and Lindsey Caperton in the hospital—and was keeping them there—but from Fritzy Krupp-Streicher Padgett and her energetic interior decorators.

Our founder and chairman's newest wife was having marble floors installed at *World Events*, pet food, and cable TV. She was having suede wall-covering put up at *Celebrity Parade*, paper products, and nondairy creamer. Somebody said *Southern Mansions* and diapers were under heavy bombardment from Chinese screens and antique furniture.

SM's edit floor hadn't been assaulted yet, but Nell said it wouldn't matter. We could easily publish out of Fu's Like Us and Eat Nam, the company cafeteria.

Lester Padgett dropped into Fu's one early evening to kill some time while he waited for Fritzy, who was upstairs arguing with two French decorators about draperies. I had a couple of drinks with him.

"Jim Tom, you old pisser-offer, I hope you're stayin' single," Les said.

I said I almost was. I saw no reason to go into it with Les that I was living half the time in Nell's apartment and half the time in my own apartment—my clothes were strewn from 72nd to 39th.

Les said, "A single man don't have to give doodly squat about antique furniture, and that's a fact. You gettin' any good pussy?"

"Some."

"See there. I bet it don't have nothin' to do with antique furniture, does it?"

"Rarely."

"Tell you something else, Jim Tom. A single man don't have to buy a painting that don't make sense, either."

"No, he doesn't."

"Is there anybody richer than a dead artist?"

"Not that I know of."

"Guess what? I got me a whole floor of dead artists upstairs. They're just hangin' there gettin' richer and there ain't nobody ever gonna look at 'em but my Nazi wife and two French sissies."

"Fine paintings are a good investment, they say."

"That's what my Nazi says. You know what I said? I said that's a hell of a deal, but as soon as them French sissies get as rich as them dead artists, we're gonna shut this shit down."

I was back in the city for two weeks before I would be going off to football stadiums on a regular basis. I caught up on expense accounts, bill-paying, surgical strikes. On the medical front, the doctors were still puzzled about what was wrong with the CEO and Lindsey Caperton. This was the topic foremost on everyone's mind. Hallway gossip said penicillin wasn't helping.

I did learn from Bryce Wilcox that Lindsey was worse off than the CEO now. Weird bacteria were originating in Lindsey's bowels, and the doctors were worried about peritonitis becoming a complication.

"Is the big tamale in much pain?" I asked.

"I gather he is but drugs are helping," said Bryce, who didn't get it.

"He shouldn't have eaten the whole enchilada."

"It's apparently not an epidemic," Bryce said. "That's the good news."

One of the Christian things I did while I was home was sell the TPG stock Fenton had arranged for me to buy. I sold it for a little more than I paid for it, which was enough to square myself with the bank and the bank's interest. It was a break-even deal.

I didn't unload the stock because our CEO was hospitalized with an unknown disorder and Rip Bellemy's wife was suing him for what would be a costly divorce, no doubt. I figured the TPG-ModeTech scam would go off uninterrupted—good old Barney Levine at Tweed, Hazard & Risk would see to *that*. I did it because it made me feel good.

It made me feel good not to allow myself to be rewarded for all the pimping I had done, as innocent and harmless as it had been in my mind at the time, and not to allow myself to be rewarded on the insider swindle that was taking place. Call me a fool for possibly blowing a hundred grand profit, but that's how I looked at it.

Of course, I didn't give back the twenty-grand raise. The raise had been two years overdue, anyhow, and richly deserved for putting up with Drones One Through Ten and Bryce's golf disease.

A letter from my son made me feel even better about life itself. Enclosed with the letter was a check from James Junior for three hundred dollars. The letter said:

Dear Dad:

I got all your postcards from the Europe zone. It sounds toxic over there. I would like to see it someday. Here is part of the money I owe you. I don't mean to lude out. You will get the balance in a month or two. I am going to keep working part-time at the Peacake Lounge this fall. I can scoop good jing at The Cake. We get a big crowd that gets latered every night.

Dad, you will be happy to hear I am dumping on the pyramids. I have decided to stick in there and get a business degree. Mom is sure happy. I am only a year from Diploma City, and guess what? I have this good buddy, Earl Otis Pottle, who will graduate at the same time and he says we can both go to work for his daddy in Atlanta. Mr. Pottle has a lot of cheese. He owns ten electronics stores. Earl Otis and me have it all planned. We will get a pad in Atlanta and chase the lovelies. Atlanta is really a good town.

I am looking forward to getting settled after all this time in school. You will be calling me one of these days to handle your complete stereo needs.

Boy, what a barf that fight was. Old Pork Chop mommied up to the canvas as soon as the bell rang.

Love, James.

I wrote James Junior back and told him how delighted I was with his decision to dump on the pyramids. I said I was very aware that Atlanta was a good town but I cautioned him to watch his step with the shapely adorables. I didn't want him to break the family marriage record.

It didn't look like I would be coming to Athens this football season, I said. I couldn't find the Georgia Bulldogs ranked in any of the Top Twenty forecasts. It looked as if the Bulldogs were light on Charley Trippis and were suffering from Under-Bro syndrome right now.

Of course, I didn't expect James to know who Charley Trippi was, so I told him. Charley Trippi was a great Georgia halfback in the 1940s. I suggested James could win a sports trivia bet with Charley Trippi's name. Charley Trippi, Old No. 62, was the only man who ever played on teams that won a Rose Bowl, Sugar Bowl, and NFL championship game. Trippi led Georgia over UCLA in the Rose Bowl after the '42 season, went into the service and came back to lead Georgia over North Carolina in the Sugar Bowl after the '46 season, and then became part of the Chicago Cardinals' "dream backfield" along with Missouri's Paul Christman, Wisconsin's Pat

Harder, and Pitt's Marshall Goldberg, and they won the NFL in '47. Trippi scored a historic double by being the MVP in both the Rose Bowl and the NFL title game.

Nobody could jack around with me on college football.

82

COLLEGE FOOTBALL WAS MY THING. IT WAS MY FAVORITE sport to write about, to be around, the sport I made the least fun of. It was a hobby as much as anything else. I kept stats and a clip file during college football season. I had perfected my own rating system to determine the No. 1 team, a system *SM* had adopted. Someday I wanted to write a decent history of college football—there had never been a good one—but that would be when I was too old to be the object of surgical strikes. I could name every All-American back to before Ted Coy, even the linemen. It wasn't enough for me to know all the Heisman winners; I could name all the runnersup. Who else but me could tell you that Choo Choo Justice was the only player that was ever runnerup for the Heisman *twice* but never won it? I could name the other members of Tom Harmon's backfield at Michigan—Forest Evashevski, Bob Westfall, Paul Kromer. Kromer was the tough one to get. I could tell you the other members of Doak Walker's great backfield at SMU—Kyle Rote, Paul Page, Dick McKissack. I could remind you that in '38, there were *two* great little quarterbacks who wore No. 8, TCU's Davey O'Brien and Southern Cal's Grenny Lansdell. If you wanted to bet me that anybody in the Four Horsemen backfield weighed more than 165 pounds, you would lose. I much preferred the college game over the pros. The cast changed. Power shifted. College coaches were more cooperative, entertaining, and intelligent than pro coaches. I made no apology for the fact that I had collected about sixty college fight songs on one cassette tape and enjoyed listening to *Go, U Northwestern* more than I enjoyed Beethoven's Symphony No.

9 in D Minor. I'm sure you could trace my zeal for the game back to growing up in Texas and seeing people reject Jesus after their team lost a big game.

In any case, I was continually on the road and fully absorbed with college football all through September. While the naive thickwit, Stewart Mason Gardner, was doing pieces for the magazine on the origin of the facemask, a Colgate fullback, and a Wesleyan coach, I was off doing columns on things that mattered more than the nation's economy, games that would have an effect on the question of who would eventually be No. 1.

I went out to South Bend for the Notre Dame–Michigan game. I loved Notre Dame. Any school that placed so much importance on winning deserved my total respect, but I also loved Notre Dame for inventing the press box hotdog, the flip card, the parking pass.

And Notre Dame's fans were hilarious. In South Bend, they had once built a bonfire out of two thousand copies of an *SM* issue in which I wrote that Notre Dame's fans were arrogant in victory, malicious in defeat.

I went down to Tallahassee for the Miami–Florida State game. I loved this rivalry. Other coaches said that when Miami played Florida State, they ought to start the game with a burglar alarm, but that was envy. Another coach once told me that when you played the Miami Hurricanes, you better not "disturb the tribe," you might get run out of the stadium.

I went down to Norman, Oklahoma, for the OU–Penn State game. I loved Oklahoma. When the Sooners didn't have a contender for the national championship, which was rare, the whole state slid into a scathing recession.

Jeannie Slay was at two of those games, and although I spoke to her on the phone, I never saw her in person, only on the TV screen. We were in different hotels in South Bend and Tallahassee and she was constantly in CBS production meetings.

She got on the air twice during the Notre Dame–Michigan game. Her job was to roam the sidelines and the stadium for featurettes. In the press box at South Bend, I saw her likeness appear on a TV monitor as she stood with a hulking Notre

Dame lineman. I dashed to the TV set to catch the audio. Jeannie was saying:

". . . and Eno Drabscik came to this country as a stowaway on a cargo ship. He knew nothing about American football until his senior year at Chicago Vocational High. Back to you, Jim."

The other time, she was up in the stands, reporting that a "Mr. O'Connell," an elderly gentleman in a James Cagney gangster cap, had seen every Notre Dame home game since the days of Marchy Schwartz.

On a TV monitor in the Florida State press box, I saw her do two other vignettes.

In one, she tried to interview a cocky wide receiver for the Miami Hurricanes, but the speedy All-American kept yelling at his coaches, "Get me the ball, get me the ball! . . . Yo, blood! You want to win this game, get the ball to *me*!"

In the other, a Florida State cheerleader explained that the school had no intention of changing its nickname from Seminoles just to satisfy a small group of "Native American" protesters on the campus. The kid said, "I just don't think it would sound right to call us the Florida State Native Americans. My fraternity would go crazy if they changed it. I bet you'd see some dead Indians around here."

Near the end of September, I was thinking of going to Fort Worth to do a column on T. J. Lambert's Horned Frogs—Orangejello and Limejello had got TCU off to a 4-0 start—but that's when two things happened that jolted *The Sports Magazine* and shook the TPG Building to its very foundation.

Lindsey Caperton was the first thing that happened.

He died, was what he did.

Yeah. Lindsey spun out. The old wordsmith went to The Big Parenthesis in the Sky.

The word got around that Lindsey had known what was wrong with him all along but had withheld the information from his doctors, which was why they had wasted so much valuable time treating him for the wrong things.

Through the first half of September, Lindsey had undergone four operations that were performed to drain the multiple abscesses that kept building up in his abdominal cavity. In a prolonged critical illness, Lindsey had always been in danger of developing blood clots, and that's what had finally occurred.

A blood clot had floated to his lung and this had been the ultimate cause of his death.

Frankly, I felt pretty rotten about it. I mean, I never wanted the guy dead—I wanted him on the rim of *The Hagerstown Herald Mail*.

Lindsey was buried in a little cemetery in a suburb of Baltimore. About a dozen staffers took the Metroliner down for the funeral and stayed overnight, mostly to get out of the office. Bryce went by limo. The mourners on the train were led by Molly Connors, the treacherous tattletale. The group included the piss-stained Reg Turner, the weeping Miriam Bowen, Marge Frack, and, of all people, Wooden Dick Webber. But I knew what Wooden Dick's intent was. He would comfort the bereaved Molly Connors, figuring he could fuck her before the night was over.

My excuse for missing the funeral was the Tennessee-Auburn game in Knoxville. Bryce delivered the eulogy and only mentioned his golf game three times, I heard later.

Fenton Boles was the next thing that happened. The oily dwarf got himself fired.

Yeah. Dismissed. History. Archives.

I didn't think it could happen in real life, that a powerful, slippery, well-entrenched, fingerprint-erasing, track-covering CEO, a master of "plausible deniability," could get his legs cut off.

But in the first week of October, soon after Lindsey's funeral, and after Fenton was well on the road to recovery, Les Padgett stormed into Fenton's hospital room and fired him in a display of fury that apparently sent nurses and interns diving for shelter.

The CEO was fired without benefit of platinum parachute for bringing indescribable embarrassment and repulsive humiliation to Les Padgett personally and the whole damn TPG company.

Bryce happened to have been in the room, visiting Fenton, when Les came in, and the managing editor recalled the chairman's words vividly.

"Here's a pink slip for you," Les shouted. "You can stick this up there with all them light bulbs and sardine cans and screwdrivers and whatever else your rectum seems to fancy! It beats any goddamn thing I ever heard of!"

83

THE GERBIL STORY RAN LIKE A GREAT FLOODING RIVER ALL through our building, all through the magazine business around New York, all through Wall Street. It rushed across the country and into newspaper offices, boardrooms, dinner parties. It traveled by phone, Fed Ex, computer screen, and fax. Evidently, the only place where it was received with a yawn was in Hollywood, where, if Jeannie Slay's information was correct, "gerbilizing" was as much a part of the film industry as some studio lawyer's latest revolutionary definition of profit.

There was no way to tell it delicately. If somebody wanted to know exactly what Fenton Boles and Lindsey Caperton had been doing, you could only say they had been seeking the zenith of orgasms, and describe it step by step.

First, they would acquire a gerbil and shoot the little rascal up with cocaine. Then they would put him in the freezer for about ten minutes, long enough for the gerbil to doze off in a frozen sleep. Next, they would slip him into a Nudom condom with a string tied to the end of it, a rip cord.

And then?

Yep. They would insert the gerbil-occupied condom into the rectum. One could only assume that this was no difficult procedure for either Fenton or Lindsey—their playrooms had obviously been introduced to other foreign bodies. Newspaper reporters who covered emergency rooms had long been acquainted with bizarre objects turning up in the rectums of wacko-sickos.

Anyhow, the idea was this: when the little rascal awakened from his frozen state—high as a bitch—he would begin to scratch and claw with intensity, and in close proximity to the prostate, and the combination of the little rascal going nuts while Fenton and Lindsey were performing other acts on each other, well . . . there you have it.

What the lovebirds hoped to achieve from this activity was said to be an orgasm of indeterminate length and unfathomable proportions.

I, myself, could not understand why anyone would want to seek such a gigantic orgasm, but of course I was only a normal heterosexual.

Fenton and Lindsey's medical problems had occurred when they had severely injured each other extracting the gerbils, by pulling too hard and too impatiently on the string. It also may have been the case that the little rascals were having so much fun at the party, they hadn't wanted to leave so soon. I ran that opinion past Nell at Fu's one evening. She laughed as she said:

"Let's stay home tonight. I'll get the wine, you stop by the pet shop."

84

THE MEMO DIDN'T MAKE ME WANT TO TAPDANCE OR STRUM the banjo, mind you, but neither did it surprise me as much as it did others. It said:

"To: The TPG Family

"FROM: Les Padgett, Founder & Chairman

"It gives me great pleasure today to announce that Clipper Langdon is the new President and Chief Executive Officer of TPG, Inc., and that Bryce Wilcox becomes Vice-President, Magazine Group, a new post.

"As you know, Clipper has been publisher of *SM* for the past seven months and has demonstrated that he is uniquely qualified to fill the very big chair left vacant by the departure of Fenton Boles, who has left us to explore and define new horizons elsewhere.

"I fully expect our company to benefit greatly from Clipper's expertise, focus, and efficiency, and to lead us in achieving continued financial success all down the line. Clipper brings with him a keen marketing sense and a strong vision of what the role of this company should be in the future.

"In his new position of 'watchdog,' Bryce will assume a number of key internal and external responsibilities where our magazines are concerned. Everyone, of course, is aware of *SM*'s enormous growth and success during Bryce's stewardship.

"One of Bryce's immediate challenges will be to select a new managing editor and publisher for *SM*.

"I am delighted to have Clipper and Bryce join me on the 33rd floor. I am sure you will give them your full support.

"I also want to assure you that despite recent unpleasant events, I am confident that with these new appointments, our ship will sail on smoothly. As Clipper said to me only this morning, 'Skipper, we won't miss a single buoy.'

"Congratulations again to Clipper and Bryce, and good luck to all of us in working to achieve our future objectives.

"L. P."

Memo-writing was a craft of its own, like textblocks for photo layouts, or ad copy. It almost required a missing gene.

It didn't take an FBI agent to figure out that Clipper and Bryce had combined their talents on the memo. Les Padgett had never written his own memo in his life. In fact, I learned later in the day that Les and Fritzy had already fled the country in the Gulfstream Four. Eileen Fincher heard from Les' secretary that Les and Fritzy had gone to Sidney, Australia, for a while to escape the gerbil laughter that had been greeting them almost everywhere they went in public.

I also didn't need an FBI agent to help me figure out why Les Padgett had chosen Clipper Langdon for his CEO. Clipper had been in on the beginning of the TPG-ModeTech caper, he was still a big pal of Rip Bellemy's, and Les was more than familiar with the whole scenario. Clipper was the man who could see it through, and the stock deal would be worth millions to the company, even after Fritzy paid the decorators.

And Bryce's reward was the lofty new job he had created for himself.

The memo wasn't on my desk all that long before I walked

around to the Bat Cave to see Bryce and put in a plug for
Wayne Mohler for managing editor.

Bryce and Eileen were cleaning out Bryce's office for the
move up to thirty-three. Eileen was putting all of the putters in
one golf bag, and Bryce was putting all the metal woods in
another golf bag.

"Congratulations, Your Excellency," I said.

"This ought to cinch Pine Valley," Bryce said. "What do
you think about the Augusta National? They take in five or six
new members a year. Why not me?"

"You're white," I said, but he missed it.

"Would that be any good? Winged Foot, Pine Valley, Augusta?"

"Who do you have in mind for publisher?" I said. I thought
it best to work up to managing editor slowly.

"Clipper has a guy. Tippy Donahue at B & M. Hell of a
guy, he says."

"I know Tippy Donahue," I said. "I met him at the Derby.
The Tipper will bring a lot to the regatta."

Bryce waggled a golf club. "Ever tried one of these? It's the
new Ginty. Fifteen-degree loft on a three-wood face, driver
shaft. Is that any good?"

"Looks like the answer. Bryce, I'm here on behalf of a
majority of the writers. We think Wayne Mohler would be a
very good managing editor."

"No way, Jose."

"Just like that?"

"I don't want to lose Wayne as a writer. I have a better idea.
I'm gonna have a contest."

"A contest?"

"I'm nominating three candidates for the job. Each one will
run the book for three weeks, maybe four. The one who per-
forms best gets the job."

"In whose judgment?"

"Mine, who else? I'm the El Commandante, right?"

I was almost afraid to ask who the three candidates were, but
I lit a Winston and did.

"Dalton, Doug, and Nell," he said, handing me an ashtray.

"Nell? Really?"

He pointed to his noggin. "Crazy like a fox, huh?"

"To coin a phrase."

"Equal opportunity, big guy. Put a woman in the running—talk of the town. She's qualified, don't you think?"

"No question," I said tamely. I didn't want to appear too enthusiastic. "She gets my vote now. Frankly, Bryce, I don't know how you can even consider Dalton Buckley and Doug McNiff—unless you want to completely destroy morale around here."

"You're too hard on 'em. Dalton and Doug are loyal. They've paid their dues. They deserve a shot."

"What do you think of this, Eileen?"

Eileen was now packing Bryce's golf instruction books in a cardboard box. "I thought Ralph Webber deserved a chance," she said.

"Ralph has too many other things on his mind," Bryce said with a wink at me.

Eileen ignored that, went on packing books.

Bryce said, "It'll be interesting. The book will be theirs. They'll be free to pick their own covers, run their own leads, make their own mistakes, take their own chances. I'll keep the scorecard."

"When does the contest start?" I asked.

"Right away. Dalton's on the tee first, then Doug, then Nell."

"Have you told them?"

"That's my next meeting today. What time, Eileen?"

"After lunch," Eileen said. "Do you want to keep *Golf Between the Ears*? It's a first edition, autographed."

She held up Cloyce Windham's book.

"No, dump it," said Bryce.

Cloyce's memoir went into the wastebasket.

I said, "What happens to the losers, Bryce?"

"Nobody loses if they do a good job," he said. "Doug could go to exec. Dalton and Nell could go to assistant m.e. Better get you one of these Gintys, big guy. It's a slam-dunk on the long par threes."

Bryce was taking his swing back to horizontal when I left his office to go blab to Nell that she had been nominated for an Oscar.

85

FOR TEN DAYS IN OCTOBER, THE WORLD SERIES INFLICTED itself on America in all of its tranquil, rustic, emerald-chessboard, game-of-inches, highly symmetrical, deeply philosophical, roots-of-boyhood, literary splendor, which to me, of course, meant that the ballplayers involved would be reading Shelley and Keats more closely as they sat naked in front of their lockers, spitting on the floor, pulling on their balls, and yanking on their dicks.

I had never quite been able to equate the baseball I had covered with the ephemeral, lyrical, hypnotically intellectual game that certain writers made it out to be. I tended to agree with whoever it was who said that if baseball was half as complicated as writers make it, baseball players couldn't play it.

Most baseball players were a sorry lot, as I had known them, basically the dumbest and lowest-rent collection of athletes I had ever encountered—pro football was loaded with geniuses by comparison, and I'm talking about white people here.

Very few baseball players had spent more than twenty minutes in college and were incapable of uttering a sentence without using the word cunt. Not that the word offended me, especially when a ballplayer used it properly, in verse.

My guess was that the intellectual writers didn't really know ballplayers. They only saw them as dots on the great emerald pasture. They didn't know that a baseball player was a guy who said the toughest part of the game was trying to explain to his wife why she needed a penicillin shot for his kidney infection. They didn't know that a baseball player was a guy who said, "I didn't know that was against the law," when he heard about another athlete exposing himself to a ten-year-old schoolgirl. They didn't know a baseball player was a guy who said, as the team plane landed back home after a road trip, to be greeted by wives, "Okay, fellows, act horny." They didn't know a baseball player was a guy who sat in the dugout, and said, "Man, that bitch has a cunt that's worn out four infields."

All this was part of the baseball player's charm, to my mind, but what did it have to do with making the game an intellectual, literary exercise?

SM's baseball writer, DeChane Moxler, was one of those "sensitive" types who couldn't turn in a piece without mentioning that baseball was "intrinsic to American society," that the game was more than the national pastime, it was "every American's shared youth," a "rock of certainty" in a world of shifting values, a game that combined crashing action with moments of "tension-packed silence."

It was up to me to bring balance to the magazine and suggest that the tension-packed silence could be described in another way. It was called STANDING AROUND.

I was willing to admit that a man who could hit, run, catch, and throw was perhaps the most highly skilled athlete in sports. More so than an NBA leaper or NFL cornerback, for example, because the NBA leaper and the NFL cornerback didn't have the faintest idea of what it would be like to stand up to a 110-mile-an-hour fastball. But I had just never been able to grasp why so many literary minds thought it was an intellectual pursuit for a guy to screw around in a whirlpool for an hour, walk around naked for two or three hours, play cards, read mail, finally put on his uniform and go out for batting practice and take infield and chase fly balls, then come back to the locker room and get totally naked again and pull on his balls and yank on his dick until it was time to suit up again and return to the field for another hour of warming up before the game, when he would then stand around for three hours, but I suppose it was more fun for a player to go to the ballpark six hours early than it was to take the kids to the mall or paint the baseboards.

Frequently, the most action a ballplayer experienced was when the trainer would spray ethyl chloride on one of his foul-tip bruises, and the player would holler, "Get the cunt numb, get it numb!"

I would argue that baseball hadn't been the so-called national pastime for years. Not since air-conditioning was invented in the thirties, an act of mercy that did away with the ballpark as the coolest place in town on a lyrical, tranquil summer's day.

And baseball seriously hadn't been the national pastime since the fifties, when football, college and pro, went on TV, which, ironically, was about the same time that Joe DiMaggio retired.

Further, I would argue that baseball would *never* have been considered the national pastime if the sport hadn't been so overcovered by sports pages and overwritten by sportswriters ever since the National League was formed back in 1876. But I understood why this had happened. Sportswriters liked to get out of the house and on the road without their wives as much as ballplayers did.

But enough of my advance column on the World Series.

In my opinion, there were three positive things about the Series this time.

One, who was in it. The Boston Red Sox and Los Angeles Dodgers. Two glamour teams. Two of only six teams in the majors that were of any real curiosity to the country as a whole, the others being the Yankees, Cardinals, Cubs, and Tigers, the only other teams that still wore recognizable uniforms.

Two, the ballparks. Fenway and Dodger Stadium. If I had to be dragged to a baseball game, I wanted atmosphere. Fenway reeked with atmosphere. Last of the old downtown ballparks, near Kenmore Square. Natural grass. The short but tall left-field fence—the Green Monster. Virtually every seat so close to the diamond you felt like you could lean over and tell the third baseman to watch out for the steal. Dodger Stadium was the first new ballpark built in my lifetime, but it was now old enough for the MTV generation to think of it as an antique, and it had housed some lore. No short fences but a lot of short movie stars in box seats.

Third, my hotels. It was a Series that would see the Ritz-Carlton in Boston, across from the Common, collide with the Beverly Hills on the West Coast.

Covering the Series, my luxury ended when I ventured out of my hotels. I wasn't a member of that armed services committee known as the Baseball Writers Association, so I had never been near the press box proper at a World Series, and neither had Richie Pace, Dub Fricker, Bubba Slack, or any other writer I knew personally.

Credentials for the World Series were always doled out by crusty gentlemen from the local chapters of the association. You could be toting around a six-pack of Pulitzers, but you would have to sit in an urgently constructed, open-air, auxiliary press box in right field, where you were surrounded by mindless, rambunctious fans and you were guaranteed to freeze to death on at least one evening.

Each time I got sentenced to the auxiliary press box, I thought of the immortal line from Ring Lardner: "Nothing on earth is more depressing than an old baseball writer."

86

THE SERIES OPENED IN THE RITZ-CARLTON—UH, BOSTON, I mean—and Dalton Buckley, the acting managing editor of *SM*, now in full throttle in his trial run, called me almost as soon as I arrived at the hotel to ask if I would do a sidebar along with writing my column.

"Dalton, I don't do sidebars," I said. "I outgrew them years ago."

"I rather imagined you might enjoy a Q-and-A with the Boston manager. I have a nice little slot for it."

Stormy Baldwin, the Boston manager, was a portly, tobacco-chewing, white-haired old fool whose "license to think," as John Lardner once put it about Leo Durocher, had been extended for these ten days of the Series. It would be difficult to print a conversation with Stormy Baldwin because *SM* was among those family publications that disallowed the use of the word "cunt."

I said, "You must have at least eight writers sitting around on their ass, doing nothing, Dalton. I suggest you assign one of them to the sidebar."

"Just trying to get your by-line in the front of the book," he said. "I'll let you off the hook this time, fella, but I must tell you, as the acting m.e., one of my goals is to get Jim Tom Pinch in the lead area."

"Maybe on football," I said.

"Who do you fancy in the October Classic, fella? I rather like the Bosox myself."

I said, "Dalton, you heard it here. It will definitely be a team of human beings."

My leading baseball authority, Richie Pace, explained to me why Boston was a falling-down cinch to win the World Series for the first time since 1918, when a young man named George Herman Ruth was a pitcher, outfielder, and first baseman for the Red Stockings. Boston was loaded with power hitters—Red Karper, Johnny Kilgore, Davey Brewster—and moreover, Boston possessed the best pitcher in the majors, the gas-throwing Al (Gas Man) Finley. The Dodgers had nothing but defense. Besides all this, it was God's will.

Down on the Fenway turf before the game, as the players stretched and spit and looked up in the stands for "sleaze kitties," Red Karper, the slugging first baseman, exuded confidence.

"We got Al going tonight," he said. "Blind people come out to the park just to listen to him pitch."

Al Finley pitched a four-hitter that night and the Red Sox might have won the first game if Red Karper hadn't let a throw from third go between his legs in the eighth inning, allowing the Dodgers to score two runs. The Red Sox might have won the second game, too, if Johnny Kilgore hadn't dropped a routine fly ball in the sixth inning, allowing the Dodgers to score two runs, an error that earned Johnny Kilgore the lasting nickname of Skillets and the Iron Glove Award in most newspapers.

We all jetted to LA for a day of rest before the Series resumed. Richie and Dub traveled on the writers' charter, but I went commercial so I could spend some of *SM*'s money and not have to listen to baseball talk.

I was warmly greeted by the staff at the Beverly Hills Hotel and by all the waiters in the Polo Lounge. I deposited money in all of the waiters' hands to ensure that my favorite booth would be available whenever I might want it. There was a new maitre d' in the Polo Lounge, an exuberant man named Enrico, but I made immediate friends with him with a twenty-dollar bill. "Yes, Mr. Preaches, it is so good to see you again," he said.

Nell had given me clearance to take Jeannie Slay to dinner. Jeannie met me for drinks in the Polo Lounge. I planned for us to go on from there to dinner at Morton's, where we could overhear studio moguls talk about the hundred and twenty-five phone calls they had taken that day, but I only saw Jeannie for forty-five minutes.

A CBS producer reached her at the Polo Lounge and desperately needed her to depart right away for the Ohio State–Iowa game in Columbus, Ohio, where a day and a half later she would explain to an anxious audience what a Buckeye and a Hawkeye were.

Jeannie asked if I was still in love. More than ever, I said, now that Nell had a shot at the managing editor's job. Jeannie knew about Nell's Oscar nomination. Nell had called Jeannie to try to entice her into doing a freelance piece for *SM*, a piece on what it was like for a woman to go into sports television. Nell was already planning the issues she would preside over when she sat in the m.e.'s chair.

"I may do it," Jeannie said. "I wouldn't do it for anyone but Nell."

"They haven't fooled around with the way you look yet, I'm happy to say."

"They think the hair needs work."

"They're wrong."

"My agent thinks I could make another two hundred grand a year if I would have my lips siliconed."

"Your agent has to die."

"This town's going crazy over the Dodgers."

"The whole thing is an unforgivable incursion on college football. Baseball should end in August."

I walked Jeannie out to the front of the hotel and stood with her until the valet guy brought her car, which was a new Nissan Z. I wouldn't have known this if she hadn't told me. "No Porsche?" I said. She said, "A Porsche lasts two weeks out here. A Porsche gets stolen going through a car wash. It never comes out." We kissed goodbye, a little beyond friendly—for old times' sake. I said I would probably see her later in the fall. Of all the football stadiums in all the world, she was bound to walk into one of mine.

87

UP TO NOW, THE ONLY HITTING STAR FOR THE DODGERS HAD been Willie James, the right fielder, who had knocked in five runs in two games, but Al Finley wasn't worried about pitching to Willie on only two days' rest. Before the start of the third game, Al Finley said, "Fuck that cunt. Drop a deuce on the spook and he bails out."

Finley surrendered a home run to Willie James in the first inning but struck him out three times after that, and the Boston bats came alive. The Red Sox won the third, fourth, and fifth games, all in Dodger Stadium, as movie stars wept, and Boston returned home to Fenway needing only to win one of the last two games to take the Series.

Red Karper was then leading the Series in RBIs with nine, but he said as he got ready for the sixth game, "I don't give a fuck about statics. What I got to know, I keep in my head."

The Red Sox surely should have won the sixth game. They went into the bottom of the ninth inning trailing by one run, but they loaded the bases with nobody out. It was here, however, that the Dodger catcher, Mickey Rouse, picked a runner off first base, and picked another runner off third base, and chased down a pop foul for the third out.

A heartbreaker for the Red Sox to lose, to be sure, but no Boston player or rooter seemed to be discouraged or overly concerned, because in the seventh and deciding game, Al (Gas Man) Finley would be on the mound again, and Al (Gas Man) Finley was confident. He said, "A man only needs two pitches—one they're lookin' for and one they ain't."

The seventh game turned out to be one of those pitchers'

duels that enraptured baseball purists, with Al Finley going the distance against the Dodgers' Hector Jiminez, a curveballer who was known to have "good location" but had often been accused of throwing salve.

It all came down to the bottom of the ninth inning. The Dodgers were ahead 1 to 0 on the strength, or luck, of a walk, a sacrifice, and a broken-bat double by Willie James, but the Red Sox slowly got runners on second and third with two out, and Red Karper came to the plate. A mere single, any kind of hit, would win the World Series for the Red Sox, and Boston's best man was up.

There was a consultation on the mound. The Dodgers' manager, Friendly Frankie Romo, went out to talk with Hector Jiminez and Mickey Rouse and discuss whether to walk Red Karper intentionally to get to the weak-hitting Pigeon Delnagro.

"Got to walk him," Richie said.

"Got to," Dub said. "They don't walk him, they deserve to lose."

I personally didn't care what they did as long as they did it soon. I gauged the temperature in the auxiliary press box at somewhere around 42 degrees.

The Dodgers decided to pitch to Red Karper. First, a ball. Then a line-drive foul down the right-field line. Now another ball. Now a swinging strike. "Wet," Richie observed. It was two-and-two.

And time-out for another consultation on the mound between Hector Jiminez and Mickey Rouse. Around us, the Red Sox faithful were alternating between prayer and lunatic screeching.

Different strategy now. The Dodgers would walk Red Karper, load the bases, and bring up the feeble bat of Pigeon Delnagro.

The Dodger catcher stepped far out to the right of the plate and took a wide pitch. Intentional ball three.

This gutless strategy was deemed totally unsuitable by Red Karper. He pointed down to his dick with one hand while he stood holding the bat on his shoulder with the other, and he seemed to yell something to Hector Jiminez, something along the lines of, "Come get your dinner, you spick cunt, if you ain't gonna pitch to me!"

The Boston slugger was still holding the bat on his shoulder when the Dodger catcher slyly squatted behind the plate, and Hector Jiminez quickly fired a called third strike.

The game was suddenly over. The World Series was over. The forlorn Red Sox had lost again.

The overjoyed Dodgers tore out of the dugout and piled on Hector Jiminez and Mickey Rouse, who were already on the ground, humping.

Red Karper stood in the batter's box in shock until he saw an angry mob of Red Sox fans spilling onto the field, coming toward him, whereupon he thought it best to sprint to his own dugout.

I accompanied Richie and Dub to both locker rooms, largely to get warm.

In the Dodgers' sanctum, Friendly Frankie Romo stood up on a bench, his hair slicked down by champagne, and was asked more than once how his team could have won this Series with almost no hitting. It was a pestering question that wouldn't go away.

Friendly Frankie Romo finally shouted, "I'll be goddamn if sportswriters can't take a perfectly good press conference and fuck it up."

Over in the Red Sox locker room, Stormy Baldwin replayed the Series.

He said, "If Red don't let the fuckin' ball go through his legs in the first game . . . if Johnny don't drop the fuckin' ball in the second game . . . if fuckin' Davey don't get picked off in the sixth game . . . *but* . . . that's how the piss runs down your leg sometimes. I'm proud of this fuckin' team. If anybody had fuckin' told me back in fuckin' July we'd be in the fuckin' Series, I'd have said they were fuckin' crazy. This is a young fuckin' team. We'll zip up our fuckin' fly and be back next year."

Red Karper sat naked in front of his locker with a towel over his lap. He wouldn't realize until he read the papers the next day that he had pulled the greatest World Series boner since Happy Jack Chesbro, the spitballing New York Highlander.

Back in 1904, Happy Jack Chesbro had thrown a wild pitch in the ninth inning of the seventh game to enable the Boston Beaneaters to win that Series.

A group of depressing old baseball writers stood around Red Karper. Now and then, one of the writers would try to console him.

"Fuck all you cunts," Red Karper said. "It hurts to lose like this, but it won't hurt so bad when it stops hurting."

88

POSSIBLY THERE HAD BEEN A BETTER COVER ON A NATIONAL sports weekly in the past five years, but I hadn't seen it. The photo caught Red Karper standing at the plate with his mouth agape as Mickey Rouse was leaping up in the air behind him holding the ball in his hand while the umpire dramatically signaled the called third strike. Unfortunately, this was the cover on *Sports Illustrated*.

Our cover, having carefully been selected by Dalton Buckley, was a portrait of the Dodgers' Willie James that might have been taken as far back as spring training.

We suffered badly by comparison, and Dalton's predictable cover billing, A POX ON THE SOX, didn't compensate much.

Shag Monti had shot the same picture that *SI* had, and from an even better angle, but Dalton even left it out of the layout inside, nor did he use Earth Dude's picture of Red Karper escaping from the fans. Mostly, he ran closeups of gloves, bats, and hotdogs.

Dalton justified these journalistic decisions by saying the Series had been such a rowdy one, he thought *SM* should do what it could to "restore calm" to the national pastime, which was, after all, intrinsic to American society.

To this end, DeChane Moxler held up his part of the bargain. His lead on the eight-page story that wrapped up the Series began:

"The baseball itself, without which a game could not be

played, is a handful of physics, a geometric force, a Mephistophelian speck, an onrushing dot, and yet an object born of the rural . . .''

That was it. As far as I could go.

One good thing came out of the whole package, however. It so depressed our watchdog, Bryce Wilcox, he removed Dalton immediately from his trial chair as managing editor.

Dalton's run lasted only two issues. He went quietly back to his job as Drone One. Now, Doug McNiff assumed command for the last October issue and the first two issues in November.

This put Nell Woodruff in the finals, many of us thought, and called for a long evening at Fu's Like Us. The group included Nell, me, Christine, Wayne, Charlotte, Wooden Dick, and Pamela, a bubbly redhead, new on the research staff at *Celebrity Parade*, that Wooden Dick had found while rummaging around the building.

We all agreed that Nell was now in a can't-lose position. Even if Doug McNiff won the managing editor's job—he did have seniority and he was a honky male, Charlotte reminded everyone—Nell would wind up no worse than an assistant m.e. or maybe even executive editor. It seemed to me that either of these was more than she might have expected a few months ago when she was still a researcher threatening to quit.

As we sat around the big round table in the corner at Fu's, Nell asked everybody for good story ideas, cover ideas, any helpful suggestions she might put to use when she followed Doug.

"Fire Molly Connors," Christine said. "Make me chief of research."

"If I get the job, that's the first thing I'll do," said Nell.

"Hire Pamela," Wooden Dick said.

"Do you like sports, Pamela?" Nell said to the girl. "Around here, you don't have to know anything about them."

"I used to date the Blue Devil at Duke."

"You dated what?"

"The guy who hops around at the games. His mother made the costume for him."

Nell glanced at Wooden Dick, who looked down at his drink.

"I have a suggestion," Wayne Mohler said. "You could run

one of my stories exactly the way I write it. It could open up a whole new world for our readers."

"Are you saying you don't need any editing at all?" I said to Wayne.

"No, I'm saying I don't need 'faster than a speeding bullet' in my lead."

"What's your position on dog to pooch?"

"Loved him, hated her."

Nell promised soft editing from all the drones during her tenure in the managing editor's chair, a downhold on the use of parentheses, a severe cutback on exclamation points, no needless tampering, saving, fixing.

She was going ballistic in another area. No more scruffy jeans and sneakers and sloppy jackets and sweaters around the office. She had raided Bergdorf's and bought four man-tailored suits and three or four cashmere sweater-and-skirt outfits and four pairs of high-heel leather pumps. Her charge cards looked like Frosted Flakes.

One of the man-tailored suits I had seen her model around her apartment had cost $2,500, but only because it was taupe. Had it been gray or beige, one or the other, it would have cost $1,000 less. But she looked stupendous in it, I admitted. The jacket was broad-shouldered with wide lapels and a deep neckline and the skirt hit her four inches above the knee. Sex exec, she called it.

In her new frocks and with her hair by Clairol, her eyes by Elizabeth Arden, and her pantyhose by Dior, Nell was ready for war, all right, but first we had to endure Doug McNiff's Stealth pencil for three weeks.

89

THERE WAS NOT, IN MY OPINION, A MORE EXOTIC CITY IN America than Miami. San Francisco liked to think of itself as exotic, and all other things wonderful, and San Francisco would have a chance to be exotic again if it could ever rein in all the wine talk. New Orleans naturally thought of itself as exotic, and New Orleans would have a chance to be exotic again if it could ever unblacken all the food. I liked San Francisco and New Orleans, of course—you would have to be comatose not to—and I had often let those cities choose a column topic for me, but I could be lured to Miami without a moment's hesitation. I suppose it was a combination of stuff. The old palm-lined avenues, the marinas popping up everywhere, the Art Deco buildings, the Mediterranean mansions, the stone crabs, The Grove, The Gables, the ethnic mix, the cups of molten amphetamine that passed for coffee, the luxury of late drinking hours if you so desired, the Caribbean thing, the hurricane thing. The air had something to do with it. Miami's air was uncommonly soft and yet it was somehow stirred with a scent of mystery and mischief. Maybe it was the Al Capone thing, too.

I slid down to Miami for a few days in early November. It was time to pay my respects to pro football. I would usually look in on pro football once or twice in the middle of the regular season, to reassure myself that it was as boring as ever, and then I wouldn't look in on it again until sometime in January, when pro football got serious.

In the past several years, pro football had been doing everything within its power to encourage intelligent people to ignore it. The yawning sixteen-game schedule, parity, overexposure on TV, a dreadful sameness to every game—who would drop the easiest passes—head coaches you had never heard of, rules that handicapped the defense, artificial turf, roofs on stadiums, greedy owners, overpaid gladiators, holding-call zebras, who were either incompetent or doing business—all these things were ruining a great game, a game that had been uplifted by such folklore heroes as Sam Baugh, Doak Walker, Bobby Layne, Johnny Unitas, Sonny Jurgensen, Jim Brown, Jake Scott, Terry Bradshaw, etc., a game that had been coached by such reliable wizards as Vince Lombardi, Paul Brown, Tom Landry, Don Shula.

Today, smart gamblers wouldn't even consider betting on a *team* in the first twelve weeks of the regular season—they disliked roulette. Smart gamblers bet the over-and-under only, taking the letdown, the menopause, out of the quotient.

Pro football had turned silly by making it possible for a team with no better than an 8-8 record to reach the playoffs and perhaps win the NFL's "world championship." An eight-game loser could be a world champion? Oh, really? Of what sport? Surely not football. But I thanked pro football for doing the collegiate game a big favor. In college football, admirably, a team was still required to wind up with a record of no worse than 11-1 after the bowl games if it wanted to stand a chance of winning the national championship in the polls. College football still made sense.

When I would express such views in my column occasionally, I would attract hate mail by the crate, but it would make me proud, make me laugh. Most of it went in the trash, but some of it would get answered. Like the person who would say, "You've got a problem, asshole." I would write back and say, "No, you've got the problem, I've got the typewriter."

The hate mail made me laugh because I realized that most of it came from those pro football fans who liked to take off their shirts in stadiums during blizzards or wear hard hats with propellers on them. Those poor people couldn't help themselves—they had been thoroughly indoctrinated by NFL shills, otherwise known as TV announcers.

I hadn't bothered to watch a pro game on TV during the regular season since Cosell and Meredith quit, but I would become mildly interested when the playoffs brought the issue down to four teams, and, of course, I was always expected to attend that overblown spectacle known as the Super Bowl. I had covered twenty-two Super Bowls and had seen a total of three good football games, but as any experienced writer could tell you, the Super Bowl was less of a sporting event than a week-long cocktail party and herpes hunt, which was why four million members of the media converged on it every year and had turned it into an overblown farce in the first place. I had it in my mind not to go near another Super Bowl, even if it was played in Miami. Not being there would do wonders for my life expectancy, and I could easily come up with a column off the telecast, provided I stayed awake.

I insisted Nell go down to Miami with me. The idea was to

try to get her to relax and take her mind off the Bryce contest for a while.

She was supposed to stay four days but left after two. Too much on her mind to enjoy it. We lounged around the pool at the Grand Bay one day, wandered through the mall in Coconut Grove, ate at Joe's one night, dined on room service one night. Gone were the days when I would leap off the plane in Miami and go straight to the Palm Bay Club or one of the convivial joints on the 79th Street Causeway in search of adventure, which would present itself soon enough in the form of a loose-ball fumble named Angela, Ashley, or Tina. For a time, there seemed to be an awful lot of Angelas around Miami.

That day at the pool, Nell stretched out in a lounge-chair in a one-piece swimsuit with no back and no stomach and I sat in a chair in my white Sahara shirt and a pair of khaki slacks with an ashtray in my lap, but there was no relaxing.

Nell said, "I want the job. I deserve it. I don't want it for the money. I don't want it for the power. I want it so we can try to put out a good magazine."

I said, "Babe, you're working yourself into a fever. I want you to prepare yourself for not getting the job. The odds are against it. Heavy."

"Because I'm a woman?"

"It has nothing to do with male-female. It has to do with history. The nitwit always gets the big job. It's true in any business. One out of a hundred, the best-qualified person gets the job."

"God gave you Ed Maxwell once, so you won't get me, is that it? One good m.e. to a lifetime?"

"Sorry I used up your luck."

"Doug could screw up, I could do great."

"Doug will be so-so. You *will* do great. But it won't matter. You're forgetting who the judge is. You're at the mercy of Bryce's judgment. If you were a five-wood, you'd have a better chance."

"I'm going to give it my best shot anyhow, if you don't mind."

"I'm not saying don't give it your best shot, I'm saying stop worrying about it. At the very worst, Bryce will make you an assistant m.e. That's not all bad.''

"All I want is what's best for the magazine, and I know I can run it better than Doug."

"I have a cover idea for you."

"Tell it to Doug."

"It's for you—during your reign. My Horned Frogs are kicking ass. They're seven-and-oh, up to fifth in the polls."

"I know. Your Jell-O people."

"Orongelo and Limongelo would make a good cover. I'll go down to Texas and write the piece for you."

"Might work," Nell said. "If the story's acceptable."

Nell was so preoccupied with the "contest," she forgot to leave me with a surgical strike before she returned to New York. I was left in Miami with nothing to do but amuse myself with pro football.

My looking in on pro football consisted of calling up an old pal on the Dolphins' coaching staff. Rod Hatcher had been an All-American tight end at the University of Texas and then an All-Pro tight end with the Jets. He was a strappingly handsome guy who had once liked to frequent some of the same saloons I did in Manhattan, which was how we had become friends.

If you want to find out anything about pro football, you go to an assistant coach. A head coach thinks of sportswriters as spies and only tells them things he wants others to hear. A player never says much, except that you don't play the game in short pants. But most assistants like to court writers—they think writers can help them find head jobs. Assistants like to spread gossip, plant rumors, drop hints that their bosses, the head coaches, are overrated saps.

Rod Hatcher came over to the Grand Bay for drinks one night. I had invited him for dinner and told him to bring along Suzi, his wife, the stew that all of New York had once been in love with, but he showed up alone. Suzi would be bored by all the football talk, he explained.

One of the first things Rod said when he met me in the hotel bar was, "Want to get some pussy?"

No thanks, I said, I was donating my share to the homeless.

"Well, let's talk fast, then," he said. "I'm out of the house for the night. I don't want to waste it."

Rod made phone calls to Ashleys and Tinas when he wasn't drawing X's and O's on napkins for me. For an hour, I felt trapped in a story that *SM*'s pro football expert, Pete Buttrick, might have written. Rod discussed control receivers, hog-down penetration, base and nickel situations, blender coverage, the wideout flood, the counter trey, corner clamp on the valves, weak-side rotation, the two-route dig, fire protection, the stutter-back dump against the Dallas hammer.

Rod looked pleased with himself when he came back from his last phone call. He said he had found the cutting horse he had been looking for. She reminded him of a cutting horse he had known in New York for a short time. He still had fond memories of that cutting horse up there in New York. Priscilla something, her name was.

"Old Priscilla," he said, nostalgically. "She could get it all done."

"Could she really?" I said.

"Shit, I'm tellin' you," he said. "I'd like to ride in *that* rodeo one more time."

Rod apologized for leaving so soon. I said a man had to keep his priorities in order. I spent the rest of the evening at the bar alone, casually observing a group of Cubans making an arms deal with a group of Al Capones.

I didn't leave my room all day and all night Saturday. I wore out room service as I watched parts of eight different college games on TV. I started at noon on TBS with Florida–Ole Miss. By one o'clock, I could switch over to ABC for Georgia Tech–Maryland. At two o'clock, it was time for Iowa–Illinois on CBS and Notre Dame–Pitt on NBC. By three thirty, I could get USC–Stanford on ABC and Brigham Young–Air Force on SNW. LSU–Tennessee started at seven o'clock that evening on TBS, and Auburn–Florida State started at seven thirty on ESPN. A man with room service and a clicker didn't need much else in his life. A dog, maybe.

Only three of those games had a bearing on the race for No. 1. Notre Dame and Southern Cal remained undefeated, but Tennessee got upset in Baton Rouge, which was good for

TCU. The Horned Frogs would move up to fourth in the polls.

T. J. Lambert's scholar-athletes played Texas Tech that afternoon in Fort Worth and won easily, although I suffered the usual five-minute scare on a network scoreboard show. Some idiot out of a communications school reversed the score on the graphic and had Tech leading 24 to 7 at the half. This happened all too often nowadays and reminded me that there had been an enormous dumbing of journalists in my lifetime.

I called the TCU press box three times during the second half and spoke to Stubby Cross, the Horned Frogs' SID, to see how Orangejello and Limejello were doing.

"Runnin' like turpentine cats," Stubby Cross reported. "My stat people can't keep up with 'em."

As the Horned Frogs beat the Red Raiders 45 to 7 and went to 8-0 on the season, Orangejello finished up the afternoon with 263 yards rushing and three touchdowns, and Limejello ran for 208 yards and scored two touchdowns.

I said, "Tell T.J. I'm coming down there next week to do a story. There's a chance to put Orongelo and Limongelo on our cover."

"They're real good kids," Stubby Cross said.

"What are they studying?"

"You mean what classes are they taking?"

"Yeah."

Stubby Cross said, "Uh . . . we'll think of something before you get here, hoss."

90

THE ONLY REASON I LIMOED OUT TO THE PRO GAME ON SUNday was to satisfy my curiosity that Miami's new stadium was located so far north of the city the home team should now be known as the Ocala Dolphins.

New stadiums. That was another grievance I had against pro football. The Dolphins had lost a lot of charm when they left the Orange Bowl. My theory was, a new stadium only got itself built in the first place so the owner could have a luxury box that looked like a two-bedroom suite in an Omni hotel. Pro football had surrendered its true identity when it left the old baseball parks and the old college stadiums and moved into clinics and insurance buildings. I was sure I would never quite become accustomed to, or totally forgive, the New York Giants and New York Jets for leaving Yankee Stadium and Shea Stadium to play their home games across the river in the Prudential Life of New Jersey lobby.

In fact, I was patiently waiting for the Cincinnati Bengals to move into Kentucky, for the Buffalo Bills to move into Canada, for the San Diego Chargers to move into Mexico, and for the Denver Broncos to erect a new stadium on the other side of the Wyoming state line, but, of course, the fans wouldn't object as long as they could wear silly hats and paint their homes in the team colors.

But maybe all this was good in a sense. A new stadium was the pro football fan's roadside recreation area, just as the new mall in town was his country club. America had nothing to lose but its crime rate.

My column had spoke, to borrow from Fort Worth English.

The Dolphin-Cowboy game on Sunday afternoon was one of those meaningless affairs in midseason that neither team wanted to win.

The Dolphin wideouts dropped flat passes all day, while the Dallas running backs tripped and fell down behind the line of scrimmage. It was an awesome display of fat-wallet, corporate football.

I was intrigued with the manner in which the Cowboys put to use their Olympic sprint champion, Robbie Morrison. Robbie Morrison, wearing No. 9.2, would streak down the sideline for a pass. The Dallas quarterback, Blake Blackman, would stand in the pocket and look. Then, no matter how fast or far Morrison ran, the strong-armed Blake Blackman would prove he could spiral the ball thirty yards over Robbie's head.

Miami's most exciting play was when Demis Mayfield, a running back, broke free and zigzagged seventy-two yards for a touchdown, but of course the play was called back for holding.

Dallas' most exciting play was when Robbie Morrison took a handoff on an end-around and dashed eighty-one yards for a touchdown, but of course this, too, was called back for holding.

All in all, the zebras had a good game. They made eight holding calls, four pass-interference calls, and three rulings that the ground couldn't cause a fumble. The zebras definitely won the day, although the final score showed Miami 17, Dallas 3.

The game had no effect on the season. Both teams were 5-6 in their conferences and headed for the playoffs.

Up in the press box, I watched a few moments of the fourth quarter on a TV set to hear what I had been missing.

The play-by-play announcer, Gary Hagan, and the color man, Hulk Garrett, seemed to agree that the game was a case of the Crimean War meeting Armageddon.

"Boom!" said Hulk Garrett. "That's a National Football League hit right there. The Dolphins are playing 'Dolphin Football' today, Gary Hagan."

"Right you are, Hulk Garrett, and the Dallas Cowboys are playing 'Cowboy Football.' Not too shabby."

"It doesn't get much better than this, Gary Hagan."

"No, it doesn't, Hulk Garrett. We've seen some good ones this season."

"And all last year."

"And the year before that."

"I can't recall that we've ever seen a bad game, Gary Hagan."

"Neither can I, Hulk Garrett."

"But that's what you can expect in the NFL."

"Absolutely. Put a bunch of great athletes down there on the field with a crew of capable game officials and what you've got is not too shabby, Hulk Garrett."

"You can say that again, Gary Hagan. It doesn't get much better than this."

CBS did a live cut-in from another game and I got to catch Jeannie Slay at a tailgate party outside the stadium in Green Bay, Wisconsin. Four people were seated at a picnic table next to a Winnebago and a grill where a man in a mackinaw and a hunter's cap was cooking hamburgers.

Jeannie was bundled up in a greatcoat with a hood as she stood ankle-deep in slush, and snow and sleet lashed across her face.

To the camera, Jeannie said, "I'm here with Skeeter Russell and his family. They say there are no bigger fans of the Green Bay Packers than the Russells. For twenty-four years, they've been parking their Winnebago in the same spot and enjoying their tailgate party before the kickoff. Lucky spot, Skeeter?"

Jeannie held the mike out to Skeeter Russell, who said:

"Naw, we parked over there by that tree one Sunday and the Bears beat us on a last-minute field goal."

"The weather is no problem today?" Jeannie said.

"Naw, the only problem I got is two want 'em rare, three want 'em well-done, and three want 'em medium-rare."

"Will you dine outdoors or indoors?"

Skeeter Russell said, "Aw, a couple of 'em are snifflin'. They'll eat inside, I reckon."

Jeannie faced America, and said, "That's the story from Green Bay. Those members of the Russell clan who like snow on their hamburgers will eat out here. Those who already have head colds will eat in the Winnebago. Back to the studio."

I talked to Nell on the phone that night. Nell had seen Jeannie's vignette. Nell thought it was worth every penny of the six hundred and fifty grand Jeannie was being paid.

I said, "There's a lowering of standards in this country that I lay directly on the doorstep of Radio-TV-Film schools."

Waiting for me back in New York was a sad little note from Janice, wife number two. She asked if I would use all of my influence to get Blubber Daniels fired as the Alabama coach. Blubber Daniels had personally lost six games for the Crimson Tide, and the whole state was suffering in ways I couldn't even imagine. Janice said she knew enough about football to know that Alabama's niggers were as good as anybody's—it had to be the numbskull coaching. Bubba Dean was so depressed he was seeing a psychiatrist twice a week, and Mr. Carpenter was so upset he couldn't concentrate on his plea-bargaining. Please do something, she said, if I cared anything about what we had once meant to each other.

I wrote back and said that in distressing times like that, I had always found comfort in prayer.

91

THE REST OF NOVEMBER WAS FILLED WITH HARROWING SOCIAL functions, which, at their best, could also be described as interruptive, and not just to the work of journalism but to the always-tricky process of getting through life. There were numerous pourings—to honor Mondays, Thursdays, Saturdays, Veterans' Day, Notre Dame losing to USC, the five-year anniversary of Fu's Like Us finally passing a health inspection, the announcement that Fenton Boles was going to teach a course in business ethics at Harvard and open his own consulting firm. There was a party in an upstairs room at "21" to celebrate the promotion of Clipper Langdon to CEO. Les Padgett returned from Australia to cohost the party with Rip Bellemy, who was now on the board of directors of TPG, Inc. The Ripper was in the throes of his messy divorce, but this didn't keep him from bringing Jackie, the high-rent bimbo, to the party. Jackie looked terrific but seemed not to recall where we had met. I think you could say that some of us were greatly relieved when Les didn't notice Fritzy Erwina Krupp-Streicher Padgett slipping into a phone booth with Wooden Dick for ten minutes, or maybe Les did notice and didn't care. Les was rumored to be keeping a young Chinese girl in a London flat, anyhow. Clipper circulated freely and referred to himself more than once as the company's "Mogulissimo." There was a party in the Rainbow Room to celebrate Bryce Wilcox's elevation to Vice-President, Magazine Group. Clipper was the host, and the highlight was watching Charlotte Murray rip off part of Achee Bromley's shirttail to apply a tourniquet to the weeping Miriam Bowen, who punctured her arm with a steak knife after Dalton Buckley told her he wasn't going to leave his

wife, after all. There was a party for Tippy Donahue to celebrate his appointment as our new publisher. Bryce threw the
party at his home in Larchmont. This was a dull affair at which
Bryce's perfect wife, Monica, in an effort to protect her Oriental rugs, followed me around all evening with the only ashtray in the house. There was, as well, Travis Steed's book
party. Here, I ventured the guess—and was proved correct—
that if you put them on the same playing field, literary folk
could eat more free food than sportswriters any day of the
week.

The party to celebrate the publication of *Is That You, Durwood?* was held on the night of November 16, a Monday,
Doug McNiff's last day in his trial run as managing editor. The
venue was a cramped continental restaurant in the Eighties on
Second Avenue. Octavia, it was called.

The name had nothing to do with the gracious fellow who
owned and ran it, whose name was Paul, and who apparently
had everything to do with the pasta being four different
colors—green, orange, red, and white.

Nell and Christine and Ralph Webber and I went to the party
together, straight from the office after work. Wayne Mohler
was supposed to go with us but we grew tired of waiting for
him. He was locked in Doug McNiff's office, arguing about a
story. Only a select few of us from *SM* were invited to Travis'
book party. The publishing house, Anarchistic Press, had limited Travis to six invitations for "sports people."

Paul was the man in the crewneck sweater with a freckled
face and wavy red hair who met us at the door of Octavia, and
said, "You *must* be some of the sports people. *Do* come in."

We pushed in, for Octavia was already crowded.

"My name is Paul," the crewneck said. "I'm the owner,
and you have a perfect right to ask why the restaurant is named
Octavia instead of Paul. Would you like to know?"

"I think we would," Nell said.

Paul said, "Octavia was my partner when we opened a year
ago. Where is he now? *You* tell *me*. That boy could have his
head turned by any mordant witch who walked in the door!
We're serving a nice white wine, but if you want something
stronger, the bartender will be glad to start a tab for you."

"We'll have whiskey," I said.

"But of course you will," said Paul. "You're sports people, aren't you?"

The small bar was just inside the front door. I wriggled into a spot between Tolstoy and Goethe and managed to get our drinks from a bartender named Josef. The four of us huddled closely and surveyed the crowd. Paul didn't need to point out that the literary men with heaping plates of fluorescent pasta were the brooding grizzlies in suits and bow ties and the literary women with heaping plates of fluorescent pasta were the rodents in granny dresses.

Although we didn't see him at first, it turned out that Travis Steed was in the room, we just hadn't recognized him in his jeans, sneakers, turtleneck, leather jacket, and Lenin cap. Travis was over in a corner, signing copies of his novel from a stack of books on a table. He wasn't signing the books for anyone in particular. No one was asking for a personal inscription.

Paul said, "Do try to enjoy yourselves—and don't be too intimidated by the verbal environment."

"We'll do our best," Christine said.

"Which one is Danielle Steel?" I asked Paul.

"Oh, that is funny," the owner said. "That is *very* funny."

We worked our way toward Travis. He looked as if he could use some company.

As we plowed through the room I overheard a reference to someone's "cultural brutality." I overheard a reference to a book that seemed to possess "a layered quality, a certain density." I think I overheard that some author in the room had written a novel that was engrossing if one cared for "mid-list drivel."

"Is that you, Travis?" Nell said to Drone Four.

"Thanks for coming," Travis said. "I feel bad about so many people in the office. The publisher didn't want too many sports people here."

"Which one is the publisher?" I asked.

"The fellow in the eye-patch."

I scanned the room. "I see three eye-patches."

334

"The tallest one," Travis said. "That's Eric. He edited my book himself. He's quite bright."

"He looks mad at something."

"Well, his own novel just got rejected by Knopf."

"Who's the woman poking him in the chest with her fork?"

"I'm not sure. I think she's a reviewer. Have you read it?"

"Read what?"

"My book."

"Oh, sure," I said. "You put me on the mailing list. Thanks. I got it last week."

"What do you think? Be honest. I really respect your opinion, Jim Tom."

"Well," I said. "It's, uh . . . it's a book. It has characters. They talk. They move around. They all seem to be up to something."

"You don't think it's too short?"

"No, I don't think you can say it's too short any more than you can say it's too long."

"Which character did you like best?"

"Well, they're all unusual, aren't they?"

"The publisher likes the grandmother."

"Oh, I can see why he would."

"I'm partial to the young boy."

"The young boy is a young boy—there's no getting around it."

"I worked hard on the boy."

"I could see where the boy took a lot of work. Didn't you, Ralph?"

"Absolutely," Wooden Dick said. He had been looking around the room with disappointment. Not a lot of pussy to pull out of *this* party. "It's full of energy, Travis," Wooden Dick added. "It really is."

"I want to read it again," Nell said.

"Do you really?" Travis said.

"Yes, I don't think I appreciated the grandmother as much as I should have."

One of the Octavia waiters took a book from the stack on the table. "These are free, right?" he said to Travis.

"Would you like for me to sign it?" Travis said.

"Why?"

"I'm the author."

"Oh," said the waiter. "Uh . . . yeah, I guess."

"Is it for you?"

"No, uh . . . just put your name."

"I can do better than that," Travis smiled.

The waiter said, "Hey, look, man, I don't want to get in a jackpot here. Forget it."

The waiter walked away, leaving Travis with the book and a pen in hand.

"Sign one for me," Christine said, sympathetically.

While Travis wrote a novella to Christine on the title page, I seized the opportunity to pick up a copy off the table and give *Is That You, Durwood?* what used to be known as the old Brentano's first-paragraph test. The novel began:

"Ker-rish, ker-rish. I can still hear the sound of my tennis shoes squishing on the dirt path, but even now, after a lifetime of consideration, I am at a loss for words to describe the land that lay between Mr. Fauver's grocery store and my grandmother's house, the land I roamed so often as a young boy, as I came home with dinner each day, my little baseball cap on backwards, smiling, clutching to my chest the liver that was always wrapped in the butcher's slick white paper. The land . . ."

I closed the book gently and placed it back on the table.

"Congratulations, Travis," I said. "Good luck with it."

"Are you going on an author's tour?" Christine asked.

Travis said no. The publisher no longer believed in such things. The publisher no longer believed in running print ads either. It was all word-of-mouth these days.

"It has a chance to do very well," I said, "if word-of-mouth spreads about the grandmother."

We lied that we had another engagement and left Travis standing alone by his stacks of books.

Outside of Octavia, we were gazing around for a nearby saloon when Wayne Mohler climbed out of a cab. He was holding a handkerchief to his nose and a sleeve of his houndstooth sport coat was all but torn off.

92

A MAN COULD LIVE WITH DÓG TO POOCH, WAYNE MOHLER moaned, but a man couldn't live with said to says—no way.

We had found an empty bar called Scuds a block from Octavia. Wayne was drinking doubles and still holding the handkerchief to his nose.

"Doug was so goddamn adamant about it," Wayne said. "I tried to reason with him. I said there was nothing constructive about it. I said you didn't gain anything by doing it. He said you gained 'urgency.' Incidentally, it's not just my piece. He did it to the whole issue."

"What do you mean he did it to the whole issue?" I said.

"Changed said to says. Well, not just says. He cajoles, he interjects, he laughs, he cries, he whispers."

"Says I?" I said.

"Says I, says he, says they, she meditates, she states, smiles he—it's pretty gruesome."

Nell said, "The whole fucking issue is in present tense?"

"Even the contents page," Wayne said, looking at the blood on his handkerchief and putting it back to his nose.

"Not my column?" I said.

"I'm afraid so, says I. The lunatic bastard has spent the last twenty-four hours making all these changes. He brought Dalton in to help him. He said he wanted to do something different with his last issue as m.e. Leave his fingerprints, as he put it."

"When did the fight start?" Christine asked.

"It wasn't really a fight."

"So how do you explain the nose?" Ralph wanted to know.

Wayne said, "My nose started bleeding when I first looked at my piece in the copy room. You know how you feel when they've done something macabre for no explainable reason?"

We all nodded.

Wayne continued, " 'Says he' was in my second sentence. 'You've got to like the 49ers' scheme, says he.' My head started to throb and felt like it was swelling up, like it might burst. I started cussing. I kicked something. Miriam heard me. When I got to the third 'says,' I was bleeding.''

Ralph said, ''If there was no fight, what happened to your coat?''

''Oh, this,'' said Wayne, glancing at his dangling sleeve. ''I did this getting in the cab. Cabs are smaller now, don't you think? Aren't cabs getting smaller?''

''How'd it end up?'' I asked.

Well, there *was* a scuffle, Wayne said. When Doug McNiff said he rather imagined Wayne would take an old-maidish attitude about the changes, Wayne leaped over Doug's desk and grabbed him by the necktie. He jerked Doug up out of his chair and, pulling on the tie, dragged him across the room and slammed him into a wall.

''Christ,'' said Nell. ''Is he all right?''

''He's fine,'' Wayne said.

''You dry-walled him?'' I said. ''Great.''

''He didn't hurt his head,'' Wayne went on. ''You know how soft those walls are. Reg Turner can knock down one of those walls with a fart. The choking bothered him for a minute, but somebody ran around and found Charlotte. Charlotte looked him over. She said he was okay. He seemed okay when I left. He was talking to Bryce on the phone.''

''What did he tell Bryce?'' Christine asked.

''He covered it up. He didn't want Bryce to think he'd lost control of the staff. He said we'd had a typical editor-writer dispute but we'd worked it out, and he wanted Bryce to hear it from him first before the story gets blown out of proportion.''

''He'll hear the details from somebody,'' Christine said. ''Was Molly Connors around?''

''Everybody was out in the hall. Bryce can fire me, I don't give a damn,'' Wayne said. ''I'm leaving anyhow if Doug gets the m.e. job. He's not an editor, he's a fucking saboteur! I can go back to the *Chronicle*. I can go to *SI*. I can freelance. I don't need 'says' in my life.''

I postponed my trip to Texas for three days. I was curious to see what Bryce would do about the Wayne-Doug incident, for one thing, and for another, I wanted to sit in on Nell's first story conference when she took over the managing editor's chair.

At eleven o'clock on Thursday morning, all of the drones and department heads assembled in the m.e.'s office and sat in the folding chairs that secretaries always arranged each week for the occasion. The folding chairs faced the m.e.'s desk. Wayne and Ralph and I stood in the back of the room.

That morning at Nell's apartment, I had watched the acting m.e. first get dressed in her sex-exec outfit, then change to a sweater-and-skirt outfit. Better to look like business-as-usual.

Before Nell opened the meeting, Bryce came in.

"Just take a minute," Bryce said to the group. "Will Doug and Wayne come up here, please?"

Wayne and Doug went to the front of the room.

Bryce said, "Differences of opinion about editorial content are a healthy thing in journalism. One of our most valuable senior editors and one of our most valuable senior writers had such a difference three days ago. It got a little spirited, as I understand it, but it wasn't personal. Wayne? Doug? Can we shake hands?"

"By all means," said Doug, extending his hand to Wayne. "Just trying to be creative, old man."

Wayne took Doug's hand. "No hard feelings . . . says I."

Light applause.

"All yours, Nell," said Bryce, exiting with a little imaginary golf swing.

On the desk in front of her, Nell looked at a printout of story proposals that had been prepared the previous week.

"Okay, let's see if we can get this over in about half the time it usually takes," Nell said. "In the lead area, I see we have USC-UCLA. I assume Stewart plans to cover it. If not, let's get him out there. I see Pete's down for Denver-Houston. That's fine. I don't think we've looked at the AFC in three weeks. I don't see Virginia Slims at the Garden on here. It should be. Screw the NBA story. This is football season. I want to switch stories in the long feature slot. We'll hold the piece on sports agents—it's good any time. I want to go with that World Series diary. We should have run it last week. In the back, we'll stay with Ralph's story on hospitality tents, but I'd like to see a better illustration to open it, Ronnie."

Nell ran through the rest of the magazine briskly—letters, sports business, book review, spotlight, update, etc.

Then she said, "After lunch, I want to see Photo about next week's cover . . . uh, Layout . . . Miriam . . . Dalton. That's it, I guess. I do have one drastic proposal for you editors. Try not to overedit. If you feel a story demands a wholesale rewrite, check with me first. I'll decide. You might want to ask yourselves this: if our writers can't write, why the fuck were they hired in the first place?

"Now, all of you know me. You've known me a long time. Any problems, I'm here to listen for these three weeks. I'm not going to turn into a bitch—the lady who's just been made head of the handbag department. Let's just have fun and try to act like we know what we're doing and, with any luck, perpetrate a good magazine."

THE SPORTS SM MAGAZINE

Mr. Rollie Ambrose
Editor, Nonfiction
Fust & Winslett Publishers
New York, N.Y.

Dear Rollie Ambrose:

Yesterday I received a wonderful thing. It was a message on my fax machine that said: "Urgently needed for catalog copy: what is your book about?"

Actually, it's about 528 pages now. It's also about a man who's writing a book for an editor who doesn't know what the fuck it's about, even though the book was the editor's idea in the first place.

This is my last letter. The next thing you receive will be Part Four. You may eventually guess that the book will have ended here because—well, among other things, there won't be any more pages after Part Four.

Onward,

Jim Tom Pinch

Jim Tom Pinch

93

EARLENE WAS CERTAIN THAT AUNT IRIS WAS SUFFERING FROM Buerger's disease—her fingers were numb and her legs were cold all the time. You would think a doctor could diagnose it, Earlene said, if somebody at Thompson's Window & Door Frame could. Uncle Elzie definitely had Bell's palsy. Earlene could barely make herself watch him try to close his right eye. And poor Otha Thompson. He had just recovered from surgery, from the kelotomy for his hernia, when the two of them had gone to the Sycamore Mall. Earlene guessed it was too much to ask in today's sorry world for two people to do something simple like to go to a movie on a Sunday afternoon without getting assaulted by dirtbags. Earlene had never heard of "white" muggers before. She didn't know such things existed. But Lord, she was thankful for the two nigger boys who scared the muggers away before they could do something worse than break Otha's nose and jerk the charm bracelet off her wrist, the one with her old DBS pin and her Paschal graduation ring on it. She gave those two nigger boys five dollars each for their bravery. Otha had gone in for his nasal septal reconstruction at the same time she had gone in for her hemorrhoidectomy, which was obviously hastened by the mugging experience, and if I didn't think *that* was painful, I could try spending five days in a sitz bath sometime.

All of this was at the top of the phone conversation after I checked into my room at the Worthington in Fort Worth. I had only called Earlene to say I was in town for a few days and ask if she had heard from our son lately.

When we got around to James Junior, Earlene said it looked like he was going to turn out just fine, no thanks to any guidance from his father.

"I know about his plans after graduation," I said. "Atlanta. Stereo equipment. His friend, Earl Otis Pottle. It sounds good. I want to see the graduation thing happen, however."

Earlene said, "You don't have any confidence in him. You never have."

The eight years of college-tuition and spending-money confidence I had shown in James Junior didn't count for anything with Earlene. What counted was that I had never taken James camping when he was a young boy and told him stories about the stars while I fried the rabbit I'd killed for dinner. I didn't think James had ever held this against me. I doubt if he would have gone camping if he had been tipped off ahead of time that there wasn't a snack bar or a TV in the woods, but neither would I, as far as that goes.

I said, "Do you have any idea what James would like for Christmas, Earlene? Is he coming home or will he work through the holidays? He has three weeks off."

"I would love to have him home, but I am very proud of what he plans to do."

"What's that?"

"James and his good friend Earl Otis are going on a scouting trip for Earl Otis' father. They are going to look for out-of-state possibilities to expand Mr. Pottle's electronics business."

"Uh-huh."

"They are going to drive all the way in Earl Otis' BMW but James promised me they will drive carefully. James wants money for Christmas, for the trip. I'm giving him two hundred dollars. I said you would give him two thousand."

"That was generous of you."

"It will be money well spent, Jim Tom. I look at it as an investment in our son's future, but naturally I wouldn't expect this to occur to you."

"Where are they going?"

Earlene said they would drive straight to Aspen, Colorado, first. After a few days in Aspen, they were going to investigate a California seaside community—Redondo Beach, she thought it was called—and then they were going to Lake Tahoe, Sun Valley, Las Vegas, and back home through New Orleans.

"Wait till I get my hat and I'll go with them," I said.

94

THE COWGIRL BARTENDER, WANDA, WAS STILL WORKING IN The Cadaver Room, and after first saying she remembered me from coming in the joint with Coach Lambert last spring, she wanted to know if my sperm was in the custody of anybody special these days.

I said I had a very good sperm-keeper in New York City.

"You live up there, really?" Wanda said.

"I do. I'm originally from here but I've been living on Manhattan Island for over twenty years."

"Why do you call it an island?"

"Because Manhattan is an island."

"Since when?"

"I'm not sure. It happened before I got there. Could I have a J and B and water, Wanda—and a cup of coffee on the side? That's not decaf, is it?"

"Honey, do I look like a decaf woman to you?"

I was leaning my elbow on the horseshoe bar as I stood between empty stools. It was around five fifteen on this Thursday, two days before the Horned Frogs would play Texas A & M in their last regular-season game at TCU Stadium. I was the only customer at the moment, other than the cellular phone salesman who had passed out in a booth in the rear. The only change in the decor of the dimly lit, linoleum-floor Cadaver Room had occurred on the walls. The walls were being eaten by things commemorating TCU's football success this season. I looked around at the purple-and-white pennants and posters, the framed photos of the twin running backs, Orangejello and Limejello Tucker, and tacked-up sports pages from the *Light & Shopper* on which the news of TCU's Saturday victories were bleeding in scarlet, marigold, and lavender.

T.J.'s scholar-athletes had won ten straight games. This was the first time such a miracle had happened to TCU since the national championship season of 1938. The Frogs had already won the Southwest Conference and were going to play Notre Dame in the Cotton Bowl on New Year's Day. The game against A & M was only important if TCU wanted to stay in the running for No. 1. The race for No. 1 was as cloudy as it always was at this point in a college football season. There were many contenders. The AP and Coaches' rankings of the current week agreed. The Top Ten read like this:

1.	USC	10-0
2.	Penn State	10-0
3.	TCU	10-0
4.	Notre Dame	9-1
5.	Michigan	9-1
6.	Tennessee	9-1
7.	Miami	9-1
8.	Nebraska	9-1
9.	Florida St.	9-1
10.	Florida	8-2

The bowl games would decide No. 1 again, and all sorts of possibilities loomed because of the matchups: TCU vs. Notre Dame in the Cotton, USC vs. Michigan in the Rose, Penn State vs. Nebraska in the Orange, and Tennessee vs. Miami in the Sugar. There was an excellent chance that the final polls would disagree, that two schools could boast of being No. 1. This was fine with me. It had happened countless times in the past. I saw nothing wrong with a little ambiguity—the more bumper stickers the better. I bitterly opposed those writers and broadcasters who cried out for a playoff every year. They didn't understand that a playoff was totally impractical in college football, and they didn't understand that there was no way for a computer or a panel of experts to arrange a "national championship game" after the bowl results without the game being a phony excuse for some TV network to sell automobiles and diet soda. It was all explained in my column.

Where TCU was concerned, it was perhaps of greater importance that the Frogs were keeping the NCAA investigators confused. Chancellor Glenn Dollarhyde's internal investigation into the alleged recruiting violations was progressing as slowly as possible.

Interviews were being conducted with all of the individuals that may have been involved, and a search was on to obtain all of the records that may have been kept. Dr. Dollarhyde had said repeatedly that TCU was cooperating fully with the NCAA, and if there was any evidence of any wrongdoing, he wanted to be the first to know about it. However, the chancellor said, these things take time. It could be many more months, or even years, before all of the facts could be uncovered and studied carefully.

Only last week, the chancellor issued a statement from his office, saying, "We intend to clean up this mess and put it behind us, but we must be cautious not to punish the wrong people."

Rabbit Tyrance, the athletic director, had announced a month ago that he was assigning his own personal "task force" to the investigation in an effort to speed up the process and get to the bottom of things and remove the cloud of suspicion that was hanging over the university's head, but he, too, cautioned that the investigation could take many more months, even years, to complete.

The chancellor and the athletic director were making every TCU graduate quite proud of them.

"Scotch and coffee, huh?" Wanda said. "Is that a New York City deal?"

"No, it's my own peculiarity. I like to be a wide-awake drunk."

"Listen to you," she smiled.

"I'm supposed to meet the coach here."

"Well, he'll be here. So will the Little Hornet."

"Who's the Little Hornet?"

"That's his rubber dolly. She's in real estate. She says she sells houses, but I don't know anybody in Fort Worth, Texas, right now today who can afford to buy a house if it has a roof on it or indoor plumbing."

"Are you telling me T. J. Lambert has a lady friend?"

"Honey, T.J.'s a celebrity. The Frogs are undefeated. He's got all kinds of scags after *his* body."

"I've known T.J. a long time, Wanda, and I've never known him to be interested in anything but X's and O's."

"Shows you what winnin' will do. The Little Hornet captured his heart six weeks ago, right here in The Cadaver Room. It was the day after we beat the crap out of those country fucks from Arkansas. I did love seein' that. They brought twenty thousand people down here and there wasn't one of 'em left in the stadium by the end of the third quarter. They throwed their pet pigs in their trucks and hauled their rural ass back where they came from."

"What's the Little Hornet's name?"

"Judy Ruth Ward. But she likes to be called Hornet now. Coach named her. Coach says she stung his heart like a hornet. They write poems to each other. Between you and me, I don't see that she's worth gettin' so excited about. Looks to me like she dyes her hair with black shoe polish, and she's got thighs like Orongelo and Limongelo—coach ought to play her in the backfield."

"Donna Lou will kill him if she finds out about the Little Hornet."

"That the wife?"

Only for the past twenty-five years, I said. Donna Lou was also the mother of T.J.'s two daughters, Anne and Beth. Anne was out of college and studying to be a nurse. Beth was in her first year at TCU and interested in the ministry.

Wanda poured herself a shot of tequila and downed it.

"I was a wife once," she said. "I would about as soon sign up for gonorrhea as do it again. Or pump gas. Roy Buchanan wanted a 'homemaker.' Of course, I didn't find that out till the dancin' was over. I said, 'Roy, how come you never talked about cleanin' toilets and cookin' veal cutlets when I was keepin' your knob polished?' He said his job was to bring home the bacon—my job was to be a woman. I said, 'Honey, I didn't buy into this shit to be a sanitation employee.' I said, 'You can get used to the fact right now that Wanda Fairchild don't have but two speeds on the stove—hot and *off*.' He didn't last long."

I said, "Wanda, there's a whole decade I don't remember

much about. Are you sure you and me were never married to each other?''

One cocktail later, T.J. came into The Cadaver Room with a big, trim, square-jawed fellow. They were both wearing purple golf shirts with the TCU logo on the sleeve and khaki slacks. They had come straight from workout. T.J. introduced me to Billy Peck, his offensive coordinator.

"Billy give our offense its name," T.J. said. "The Run and Scoot."

"Are we ready for the Aggies?" I asked.

Billy Peck said, "We've got a good scheme for 'em. It's all up to the kids. If our kids don't run with their flaps down we'll be all right.''

Wanda fixed a Jack Daniels on the rocks for T.J. and pulled a draft beer for Billy Peck. It quickly became evident that Wanda and Billy Peck were in love. The offensive coordinator went behind the bar to kiss Wanda and massage her tits.

"This one right here is my rubber dolly," Wanda said to me, as she and Billy Peck squeezed around on each other.

"She's somethin', ain't she?" Billy said. "She don't even want me to get a divorce. That's what I call an all-conference woman.''

T.J. said, "She may be all-conference but them tits is goin' to Canton, Ohio.''

Wanda turned loose of Billy's crotch long enough to draw something on a napkin with a ballpoint pen. "Have you seen TCU's offense, Jim Tom?''

"Aw, hell, he's seen that," T.J. said. "He's been to the Southeastern Conference. That's where it come from.''

"What is it?" I asked.

Wanda finished printing the letters on the napkin and handed it to me. I read:

"NRL . . . NRR . . . SPDN . . . WBKP.''

"I must be dense," I said. "I don't get it.''

Billy Peck fell across the bar in laughter as Wanda deciphered the letters for me. "Nigger Run Left . . . Nigger Run Right . . . Same Play, Different Nigger . . . White Boy Kicks Point.''

I looked at T.J. "Have you shown this to Orongelo and Limongelo?"

"As a matter of fact, I have," T.J. said. "And don't look at me like that, Jim Tom. You know goddamn well I ain't no racist. It's about time people learned to take a fuckin' joke. I've had them kids in my home for dinners. I've kissed 'em when they scored touchdowns. Orongelo and Limongelo are good kids. They laughed harder than anybody at this thing."

T.J. wadded up the napkin and tossed it at a wastebasket.

I said, "Was that before or after they burned down your house and married your daughters?"

95

THE LITTLE HORNET WASN'T ALL THAT LITTLE, AS WANDA promised, but she seemed sociable enough. She planted a kiss on T.J.'s cheek, put her purse down on the bar, took out a sheet of paper, and said she loved Auburn, give Georgia the six and a half. She loved Stanford with three and a half over Cal— Stanford could win the whole game—Michigan minus five over Ohio State was like going to the candy store, and TCU giving thirteen and a half was a mortal lock because T.J. was gonna lay wood on A & M's maroon ass.

"Hornet likes her sports," T.J. said.

"I can see that," I said.

Wanda served the Little Hornet her usual, a vodka on the rocks.

"I don't bet big," the Little Hornet said. "It's only a hobby. I *am* up about six grand this year."

"What's your system?" I asked.

"I bet coaches. I bet quarterbacks. I like an underdog away from home with seven and a half to ten points. It's usually an overlay."

"You're not betting the quarterback in TCU's case," I said. "We don't have one, do we, T.J.?"

The Little Hornet didn't give the coach time to answer.

"We don't need a quarterback," she said. "All we need is a ball dispenser, and that's what we got. Randy Skenk takes the snap and dispenses it to them two Cadillacs."

The coach, the Hornet, and I moved to a booth with our drinks. We left Billy Peck at the bar with Wanda.

"Hornet likes her baseball, too," T.J. said.

"I *love* my Texas Rangers," she said. "I never miss a home game. We'll be better next season. We need hitters, of course. We don't have but one old boy who can give it a ride. The rest of 'em are scratchin' around in the rock pile, but we've got the pitchers. McMillan throws cheese, Boatman can paint the slider real sweet, and Davis is the best purpose man in the American League. Talk about your brushback. He can bust it under the hitter's nose so he can *smell* it."

The Little Hornet wanted to know how I thought TCU would do against Notre Dame in the Cotton Bowl.

"We don't want to make 'em mad," I said.

T.J. said he would worry about Notre Dame when the time came. Right now, he was worrying about the Aggies on Saturday. "We beat A & M, we wind up eleven-and-oh. We in the national championship picture. They can't ignore us."

The Little Hornet said, "Oh, T.J., you're gonna warp the Aggies. You know it and I know it."

"Football ain't round," the coach said. "It can bounce funny on you."

The Little Hornet gave T.J. another kiss on the cheek, and said, "Sweetheart, you just give that old football to Orongelo and Limongelo and you sit back and watch the man on the scoreboard try to keep up with the arithmetic."

I drank with them for another hour, till the off-duty nurses came in. Then T.J. walked me to my rental car.

"I was with you tonight," T.J. said, "in case the subject ever comes up. We were out pretty late, talkin' football."

"Was Billy Peck with us?"

"Naw, he had to go to his Bible study group."

96

FRIDAY WAS A LONG DAY AND THERE ARE THOSE WHO WOULD say it was more eventful for the TCU coaching staff than it should have been.

I went out to the coliseum about ten o'clock in the morning. The coliseum, at the south end of the stadium, was where the athletic offices were located. For a while, I drank coffee and visited with Stubby Cross, the SID, in his basement office, the only office that didn't have purple carpet. Stubby loaded me down with facts and figures about Orangejello and Limejello Tucker. The All-American selections were out, and neither of the twins had made first team, and Stubby said this was a rotten shame inasmuch as their stats were so impressive. Orangejello had rushed for 1,823 yards. Limejello had rushed for 1,669 yards. They ranked one and three in the nation in this respect, but it just goes to show you, Stubby said, how a school like TCU has to suck hind tit when it comes to national publicity. Stubby said he thought Orangejello should win the Heisman Trophy, but he guessed it would go to that Notre Dame quarterback, Skeego Kaskanovick, because of his golden helmet and all the priests who get to vote.

A photographer from my magazine had showed up yesterday, Stubby said, and shot Orongelo and Limongelo in their game suits. The photographer was no one I had ever heard of. Stubby said the photographer posed the twins for portraits and would also be shooting them in the Aggie game.

"It could be a cover," I said, "if he had any film in the camera."

Stubby took me to lunch in the dining room of Big Ed Bookman Hall, the athletic dorm. We sat with Orangejello and Limejello, who were dressed for the occasion. They wore button-down shirts and pressed jeans and carried an armload of textbooks. I watched each of them eat three chicken fried steaks with side dishes of corn, green beans, pinto beans, mashed potatoes, French fries, mustard greens, macaroni and cheese, a gallon of milk, and an entire chocolate ice-box pie.

I didn't get much in the way of quotes from the running backs. They said their offensive line was a real good one. Orangejello said his best play was called "Orange Right." Limejello said his best play was called "Lime Left." Coach Lambert liked to keep it simple.

Orangejello said he was studying geography, as was Limejello. "We like to look at maps and shit," he said.

Limejello seemed relaxed about the A & M game. "You know, it's do-or-die," he said, "but it's not a matter of life or death."

After lunch, Stubby Cross took me to the coaches' film room back in the coliseum. Billy Peck had prepared a highlight film to be used for Cotton Bowl pregame publicity. Stubby thought it might be helpful to me.

Scott Shelton, another assistant coach, ran the projector while Billy Peck and Stubby provided insight into what I was watching on the screen, which was mostly Orangejello and Limejello knocking tacklers down, stepping on them, dancing away from them, and running for touchdowns, all of it in slow motion.

"Look at this right here," Billy Peck said. "Orongelo puts his hat on that Baylor linebacker. Heh, heh. That old boy will be diggin' his dick out of the dirt for a while. Wait a second, Scott! Run that back!"

The film backed up. Billy Peck squinted at it. "Run it back again."

The film backed up and ran forward again.

"Stop it right there," Billy Peck said. "Gimme a closeup on those people in the stands, up there in about the tenth row, behind the Baylor bench. That's it."

Prominent on the screen was a pretty young woman in a red wool coat with a fur collar. She was embracing and kissing the man next to her.

"Son of a bitch!" Billy Peck said. "That's Mary Elizabeth!"

"Who's Mary Elizabeth?" I asked Stubby Cross, quietly.

"His wife," Stubby whispered.

"Want to see it any closer up?" Scott Shelton asked Billy.

"No, I don't want to see it closer up!" Billy said. "God-damn that no-good, cheatin' tramp! She's got some explaining to do!"

Billy raced out of the room.

I wasn't quite sure what to do in that awkward moment. I wanted to laugh but thought better of it. I said I guessed I'd seen all the highlights I would need for my story. I thanked Scott Shelton for his trouble.

Stubby said to Scott, "What will Billy do? Go home and beat her up?"

"She ain't home," Scott said, looking at his wristwatch. "She's out at the Ramada with Kirk."

"Who's Kirk?" I asked.

"Kirk Norton," Stubby said. "He's our defensive coordinator. You're not gonna write any of this, are you, Jim Tom?"

"Of course not," I said. "But 'Run It Back Again' would be a good headline."

Two hours later, down on the stadium field where the Horned Frogs were running through a light workout in their game suits without shoulder pads, Billy Peck was taking out his domestic frustration on the players, yelling at them, cussing them, calling them lazy motherfuckers.

I was a little afraid to ask Billy what he had done to his wife, but T.J. said he hadn't found her yet. T.J. said he was certainly disappointed in Mary Elizabeth; she had always seemed like a real nice girl to him.

I said it only seemed fair to me. Billy Peck was jacking around with Wanda, the barmaid. Why shouldn't Mary Elizabeth have some fun?

T.J. looked at me as if he couldn't believe what he heard me say. "I'll tell you what, Jim Tom. Livin' up there in New York City for so long has give you a strange set of morals, if you don't mind me sayin' so."

About ten minutes later, I was still standing with T.J., watching the Frogs run through their offensive sets, when we heard Donna Lou's unmistakable voice behind us. She was reading poetry.

"How do I love thee, darn it?

"This is your Little Hornet.

"I love your eyes of blue

"Like you love TCU

"And I love you more each mornet."

Donna Lou was holding a batch of envelopes and letters. "You dumb shit," she said. "It might have been a little smarter of you not to file these under 'P' for poetry. How are you, Jim Tom?"

"Fine, Donna," I said to the ex-Tennessee majorette in the dark-brown bangs. "Good to see you again."

T.J. said, "What the fuck was you doin' goin' through my desk at home?"

Donna Lou said, "Who the fuck is the Little Hornet? That's a better question!"

"I want to know what you was doin' in my desk?"

"I was lookin' for the checkbook as usual. Who is the Little Hornet?"

"Woman, I got me a football game to win—can't you see that?"

"Who is she, T.J.? I want to know right now!"

"I wish I knew," the coach said. "She's a crazy person. She writes me them poems, she calls me on the phone. I didn't want to worry you. She's threatenin' our lives. I'm savin' all them poems as evidence for the police."

I found myself gaping at T.J. with awe.

"You can ask Jim Tom here. I told him about it last night."

Donna Lou turned to me.

I said, "The Little Hornet was definitely on his mind last night."

"Have you called the police?" Donna Lou asked.

"Not yet," said T.J. "I want to win this football game, then I'll call 'em. I don't want this hangin' over our heads when we go to the Cotton Bowl. Now you go on home, put them poems back where you found 'em, and let me get on with my bidness."

Remarkably, Donna Lou seemed satisfied with T.J.'s explanation. She asked what the coach wanted for dinner.

"I won't be home for dinner," T.J. said. "Me and the staff

got a lot of film to look at tonight. I'm gonna put me in a shovel pass tomorrow."

Donna Lou stuck the envelopes and poems in her purse, smiled a goodbye to me, and walked away toward a stadium ramp. I lit a cigarette and waited for T.J. to say something.

He said, "You see, Jim Tom, a great coach is a man what can design a good defense under stress."

I spent the evening with room service and the geezer-codger portable, writing two thirds of my story, talking mostly about the glorious history of TCU football. I wrote more about Sam Baugh and Davey O'Brien than anything else. Circumstances left me no choice.

97

A RICH MAN CAN COMMIT ALMOST ANY SIN IN THE STATE OF Texas and get away with it, except for one—he's not allowed to go broke.

I was reminded of this in a conversation with Big Ed Bookman in the chancellor's luxury box. The box was carpeted and outfitted with comfortable leather swivel chairs and well stocked with food and drink and protected by glass and heat from the norther that had turned the sky as purple as the TCU jerseys. Billy (Whip-Out) Murdock was conspicuous by his absence. Billy was usually a fixture in the chancellor's box on game days, but Big Ed said that Billy had made himself disappear after building four office towers downtown that stayed empty. Billy now owed the banks three million a month in interest alone, and Big Ed said it wasn't right for Billy to embarrass the university by going broke like that. The chancellor, quite rightly, had kicked Billy off the Board of Trustees, and Big Ed had kicked Billy out of the Lettermen's Hall of Fame. Billy had bought his way into the school's Hall of Fame in the first place. Big Ed recalled that Billy had never been anything more than a second-string defensive back at TCU who let every weak-armed fag in the conference throw touchdown passes over his head. He had never hit a ballcarrier as hard as he had hit the banks and the S & L's, and the economy would be better off without pretenders like Billy Murdock around.

Big Ed was wearing a purple suit and white Stetson and purple boots, and his purple tie was held by a little gold oil derrick tieclip. His daughter, Barbara Jane, was another famous TCU alumni. She was married to Billy Clyde Puckett, who was holding his own as a TV sports announcer, while she was starring in a new sitcom, *Single Parent*. Big Ed said Barbara Jane had made him happy by turning down the lead in a movie called *Marsh Bitch*. "One of them horror deals," he said.

This gossip was more interesting to me than anything that was happening down on the football field. TCU was winning a lackadaisical game by the score of 21 to 7, a game in which Orangejello and Limejello Tucker were having a few good moments but seemed to be saving themselves for Notre Dame in the Cotton Bowl. They ran like themselves on only one long drive. The rest of the time they seemed more concerned with avoiding injury than tromping on Aggie tacklers. But maybe it was the cold weather.

I sat with Dr. Glenn Dollarhyde for a while before I went back down to the press box on the level below. The chancellor introduced me to his special guest for the day, Gus McCalip, the computer tycoon. The chancellor, who was known for his fund-raising more than anything else, had hunted down the wealthy Gus McCalip and had brought him into the "TCU family." Gus McCalip was a little bald-headed man in wire-rim glasses who didn't have much to say, not to me, anyway. The chancellor walked me to the door of his luxury box when I left. He said Gus was going to be very important to the university in the future. At this very moment, Gus McCalip was trying to decide what structure on the campus he would like to see his name on. A new dorm went for three million. An academic hall went for five million. He could have the stadium for ten million. The chancellor said the Horned Frogs might well be playing football in Gus McCalip Stadium next season, a small price to pay for such a large contribution to higher education.

I said, "You run a nice whorehouse, Glenn. Why don't you sell him the 'C' in TCU? He could have that for twenty million, couldn't he? Texas McCalip University . . . TMU. All you lose is your logo."

The chancellor laughed. "You're a funny fellow, Jim Tom. See you at the Cotton Bowl."

The game was over in time for me to catch a six o'clock flight to New York. I tried never to fly at night, being a big fan of visibility, but I wanted to be back in the office on Sunday to have a say in the selection of the TCU cover photograph. My flight was held for two hours over LaGuardia, due to an air traffic controllers' slowdown, so it was midnight by the time I got to Nell's apartment. I crawled into bed with her, and said, "Don't ever let me go to Texas again without you." She said things were going smoothly at the office. Nobody had put roach powder in her coffee yet.

We went to the office together Sunday morning. I finished writing the piece while Nell did her m.e. chores. Around three in the afternoon, I was called into the mockup room to look at two cover tries that Ronnie Zander, the art director, had come up with. Nell was in the room with Ronnie and Dalton Buckley, who was "catching" my story. They were all studying the two dummy covers when I entered.

I approved of one cover and laughed out loud at the other. The one I liked was a game-action shot of Orangejello carrying the football on a sweep, coming directly at the camera, stepping on an Aggie's throat, as Limejello led interference for him. The other was a graphics stunt the art director was quite proud of. Orangejello and Limejello were leaning on either side of a large object, grinning at America. The object was an enlargement of a box of Jigglers Jell-O.

I took Nell aside for a second, and said, "If you run that Jell-O thing, I'll have to leave the country—and so will you."

In the interest of romance, to say nothing of journalism, Nell selected the game-action shot for the cover.

98

NELL'S LAST ISSUE IN HER TRIAL RUN AS MANAGING EDITOR ran in the first week of December, and I think it would be fair to say that the cover subject she chose was, where I was concerned, a smote-the-forehead thing. Ralph Webber called it suicidal. Wayne Mohler called it militant. Christine Thorne called it risky. What Nell did was put Jeannie Slay on the cover.

The cover photo was posed and shot by Shag Monti in a long portrait session in a studio with many lights and reflector screens and props. There was Jeannie on *SM*'s cover with a wry smile, sitting on a barstool in a rust shawl-collar cashmere sweater and designer jeans, holding a CBS microphone in her hand, with college and NFL helmets and footballs littered all over the floor beneath her.

Nell wrote the cover billing herself, which was: WHO IS THIS GIRL AND WHAT IS SHE DOING AT THE FOOTBALL GAME I'M WATCHING ON TV?

Jeannie's story inside was even more provocative than I had expected. It dealt with her first three months as a broadcaster. She didn't go out of her way to put all of her producers and directors and fellow announcers to death; she merely wrote the truth and let them put themselves to death. She quoted a producer as saying, "Jeannie, be ready because we're coming to you on rockets' red glare." She quoted a director as hollering in her earpiece, "Get out of it, Jeannie, we're five seconds over commercial!" She quoted an anchor monster as saying to her in private, "Never correct me on the air again—and I mean *never*."

The Jeannie cover scored two big upsets. Clipper Langdon liked it, which meant that Bryce Wilcox liked it. Clipper sent Nell a note of congratulations, saying she had struck a mighty blow for women, particularly women shoppers. Clipper's wife had already inquired about the sweater and jeans Jeannie was

357

wearing in the photo. And the CBS brass liked it. They said it didn't matter that the story was a bit caustic; the important thing was that the CBS "eye"—the logo—was clearly visible on the microphone on the cover.

When the issue came out, Jeannie called from LA. She said, "I don't know what you think, but it's the best cover *I've* ever seen."

She asked what I thought of her story.

It was full of energy, I said. I actually liked it a lot, but I didn't need to go into that very deeply because she told *me* how good it was.

There was a good deal of Richie Pace in Jeannie, which, I suppose, was the reason she had wound up in television.

I complimented her on the lead. Her story began:

"They said I was 'cosmetically correct,' with a few minor reservations, but when they discovered that I knew there was a goalpost at each end of a football field, their sigh of relief could be heard from South Bend to Palo Alto."

"When are you going to the Cotton Bowl?" Jeannie asked.

"A day or two after Christmas."

"Bring Nell."

"I am."

"Does TCU have a chance?"

"Not if they make Notre Dame mad."

"What does T. J. Lambert think?"

"You know coaches," I said. "T.J. says, 'We're gonna run through them Golden Domes like shit through a small dog.' "

Jeannie wasn't sure she could get that quote on the air.

99

THE ORDER CAME FROM CLIPPER LANGDON HIMSELF, AND since Clipper was the Mogulissimo—*n'est-ce pas?*—Bryce simply passed the news on to us in the form of a cheerful memo. The way Bryce handled it was no big surprise. He was hardly known as a man who would hurl his body in front of a moving superior for the piddling sake of journalism. The "contest" to find a managing editor for *SM* was being extended through December, and there was a new candidate. The new candidate was Whipwell (Whipper) Crimbley, a young man of thirty out of Princeton who just happened to have an abiding interest in sports, who just happened to want to run his own sports magazine, and who just happened to be Clipper's nephew.

Whipper Crimbley was a tall, body-building float-brain in a Brooks Brothers suit with wet-look hair who called a staff meeting his first day on the floor to announce several policies that would be in effect during his stay. No smoking was one. You could smoke in your own office but not if anyone came in and requested that you not smoke. The lunch break would be limited to one hour, strictly. Any staff writer who was not up to date on his or her expense account would be denied a travel advance, even if it meant the magazine couldn't cover an important story. Where copy was concerned, Whipper Crimbley wanted to see a more widespread use of the parenthesis. "I see the parenthesis as the ammunition dump of a paragraph," he actually said. The parenthesis even looked sporting. Think of the parenthesis as two athletes straining to engage one another in conflict—"It's the curvature, you see?" As for pictures, he wanted to see more rippling muscles. Nothing could be more stunning on a cover than a rippling muscle, unless it was two rippling muscles.

And since we were a sports magazine, Whipper wanted to see more sporting activity around the place. He would be available for any touch football, half-court basketball, or softball game that anyone might organize. Cleats would be permitted in the outdoor games. He would be wearing cleats himself.

Whipper Crimbley came to us with exciting credentials. His first three years out of Princeton had been spent as a researcher at *Sports Illustrated*, checking lacrosse and archery stories and trying to cleat female staffers when he slid into second base. Restless because he hadn't been promoted, he moved into ad sales at *GQ*. There, he was noted for his pass rush in touch football games. Still restless, Whipper had been offered an opportunity to prove himself in journalism in Duluth, Minnesota. For the past four years, he had been mastering the sport of dogsled racing while working as the assistant editor of *Scroom, the Authorized Liquidator*, a confidential surplus mail-order catalog.

Whipper was your man if you needed someone to write: "Watch your fish swim around the world in this 2.2 gallon global aquarium. Includes undergravel filtration, built-in light, air pump, lifelike greenery. Plugs into any AC outlet. 30-day factory warranty. This aquarium makes a great conversation piece for your home or office. Price Blitz . . . $39. Item J2591-8175."

It was Nell who quickly obtained copies of *Scroom, the Authorized Liquidator*, and saw that they fell into the right hands around the office. Then it was Wayne Mohler who introduced the game.

On the bulletin board in the main hallway, the following things began to turn up mysteriously:

"In my younger and more vulnerable years my father gave me some advice that I've been turning over ever since on my dual floppy turbo laptop w/ supertwist backlit display for only $688."

"You know how it is there early in the morning in Havana when you don't have your Mulch Monster that mulches and aerates your lawn and garden."

"An unassuming young man was traveling, in midsummer, from his native city of Hamburg to Davos-Platz when he was distracted by the sight of a real worksaver, an 85-watt airless paint sprayer, which made him forget all about those tedious brush applications."

On a dare from Wayne, I took it all the way to my Heisman column.

"For a versatile look on your football team, don't miss this four-piece quarterback kit, the Skeego Kaskanovick, manufactured in Bethlehem, Pa. Includes throwing arm, voice activator for audibles, strong steel legs, spare spark plug. Enjoy professional results now! Undisclosed price if ordered by Notre Dame recruiters."

Many of us hid out in Fu's through the rest of December, letting the magazine more or less produce itself. It could do that if everybody went about their routine jobs. Old stories that had been rejected were pulled out of junk heaps and thrown in to fill up blank spaces. Whipper stayed busy inserting parenthetical facts, sometimes two, into every lead, and looking for veins and bulges and ripples to put on covers.

Nell, of course, was more depressed than anyone else. Our lives at *SM* were going to be misery from now on. We had better start looking around for new employment. It was in the cards, she said, that the Princeton donut-hole, nothing-burger, clueless dork of a Whipperwad was going to get the managing editor's job.

"There's a bright side," I said at Fu's one night. "He knows absolutely nothing, so maybe we can lead him in any direction we want to. I'd rather have somebody who's totally stupid than somebody who's half-smart."

Wayne Mohler said, "I don't see a problem. Book yourself for three months of assignments at a time, stay out of town, take their money, never read the magazine."

"That's been my theory all along," Ralph Webber said. "Stay out of sight. Never look at your story after it goes in the magazine."

Nell said, "That's exactly the attitude I was hoping to change."

One evening after we left Fu's and went to Nell's apartment to relax in front of the fire, I instigated a mutual defrocking and joint-venture surgical strike.

"I don't understand magazine people," Nell said, as we went about the business at hand, sliding off the sofa and down onto the carpet in front of the designer log roasting in the fireplace. "I've been around magazine people for fifteen years and they still bewilder me."

"I don't see why," I said. "You know they're fuzzy-minded."

"They can be so smart on one subject and then completely idiotic on another. Doug's like that. Dalton's like that. Reg Turner's like that—when he's awake. God knows, Bryce is like that. Lindsey was that way. It's like they can't make sense on two subjects in a row."

"Fuzzballs. You work around it pretty well."

"Perfectly perceptible one minute but diametrically opposed to anything logical the next—and stubborn about it."

"They have tape gaps," I said. "In the mind. How do you unhook this?"

"I'll do it. Their brains are dented. They have this little dent. Somewhere along the way, they got hit in the head with the naive axe."

"There's not much street-smart going around."

"But why? Somebody steered them into the business. Who told them not to bring but half their luggage?"

"Most of them don't come with any newspaper experience. There's some dues they've never paid. You're an exception."

"God, some of them are obtuse."

"Don't forget deceitful. Can I get on my left side?"

"What for?"

"I'll stop breathing if I don't."

Nell was a good scout about positions.

100

CHRISTMAS SNEAKED UP ON THE WORLD AGAIN AND WROUGHT its usual havoc on the human race, turning millions of normally calm and sensible people into snarling terrorists.

The only thing I really liked about Christmas was the turkey, dressing, mashed potatoes, and giblet gravy, and I learned a long time ago to have the food catered if I wanted to enjoy it. This time, I was going to have the feast with Nell, so I did both of us a favor. I called up the caterer, Mrs. Dobbs' Taste Treats, and ordered the heat-and-serve turkey, cornbread dressing, mashed potatoes, and giblet gravy to be delivered to Nell's apartment on December 24, a Friday. I instructed Mrs. Dobbs to leave off all the silly things nobody ever ate. The aspic and shit.

The thing was, I remembered too many Christmases in the past when the women in my life—my mother, my mother's mother, Earlene, Earlene's mother, Janice, Janice's mother, assorted aunts—turned into ovenwhipped kitchen victims when they cooked the feast. This was because they didn't have any help and they were already exhausted from shopping for things nobody wanted, from slaving over the gift wrapping, making sure the paper was the right color and the bows were in the right place, before people ripped it apart and threw it on the floor, and from decorating trees that nobody ever noticed. They had a perfect right to turn cranky when they were so oven-whipped after becoming kitchen victims and having to do all the cooking alone while the men were off playing golf, but what I couldn't understand was why they kept doing it year after year.

I also remembered too many Christmases when James Junior was a little kid. Those were the years when I came to the conclusion that a merchant ought to be hung upside-down like Mussolini for selling you a Christmas tree without a stand on it. In my whole life, I'd never managed to make a tree stay put in the stand I had bought from a hardware store or a dime store. Five minutes after the tree would be up and decorated, it would topple over and crush a cat to death, or break a vase on a table, or set fire to a curtain.

In those joyful days, there was also the thrilling but hopeless search for the piece of track that was missing for the electric train, as well as the journey to find a store that not only would be open on Christmas day but would have in stock the elusive nine-volt battery. My argument that Jesus never complained about not having any batteries on Christmas day never made an impact on Earlene.

Wayne Mohler was the only person I knew who liked Christmas shopping, but, of course, he had it honed down to a fine art. Wayne would find a boutique in the same block as a bar, one of those boutiques that sold bird statues and plates and a few leather things. He would go in, give the fag three grand, and tell him one wife, two mothers, two sisters, three aunts, one uncle, and six friends. He would go get drunk and come back four hours later. Everything would be gift-wrapped and ready for mailing.

Journalism does Christmas, Nell called it.

I had pretty much licked the shopping thing in recent years.

Most of my friends—Richie Pace, Dub Fricker, Wayne, Ralph, and a dozen others, along with a few distant relatives—all got the same smoked turkey from the same smokehouse in Texas. Well, some of them got hams.

I had sent Jeannie Slay some rare books I had heard her mention she was in quest of and couldn't find. They happened to be in my own library. I had already given Christine a cashmere sweater. I had sent James the two thousand dollars Earlene had promised him. I had sent Earlene the five hundred dollars she had come to expect. These funds came out of the six thousand dollars I had already drawn from Marge Frack in finance, my Cotton Bowl advance.

Nell and I chose the day of an ice storm to do our shopping for each other, figuring there would be fewer shovers, elbowers, shouters, and rib-jabbers in the stores; fewer people threatening to commit murder over taxis and parking spaces. "Fuck you, you cocksucking asshole!" was the most familiar carol to be heard near any shop window in Manhattan amid the jingle of bells from sidewalk Santas.

The day we shopped, we mostly had lunch and then tea and then cocktails, but there was an hour when we parted, Nell to go buy me the new Dunhill lighter and Dunhill windbreaker I wanted, me to go buy her the antique pearl earrings and antique harem ring she liked but said were too expensive. That took care of the balance of the Cotton Bowl advance, and then some.

During Christmas week, we resisted several invitations to parties in the suburbs. This was the nastiest trick anybody could play on a person who lived in Manhattan. Going to a party in the suburbs involved being a slave to train schedules or renting a car, and for what? To be bored into cement by small talk, drink a goofy brand of Scotch, and eat the one bite of lean meat on a lamb chop. Give me a choice of going to a dinner party in the suburbs or walking barefooted across Arizona and I would choose the walk every time.

We did attend the magazine's annual Christmas party on the night of December 22. It was held in a private ballroom at The Plaza. Once again, it was an opportunity to observe many staff members in their finery, dancing to big band sounds, vomiting on their best shoes. A few gifts were exchanged before the staff members began to throw up, pass out, burst into tears, or lapse into jealous rages and disappear. Marge Frack was on my smoked-turkey list—a man wouldn't ignore the lady in finance. Marge usually gave me a carton of Winstons, but this time, she came up with something more inspired. It was a message T-shirt she'd had made up especially for me. The message was:

BREAKFAST	$ 24.99
LUNCH	$ 24.99
DINNER	$678.37

Marge saw that the T-shirt was shown all around the party. I was pointed at, frowned upon, applauded, saluted, and bowed to.

A group of us staked out a big round table in a corner, as far away from the dancing, crying, and vomiting as possible. The group included me, Nell, Christine, Wayne, Ralph, and Pam, the researcher from *Celebrity Parade*. Ralph slipped Pam into the party, which was supposed to be for *SM* people only. I deduced that Wooden Dick was getting close with Pam but he wasn't there yet; otherwise he wouldn't have brought her along.

Pam informed us that she had been to six different TPG Christmas parties in the last ten days. Ours was nice but pet food's was the best, she said.

"Where was pet food's party?" Christine asked.

"Bermuda."

Reg Turner intruded on our table. He fell into a chair with a glass of gin in his hand and instantly nodded off. Wayne and Christine gave Reg plenty of room. They shifted one chair away from him on either side.

The empty chair enticed Whipper Crimbley and his wife, Jane, to join us briefly. They arrived in black tie and gown, each holding a glass of white wine. Whipper introduced us to his wife, a vapid girl with only a mild case of the Señorita Bloat.

"Rather a nice do," Whipper said, glancing around.

"The orchestra is so *old*," said Jane.

"You'll select the music next year, darling," Whipper smiled.

I couldn't look at Nell.

Presently, Whipper turned to Reg Turner. "Not to talk shop, old sport, but what provisions have you made for our bowl coverage?"

Reviving for a moment, Reg said, "Windy boy . . . windy boy."

Whipper raised an eyebrow as he stared at Reg. Jane looked away, pretending not to have heard or smelled anything.

Wayne Mohler said, "Merry Christmas, Reg."

"Windy boy," Reg mumbled. "Windy boy."

"Would you care to dance, darling?" Whipper asked his wife.

"I would love to dance, dear."

They danced away, never to return to our table. Not while we were there, anyhow. Which wasn't very long. We left Reg with his chin on his chest and moved downstairs to the Oak Room.

Nell and I spent Christmas Eve in a Third Avenue bar with Wayne and his wife, Marilyn, and their English springer, Jessica. Their dog was a good listener. Jessica was quite accustomed to hearing Wayne tell her horror tales about editing. We all got lathered and stayed out so long that Nell and I slept till noon on Christmas day.

We lounged about with coffee and read the papers and opened our gifts. Nell talked to her parents in San Francisco and thanked them for the comforter. James Junior called me from Aspen and thanked me for the jing and said Aspen was cosmic. Nell heated up the feast and we dined. Then we took in an afternoon movie, and then an evening movie to erase the bitter disappointment of the afternoon movie. Then we went back home and practiced the final rite of Christmas, which was throwing away all of the unopened fruitcakes that had been arriving for two weeks.

101

THE WEEK IN DALLAS AND THE WEEK THAT FOLLOWED IN New York seem in retrospect to have a director-rewrites-novel-for-movie quality to them. Nothing went quite the way it was expected to go.

First of all, I didn't feel like I was in Texas half the time. Dallas can do that to you. Except for the Cotton Bowl stadium out on the State Fairgrounds, and the old original Neiman-Marcus Building downtown, and the Texas Schoolbook Depository, or whatever they call it now, everything in Dallas looks as if it's been built in the last thirty minutes. Dallas can drop a glass office tower on a field of mesquite for you while you're stuck on a freeway. The city has always been known for its progress, not to overlook its bombast. If the Alamo had been in Dallas, it would be the Hyatt-Alamo today. Dallas fancies itself as the center of style and culture in the Southwest. It has never grieved for a second that Fort Worth, thirty miles west, was an Indian fort ten years before Dallas became a town. Fort Worth is still an Indian fort, Dallas businessmen like to say—if you want to look at money, come to Dallas.

Dallas was overjoyed to have Notre Dame as the "visiting team" in the Cotton Bowl. Every one of the seventy-five thousand tickets had been sold because of Notre Dame. This would save image conscious Dallas the embarrassment of having a partly-empty stadium shown on national television. TCU was no draw at all. The Horned Frogs would be lucky to have fifteen thousand fans cheering for them.

T.J. moaned about the situation in private all week. "We outnumbered," he kept saying. "Them Catholic fuckers don't never play a game away from home."

Nell and I and Richie Pace went down to Dallas on the same flight on December 28. It was the same day that Jeannie Slay came in from California and Dub Fricker came in from Florida, the same day the two teams arrived.

We were all in the same hotel downtown, the fifty-story Regal Atrium. The Regal Atrium was not unlike the Summitorium in Atlanta. There were restaurants and bars everywhere, all over the lobby and mezzanine—in orchards, gazebos, botanical gardens. Those of us fortunate enough to have rooms on the front of the hotel were dazzled by a view of the Texas Schoolbook Depository and Dealy Plaza.

After checking in, we all held a reunion with Jeannie in a bar in an orchard. It wasn't easy. Jeannie Slay, *SM* covergirl and network celebrity, signed autographs the whole time.

"Amazing, isn't it?" Jeannie said. "Just because your face is on TV, people think you're somebody important. I never signed an autograph when I wrote a column. Most people thought my name was 'Johnnie Slab,' anyhow."

"It's petrifying," Nell said, as Jeannie signed a business card for a man in a Notre Dame sweatshirt.

The man left with a smile and Jeannie said, "I was on this panel show in LA the other day. Local show. A discussion about women in TV. A weather girl and a woman on a shopping channel signed more autographs than I did. A man in the studio audience came up to me after the show and asked me to sign something. He said, 'Who *are* you, anyway?' "

"That was going to be my next question," I said.

Jeannie said, "I hate to say this, guys, but I'm starting to like it. You know why? When the game's over and somebody wants to go to dinner, I can go. I don't have to write. I'm not in the press box for three more hours. I have a life now. I even have time for dates."

"Who are you dating?" Nell asked.

"Nobody—but I have time."

Richie said to Jeannie, "I read this statistic in *USA Today*. A girl your age has a better chance of getting killed by terrorists than she does of getting married by the time she's fifty."

Jeannie laughed. "I'll take a terrorist, if he's straight."

Bowl games are an opportunity for a city to show itself off to visitors, but Dallas doesn't have an abundance of movie studios to tour, as the Rose Bowl does, or a lot of French Quarters to get lost in, as the Sugar Bowl does, or a lot of Biscayne Bays to cruise around, as the Orange Bowl does.

What Dallas offered to the visiting teams and press were luncheons and speeches and dinners and trips to South Fork and Maverick games, all of which we skipped. Nell and Jeannie did make it to Neiman-Marcus once, and two days before the game, we all piled into my rented Lincoln, the five of us, and I drove Nell, Jeannie, Richie, and Dub to Fort Worth to show them my hometown. They were all impressed by the old stockyards, the murder trail, the barbecue, and the eerie peacefulness of the downtown area. Richie asked if I knew a real estate agent in Fort Worth—he was interested in beachfront property.

The rest of the time we hung around the hotel's gazebos and the Cotton Bowl press room in the hotel and listened to TCU's Stubby Cross and Notre Dame's Vinnie Tarabello, the SIDs, and all of the other writers discuss all of the possibilities of the national championship dilemma. There were many. If USC won in the Rose and Penn State won in the Orange and TCU won in the Cotton, who would the voters choose? USC or Penn State, probably. More likely USC. Both teams had played a tougher schedule than TCU. But what if Michigan upset USC in Pasadena and Nebraska upset Penn State in Miami and the Irish beat TCU? There would be no undefeated teams left. Who then? "They would have to give it to us," Vinnie Tarabello said. "We had Knute Rockne." What if USC and Penn State both lost but TCU won? TCU would be the only unbeaten team left, but Michigan would have knocked off USC, which was No. 1 going in. Michigan would be 11-1 and TCU would be 12-0, but Michigan was Michigan and TCU was TCU. Wouldn't the Wolverines outpoll the Horned Frogs? "Your schedule works against you," I said to Stubby Cross. "We can't help who we didn't play," he said.

The season records of TCU and Notre Dame were displayed prominently on large posters in the press room.

TCU (11-0)			*NOTRE DAME* (10-1)		
62	Kansas State	7	17	Michigan	14
44	Vanderbilt	6	21	Mich. State	3
52	SMU	12	41	Purdue	7
40	Arkansas	3	13	Stanford	10

33	Wash. State	10		23	Air Force	9
27	Rice	0		20	Florida State	17
31	Houston	14		34	Pitt	7
17	Baylor	3		69	Navy	0
45	Texas Tech	7		40	Duke	0
28	Texas	13		18	Alabama	3
21	Texas A&M	7		10	USC	16

Each afternoon, the head coaches held post-workout press conferences in the hotel press room.

Notre Dame's coach, Mike Kercheski, the uncle of Notre Dame's Heisman quarterback, Skeego Kaskanovick, began each press conference with the same words: "We're just happy to be here. We just want the kids to enjoy the experience."

Mike Kercheski would then lavish praise on TCU's team, talk about the crippling injuries that were affecting his key players, discuss the vital role that academics played in Notre Dame football, thank the sportswriters for all of their past kindnesses, and close by saying he didn't see any way for his crippled and outweighed Fighting Irish to stay on the same field with the Horned Frogs, which meant that he expected Notre Dame to win big.

T.J. outdid himself in his public appearances.

On Wednesday, three days before the game, he said to the press: "We're a deeply religious team. Our kids held a prayer meeting last night. They're dedicating the game to our seniors."

On Thursday, two days before the game, he said: "This is the greatest honor of my career, to be playing Notre Dame. College football wouldn't be college football without Notre Dame. I just hope our kids aren't in too much awe of Notre Dame's reputation and we can make it interesting for them."

On Friday, New Year's Eve, at the last official press conference, T.J. said: "The squad made a special request of me last night. They wanted to go to their regular church. We went to Fort Worth for a special service at Worth Hills Christian Church. We prayed that nobody on either team would be injured tomorrow."

T.J. made a special request of me after his press conference.

The Annual Cotton Bowl New Year's Eve Gala was to be held that night. This was the biggest social occasion of the year for the Southwest Conference. The party would be in the grand ballroom of the hotel, an exclusive black-tie function. An elaborate six-course dinner would be served and champagne would flow and there would be an orchestra and dancing and table-hopping and the presentation of the Cotton Bowl Queen and her princesses. All of the chancellors and athletic directors and head coaches and coaching staffs and their wives would be there, including Donna Lou Lambert and Mary Elizabeth Peck, along with the Notre Dame people and the CBS people and several of Dallas' most important business leaders and all of the sportswriters who were covering the game—and the Little Hornet and Wanda from The Cadaver Room. Could the Hornet and Wanda sit at my table?

I said, "You're taking your bimbos to the Cotton Bowl party?"

"No, you are," T.J. said.

"Don't you have enough on your mind with Notre Dame?"

"Me and Billy promised. They've went out and bought new dresses. They got rooms here in the hotel. When you're ready to go to the party, call five-oh-one and five-oh-three."

"How do I introduce them if it comes up?"

"They know to play like they're sportswriters."

I laughed.

T.J. said, "It'll work. Hell, sportswriters can look like any fuckin' thing, Jim Tom—you know that."

102

THERE'S SOMETHING ABOUT A LOUD, FLOWERED-PRINT COCK-tail dress that fits too tight in places and pulls at the seams that makes me think: I don't want this person in my life. But I had two of them at the table, Judy and Wanda. The dress on Judy Ruth Ward, better known as the Little Hornet, was bright red and bright blue. Wanda's dress was bright green and bright yellow. They both wore fishnet stockings and their heels were so high they could have been seriously injured if they had fallen off their pumps. The Hornet's hair was big and round and shiny black. Wanda's hair was big and round and reddish brown. To touch the hair on either one of the ladies was to run the risk of getting electrocuted. And there we were.

God was good to us on one count. As you came in the door to the Regal Atrium's grand ballroom, our table was far to the left—over there by Baylor and Texas A & M. It wasn't near the dance floor in the center, which was where you could find TCU and Notre Dame and CBS. This helped some, to be hidden. But not enough to keep Richie Pace and Dub Fricker from acting as if they weren't really with us, and gutlessly spending most of the night at a standup service bar over in a corner.

Nell and Jeannie each looked smashing in tailored skirts and jackets, Nell in her antique pearl earrings. They both said I should have worn a tux. I said the Cotton Bowl was lucky I brought along my black blazer and a pair of dark gray slacks.

Jeannie sat at our table the whole night to escape from Gary Hagan, the play-by-play announcer, and Hulk Garrett, the color man, and a producer, director, and associate producer, all of whom were intent on listening to Hulk Garrett spin the same yarns about his playing days with the Rams.

Nell and Jeannie were good with the Little Hornet and Wanda. They drew them into conversations and did their best to make the Fort Worth ladies feel comfortable in the high-flown surroundings, which, one could only guess, were more cultivated than those to which they were usually accustomed.

Nell let the Hornet and Wanda know that she, Nell, and Jeannie knew the score about why the Hornet and Wanda were at the party. Nell said, "If wives don't know any better, they deserve what they get." Wanda said, "Honey, you can swing that in ragtime." I said I thought Mary Elizabeth Peck was getting her share, but I didn't know about Donna Lou Lambert.

I could only admire Nell's patience in listening to the complete history of all of Wanda's kitchen appliances and the problems with many of the automobiles she had owned. In the meantime, Jeannie heard the Little Hornet liked Michigan with three and a half over Southern Cal, Nebraska with six and a half over Penn State, and the Frogs with six over Notre Dame.

I did my PR duty. I left the table to visit with some of the conference coaches. I paid my respects to the Notre Dame table. I said hello to some of the Dallas business leaders. I asked one of them, Steely Bob Brunson, a banker, if the Dallas economy was as bad as Fort Worth's. "Don't worry about Dallas," he said. "Dallas is the last to go and the first to come back."

I sat for a while at the TCU table with T.J. and Donna Lou and Billy Peck and Mary Elizabeth and Dr. Glenn Dollarhyde and his wife, Ruby, and Rabbit Tyrance and his wife, Modene.

Mary Elizabeth Peck, a curvy blonde, definitely looked like trouble. She held my lighter hand as I lit her cigarette, and said, "I see you are surrounded by women over there, Jim Tom. You must have something we don't know about."

"I know how to bribe a waiter to keep the drinks coming," I smiled.

"Who are your lady friends?"

"Sportswriters."

"*Women* sportswriters?"

"There are quite a few of them around these days," I said.

"I'll bet they have fun in the locker rooms."

"Not really."

"Who do those women write for?"

I said, "One of them is an editor at my magazine. One of them is on TV, actually. The other two I only met tonight. They were assigned to our table. I'm embarrassed to say I can't remember their names."

The next moment was heart-stopping. I looked up to see the Hornet and Wanda coming toward the TCU table. They were, by now, a little ripped on champagne.

"Hi," said the Hornet. "I'm Judy Ruth Ward. This is Wanda Fairchild. We're with *Pigskin Weekly*. We're doin' a story on which coaches in the conference are the best dancers, and we thought we'd start with TCU."

The Hornet took T.J. by the hand and Wanda took Billy Peck by the hand. T.J. and Billy stood up.

Donna Lou said, "T. J. Lambert, you haven't danced in twenty-five years!"

"This is bidness," T.J. said. "It's for publicity."

The two couples moved to the dance floor.

"I'd like to dance, too," Mary Elizabeth said, taking my hand.

"No, I don't think I . . ."

But she pulled me to my feet and dragged me out to the floor, and the next thing I knew, her body was pressed snugly against mine.

"What do you think of their girlfriends?" she said.

"Who?"

"Drop the shit, Jim Tom. I know about Wanda. I know about the 'Little Hornet.' I have friends on the coaching staff."

"So I hear."

"I would never say anything to Donna Lou. If she wants to be stupid, that's *her* problem. What room are you in, baby?"

"Why?"

"I thought I might come up later. You can tell me all about sportswriting."

"I'm sort of with somebody," I said. "I'm sharing a room with that editor sitting over there."

"She's cute. Your business looks like fun. So gimme a call next time you're in Fort Worth alone, lover."

"I understand you're not home much."

She gave me a look, then grinned. "I can juggle my schedule around for you."

I pleaded a cramp in my leg and took Mary Elizabeth back to the table. T.J. and Billy were still dancing with the Hornet and Wanda. I wished the chancellor and the athletic director and their wives and Donna Lou a happy New Year and good luck in the game tomorrow and returned to Nell and Jeannie, who had been rejoined by Richie and Dub as soon as the Hornet and Wanda left the table.

In the next hour, we watched the Hornet and Wanda make a spectacle of themselves. They solicited the party photographer and made him snap their pictures sitting on the laps of all the head coaches in the conference. Wanda took up on the dance floor with the Aggie coach, Whimpy Dupree, who was said to be separated from his wife and was at the party stag. The Hornet took up on the dance floor with Hulk Garrett, whose wife was in California. They were all quite a sight, doing an old-fashioned twist.

T.J. came over to our table and took me aside. He said, "They're tryin' to piss me and Billy off, Jim Tom. And you know what? They've done it. You can tell 'em for me that they've done lost their scholarships."

I didn't get a chance to pass along the information. Wanda never came back from the Aggie table. The Hornet never came back from the CBS table.

The band rang in the New Year with the old familiar refrain. I embraced Nell and we kissed and professed our love for each other. Jeannie gave Richie and Dub a hug and kiss. The fellows all shook hands and wished each other good stories and better bosses in the coming year. Jeannie and Nell hugged. Then Jeannie said, "Mind if I give this big lug a kiss?"

"If you keep your tongue to yourself," Nell said.

Jeannie and I kissed and squeezed on one another with affection.

"May the New Year bring you an anchor job," I said.

Jeannie said, "Oh, Nicky, if you can paint, anything is possible."

We stood around for another twenty minutes. The party wasn't over for most of the guests, but it was over for those of us who faced a long trying day of seeing who was going to be No. 1 in college football tomorrow.

Gary Hagan, the play-by-play man, shook my hand on his way out of the grand ballroom. I was slightly distracted by the amount of makeup on his face but I did hear the question he asked.

"Who's going to take it tomorrow, Jim Tom?"

103

As was customary with life on the road, the phone rang the next morning at the same time that room service arrived. I took the call from Whipper Crimbley while Nell pointed out to the waiter that we ordered our eggs scrambled, not fried, sausage patties, not raw bacon, biscuits and cream gravy, not apple Danish, tomato juice, not orange juice, and real coffee, not decaf—but never mind, we would make do, if he would just come back with the real coffee and some salt and pepper and sugar and perhaps some knives and forks.

Whipper Crimbley first said, "Happy New Year, Pincher."

"Same to you, Whipper," I said.

The mention of Whipper's name drew Nell's attention.

"How's the weather?" Whipper asked.

"I don't know, the drapes are closed. Want me to look? It's supposed to be clear and chilly."

He said, "Sorry to trouble you, old man, but we're still trying to catch the tails of these darn bowl games."

"They're elusive devils." I peeked out a window. The sun was shining on Dealy Plaza.

"The thing is," he said, "I'm here in the office and a while ago, rather fortuitously, I might add, I ran into this chap from Photo. He told me we don't have any photographers assigned today."

"*No* photographers have been assigned to shoot the games today?"

I said it loudly—for Nell. She fell into a chair and started laughing.

Whipper said, "Bit of a misfire in communications, the way I read it."

"Bit of a misfire in communications around the office, eh?"

Nell tumbled onto the floor in her hotel terrycloth robe and beat her fists on the carpet, laughing harder.

Whipper said, "Yes, apparently what happened was, Reg

rather imagined Dalton handled it, and Dalton rather imagined I handled it. I rather imagined it was a departmental responsibility. One of those things. Nothing we can't overcome, however. I'm just wondering if you can hire a newspaper photographer to shoot three rolls for us at the Cotton Bowl today? We'll pay generously, of course. I'm going to ask Stew Gardner in Pasadena and Wayne Mohler in Miami to do the same thing. It's the photo department's idea, but rather a good one, I think, considering the emergency."

"I'll turn the job over to Nell Woodruff," I said. "She's good in emergencies."

"Oh, is Nellie down there?"

"Nellie's here, yes."

Nell looked up. "Nellie . . . ? He didn't say Nellie?"

I confirmed it with a nod.

"Oh, God," she said, rolling over on the carpet. "Oh, my God."

"Rest at ease, Whipper," I said. "Nell will handle it. She'll line up a shooter and tell him exactly how to label the film and ship it."

"Excellementé," said Whipper. "You'll be filing later?"

"Probably not till after the game. It's an old habit I've developed."

"Quite so. Who is it Notre Dame is playing?"

"TCU."

"Uh-huh. Well, have a good one."

The second I hung up the phone, Nell said, "Those jerks! Those fools! Nobody thought to assign photographers today? What have they been *doing* up there all week?"

I said, "Oh, you know how it is in the helter-skelter world of weekly magazine journalism. These darn things can slip through the cracks."

The Cotton Bowl is only four miles east of downtown Dallas. It sits on the State Fairgrounds amid some Art Deco exhibit halls that were built for the Texas Centennial of 1936. The stadium is an old gray oval, upper-decked on both sides, that has a lusty history. Almost sixty years of New Year's Day games and Texas-OU games. SMU once played there, as did the Dallas Cowboys. I had been in the Cotton Bowl enough times in the past to think of it as a time-share condo.

Nell and I drove out to the stadium two hours before the one-thirty kickoff. Time enough to have the barbecue lunch in the press box. Time enough for Nell to hire a photographer from *The Dallas Morning News* to shoot some rolls for us.

I went down on the field thirty minutes before the game, which is something I like to do at Poll Bowls. The electricity that fills the air in the final countdown before a big football game is unique in sports. I liked to hear it, feel it, savor it.

Over in a corner of the stadium, Jeannie was hooked up to a mike and facing a hand-held cameraman while an associate producer stood by. She had been there for a couple of hours, doing "bumpers." A bumper is a ten-second lead-in to a commercial, some sort of historical fact that would run with film footage.

I listened to Jeannie do a bumper: "One of the greatest football players in history came from Dallas. His name was Doak Walker. Three-time All-American and Heisman Trophy winner at SMU. They call the Cotton Bowl, 'The House That Doak Built.' "

"Very nice," said the associate producer.

Jeannie did another one: "Texas Christian University was the host team in the very first Cotton Bowl game on January 1, 1937. The star for the Horned Frogs that day? None other than Slingin' Sam Baugh."

"Good one, Jeannie," the associate producer said.

She saw me grinning.

"Back-breaking labor," she said. "I don't see how we do it."

Owing to our special friendship, T. J. Lambert permitted me to come into the TCU locker room and hear his last-minute pep talk. No other writer was allowed in.

I watched the TCU players move about quietly, slowly, glancing in a mirror on a wall, one by one, casually, to see if their wristbands and their towels were just right, if their dark purple jerseys were tucked in just right, if the purple stripes running down the sides of their glistening white pants were just right. Their socks were taped up, their purple helmets polished. They were ready for a game on national TV.

T.J. gathered the squad in a circle, some kneeling, some sitting, some standing. The coach paced back and forth among them as he spoke, his voice low at first but soon to build into a coach's crescendo before he sent them storming out the door and onto the field.

"Awright, men," T.J. said. "This right here is a football game you get to play once in a lifetime. What you do out there on that field today will be with you the rest of your life. You got your Notre Dame waitin' for you out there. It's the Notre Dame you've heard about your whole life. They *are* college football. Ain't no doubt about it. But you know what some of their players asked me this week? They asked me what TCU stands for. Naw, they never heard of TCU. Well, I don't know about *you*, but that makes me pretty goddamn *hot*. Let me tell you somethin' else about 'em. They may be Notre Dame and they may wear them gold hats, but they're just kids like you. They're the same age and they ain't no bigger and they ain't no faster. They human. They jack off in the shower just like you do. Now, we know what our game plan is. We're gonna run them fat tackles of theirs till they're beggin' to go back to Poland. Our defense is gonna punish 'em for ever pass they catch. And don't worry about the Catholic shit. You hit 'em hard enough—and keep hittin' 'em—they'll feel it over there in the Vatican. We'll knock that beanie off the little Pope's head, is what we'll do. Okay, who wants to lead us in prayer today? Orongelo?"

Orangejello Tucker shuffled out from the crowd and bowed his head. The other players bowed their heads. Orangejello mumbled something I couldn't hear.

"That's enough," T.J. said, butting in. "Awright, men, let's go KICK SOME FUCKIN' ASS!"

The players hit the locker room door, yelling and whooping.

104

A FOOTBALL TEAM CAN BE SO TIGHTLY WOUND, SO INTENSE, so preoccupied with trying not to make any mistakes, it can sometimes forget to play football. In the first half of the Cotton Bowl game, T.J.'s scholar-athletes were all of those things in addition to being, for want of a better word, inept. Orangejello Tucker fumbled the opening kickoff and Notre Dame recovered the ball at the TCU five-yard line. That gave the Irish their first touchdown. Later in the first quarter, Orangejello fumbled at his own ten-yard line. Notre Dame recovered. That gave the Irish their second touchdown. In the second quarter, Limejello Tucker fumbled at his own seven-yard line. Notre Dame recovered. That gave the Irish their 21 to 0 lead. The score could have been worse. Two long Notre Dame drives failed to produce any points when the Irish quarterback, Skeego Kaskanovick, insisted on throwing incomplete passes down near the TCU goal when he could have run keeper plays, as he had earlier, and probably walked into the end zone. The TCU defense looked as if it had never seen a quarterback keep the ball on an option play. All of this made Richie Pace something of a pest in the press box. He kept coming down the aisle to where Nell and I were sitting to share his wit and wisdom with us. After Notre Dame's second touchdown, Richie said, "Let me see if I understand this. Your school is the one that's playing without the football, right?" When the Irish scored their third touchdown, Richie said, "I knew it wouldn't be any fun if they kept score." Nell gave me a sympathetic pat, and said, "It's only a game." I said, "Notre Dame's in big trouble now. We've lulled them to sleep."

I noticed from the middle of the first quarter on that T.J. wasn't himself down on the TCU sideline. He wasn't the T. J. Lambert who would normally be cursing his players and slapping them on the sides of their helmets and kicking over water buckets and yelling threats at the zebras. He was so stunned by his team's inferior performance and Notre Dame's quick three-touchdown lead, he looked as if he had given up. He either stood around with his arms folded or wandered along the side-line with his hands in his pockets. I wondered if the trainer had given him a couple of Valium.

Although I knew I would miss the Kilgore Rangerettes, I went down on the field about three minutes before the half, and then walked around to the tunnel and entered the TCU locker room with the team. The players bitched at each other and slammed their helmets down and took pisses. T.J. calmly sat down in a chair and crossed his legs and called a squad meeting.

"Well, I missed my guess," he said to the team. "I thought they'd be so far ahead, we could go home by now, but we've got to play thirty more minutes. Looks like we've got a good chance to break the Cotton Bowl fumble record. That'll be somethin' we can be proud of. I don't blame none of you. I take full responsibility for the way you played. I forgot to tell you to hold your hands over your hearts when they played the fuckin' anthem. That got us off on the wrong foot right there. I ain't got no strategy to change. I think we ought to just go out there in the second half and play with our dicks like we been doin'. Bowl games are supposed to be 'fun,' so let's see how much more fun we can make it for Notre Dame. But I don't want none of you to play so hard you get hurt. We better pray to that. Billy Ray, why don't you lead us in the Lord's prayer?"

Billy Ray Deakins, a three-hundred-pound, six-six offensive lineman—white boy on steroids—moved into the middle of the players and bowed his head.

"Now I lay me down to sleep," he began. The squad broke into laughter, and T.J. threw up his arms and went to take a leak.

I walked back out on the field with the coach. He had nothing to say until Jeannie Slay grabbed him for one of those sideline comments just before the second-half kickoff.

Jeannie said, "Coach, what's your biggest problem in getting back in this game?" She held the mike up to T.J.

He said, "Our problem is, we're playing a great football team and there ain't a damn thing we can do about it. But that's fawright. We're just happy to be here. We just want our kids to enjoy the experience.''

Notre Dame kicked off to TCU while I walked up the steps of the lower level of the west side stands, reached a portal, and went on to the press box elevator that took me up to the box perched over the upper deck. By the time I got to my press box seat, TCU had driven down to Notre Dame's ten-yard line.

"How?" I asked Nell.

"Two pass interference calls and a facemask.''

At this moment, Orangejello ran a pitchout wide to the right and fumbled at the Notre Dame two-yard line, but the officials ruled no fumble—the ground can't cause a fumble. On the next play, Orangejello dived into the end zone for a touchdown. When TCU's placekicker, Olaf Amangergening, a soccer-style placekicker of unknown nationality, added the extra point, it was 21 to 7, Notre Dame.

The Irish came back with an eighty-five-yard drive, all on the ground, that consumed ten minutes on the clock, but from the TCU six-yard line, Skeego Kaskanovick threw three incomplete passes and a bad snap cost Notre Dame a field goal. This stroke of good fortune seemed to awaken T.J., get him back into the game. He put on his headset to communicate with his coordinators upstairs and started sending in plays.

Limejello Tucker, on the first play of the fourth quarter, broke loose on a double reverse and ran sixty-five yards to the Notre Dame twenty-three. TCU tried four straight running plays from there and got close to the thirteen-yard line for a first down. It looked short by half a yard, but the measurement gave the Frogs new life. A dive play got nothing, a sweep got nothing, but on third down, Orangejello banged down to the Notre Dame two-yard line. He fumbled when he was hit high and low, and the replay showed that it *was* a fumble, which Notre Dame recovered, but the zebra ruled Orangejello was down—and the ground couldn't cause a fumble. On the next play, Limejello scored on a pitchout and Olaf Amangergening kicked the point, and it was 21 to 14, Notre Dame.

Richie Pace came down the aisle to say, "I've always said the zebras do a great job.''

The Irish mounted another long drive that carried them to

TCU's fifteen-yard line. Skeego Kaskanovick completed two touchdown passes from there, but the zebras ruled that both receivers were out of the end zone when they caught the ball. A fourth-down pass failed and Notre Dame came away with no points again.

There were now only three minutes left and TCU was deep in its own end of the field, but Notre Dame's prevent defense allowed Randy Skenk, the TCU quarterback, to hit Orangejello and Limejello with flat passes and move the ball out to mid-field, where there was only one minute left to play and TCU faced a third-down-and-eight problem. That's when T.J. sent in the trick play, a play he called the "Fuckerooski." Others called it the "Fumblerooski."

The Frogs lined up in a shotgun formation with four receivers split wide. Obvious passing down. But the TCU center only pretended to snap the ball and Randy Skenk only pretended to take the snap and fade back. The center moved the ball a foot to his right, on the ground, and Billy Ray Deakins, the offensive guard, picked up the ball unnoticed and suddenly he was lumbering toward the Notre Dame goal.

A three-hundred-pound offensive lineman can take a week or so to run fifty yards, and Notre Dame's safety and cornerback caught up with him at their twelve-yard line. One defender jumped on Billy Ray's back and the other one grabbed him around the waist. Billy Ray lugged the two tacklers forward for about seven more yards, and just before he went down, he lateraled the ball back to Orangejello, who was trailing the play, and Orangejello pranced into the end zone for a touchdown. Orangejello celebrated the touchdown by doing a moon walk and a knee-wiggle dance step before he knelt in prayer.

T.J. called a time-out before the conversion to talk things over with his staff on the field and on the headset. There were only two seconds left. No time for Notre Dame to retaliate. It was all up to TCU. The Frogs could go for two points and try to win the game or kick the extra point and settle for a tie.

The TCU coaches seemed to argue among themselves for a moment, but T.J. put an end to it by shoving one of the coaches into a crowd of players and sending in Olaf Amangergening to placekick the point, which he did. The Cotton Bowl ended in a 21 to 21 tie.

In a flash, Richie Pace was standing behind us. "So this was kind of like it was at the Alamo, wasn't it?" he grinned. "Davy Crockett said, 'I know what let's do, gang. Let's play for a tie.' "

"That your lead?" said Nell.

I said, "It was the percentage play. The Frogs are still undefeated. They've still got a shot at number one. Frankly, I didn't think T.J. was that smart."

T.J. defended his controversial decision in the locker room as the writers badgered him about going for the tie. He finally grew tired of explaining how his team had fought back from twenty-one points down and didn't deserve to lose on a gamble at the very end, and said, "I'll put it another way. You sportswriter fuckers don't know shit about nothin'."

I wrote hurriedly that TCU's Billy Ray Deakins, on any given day, could probably outeat the Four Horsemen, and that the Frogs didn't tie one for the Gipper, they tied one *on* the Gipper, and then Nell and I rushed back to our hotel room at the Regal Atrium to watch the second half of the Rose Bowl and all of the Orange Bowl on TV.

We ordered a gross of cheeseburgers and some whiskey to the room and Richie and Dub Fricker joined us. Jeannie called the room to say she was on her way to the airport—she had to be in San Francisco to win an Emmy at an NFL game tomorrow. I said, "Here's looking at you, kid." She said, "And now to Australia and a crack at those Japs."

I made Nell and Richie and Dub root for Michigan in the Rose Bowl and Nebraska in the Orange Bowl so my alma mater would have a chance for the national championship in the final wire-service polls. It was after the Wolverines beat the Trojans 22 to 17 and Nebraska upset Penn State 14 to 3 that I instructed Richie and Dub on how to vote in the AP poll tomorrow. TCU (11-0-1) first, Michigan (11-1) second, Notre Dame (10-1-1) third.

"I'll take it under advisement," Richie said, "but right now, I'm leaning toward Michigan. Love their helmets."

Nell and I caught an early flight to New York the next

morning. We wanted to get back to the office to do damage control on the magazine's bowl coverage. Around six o'clock that Sunday night, I called some friends at the AP and USA *Today* offices to see if the results of the final polls were in. The news was good enough. In the Coaches' poll, the panel of experts voted Michigan No.1, but in the AP poll, the writers voted TCU No.1. Both schools could claim the mythical national championship. Dueling bumper stickers.

I reached T.J. at home and delivered the happy news. "Split vote don't bother me none," he said. "It's like the Bear once said. All you need to win is one, then you can act like you won 'em all." T.J. said he would go congratulate his players right now. They were all over at the church.

105

FOR THE NEXT FIVE DAYS WE WERE A SHIP WITHOUT A RUDDER in the ocean of journalism, a yacht without a keel in the sea of magazines. Whipper Crimbley wasn't at work. No one thought much about it for two days, but when he didn't show up on our floor on Wednesday, Doug McNiff called his home to see if he was sick with the flu or something. His wife said he was just fine, he had gone to work, and the reason he hadn't been on the floor at *SM* was because he was involved in some important meetings with Bryce Wilcox and Clipper Langdon. Assuming he was the next in command, Doug moved into the managing editor's office on Thursday and conducted the weekly story conference. Someone mentioned at the story conference that Whipper had been seen in the hallway at both *Celebrity Parade* and *Southern Mansions*. When the Whipper still wasn't in our office Friday morning, I called Bryce to ask what the hell was going on.

"Stay loose, big guy," Bryce said. "Everything will be settled by this afternoon."

"What is everything?"

"Whipper is trying to decide whether he wants to be m.e. of

Celebrity Parade or *Southern Mansions*. Clipper says it's Whipper's call.''

"He doesn't want *SM*?" I said, doing my best to hide the ecstasy in my voice.

"No," Bryce said. "It has to do with Reg Turner. Whipper and his wife talked it over. They both felt Whipper wouldn't be happy over the long haul working around somebody as, well, flatulent as Reg. Of course, I can't make Reg move to another book within the company. You may not know this, big guy, but Reg has been with TPG for thirty-three years. He's quietly been putting his profit sharing back into the company. He owns almost as much stock as Les Padgett—and he likes it where he is."

"God bless Reg," I said. "Who are we going to get?"

"Clipper and I will have one more meeting over lunch today. We haven't really decided. It's a tough one."

I said, "I'll tell you how I feel about it, Bryce, copy-wise. If it's a choice between Doug McNiff and the Hillside Strangler, I'll take the Strangler."

The first memo came around at three o'clock. It announced that Whipper Crimbley, who had always had an abiding love for show biz, was the new managing editor of *Celebrity Parade*, and that the present managing editor was being transferred to Oban, Scotland, where he would be in charge of the overseas diaper division.

The second memo came around at four thirty. It said:

To: The Staff
From: Bryce Wilcox

I am very pleased to announce the appointment of Nell Woodruff as Managing Editor of *The Sports Magazine*, effective immediately.

Nell's appointment is perhaps a paradigm for our aim of graduating loyal staffers and promoting them as they mature.

Nell's editorial tenure for the past eight years at *SM* has been distinguished and uncompromising, as all of you know.

It also should be said that this makes Nell Woodruff the

first FEMALE to become the Managing Editor of a TPG publication. As Clipper Langdon, our CEO, remarked today, "This fact alone will see all of us walking a little taller around the promenade deck."

Clipper and I have no doubt that Nell is fully capable of helping us attain even higher orders of achievement and entrenching *SM* as the conscience of sport.

B. W.

Needless to say, there was quite a celebration at Fu's Like Us that night. Most of us got overserved. Nell was so happy she didn't bring up the fact that her m.e. salary of two-fifty was a hundred thousand under the amount they would have paid a member of the male population. She would complain about that in due time. I had a bit of a problem getting her in and out of the cab after she had put the last majestic grand-final cocktail down her neck, on top of the single fried wonton that presented itself for dinner in an earlier hour.

The next morning, while Nell was gobbling Anacin and wishing for a Visine shower, she asked if I wanted to sublet my apartment and move in with the m.e. to be close to the seat of power. I said I thought it sounded like a good idea—I hadn't seen my apartment in months, except to pick up the mail and tip the staff. Her apartment was the one with the fireplace, after all.

The announcement of Nell's promotion to managing editor of a national sports weekly was big-deal, feminist, gender-based stuff, of course. It made the front page of *The New York Times* and *USA Today* and numerous other papers. Talk-show people immediately started trying to book her for appearances, but she granted only one TV interview, and that was to Jeannie Slay.

Jeannie called Nell to congratulate her the minute she read the news on the wire. Jeannie also suggested the TV thing. It would be taped and would play sometime in connection with a Super Bowl preview. Nell agreed. So Jeannie came to New York and turned up in the office with a hand-held cameraman, an audio man, a lighting man, and two members of a union who did nothing but stand around. The interview was done in

Nell's office, which was no longer known as The Bat Cave. Some office wit had already named it The Lib Crib.

I sat in on the interview and thought the outtakes would make a better show. With the camera rolling, Jeannie said, "Just be natural, Nell. Pretend I'm Barbara Walters and you're Cleopatra." Nell looked straight into the camera and said, "Hi, I'm Nell Woodruff. I'm a highly educated person, I come from a very well-to-do family, and I've always wanted to do something for the little people."

Nell and Jeannie laughed so much on camera, it was amazing that Jeannie got two minutes out of the interview that was usable. Mainly, Nell said she hoped to give the magazine back to the writers.

The three of us went to dinner that night, to an unfamous Italian restaurant on 49th Street that I liked for the simple reason that the chef didn't make a habit of squirting tomato paste all over the pasta. I won't divulge the name because the notoriety might ruin it. The place would become loud and crowded and the food would turn the color of an Alabama football jersey. Anyhow, this was the night Jeannie confessed that she had found someone to date. He was a divorced CBS programming executive in the LA office who seemed to have all the traits of a future network president.

"It's bad luck to fuck laterally," she explained.

Nell assembled her SM team rapidly over the next few days. She reinstituted the position of executive editor and named Wayne Mohler to the job. Wayne didn't really want to give up writing but Nell money-whipped him into a daze. She promoted Ralph Webber to assistant managing editor, eliciting from Wooden Dick the promise that he would assistant managing edit as often as he practiced his hobby. She kept Doug McNiff and Reg Turner on as assistant m.e.'s, having no choice in Reg's case. She gave Molly Connors the option of resigning or moving elsewhere within the company, if any other division would take the deceitful little bitch. Molly found an opening in pet food as a label designer. This cleared the path for Christine Thorne to become chief of research at a salary that would enable her to afford her own apartment. Nell then created the post of deputy chief of research for Charlotte Murray. The new managing editor even said I could have a new column picture, one that looked more like the man she loved and less like a man who thought the world was doomed.

So it was happy endings all around, the only known happy endings in the modern history of magazine journalism, and I said to Wayne one night in the neighborhood tavern that if Nell could see to it that my column went another three whole months without a parenthesis in the lead, I just might marry that girl.

DITKA

MONSTER OF THE MIDWAY

Armen Keteyian

"(voice at full scream) I don't want a book done on me! You have no right to write this book! You want to write an article like the rest of the clowns in this city, fine, but you don't have the right to write a book. You do whatever you got to do, as long as you know my feelings...."

—Ditka on <u>DITKA:Monster of the Midway</u>

POCKET
<u>BOOKS</u>

Available in hardcover from Pocket Books   620

THE UNAUTHORIZED
INSIDE LOOK
at the
U.S. OLYMPIC
BASKETBALL TEAM

★★★★★★☆☆☆☆☆

THE GOLDEN BOYS

☆☆☆☆☆★★★★★

by CAMERON STAUTH

POCKET
BOOKS

Available in hardcover
from Pocket Books